Praise for Stella Chaplin

It's a Wrap

'A hugely enjoyable insider's view on the not-so-glam movie world'   *Company*

'A funny, addictive read with plenty of sex, mayhem and lies'
New Woman

'This is an hilarious, riveting read'   *Hot Stars (OK)*

'Stella has penned a scarily realistic tale of life on the set of a Brit Flick. The affairs, the arguments and the strange behaviour of the leading ladies makes her second novel a compulsive read'   *Sunday Mirror*

'A wickedly funny chick-lit read, set in the British film industry'
Heat

'If you ever wondered what shenanigans can ensue on a film set, take time to read this . . . Every page is filled with backstabbing, plotting, dangerous liaisons and great humour which makes for a thoroughly entertaining read'
Woman (Summer Special)

Lip Kisses

'Imagine a one-woman *Sex in the City*, set in Maida Vale. Add a dose of Bridget Jones-style champagne alcoholism and a dash of early Jackie Collins. This will give some idea of what Stella Chaplin's debut novel *Lip Kisses* is all about . . . This is the perfect airport-to-beach novel'   *Sunday Express*

'A witty, insightful book with a cast of over-the-top characters that'll have you chuckling out loud on the bus to work'   *Heat*

'A witty read which manages to be light-hearted *and* gripping'
Company

Stella Chaplin lives in London. *It's a Wrap* is her second novel.

By Stella Chaplin

It's a Wrap
Lip Kisses

It's a Wrap

Stella Chaplin

ORION

An Orion paperback

First published in Great Britain in 2003
by Orion
This paperback edition published in 2004
by Orion Books Ltd,
Orion House, 5 Upper St Martin's Lane,
London WC2H 9EA

A CIP catalogue record for this book is available
from the British Library.

ISBN 0 75284 599 3

Printed and bound in Great Britain by
Clays Ltd, St Ives plc

www.orionbooks.co.uk

one

'Are you nervous?'

'A little.'

'That's OK. We're all a little nervous too.'

Emma smiled gratefully, but the other two people sitting at the table had already heard this joke eleven times that morning and didn't laugh.

'Look this way.'

The flash of the camera captured Emma's expression at the midway point as it shifted from an eager-to-please smile to gaping surprise. The dark-haired woman in the black dress stapled the Polaroid to her CV while it was still developing and scribbled something in the margin. That was the best thing about Emma's CV. There was plenty of space on it for making notes, even though Emma had listed all of her hobbies, interests, accents and special skills to take up more room.

'Can you turn to the left, please? And now to the right? And face front.'

Emma smiled again at the man sitting in the middle chair who seemed to be in charge.

'Let me tell you a little about the film,' he said. 'It's a love story and a thriller. A roller coaster of comedy and action. With music. And the part we'd like you to read for us today is Eddie's girlfriend, Roxanne. Eddie wants to be a rock star and you love Eddie. Madly. Passionately. You'd die for Eddie. You'd kill for this man. He's everything to you. Your sun, your moon, your stars. Do you understand?'

Emma nodded. She couldn't remember if the other man in the blue T-shirt had said he was the director or the producer. She smiled at him anyway, but he was trying to file some pages back inside a ring-binder and didn't look up.

'So here we go then. Just play it how it feels. Relax. Have fun with it. I'll be reading Eddie's part. Are you ready?'

Emma nodded again and swallowed hard.

'Just ignore the camera. Pretend it's not here.' He took a sip of water and pushed a wayward dark-brown curl back off his face. 'It's no good, Roxanne,' he read. 'I want to love you but I can't. It's not you. It's me.'

'But Eddie!'

'Oh-kay. Thank you, Emma. That was very nice. Now is there anything you'd like to ask us?'

Emma's eyes flickered across the three faces looking back at her and her mind went blank. They were waiting for her to say something.

'When is this going to be on TV?' she asked.

'It's a feature film,' explained the man in the middle chair. 'For the cinema. Can you send in the next girl on your way out?'

Emma opened the door and a tall girl with long brown hair and sleepy eyes eased herself out of the first green plastic chair in the corridor to take her place. There were six other girls still waiting, fanning themselves with their CVs, skinny legs in short skirts and tight trousers, chewing gum and smoking and listening to Moby on their minidisc players. They glanced up at Emma as she walked past, scrutinising her intensely, without making it obvious they were checking her out.

'What did they ask you?' said one girl. She had a dazzling smile, a blue halter-neck top and long blonde hair. Extensions, Emma decided. Quite nicely done.

'I can't remember.'

'Oh, I'm sure you'll get it,' the blonde gushed, patting her arm. Emma recognised the type – straight out of Sylvia Young's, and so manically confident about getting the part they always made a big show of being supportive to everyone else. Her dad was probably Ridley Scott.

'Thanks,' said Emma and started down the four flights of bare concrete stairs that led to Dean Street. Slowly, calm at first, then running as soon she'd passed the first landing. There was a pile of unopened dusty mail on an old chest of drawers and she pulled open the front door with such violence that half of it was blown onto the floor.

'That was terrible. Terrible, terrible, terrible,' she wailed.

Two words. Why had she done it in a Scottish accent? 'But Air-die!' She'd blown her chances now. She should have smiled more. Why didn't she ask them questions about her character? Maybe she should have done it in Geordie. Or Scouse. Everyone loves a Scouser.

She'd promised to ring Irene, her agent, and tell her how it had gone. But as usual, she got the answering machine which Irene couldn't set properly, so you could never be entirely sure whether you were leaving a message or not. Instead, she rang Jason.

Jason was her boyfriend and he was a proper actor. Or, more to the point, he was an actor with a job. He'd never actually had any formal drama training but he'd done a bit of modelling (catwalk and a lot of work in Japan if anyone asked; the Lunn Poly winter-sun brochure if they demanded proof) which was the only qualification he needed for *Shelby Square*. He'd been in the teen-soap for two years and was starting to be a tiny bit famous which was great. But *Shelby Square* was made in Sheffield, which was bad, because it meant Emma only got to see him at weekends. She had one of his old modelling photos sticky-taped to the back of her mobile phone.

'Hi, baby!' she squeaked when he answered. 'I've just come out.'

'Come out of what?' He sounded like he was chewing.

'The casting. What are you eating?'

'A ham and cheese croissant. How'd it go?'

'Awful. I don't think they liked me.'

3

'How could they not like you? You're gorgeous.'

Emma smiled, although she'd known he was going to say that. They had this identical conversation every two or three weeks – sometimes more often, if Irene was on a sugar rush and had faxed off her CV all over the country. 'You're so lucky never having to go to auditions,' she sighed. 'You could stay in *Shelby Square* for ever if you felt like it.'

'Well, don't let it get you down. It wasn't a big part, was it? What was it – two lines?'

'Two words. But it was still something. They said it was a feature film. It's just really discouraging to keep getting turned down all the time. You know?'

There was the sound of more chewing and something that sounded encouraging that Emma didn't quite catch.

'Still – I'll get the next one, won't I?' she pressed on. She could do the whole conversation by herself now and she knew all of Jason's lines as well. 'I'm probably about to get offered something totally fantastic and then I'll be really glad that I didn't get this won't I?'

'Absolutely. It's all experience. It's just a great big learning curve. You've got to keep going out there and believing in yourself and one day it's all going to happen for you.'

Emma looked at her watch. 'I've got to go. I'm late for work. I miss you, baby. Call me later?'

It was already a quarter to twelve. She unlocked her bicycle from the railings and pedalled off through Soho in the direction of Covent Garden, shouting: 'Toot toot!' at the pedestrians who leapt off the footpath and straight out in front of her as though she didn't exist. She used to have a bell but the kids in her street had unscrewed it and even though she could hear them playing with it, she was afraid to ask for it back because they looked like the type who'd slash her tyres.

'How was it? asked Donna as she ran into the salon ten minutes later, coaxing her flattened helmet-hair back into shape.

'Not too bad. You know.'

4

'You're very brave. I can't stand dentists.'

'Me neither.'

'Anyway, my twelve o'clock's here already.' Donna pointed her jewelled pen towards a redhead with a tell-tale grey parting who was reading *Tatler*.

Emma helped the woman into one of the salon's black gowns and tied the sash behind her back. 'Can I get you a cup of coffee?' she asked.

Three years out of drama school and here she was, still at the same salon where she'd worked as a Saturday girl and during the holidays. So much for her career. At this rate, she'd still be paying off her student loan when she was sixty. She'd graduated from sweeping the floor and folding towels to shampooing and colouring, but the highlights of her acting career so far were Meningitis Girl in *Holby City* and two lines in *The Bill* – 'Get your hands off me!' and 'I never touched nuffink!'

'You think it's tough now!' Irene, kept telling her. 'You wait till you hit forty! I've got some of the best actresses in the country on my books and they're over the hill at thirty-eight. You've got it easy compared to them. What happened about that demonstrating job at the Ideal Home Show? You shouldn't be so picky.'

Secretly though, Emma was beginning to wonder if Irene was all she was cracked up to be. She'd been to Irene's office only once and it had turned out to be a desk with a telephone and a manual typewriter in the living room of a basement flat in Romford. When Emma had looked in through the net curtains, she'd found Irene asleep on the sofa at half past three in the afternoon, still in her dressing gown, with the TV and all the lights on and six of Irene's eleven cats asleep around her.

Emma had stopped telling the other girls at the salon when she was going for an audition – even Donna who she shared a flat with. It had become slightly embarrassing the way they always got as excited about it as she did – forever asking, 'Did you get it? Did you get it?' And it was depressing having to keep telling them that no, this time she'd been too young, or too old, or too short or not blonde enough. Or that they'd really been looking for *a name*.

She was twenty-four already and, by Irene's reckoning, she only had sixteen years to go before she was over the hill. And she hadn't even started! If it wasn't for the unmistakable adrenalin high she felt on those rare occasions when she was allowed to act – that transcendental feeling that she was in the right place at the right time doing the thing she was supposed to be doing with her life – she might have thought about giving it all up. The only tiny problem was that the thousands of other out-of-work actresses in Britain all felt exactly the same way.

Michael, her boss, was cool about her taking time off for auditions because he fancied having a crack at showbiz himself – transforming traffic wardens and dinner ladies on daytime TV. He was every bit as good as that Nicky Clarke, he reckoned.

'Why don't you just lie?' he'd suggested when she'd shown him her CV. 'Why don't you say you were in *Titanic*? There were thousands of people in that. Do you really think anybody's going to remember whether you were one of them? If they ask what it was like, just tell them it was cold and wet. They can't argue with that.'

Irene was all in favour of lying too. 'If they ever ask if you can do something, always say yes,' she told her. 'If the part calls for a thirty-year-old, tell them today's your thirtieth birthday. If it's for a schoolgirl, say you're sixteen but you've had a hard life.'

But Emma couldn't lie. She was the worst liar in the world. Sometimes she wondered if the reason why she wanted to act in the first place was because it was the only time she could get away with not telling the truth.

'Yes, I'd love a coffee,' her client said. 'You don't mind if I smoke, do you?'

'No, go ahead,' blushed Emma, and stifled a cough as she went to put the kettle on.

two

Ben stretched out his legs and lit a cigarette. This was the part of the job he knew he was going to look back on with nostalgia – the calm before the storm, before he had to get up in the dark and spend twelve hours a day, six days a week, making a hundred snap decisions every minute, compromising every image he held dear because he would never have enough money or enough time or enough talent to make the perfect movie he had in his head.

He was about to voluntarily spend two months of his life in a permanent state of anxiety, terrified that it would rain, or the lab would scratch his negatives, or that the generator would break down and he would never get his movie shot on time. But now, right now at this precise second, everything was still OK.

This morning, for instance, he'd been able to stroll into the office around nine, and an eager production assistant had brought him a double grande latte from the place on the corner – *without him even having to ask* – and then he had spent the morning watching beautiful, stunning, perfect young women parade through his office, and the most amazing thing of all was that every single one of them was absolutely desperate for him to like her. It was a shame he would have to put an end to this idyllic arrangement by actually shooting a movie.

'Well, what do we think?' asked Angela the casting director. 'Personally, I liked Amber and Sophie.'

'Did we see someone called Amber?' asked Ben, flicking through his notes.

'I can't remember who we've seen,' said Patrick. 'It's all just a lovely blur. I've had to keep my folder on my lap or I would've poked them in the eye.'

Angela was already rewinding the tape. 'Do you mind?' She'd only agreed to cast this film as a personal favour to Ben because she had him pegged as a talent on the way up and a good investment for her future. She didn't have much time for Patrick McKay, a producer whose star now looked unlikely ever to rise beyond the hand-to-mouth, penny-pinching, raggedy-arsed low-budget end of the business. 'Let's take a look at them again,' she said.

'Turn the sound down,' said Ben. 'Don't make me listen to my terrible line reading. Please. It's only two words. They can all speak English.'

So they watched in silence as the would-be Roxannes paraded across the screen for Patrick and Ben's viewing pleasure.

'Oh my God, what has she come as?' jeered Patrick as a girl with blue highlights and a leather mini dress displayed her left and right profiles.

'Next!' echoed Ben.

'Yes please, love,' leered Patrick, as a tiny dark-haired girl with an enormous bust paraded across the screen. 'And bring those boots.'

'But her teeth are terrible,' said Angela. She scribbled the words FANG ALERT! on the girl's CV in red ink and underlined it three times.

'If you say so,' sighed Patrick.

'Now this is Amber,' said Angela as the next girl appeared. 'She was terribly good.'

'No, too skinny,' said Patrick. 'I've got bigger tits than she has. Next!'

'I don't even remember this one,' said Patrick as a startled looking girl with light-brown hair and blue eyes appeared on screen.

'No, she looks almost normal,' agreed Ben. 'What's her name?'

'Emma Buckley,' said Angela. 'I've never heard of her.'

'Oh, right, the one with the terrible Scottish accent,' said Patrick.

Emma smiled again towards the side of the camera where Patrick had been sitting and he felt a familiar ping in his groin.

'She hasn't done much,' said Angela. 'She's with Irene Hamilton.'

'I thought she was dead,' said Patrick.

'Only from the neck up.'

'Yeah, maybe she's a bit of a gamble,' Ben agreed. 'But she's got a bit of a spark.'

'Oh look,' said Angela, interrupting. 'Now this is Sophie.'

The girl with the long brown hair smouldered at the camera, her black liner giving her sleepy green eyes a cat-like appearance.

'Well, there's our Roxanne,' said Patrick.

'She's head and shoulders above the others,' said Angela.

'Literally,' Patrick agreed. 'What is she, seven foot tall?'

'Five eleven.'

'I'm not a hundred per cent convinced,' said Ben. 'She's not an actress. She's a model.'

'Well, you did say you wanted a bit of glamour in your movie,' Angela reminded him. 'And I'd grab her now if I were you, because in a month's time her bra campaign is going to be on billboards all over the country.' She handed Ben and Patrick a black and white ten-by-eight.

Ben stared at the picture of Sophie with one finger in her open mouth and the little finger of her other hand nonchalantly tucked just inside the lace of her knickers and the area of his brain labelled 'Artistic Integrity', which was already battered by wafer-thin budgets and pounded constantly by the growing realisation of his own inexperience, was finally demolished by a tidal wave of testosterone. Meanwhile, in an adjacent part of his brain marked 'Lifetime Goals', he had a vision of his name, in letters ten feet high, on the hoarding above the Odeon Leicester Square next to this photo. He saw Sophie standing beside him on the podium as he stepped up to collect his Oscar. She still had her finger in her mouth. 'Well,' he said. 'It's just one line of dialogue.'

'Piece of piss,' agreed Patrick.

'And we can always re-dub it if she's really bad,' Ben continued.

'So is that a yes for Sophie?' asked Angela.

'Well, it's entirely up to you, Angela,' said Ben, thinking that if it all went tits-up, so to speak, he would need someone else to pin the blame on. 'If you're sure she's right for the part—'

'I'll get a contract out to her straight away.' Angela stood up to go back to her desk and Patrick quietly slid Emma's CV from the top of the reject pile and slipped it into his folder before anyone could see.

'So,' he said, turning to Ben and giving him a playful kick with his Caterpillar boot. 'Have you had a chance yet to meet up with the lovely Liz?'

Ben groaned. 'You had to go and spoil it, didn't you? You couldn't just let me enjoy my last few days of peace.' He tapped the last cigarette out of the packet and lit it up anxiously.

'All I meant was—'

'I know what you meant, you Scottish bastard. She's coming in tomorrow. Eleven o'clock.'

'Will you be needing a chaperone? A bodyguard? The last rites?'

'It'll be fine. It's been six years. It'll be absolutely fine.'

'I predict tears and sick followed by a swift castration.'

'Fuck off, Patrick.'

But when Patrick had gone, Ben hoped he wasn't right.

Ben had just been a humble focus puller when he met Liz. Actually, not so humble, he had to admit. Every person on every crew he'd ever worked with from the runner on up had ambitions to direct, but Ben was determined to be one of the few who would actually make it. He'd dropped out of his economics degree and badgered production companies for work as a runner. He'd worked for free, made more cups of tea than he cared to remember, been enthusiastic and hard-working without being too much of a pain in the arse about it, and had made friends with a couple of camera operators and persuaded them to take him on as a trainee.

Nearly five years later, he'd worked his way up from loader to focus puller and whenever he wasn't working he was writing, because he reckoned that was his best shot at getting a chance to direct. His scripts were all still terrible but he thought they were getting better.

He'd met Liz in Crete shooting a fruit juice commercial. He remembered that he'd never been so hot as he had been that morning. All of the crew had taken their shirts off and he could feel Liz's eyes on him even before he saw her. She was wearing an orange bikini top and a tiny wrap-around skirt and he could still remember the way she flicked her long flame-coloured ponytail over her shoulders as she strolled languidly backwards and forwards adjusting costumes.

At lunch, she'd sat next to him on the sweaty plastic chairs, secretly stroking his leg under the table, and then she'd got up, as cool as you like, and just walked back to the wardrobe trailer. She still hadn't spoken a single word to him.

That night, he'd had a glass of ouzo in the hotel bar to get his nerve up and then gone and knocked on her door. All he'd intended to do was ask if she wanted to come out for a drink, but the moment Liz opened her door in her orange bikini the only thought left in his mind was that he had to get her into bed immediately. Which was precisely what he did.

Ben was twenty-four then, and Liz was twenty-eight. He found it incredibly sexy that she was technically an older woman. Hell, when he was twenty-four, he found everything incredibly sexy. It was incredibly sexy that she had long red hair and a tattoo of a dragon in the small of her back. It was incredibly sexy that she was more successful than he was. It was incredibly sexy spending the whole of his day off in bed with Liz.

It was the best sex he'd ever had in his life by a million miles and that was the part he still liked to think about. Before it all got messy. But then no relationships end well, do they, he told himself. That's why they end. And there had been plenty of other girls before Liz and since Liz. Meet 'em, fuck 'em, get bored of them and dump them. That was the rhythm his sex life had tapped out roughly every three months. His ten months with Liz was still a record.

Just a few weeks ago, his most recent affair with a fiery Spanish dancer called Pilar had crashed and burned in a volcano of Spanish expletives the third time he said he couldn't go clubbing with her because he had to write.

'Write! Write!' she'd spat at him. 'What are you writing always that is so bloody important? Eh? This feelm you say there is not even a part for me in, eh?' And she'd picked up his laptop, yanking the plug out of the wall and letting it crash to the ground before flouncing off in a never-to-be-seen-again tempest.

Ben didn't have time to chase after her because he was on his hands and knees inspecting the damage to his laptop and praying that there was life in the battery because he hadn't saved his changes. The casing was cracked and he would never again be able to use any words that had a Q in them, but at least he was able to save the latest version of his script to disk. Pilar was just a girl, but this screenplay was his whole future.

As for Liz, he hadn't worked with her since they broke up. The film industry was a small, incestuous village and he didn't usually go to such extraordinary lengths to avoid his ex-girlfriends. So maybe it was guilt about the way he'd ended it that made him always check who the costume designer would be before he accepted any jobs. Not that he ever let on that's what he was doing of course. No, he'd just ring the production office to check start dates and casually ask who else was already attached to the project – just out of professional curiosity. Once or twice Liz's name had been mentioned and he'd pretended to check his diary and suddenly realise that he wasn't going to be free on those dates after all. It had cost him one really good film which he still regretted not taking. And now, here he was, deliberately hiring her on his very first feature as director. He wasn't mad, he reminded himself, just desperate.

He'd fully intended to give the job to Justine Burgess and they'd had long talks about it, and she'd said yes. But that was months and months ago and before Patrick had got all the money together, she'd been offered a huge sci-fi epic at Pinewood. She was really, really sorry, she said, but she couldn't afford to hang around for some half-arsed project that might never happen. She didn't actually say half-arsed, but Ben knew that's what she meant. He didn't blame her. He'd have done exactly the same thing.

So then he'd tried Sara Pollard, but when he'd told her how much he could afford to pay her, she'd laughed for about three minutes and pointed out that she could earn that in two days on a commercial, thanks all the same.

And then he'd called Ginni Ferrari who wasn't even in the country and then, just when he was getting really desperate, he'd got a call out of the blue from Liz. She said she'd heard about his film and she just happened to be available and she'd be willing to do it for a fraction of her usual rate as a favour to an old friend. In fact, she said, he'd be doing her a big favour because the film she'd been on had folded after just two weeks and her whole team needed work.

Ben had wanted to say no. He wanted to say that he'd spent the last six years doing his utmost to avoid her and that even though they were due to start shooting in three weeks and he was absolutely desperate, he wouldn't want to work with her if she was the last costume designer on earth.

So he had lied. 'Wow, that's great, Liz,' he'd said. 'I'd love you to do it. You know, the only reason I didn't ask you in the first place was because I didn't want to insult you by offering you such a poor deal. We really are working on a shoestring here. Half a-shoestring. But the thing is, the thing is . . . I've already offered it to Ginni Ferrari and I'm waiting for her to get back to me. It's such a pity.'

13

'Oh, didn't you know?' said Liz. 'Ginni's in Mexico doing a film for HBO. I had an e-mail from her just the other day. She's not back until September.'

She had him by the balls. He still couldn't lie to her.

'No,' he said lamely. 'I didn't know that.'

'So, I guess you do need me after all?' said Liz.

And Ben had said yes. He had even said thank you.

Now Ben sat in his rented Soho office and looked again at the spreadsheet he'd drawn up on his new Apple G4. It only had two columns. The first column was headed: Reasons For Hiring Liz, and underneath he had typed:

1. She's an excellent designer
2. She's available
3. She'll do it for the money
4. It's too late to get anyone else good
5. I owe her a favour

The second column was headed: Reasons To Not Hire Liz. And underneath that he had typed just one line:

1. She used to be in love with me.

But that was six years ago, he reasoned, and she'd be over him by now. In fact, he knew she was over him. From time to time, people he worked with would say, 'I had an e-mail from Liz the other day', or, 'I bumped into Liz last week', or, 'Guess who was at the party last night?'

'Is she seeing anyone?' Ben would ask and he'd be relieved when they'd say that yes, as a matter of fact, she'd been with some Danish guy called Stefan, or that they'd heard she was seeing a cameraman, or an investment banker. That was a relief. He didn't want to think that he'd broken Liz's heart. He was glad to hear that she was well and truly over him because it meant he was off the hook. Somebody told him they'd heard she'd become a Buddhist and Buddhists were famous for being laid-back. And on the phone she'd sounded really happy. Normal. He didn't want her to think he was sending her mixed signals, but he was sure she understood that this was strictly a professional arrangement. Besides, nobody carries a torch for six years, do they? It was just like he'd told Patrick: everything was going to be absolutely fine.

three

Liz closed her eyes as the cotton ball dipped in acid was dragged gently across her forehead.

'Now this is going to tingle,' said the nurse. 'Let me know if it's unbearable and I'll neutralise it right away.'

Liz liked the tingling. It was a sign that something was happening. No pain, no gain. As the acid was dabbed on her chin, around her mouth, and over her cheeks, she imagined all her dry, sluggish, sun-damaged skin cells being tingled into oblivion. This was her fifth treatment and already she thought her skin felt softer than it had a month ago.

'How does that feel?' asked the nurse.

'Wonderful,' Liz replied. When this course of treatment was finished, she'd ask for the acid solution to be increased to 90 per cent.

After eight minutes, the acid was quickly wiped away with damp pads of cotton wool. Then came the moisturiser and Factor 30 sunblock was smoothed gently all over her face. Liz examined her face in the mirror the nurse was holding. The pinkness would wear off by tomorrow. She certainly didn't look thirty-four.

She tried to frown and was annoyed to see that the Botox hadn't kicked in yet. Three to five days, they'd said, and here it was, four days later and still her brow crinkled and furrowed just like it always did. She had until exactly eleven o'clock tomorrow morning to achieve a paralysed and serene forehead. But she didn't feel serene. Perhaps her Endermologie treatment would relax her, she thought, as she walked down the corridor to the adjoining treatment room.

She undressed and slipped into the tight, white nylon body-suit and lay down on her stomach so that the beautician could start rollering her thighs and bottom. The hum of the machine always soothed her. She never thought about the cost. It was an investment. What better way to spend her hard-earned money than on herself?

Six years ago, she hadn't had to worry about cellulite, or frown lines, or a dull, sluggish complexion. She hadn't needed botulism germs, or glycolic acid or two forty-five minute sessions a week of pinching and pummelling to be beautiful. Six years ago, she'd had Ben. She'd wanted him since the moment she first saw him across the beach, mopping the sweat off the back of his neck with a wet-wipe he'd cadged off make-up. She closed her eyes and remembered how his skin had looked as sweet as golden syrup. God, life had been easy then . . .

She loved the sun. She loved the way it put splashes of gold in her hair and turned her skin to honey. She loved the hot breeze caressing her bare arms after a dark English winter hidden away in fleeces and waterproofs. She loved the feeling of fresh air on her legs again, the bite of the white sand between her toes. She loved her job. She loved her life. She loved being tall enough to look any man in the eye and strong enough to wrap any one of them around her little finger. Most men were a little afraid of Liz and she liked that. The ones who weren't afraid of her she liked even more. She wanted to be pursued. She wanted them to make the running, but she wasn't afraid to give them a little shove to get the ball rolling.

That morning when she'd seen Ben solemnly measuring lens distances and winding in his tape, she'd approved of the way his broad shoulders tapered down to narrow, boyish hips in his long baggy shorts and thought how nice it would be at the end of a long, hard day, to touch the spot where his eyebrows almost met in the middle but didn't, and to rest her head on those shoulders and lick the sweat from his throat like a cat. He still hadn't noticed her because he was concentrating on his work, but that was OK. There was plenty of time. She smiled to herself. The sun was still making its way to the top of the sky.

'Could you roll over onto your side now?'

Liz awoke and arranged herself on the narrow bench so that the beautician could work on her inner thigh. Julian. That was the cameraman's name, she remembered.

'Julian!' Liz leaned over his shoulder and kissed him on the cheek. 'How are you, darling? I haven't had a chance to even say hello to you today, I've been so busy.'

'Hi, Liz,' Julian motioned with his hand to the empty chair opposite him. 'Join us.'

Liz put her plate down on the table and slid elegantly into the vacant seat beside Ben.

'Do you know Ben?' Julian asked.

'Yeah, we met at the airport,' said Liz, with just the briefest of polite smiles in Ben's direction. 'So how are Caroline and the baby? Have you chosen a name yet?'

'Molly,' said Julian. 'She's absolutely amazing. Thanks for your card by the way.'

'I can't wait to see them.' As Liz lifted a piece of grilled swordfish to her lips, her left hand, which was resting on her lap under the table, strayed over to Ben's leg and she began casually but unmistakably sliding her finger along the top of his thigh. 'Is Caroline planning to go back to work?' she asked. She could feel his quadricep muscle tense under his shorts.

'I don't think so,' said Julian. 'Not for a few months. I think she'd be quite happy to stay at home for a couple of years if she can.'

'Oh, how lovely,' said Liz, as the back of her finger reached the inside of Ben's bare knee. 'I must call her when we get back to London.'

'Yeah, come over for dinner, that'd be great.'

'Do you know what you're going on to after this?' Liz's finger began slowly working its way back up Ben's thigh.

'A documentary for Channel 4. It's not very interesting, but it'll keep me in London for four weeks which is the main thing.'

'Oh yeah, you don't want to miss a minute of it, do you?' said Liz, making delicate little circles on Ben's leg. 'They're so gorgeous when they're babies.'

'What about you? You getting broody yet?' Julian asked.

'Me?' Liz laughed. 'I don't think so. Where on earth would I find time for a baby with this job? I don't even have time for lunch. I've got a Carmen Miranda head-dress to glue back together.'

She stood up, her meal scarcely touched, and went to put her plate in the washing up bowl. She didn't even glance back at Ben. She didn't need to.

The machine vibrated gently and Liz visualised all her fat cells marching obediently into her lymph passages and being herded out of her body.

'OK. Other side now,' the beautician told her. 'You know, it doesn't really look like you have any cellulite at all.'

'No, I don't,' agreed Liz, 'and I don't intend to get any.'

She turned over and smiled to herself, remembering how she had ignored Ben all that afternoon. After an hour of walking backwards and forwards and standing where she was sure that he could get a good look at her, she'd sent her assistant on set and gone back to the wardrobe tent to dress all the extras, knowing it would drive Ben crazy, wondering where she'd gone.

Later, back in the hotel, she'd showered, pinned up her hair and hadn't even pretended to be surprised when she'd opened her door and found Ben standing in the hallway. Men! They were all so easy.

'And now on your back.'

Liz obediently rolled over with a blissful smile on her lips as the machine began to roll and suck at the front of her legs.

What a fantastic night that had been. Ben had made love to her with the dedication and enthusiasm only a twenty-four-year-old man who is fucking a total stranger can muster. As he'd dragged her from one corner of the bed to another she'd been fascinated by the reflection of their two lean, perfectly matched bodies in the cheap dressing-table mirror. They might have been brother and sister.

She hadn't expected him to stay but they'd spent the night curled up together, face to face under the cotton sheet, taking it in turns to swat the mosquitoes that buzzed around their ears. Before the alarm had rung at six, he'd kissed her awake and that was when Liz opened her eyes and fell in love with the kind, unshaven face looking back at her.

'Morning,' Ben had said, then rolled gently on top of her, still smiling. Liz pushed his hair out of his serious grey-green eyes and, for the first time in her life, found herself wondering what their children would look like.

four

The kitchen was a mess as usual. The remains of an unsuccessful fry-up were still on the stove and a trail of beans and tomato sauce led to the counter. Emma looked around for a clear surface to put down her shopping bags, then gave up and dumped them on the floor, emptying the milk and salad and pasta straight into the fridge.

Chris, Donna's boyfriend, appeared in the doorway, looking like he'd just woken up.

'Hey, I was going to do those dishes later,' he mumbled. 'I'm just off down the pub to meet Donna. Want to come?'

'Mmm. Maybe later.'

'OK. See you.'

She could hear Chris clumping around in the hallway and the front door closing behind him. Chris and Donna were OK, but the chance of having the flat to herself for a couple of hours was too good to pass up. She'd worked till the salon closed at seven to make up for coming in late and all she wanted to do now was put her feet up, have something comforting and stodgy to eat, and watch bad TV. She wasn't going to think about the audition at all. It was only a two-word part and it really wasn't worth getting worked up about anyway.

She was starting to realise what a strange game acting was. It expected you to be incredibly sensitive and at the same time willingly put yourself into situations where you'd be rejected time and time again. Emma tried to be philosophical about it and chalk it all up to experience, but with every knock-back she could feel herself shrinking, bit by bit, and she was afraid that one day she'd wake up and there'd be nothing left of her at all.

Jason said acting was all about luck. And it was very bad luck indeed that only a third of the students in her year had been signed up by one of the agents who came to see their final production. The previous year, all the students had got agents, so it had never occurred to Emma that she'd leave drama school with no agent, no prospects and that the only jobs she'd be able to get were the kind that didn't actually pay any money. So far, she'd managed to avoid selling her soul to the travelling children's theatre – 'Do you have any *experience* of playing hedgehogs?' they'd asked her – but it was surely only a matter of time.

Irene had come to see her when she'd been doing a five-week run at a fringe theatre in Chelsea where they didn't even pay her bus fare. She'd rush out of the salon on the dot of six every night and cycle in the rain to the Kings Road just in time to do her own make-up at six thirty for curtain-up at half past seven. She didn't know of any other industry that expected you to be quite so grateful to work for free. But she was trapped. She needed work to build up her CV, but if she wanted to stay in London where most of the work was, she also needed money to survive. So her Saturday job in the salon had gradually stretched to full-time. At first, she'd thought she'd be there just a couple of weeks until her career took off, but it had been three years now, on and off. The pay was peanuts but at least it was regular peanuts.

She poured the boiling water into the saucepan, added a pinch of salt and a long handful of spaghetti. She looked again at the dishes stacked around the sink and sighed. There are two kinds of people in this world – the kind who can walk away from a pile of dirty dishes and just go to the pub, and the kind who can't.

Emma was definitely the kind who can't. She scraped the dirty plates and frying pan into the bin, pushed the last of the spaghetti right down into the saucepan and rolled up her sleeves. Never mind whose washing up it was. Never mind that Chris had been at home all day again and that her own fingers were still pruned after an afternoon of shampooing, it was easier and less stressful in the long run to just do it herself. She'd liked it better before Chris had moved in with them. But it was Donna's flat and she could move in her boyfriend if she liked. But it was such a small flat, and Chris seemed to fill every corner of it with mess and noise.

Jason never stayed over because the box room she rented from Donna was scarcely big enough for two people to stand up in at the same time. The first time he'd visited her, he'd had to open his overnight bag in the hallway. Then he'd made a big song and dance about not being able to sleep because, he claimed, the walls were closing in on him and he'd insisted that they get up in the middle of the night and check into a hotel. Emma hated to see him flash his money around like that but he was right. The room was titchy, but what did you expect for thirty pounds a week? Donna was doing her a huge favour. Emma had hoped that after they'd been going out for a year, Jason would ask her to move in with him so that she wouldn't have to eat spaghetti on her own every night. She wouldn't mind moving to Sheffield and she could probably get as much work there as she did in London. She could hardly get any less.

There was a ringing sound coming from the kitchen table and she drowned her handbag in suds as she reached inside to grab her mobile phone. Irene wouldn't be calling her this late, would she?

'It's probably just Jason, or Mum,' she told herself. 'Don't get your hopes up.'

'Hello. Is that Emma Buckley?' Emma didn't recognise the voice – it was male, with a faint Scottish accent.

'Yes.' Water was running down her phone arm and inside her rolled-up sleeve.

'You came to see us this afternoon at the casting for *Brighton Rocks*. This is Patrick McKay, the producer.'

Emma's heart was racing. She hardly dared imagine what he

was going to say next. Please let it be yes, please let it be yes, she thought.

'There's a chance that we might have a part for you, but we'd like to see you again. I don't suppose there's any chance you're free this evening?'

'What? Now?'

'Just for an informal chat.'

'Yes, of course!' Emma ran to the stove to turn off the gas as the water in the saucepan began to bubble over.

'Tell you what, why don't we meet around the corner from the office at the House? At, say, nine o'clock? How would that be for you?'

'That'd be great! Fantastic! Where do you live?'

Patrick chuckled. 'Sorry, I meant Soho House, of course.'

'Oh. Of course.' Emma winced and wanted to kick herself. She'd been to Soho House once with Jason – a surprise party for one of his friends and she'd seen Cat Deeley having lunch – but now Patrick was going to think she was just a hick from the sticks.

'I'll see you there,' said Patrick.

'OK. Goodbye. Thanks!' A call-back! It was too good to be true! Oh God, she hadn't sounded too keen, had she? They were supposed to think this was just another part for her – not her first film ever. She ran to her bedroom and flung open her cupboard doors, looking for a smart, clean top. How about her denim skirt and pink T-shirt? Was that the sort of thing you'd wear for an informal chat with a producer and casting agent? Would the director be there too? Ben thingy?

She washed off her old make-up and splashed her face with cold water, wondering what they wanted to chat to her about. They'd probably want to know about her background. Emma hadn't been in this business long, but she knew that she was the only girl at her drama school who'd grown up on a sheep farm in the middle of nowhere.

People from her village didn't become actresses. Agriculture – that was the thing. Or Equine Studies. Or they became vets like her brother. Her family had tried to be supportive, without being entirely sure what it was they were supporting. Even her careers adviser at school had tried to push Emma into teaching, before reluctantly finding an out-of-date list of drama schools and suggesting that Emma phone them herself to find out how to apply.

Her first trip to London for auditions had been a revelation. She remembered being surprised and a little disappointed to discover that the buildings in Leicester Square, Piccadilly and Coventry Street weren't yellow at all like they were on her Monopoly board, but made of ordinary coloured bricks, just like the buildings back home.

Walking down Shaftesbury Avenue for the first time, the names of the stars above the theatre hoardings had seemed like gods to her, even though she had never heard of most of them. She'd never even been to the theatre – apart from panto – and neither had any of her family. She'd always imagined that you would somehow have to be invited. She'd seen photos in the papers of celebrities arriving to see plays in the West End. Surely they wouldn't let in just anybody?

So no-one had been more surprised than Emma to get the letter saying she'd been accepted at the drama school of her choice. It was the least-grand sounding school on her list – she was afraid the posh ones would only laugh at her – but their fees had turned out to be just as high.

Now, at five minutes to nine, she came out of the tube at Tottenham Court Road, wearing her best denim skirt and pink T-shirt, and walked towards Soho Square trying to think calm thoughts. As she passed Waterstones, she stopped and smiled at her reflection in the window to rehearse looking relaxed and informal. 'Ben!' she smiled at herself. 'Patrick! Hello! So nice to see you. And Casting Lady Whose Name I Don't Know. Hello!'

In Greek Street, she checked the numbers on the shops looking for the right building and found herself standing in front of a scruffy doorway. She pressed the buzzer.

'Hello? I'm meeting Patrick—' and she realised she'd completely forgotten Patrick's surname.

'I can't hear you. Patrick who?' said a crackly voice.

'I can't remember.' The audition had been such a blur, all Emma could remember was his hair. 'He's got collar-length mid-brown hair with a slight wave to it, there's just a tiny bit of grey and I think he uses styling gel. He's a producer.'

'That sounds just like me,' said a voice and Emma turned to see Patrick standing behind her. 'What's the matter? Won't they let you in?'

'Sorry. I couldn't remember your second name,' Emma admitted.

Patrick flashed a swipe-card and the door buzzed to let them both in. 'I don't think I've ever heard my hair described in quite such detail,' he told her.

'Oh. I guess I just always notice people's hair first,' Emma said quickly. She'd hate Patrick to think she was just a hairdresser. While they queued at the bar, she looked around the crowded room for a familiar face. 'Where are the others?' she asked.

'The other what?' said Patrick.

'I thought Ben and the casting lady wanted to see me again.'

'Right. Yes, they did but they're very busy back in the office. So they asked me to pop out and meet you on my own. You don't mind, do you?'

'No. Of course not.'

'I got you white,' he said, handing her a glass. 'Shall we go through?'

Emma took her drink and followed Patrick backwards and forwards up and down stairs, through a maze of interconnecting rooms and corridors, until he found a couple of armchairs in a quiet corner that he liked the look of. Emma sat down and sipped her wine cautiously, remembering that all she'd eaten was a carton of tomato soup and an apple at around two o'clock.

'So. Emma Buckley,' began Patrick. 'What part of Scotland are you from?'

Emma blushed, remembering her audition. 'I'm not,' she confessed. 'I just thought Roxanne might be Scottish.'

Patrick pretended to look surprised. 'Oh, I get it! Acting, were you? I suppose your name's not Emma Buckley either?'

Emma was a little taken aback. 'No. I mean, it is.'

'Well, it's a very good name. A good movie name. I like it.'

'Thanks.'

'I'm surprised I haven't heard it before.'

'Well, you know, I haven't done very much. I don't expect anyone to have heard of me.'

'That's a pity,' he said, 'because the camera loves you.'

Emma chewed her lip, thrilled to bits. 'That's very kind of you.'

'I'm just telling you the truth. I'll have to show you your audition tape some time. You light up the screen. Do you have family in the business?' he asked.

Emma shook her head. 'No. They've got a farm. My middle brother's a vet.'

'Really!' Patrick was fascinated but slightly queasy as well. The countryside made him nervous. All that fresh air.

A waitress wafted a plate of fish cakes and fries past Emma's nose and she wished that she'd had time to cook her spaghetti before Patrick phoned. Perhaps they could get some nuts or something.

'So,' she said, hoping she wouldn't sound too pushy, 'you said on the phone there might be a part for me?'

'Right, right. Have you seen any of the other films I've produced?'

'I'm not sure,' she admitted.

Patrick reeled off the names of half a dozen titles. Some of them Emma recognised from the shelves of her video store but hadn't actually seen, so she tried to ooh and aah in all the right places, as Patrick explained the long and convoluted process by which Ben's first script had got this far. Emma didn't under-stand half of it, especially the part about lottery money, but she nodded a lot and said, 'I see', in what she hoped was an intelligent manner. Another waitress appeared with menus and Emma breathed a sigh of relief.

'I'm very hungry,' she confessed.

'Good! Good!' said Patrick. 'Young, hungry, keen to get on! That's what I like to hear.'

He handed the menus back without looking at them and ordered another round of drinks even though Emma's wine was largely untouched. 'Did you know I produced that vodka commercial Ben won the award for?' he asked.

'No, I didn't,' sighed Emma. 'So, did I pass the audition?'

'Well. The good news is, we've narrowed it down. It's between you and one other girl.'

'That's great!' Emma didn't know whether this was good news or not. She hoped it was good news.

'Sophie Randall,' he said. 'Do you know her?'

Emma shook her head.

'She's a model,' said Patrick. 'Stunning girl, really quite stunning . . .'

Emma's hopes started to ebb away.

'. . . but sometimes, it's nice to take a flyer and go with a new face,' he went on. 'Know what I mean?'

And her hopes sprang back to life.

'So that's why I wanted to meet you again and see if my instincts were right.' He picked up her right hand and turned it over to examine it. 'Did you know I can read palms?' He turned her hand onto its side and pointed to two creases just underneath her little finger. 'See that? That means you're going to have two children.'

'Really?' exclaimed Emma. 'That's wonderful.'

'And this line here? This is your head line.' He traced the line thoughtfully with his finger tip. 'I can see you're a clever girl, Emma. The sort of girl who's going to get on in life. The sort of girl who knows who her friends are. Do you know what I mean?'

Emma looked up to find Patrick studying her intently. He was still holding her hand but he had turned it over now and was casually resting his own large hand over hers, stroking the back of her fingers with his thumb.

Emma smiled, slightly embarrassed. It was only fair to let Patrick know straight off that she wasn't in the slightest bit interested in him in that way. He was at least forty and although you could tell he'd been quite good-looking once, he'd let himself go soft around the edges. 'I've got a boyfriend you know,' she told him as gently as she could and sneaked her hand away.

'I'm sure you have,' said Patrick. 'I never imagined for a second that a beautiful girl like you would be single. But that doesn't mean we can't be friends, does it?'

'No, I suppose not,' Emma agreed, thinking Irene would be pleased she'd made friends with a producer who thought she lit up the screen.

'I tell you what,' said Patrick, as though the idea had just flown into his head. 'Why don't we go back to the office now and do another screen-test? A bigger part this time. Something you can really get your teeth into.'

'Will Ben be there?' she asked.

'Everyone will be there,' said Patrick, getting to his feet. He took out his wallet and left fifteen pounds on the table. 'Come on.'

Reluctantly, Emma got to her feet, looking longingly at the fish cakes on the next table, then followed him back through the maze and down to the street. She hoped Patrick would have some crisps in his office or a packet of biscuits at least.

Patrick unlocked the front door of the building and jangled the keys in his pocket as he pressed the button to call the lift. He was still wearing the shabby blue T-shirt he'd been wearing that afternoon and Emma could see he was getting the tiniest bit of a paunch. Days of high stress and nights of expensive wine and rich food had given his face a split personality. He had a permanent frown line between his eyebrows – just like George Michael, Emma thought – while the bottom half of his face had settled into fleshy, comfortable jowls. There was something else too – a watchfulness in his eyes, as though he couldn't look at the world without mentally calculating his percentage.

At the fourth floor Patrick led the way down the corridor to the production office, reached into his pocket again for his keys and unlocked the main door. As he pushed it open, Emma could see the office was in darkness.

'Oh, that's bad luck,' she said. 'The others must have got tired of waiting for us. I can come back tomorrow, if you want.'

Patrick made no sign that he'd heard her, and reached around the door frame to switch on the inside light. The fluorescent tubes slowly flickered into life as though they were surprised and a little embarrassed at having been woken up at this hour.

'Well. Come on, then,' he said impatiently.

Emma took a few steps back.

'What's the matter? You're not afraid of me, are you?'

Emma shook her head, although her heart had started to thump wildly. She realised that no one else knew she was even there. No one had seen them come in. The building was completely deserted. 'No, I'm not scared,' she said, trying to stop her voice from shaking. 'I'd just like to go home now. I haven't had any dinner.'

Patrick sighed. 'Look, do you want to be in this movie, or don't you?'

Honestly, thought Emma, the cheek of the man! Just what does he take me for? 'Do you mean will I have sex with you just to get a crummy two-word part?' she said in what she hoped was her haughtiest voice. 'The answer's no. You'll have to keep your casting couch for some other girl.'

Patrick started to laugh. 'My *casting couch*?' he repeated sarcastically. 'How very 1950s of you. I think you've been reading too many Jackie Collins novels. I'm afraid all I've got is a two-seater sofa from IKEA.' He stepped closer. 'Come in and have a look, if you don't believe me.' He reached out his arm towards her and Emma panicked. She half turned to go, stepping backwards and tumbled ungracefully down the first three stairs.

'Oof!' she gasped as she landed on her hands and knees and the contents of her bag scattered all over the landing. She froze, staring up at Patrick in alarm, expecting him to pounce at any minute. And then, as she began frantically grabbing her lipstick and keys, he leaned over very slowly, picked up a stray Tampax and handed it to her.

'I think you dropped this,' he said politely.

Emma scrambled to her feet and fled back down the four flights of stairs to the street with Patrick's laughter ringing in her ears.

five

Ben rolled over for the tenth time and realised that he'd been thrashing about for ages. Every night it was the same. Every night he'd fall asleep around midnight and then wake up with a jolt precisely three hours later, bathed in sweat with a horde of unspeakable anxieties galloping through his mind. The 3 a.m. horrors, he called it, and at the root of it all was this one thought: he was a fraud. And on day one, when the camera turned over for the first time, he was going to be found out.

Meanwhile, he tossed and turned, a million different fears competing for his attention. His script was full of plot-holes – why hadn't he realised this before? – and the ending was hopelessly weak. The schedule was impossible; his storyboards were incomplete, and he still hadn't done a shot-list; the budget was a joke, and he was already getting pressure from Patrick to cut all the crane shots. He rolled over again, tugging the duvet up around his ears.

Three major parts were still uncast. They still hadn't found a suitable location for Scene 133 and, if the weather was bad, the whole of week two was doomed because it was all exteriors and there was no weather cover. And he just knew he was going to have major problems with Hugo, his director of photography. Ben could tell from the way Hugo had acted in that meeting yesterday that he was going to steamroller him and try to direct this movie himself, the arrogant piece of shit. Nobody was going to listen to him. What right did he have to direct a movie?

'I've got to get some sleep,' he told himself. 'I've got to. I can't lie awake like this every night – I'll go mad.' He tried lying on his back with his palms facing upwards – the corpse pose, they called it in his yoga class, which now seemed particularly apt – and started counting backwards from a hundred to quieten his mind. He got as far as ninety-four when he remembered that Liz was coming to see him in the morning. His eyelids shot open again and he stared blankly up into the darkness.

Sometimes late at night, his phone would ring and there'd be no one there. The line would be silent, and after he'd said hello, he'd hear the click of somebody hanging up. He couldn't explain why, but he'd always wonder if it was Liz. He'd tried dialling 1471, but always it was the same message: 'The caller has withheld their number.' It could have been anybody of course. He had no reason, really, to think it might be Liz, just a strange feeling in the pit of his stomach.

And there was something else too. One night, a couple of years after he and Liz had split up and he was seeing a girl who produced music videos, he'd gone to close the curtains in her bedroom and, when he looked out of the upstairs window, he'd seen, standing on the pavement on the opposite side of the road, a tall figure in jeans and a black hooded top looking straight up at him. The person stared at him for a second and then turned and walked quickly away. It was too dark to see their face – he couldn't even be sure if it was a man or a woman – but something about their silhouette reminded him of Liz. Or maybe he was just imagining it. Why would she be watching him? How would she even know where he was? It was pure vanity on his part, he told himself, to imagine that she was even thinking about him. It must have been his guilty conscience just playing tricks.

Ben turned his bedside clock so that the streetlight filtering through his wooden blinds lit up the numerals just enough for him to tell the time. Twenty-three minutes past four. In less than seven hours Liz was going to be sitting in his office again. He positively, definitely had to get some sleep.

Jamie, the first assistant director, was programming all the crew's phone numbers into his mobile; Piers, the location manager was trying to figure out where he was supposed to park twelve trucks in Brighton city centre; Dominic, the second AD, was persuading his sister who taught English as a second language that it would be a good learning experience for her students to spend three days working for free as extras on a film; Vanessa, the production manager was describing the symptoms of her wheat allergy to the caterers and making sure they would stock up on corn pasta; Georgina, the third, was poking a letter opener into the mouth of the photocopier in an attempt to undo a paper-jam; Flick, the production assistant was pleading with the hotel who were claiming to be double booked and Ben was hiding. The door to his office was shut and he was pretending to do a shot list for Scene 82. On the sofa opposite, Patrick was going through the art-department budget dividing all their estimated costs by two.

Poppy, the art department assistant stuck her head around the door. 'Sorry, Ben, the flashback scene – how many years ago is that meant to be?'

'Six?' said Ben off the top of his head. Poppy's head disappeared again and was immediately replaced by Flick who came in, sat down on Patrick's lap and helped herself to a cigarette from the packet in his top pocket.

'They can do you a sea-view with a bath, but not a shower,' she told Ben, lighting up. 'All the rooms with a shower are on the other side of the corridor. Whaddya reckon?'

'Take the view,' said Patrick. 'But tell them we want a discount.'

'They're already giving us 30 per cent off,' said Flick.

'They're lucky we're giving them any money at all,' said Patrick. 'That hotel should have been condemned ten years ago.'

'I'll take the shower,' said Ben.

Flick slid off Patrick's lap and settled on the sofa to finish her fag.

'This is a no-smoking office,' Patrick pretended to scold her.

'I know, that's why I've come in here,' she said pointing at the mound of grey butts in Ben's ashtray.

Ben went back to typing up his shot-list. It gave him a sense of being in control, seeing it all laid out neatly on his screen like that as though he had broken the back of the work just by putting it in writing and committing it to celluloid would now be a mere formality.

'I'm not late, am I?'

Ben froze at the sound of Liz's voice, and for a second he toyed with the idea of pretending he hadn't heard her. If he managed to ignore her, was there a chance she might magically disappear? But it was too late. Patrick was already on his feet to give Liz a kiss.

'Hello, stranger,' he said warmly and Ben had no choice but to look up and acknowledge her presence.

She looked younger than she had six years ago and he wondered how this could be possible when he felt about a hundred years older. And she was taller than he remembered, but this was more easily explained by the three inch spike heels on her black leather boots.

She was dressed in a tiny pin-striped kilt, a crisp white shirt with discreet ruffles, and a broad black belt slung across her hips. He was prepared to accept that this must be cutting edge fashion because, unless she'd changed, Liz wouldn't be caught dead in anything less. Her trademark flame-coloured hair hung in a silky curtain to her shoulders and her skin was several shades paler than it used to be. It suited her. Alabaster is the new tan – he would have to make a note of that.

'Liz!' he said, in a voice that he hoped sounded pleasantly surprised. He dithered over whether or not he should get to his feet, but he failed to commit his whole body to the movement and just ended up rocking forwards slightly in his chair.

'Hello, Ben,' she said, but made no move towards him, or, for that matter, up or down. He was relieved to see that she was, at least, smiling.

'Would you like a coffee?' he suggested.

'Yes please.'

Patrick and Ben looked pointedly at Flick who returned their look with wide eyes. 'Oh right. That'll be me, then,' she said, stubbed out her cigarette and clomped off to do battle with the coffee dispenser.

'I'll leave you two to get on with it, shall I?' said Patrick.

'No – stay!' said Ben, but Patrick was already heading out the door, leaving it open just enough so he'd be able to eavesdrop on their conversation from his desk.

'So. Have you got your deal sorted out yet?' asked Ben nervously. What did she have to come in and see him for anyway, he wondered. Couldn't she just get on with it?

'Vanessa's doing my contract now,' Liz replied. She was wandering around the room looking at the cast photos drawing-pinned to the walls.

'Good-looking boys,' she said approvingly, looking at his four main leads. 'How did you manage to get Danny Parker?'

'I did the video for their first single.'

'Nice one. Can he act?'

'Of course he can act.' Ben was forced onto the defensive. Liz hadn't been in the room two minutes and she'd already found his Achilles heel. 'You don't think I'd have cast him just for his name, do you?'

'No, of course not,' Liz assured him, and Ben laughed to emphasise just what a ridiculous suggestion that was. He certainly hoped Danny Parker could act or he was going to be well and truly up shit creek.

'So you've had the script?' he asked to get off the subject.

'Yes. Congratulations. It's absolutely brilliant.'

'Do you really like it?' He'd been through so many rewrites he was desperate for any crumbs of praise he could get – even from Liz.

'I do. Very action-packed.'

'I hope so. That's the plan, anyway.' He pretended to be reading something urgent on his computer screen so that he wouldn't have to look at her. He'd told himself he could handle Liz but her cool self-possession was unnerving. 'And you're happy with your costume budget?'

'No, of course I'm not happy with it,' she snapped, and Ben was slightly alarmed. 'They're only giving me enough money for one assistant and your entire cast are going to be wearing Top Shop, but I expect I'll manage. I always do.' She smiled to let Ben know it was a joke but honestly, what was she supposed to do with six thousand pounds? The clothes she was standing up in came to nearly half that.

'Would you like to see my reference photos?' Liz took a folder out of her bag and Ben turned the pages slowly without focusing on any of the pictures. He looked up briefly to comment and quickly looked down again when he realised that Liz's bare thigh was just inches from his nose. He could feel the blood pumping through his ears. She still looked exactly like the kind of girl you wanted to do it with right here, right now, on the desk with the door open. But he wasn't going to go down that road again.

'Oh look, here's your coffee,' he said, relieved, as Flick returned with two plastic cups, one inside the other, and handed them to Liz. 'That all seems great.' He passed her folder back and hoped she would take that as her cue to leave. Instead, she sat down on his sofa and carefully crossed her legs.

'So, how have you been?' she asked casually.

'I haven't been avoiding you,' Ben blurted out without realising he was going to say it.

Liz just laughed. 'Avoiding me? Why ever would you say that?'

'I've been fine,' said Ben and realised that he was now one question out of sync. 'How've you been?'

'Me? Great. Absolutely great.'

'Congratulations on the BAFTA nomination last year.'

'Thanks,' said Liz. 'It was two years ago, actually.'

'Really? Time flies, doesn't it?'

'Are you OK, Ben? You seem a little nervous.'

'Do I? I'm just a bit stressed, I think. Because of the film. All the pressure.'

As if on cue, there was a knock on his door and Angela came in without waiting to be invited.

'Sorry to interrupt your meeting, Ben, but there's bad news. We've lost Zoe Langridge.'

'What? How can we have lost her?' Ben was aghast. Zoe Langridge was playing Jasmine – his female lead. 'I thought she'd signed.'

Angela shook her head. 'The contract went out to her agent but she says she's changed her mind. She says she doesn't want to play a cloakroom girl because it's too demeaning.'

Ben couldn't believe his ears. '*Demeaning?*' he spluttered. 'That's insane! In her last film she murdered her husband!'

'I'm just telling you what they told me.'

'And in the one before that she was a heroin addict!'

'Crack,' said Liz.

'What?'

'She was a crack addict. Not a heroin addict.'

'Well whatever she was – how is that better than working in a nightclub cloakroom?' Ben demanded. 'We start shooting in ten days time. Is there time to call anyone else in?'

'You've already seen everyone who's available. I'll go down the list right now and start making some calls. Don't worry, Ben. I'll find you someone just as good.'

When Angela went out, Liz unfurled herself from the sofa, unpinned the photocopy of Zoe Langridge's Spotlight photo from the wall, and put it helpfully on Ben's desk.

He clapped his hand over his mouth and chin and stared desperately at the big empty space on his noticeboard under the label 'Jasmine', praying for divine intervention or to wake up and find this was all a horrible dream.

'That's a shame,' he heard Liz say sympathetically. 'I worked with Zoe on *Life Kills*. I'd already picked out some gorgeous things for her.' She gathered up her belongings and tossed the full cup of coffee into the bin. 'Sorry. I can't drink this. It tastes of chicken soup. Now, if there's nothing else you need to talk to me about, I'll have to get going, because I've got a fitting this afternoon.'

This time Ben managed to get all the way to his feet. He was going to kiss her goodbye in the same way that he'd kiss any female colleague he hadn't seen in a while. He'd rehearsed in his head how it would go. Step in, peck on cheek, step back. No body contact. Efficient, clean, precise – he'd done it a million times before. But Liz was walking across the office and it was too risky, he realised with relief. He couldn't be expected to land a clean kiss on a moving target.

'Well, it's good to see you again, Ben,' she said, and, with a little wave, she was out the door.

Ben went back to his desk and watched through the doorway as Liz kissed Piers, the location manager, on her way to Vanessa's desk. He could see her quickly scanning her contract, signing it with a flourish, and then filling in her National Insurance number, VAT number and bank details on her start form. Then she kissed Vanessa goodbye, walked over to give Patrick another kiss, gave the office a general wave, and her heels clicked off down the corridor.

Immediately she'd gone, Patrick came running into Ben's office and shut the door.

'Well?' he demanded. 'Are both your testicles still attached?'

Ben shrugged his shoulders. 'I dunno. I think it went OK. She said she liked the script and she didn't like the coffee.'

'Hmm. Two out of two. So are you going to give her one?'

'No!'

'Then, do you mind if I – ?'

'Fuck off, Patrick.'

'S'all right, I'm only joking. She's still very, very tasty though.'

'I didn't notice,' Ben lied. There was absolutely no way he was going to get mixed up with Liz again. That was the one thing he knew for certain.

six

The tranquil pocket of St John's Wood where Ronald Gasch had lived in great comfort since 1967 was a bugger for parking. But it was only after his wife had died that he'd taken the drastic step of uprooting the monkey puzzle tree and laying part of the spacious front garden to gravel so that visitors could drive in through his imposing iron gates and park off the street. It reminded him of a bloody doctor's waiting room out there, as he peered gloomily out through the curtains at Liz retrieving the Selfridges carrier bags from the back seat. He imagined, as he often did, for he was prone to Eeyorish bouts of depression, what the garden would look like when the hearse parked there to finally carry off his old, dead body.

He sighed, turned away from the window, and called out to Mary to make them some tea. She came 'to do' for him twice a week and, apart from her insistence on leaving his radio tuned to Terry Wogan and her constant, mystifying requests for 'more tick bleach', he enjoyed the human company. He dislodged a troublesome bit of phlegm from the back of his throat and smoothed back what remained of his silver hair before opening the door to Liz.

'Do let me help you with all those bags,' he said and paused in the hallway longer than was probably necessary to rest a suit hanger over his arm, so that she would have time to appreciate the series of framed photographs of his own glorious theatrical heyday that lined both walls.

Liz leaned forward to examine a portrait of a fair-haired

young man with finely chiselled features in Elizabethan costume and said the same thing that everybody under the age of fifty always said: 'Is that you?'

'Four seasons at the Old Vic for my sins,' he sighed again, hoping that she would take particular note of the way the tights hugged the firm arc of his thighs. 'I wasn't always a decrepit old fart, you know.'

'Don't be silly,' said Liz briskly, although privately she thought that old fart was a pretty accurate appraisal and she vowed again that she would never let herself get old with liver spots, turkey skin and rheumy eyes.

She followed him through to his chintzy living room where his two overweight Siamese, Goneril and Regan, were persuaded to relocate further along the sofa so that she could lay out the suits she had brought for him to try on.

Ronald was playing the heavy in Ben's film – a thuggish concert promoter whose name was Larry Turpin but who was inevitably nicknamed Dick. Liz had selected suits that were well cut and yet subtly tasteless, and she planned to get double-duty from the trousers by teaming them with leather bomber jackets. Ronald had given her his measurements over the phone, but seeing him now in the flesh for the first time, she suspected that he'd deliberately lied to her about having a thirty-four inch waist and that she'd have to make yet another run to Selfridges to get a larger size.

Ronald disappeared modestly upstairs to try on the first suit – it wouldn't do for Mary to find him in his skivvies – and Liz, who had no desire to follow him into his bedroom, remained on the sofa where she could relive every moment of her reunion with Ben.

It had gone, she thought, even better than she'd hoped. She had been professionalism itself. Untouchable. Magnificent. Ben wouldn't have had the faintest idea of the turmoil she'd been living in for the last six years. And if all went according to plan, he never would.

Maybe one day she would ask him: 'Why did we waste so

much time apart?' But he would take that in a spirit of sweet nostalgia and not the churning, unbearable bleakness that had become her life. He wouldn't know that every moment of every day for the last six years she had been waiting for the moment when he would come back to her.

Liz had always believed that if you wanted to get ahead in life, you had to have a plan. You couldn't just drift along, vaguely hoping that something would turn up. You had to make things happen, and up until the day she met Ben, she'd planned her life brilliantly. She wasn't going to end up like her mother who'd drunk her good looks away and worked on an assembly line in Sunderland putting car dashboards together. As for her father, she'd met him only once when he'd turned up a few days after her sixth birthday – a ruddy-faced bear of a man with a rough, ginger beard that scratched her face when he tried to kiss her. He'd given her a Barbie in a nurse's outfit, shouted at her mother for an hour and then had to ask her for the train fare back to Durham. Liz kept the Barbie, but she never mentioned her father again.

She escaped to London the moment she could. She'd decided to be a costume designer after reading a magazine article when she was sixteen and she trained at Wimbledon College of Art, working towards her goal with single-minded determination. Some people called her a control freak. She preferred the word perfectionist. She'd travelled all over the world. She'd saved money, got a mortgage, and the next item on her agenda was marriage and children.

She knew of women who'd started families in their forties but even if such a thing were biologically possible, she had no desire to be an old mother. Or an old anything. Her first child – a boy, she hoped – would be born before her thirty-first birthday. The second – a girl – would arrive a year to eighteen months later. She knew it was going to be hard work looking after a baby and a toddler so she intended to employ a live-in childminder who would start a couple of months before the second one was born. It made sense to get childbirth out of the way as soon as possible and it would be nice for the children too, she thought, having a brother or sister around their own age to play with. While they were little, she'd work a couple of days a week – doing dailies, or assisting on commercials or pop promos which would mean OK money and not too much responsibility – until the youngest one started school and then she'd go back to work full-time. She'd still be just thirty-six or thirty-seven then and young enough to pick up her career where she'd left off. Her husband would of course be earning enough money to support them all in the meantime.

And then, at twenty-eight, right on schedule, she'd found the man she wanted to marry. It was Ben Lincoln.

'Will I do?' asked Ronald Gasch, coming downstairs in a navy suit, purple shirt and lilac tie.

Liz snapped out of her reverie and knelt at his feet to pin up his trouser legs that were dragging on the floor. The close-up view of Ronald's clammy white feet repelled her and as she drove away, she was still struggling, unsuccessfully, to get the image of his deathly pale toes out of her mind. She would never – ever – let herself get old if she could help it.

Her bedside cabinet had been filled once with the soft-porn Polaroids she and Ben had taken of each other. She wanted them to always remember how perfect they had been then – their taut, young skin, their healthy white smiles, their thick, lustrous hair. When they'd got back to London after filming in Crete, Ben was supposed to be flat-sitting for a friend who was filming in Morocco, but he began spending almost every night at Liz's flat in Clapham where it was light and airy, the walk-in shower was big enough for two, and Liz's cleaning lady came every week to arrange white arum lilies in tall glass vases.

Liz's favourite moment of every day was when she would slide into bed onto her crisp, white Egyptian cotton sheets, and feel the thrill of Ben's skin against hers. And three months later, when Ben's friend returned from abroad, it seemed only natural that Ben move into Liz's flat until he had a chance to find a place of his own.

The more she got to know Ben, the more certain she became that he was The One.

'Look at us,' he said one morning as they brushed their teeth before work. They were both wearing Paul Smith moleskin jeans and grey T-shirts. 'We look like twins.'

Liz smiled. They'd started to dress alike without even thinking about it. They *were* alike. They were soul-mates, of that she had no doubt and she remembered he had kissed her then with the toothpaste still in his mouth and it had tasted like she was kissing herself. Sometimes she couldn't decide whether she wanted to fuck him or be him.

And that was the same day that Ben rang her with the news.

'Guess what?' he told her. 'I've been offered a film in Mauritius. It's a twelve-week shoot. You don't mind, do you?'

'Mind? No. That's a fantastic break for you,' Liz said, but she was shaking with panic. She'd been dreading the inevitable day when one of them got the call that would keep them apart for more than a few weeks at a time. But perhaps there was still a way they could be together. 'Who's doing the costumes?'

'I don't know. You aren't thinking of doing it, are you? What about your series?'

Liz was halfway through a period drama for the BBC. 'Don't worry about that,' she said. 'I'll find a way to get out of it. You don't want to go all that way without me, do you?'

'No, of course not,' said Ben and gave her the number. 'It'd be great if you could come out. But they must have a costume designer on board already if they're about to start shooting.'

'Well, they can always use some help, can't they?' said Liz.

But when she rang the production company, it was just as Ben had said. The wardrobe department were already fully staffed and most of them had been out in Mauritius for weeks. The only other people they'd be taking on would be local labour at a fraction of what they'd pay the British crew. Liz

45

couldn't possibly stoop to such an indignity. Especially not if it meant breaking her BBC contract. She was trapped.

Twelve weeks. That was about a third of the total time Ben and Liz had been together. Could she trust him for three months on his own? She knew only too well what film crews were like once they got on foreign soil. Half the crew would come back with Mauritian brides or girlfriends and the other half would leave broken hearts and coffee-coloured babies behind. And even if she trusted Ben, she certainly didn't trust other women to keep their mitts off him. Liz always felt uneasy whenever Ben went away – even if it was just a boring one-day corporate shoot in Inverness. Ben was too gorgeous and eligible to be allowed out on his own. When he'd gone to Prague for ten days, she'd flown out for a long weekend to keep an eye on him, but Mauritius was too far away for that. Where the fuck was Mauritius anyway?

She grabbed her British Airways schedule from her office desk and tried to find it on the world map inside. Jesus Christ – there it was – a tiny dot in the middle of the Indian Ocean! And it was supposed to be beautiful. A make-up girl she knew had gone there on her honeymoon a couple of years ago.

Suddenly Liz realised that was it. The answer to everything. They could have the wedding in Mauritius. She turned the idea over in her mind to make sure she wasn't just being fanciful and she realised it was absolutely possible. In fact, it was more than possible, it was perfect.

Her BBC job would finish about five weeks before Ben's film. Between now and then, she'd organise everything. She was a champion organiser and she'd even have time – just – to make her own dress. She'd fly out to Mauritius a week before the wedding and a few days later, their families could join them, plus half a dozen of their friends. They'd get married on the beach under the palm trees and have a small reception afterwards under a white silken canopy. She was already sketching a rough Bedouin tent design on the back of the BA schedule.

It wouldn't be the big church wedding she'd always planned,

but it would be even better. They'd met on a beach, and they'd get married on a beach. And they'd stay in Mauritius for their honeymoon. Liz would be twenty-nine by then and she'd be ahead of schedule. It was the most perfect plan she'd ever made. Ben would love it. She could hardly wait to get home that night and see him. Where should she propose? In bed? Over dinner? She had never planned this part of it before. In her original plan she was always the one being proposed to, but the secret of a good plan is flexibility and all she was doing was giving Ben another gentle nudge in the right direction.

There was one thing she was sure of. She knew she wanted to be naked when she asked him. When they grew old together and reminisced about the day they had pledged to get married, she wanted them both to be reminded of their youthful, golden perfection. That memory would be her first wedding present to Ben.

She made sure she got home before he did and filled the bedroom with fresh white flowers. She chilled champagne and brought two glasses into the bedroom. Ben came home and wanted to make love to her in the shower, but she teased him and made him wait, working him into a lather until he could hardly bear it.

'Come on,' she said, and led him into the bedroom while they were both still wet. She lay on the bed on the white towels she had arranged and Ben lunged at her. It took all her self-control to push him away.

'Sit up,' she told him, and grabbed the Polaroid camera from her bedside table. 'I want to take a photo of you.'

He laughed and sat up and she leaned back, turning the camera on an angle to fill the viewfinder with every inch of the man she loved.

'My turn,' he said and Liz smiled so he could capture every aspect of this historically intimate moment for ever.

The camera flashed and he dropped it onto the floor.

'I've got something I want to ask you,' she said, and moved closer to him so that they were now both sitting up in the middle of her bed. Liz was cross-legged and Ben automatically wrapped his legs around her waist. Her nipples brushed tantalisingly against his chest as they breathed. They sometimes sat like this for ages, testing each other to see who could resist the longest.

'What is it you'd like me to do?' he smiled. He very much hoped it would be anal sex again.

Liz looked him straight in the eye. 'Marry me,' she said.

The moment she said it, she wanted to take it back.

She had expected Ben to say, 'Yes,' without a second's hesitation. But the look she saw in his eyes was one of fear.

'Well. Say something,' she said when he'd been silent for too long.

He tried to laugh. Not very convincingly. 'You don't want to get married, do you?' he said at last. 'I mean, we're fine just as we are, aren't we?'

'Yes, we're fine,' said Liz. 'Better than fine. That's why I want to spend the rest of my life with you.'

The fear in Ben's eyes turned to panic. He struggled to unhook his legs from hers and as he slid across the bed, Liz felt an icy chasm open up between them. If she didn't hold on tight she would be sucked into it and disappear.

'Look. Liz,' said Ben, 'you know that I like you a lot, but . . .'

'But what?' she demanded. *This wasn't the way it was supposed to go.* There had been no buts in Liz's plan. No buts at all.

'But. I don't think I want to get married yet. I'm only twenty-five.'

'Oh that's right. You're only twenty-five,' Liz couldn't hide the coldness in her voice. 'Well, it may have escaped your notice, but I'm not twenty-five any more. I'm twenty-nine, and I don't intend to hit thirty as a single woman.'

'That's crazy,' he laughed, and she would never forgive him for trying to make a joke of it. 'Who cares how old you are? There's no law that says you have to be married by the time you're thirty.'

Liz could hear the break in her voice as she tried to lay out before Ben the cast-iron reasons why he simply had to say yes.

'That is so easy for you to say. Sitting there in your twenty-five-year-old male skin. You have no idea what it's like for women, do you? You can't even imagine what it'll feel like to turn thirty, can you? That's years away. You think it's never going to happen to you, because you think you'll be young for ever, but it will. One day you're going to get old and ugly, and your skin will sag and your hair will fall out and you won't be able to walk upstairs without wheezing and nobody will care or even remember what you look like now when you're perfect. But I will. Do you understand what I'm trying to say to you?'

'No. Not really,' Ben admitted.

'I want to have children,' said Liz, her voice gentler now, stroking his back. Perhaps that was the way to get through to him. 'I want to have *your* children. And I want to have them soon – not when we're too old to enjoy them. Can you imagine how fantastic our kids would be? Yours and mine?' She brought her face close to his and waited for him to kiss her.

'I'm not ready for kids,' said Ben. 'I'm sorry, Liz. Maybe one day. But not right now.'

'Well what am I supposed to do?' yelled Liz. 'Just sit around and wait for you to be ready? Is that it?' She wasn't going to cry. She had never let a man see her cry.

'Liz. Don't. Please.' Ben got up and put his arm around her. 'I don't know what to say. The last few months with you have been fantastic, but this is all a bit of a surprise to me. I thought we were just having fun.'

'And you think being married to me won't be fun?'

'It's just too soon. Too much. For me, anyway.'

'What's the matter?' Liz demanded. 'Don't you love me?'

Ben thought about it.

'Oh well, Jesus Christ,' shouted Liz. 'If you have to think about it, don't even bother answering.' She leapt off the bed looking for her kimono to wrap around her but it was out of reach.

49

'Liz, I'm sorry,' said Ben.

'I just don't get you,' she said. 'What we've got together is perfect. What else is it that you want?'

'I want to direct,' said Ben.

She had loved him because he was young, but he had been too young – she could see that now so clearly. And so she'd waited until after he turned thirty before making her move so that he would understand – as she had always understood – that we're not meant to go through life without a soul-mate. She would rather die, she vowed, than end up old and alone like Ronald Gasch.

seven

Emma was grateful they were busy at the salon because every time she had a moment to herself to think, she went hot and cold with humiliation remembering her evening with Patrick.

This is what happens, she thought, when you try and get above yourself – life sneaks around to give you a kick up the arse and you end up flat on your face. Maybe it was a sign. Maybe she really wasn't tough enough for this business. She'd rung Irene that morning just to see if anything else had come in for her.

'What are you doing ringing me this early?' Irene snapped. It was a quarter past ten. 'Oh, and I've put you up for *Cats*.'

'But I don't sing or dance.'

Irene sounded suspicious. 'Don't you? Are you sure? Well, perhaps it's time you learned. And there's been no word from that film, so it looks like a No.'

'Oh.'

'Don't take it so personally.'

'Well how am I supposed to take it?' Emma didn't tell Irene about her second meeting with Patrick because she half suspected Irene would shout at her for not sleeping with him anyway.

'It's only sex,' she could imagine Irene saying. 'Don't tell me you don't do that either! You want to buck your ideas up, my girl!'

Maybe that's what other girls did. Maybe she should just have slept with Patrick and he would have given her the part and then she would have been celebrating instead of going home with scabby knees on the Central Line. Maybe she'd just been hopelessly wet about the whole thing and deserved to be an out-of-work actress for ever.

On Saturday night, as she sat on the train to Sheffield, she toyed with the idea of telling Jason, but she wasn't sure how he'd react. He might think it was her fault and that she'd been leading Patrick on somehow. He could be terribly jealous sometimes even though he had absolutely no reason to be. Emma hadn't so much as looked at another man since she'd met him and why would she? He was everything she'd ever wanted and she was so proud of him.

They'd met when Emma got a one-day contract with *Shelby Square* playing a juror in a murder trial. She'd had to pay the train-fare up to Sheffield herself – the show only used local extras and wouldn't pay her any expenses – but Irene had said it would be worth it to let the producers have a look at her and good experience to see how TV studios worked. They didn't teach you that at drama school.

Jason's character, Troy Harding, was giving evidence and he probably wouldn't have noticed Emma were it not for the fact that halfway during his scene, Emma was trying to quietly stretch her legs, and accidentally pushed so hard on the front of the jury box that the nails holding the sheets of plywood gave way and the whole thing collapsed. She would have got away with it too had she not immediately squealed, 'I'm so sorry! I thought it was real!' and jumped up to try and repair the damage herself.

While the carpenters were putting the set back together, Jason wandered over to her.

'Did you do that just to get my attention?' he asked. It wasn't entirely a joke, because since he'd been on TV, Jason had noticed that girls were suddenly going to quite extraordinary lengths to get his attention. Usually this involved some variation on taking their tops off in nightclubs, drinking too many Bacardi Breezers and unzipping his trousers. Destroying the scenery may not be subtle, but it was at least original.

'No, it was an accident,' protested Emma. 'It was really cramped in there and I got pins and needles.'

So naturally then, Jason had glanced down and seen a small, ever-so-lightly tanned foot, five tiny slim toes dusted with a shimmer of silver polish and tender, baby-smooth skin lightly clasped by the narrow straps of Emma's sandal.

Jason had never thought much about feet before and so he had never realised that a foot could be pretty. His own feet had black hairs sprouting from the toes, his toenails were yellow and horny and produced a mysterious cheese-like substance, the skin on his heels was hard and flaky, and the way the bones on the top of his foot stood out always put him in mind of a large flightless bird.

That was when Jason decided he'd probably give her one that night. He knew she wouldn't knock him back. Girls never did these days. 'Where are you staying in Sheffield?' he asked her. It was as simple as that.

Or so he thought. Emma couldn't jump into bed with someone she didn't know – she just couldn't – even if they *were* on the telly and she had the weirdest feeling that she'd known them for years.

But Jason was so good-looking. He had short, dark-brown hair, serious brown eyes, gorgeous dimples, and an olive complexion – his mother's side of the family were Welsh but people often mistook him for Spanish and he didn't contradict them.

He took her to a very noisy pub and after a couple of hours straining to hear his life story, she simply had to tell him, 'You know, you're just like Troy.' And Jason had taken that as praise because in all his time on the show it had never once occurred to him that the reason he'd been cast as Troy in the first place was precisely because he *was* like Troy. And as time had gone on, and the writers got to know Jason a little, they'd taken some of his other personality quirks – like his obsession with cars and his habit of saying, 'as it goes', and given them to Troy as well. It was less work, they discovered, than making stuff up.

Recording three twenty-four-minute episodes a week meant

there was no time for rehearsals and doing more than two takes was a luxury they couldn't afford. So casting people who were exactly like their characters to begin with made life a lot easier for everybody – except, that is, for the actors who, once they'd seen their faces in enough magazines, took this as a sign that they'd outgrown *Shelby Square*. But once they left the studio car park and turned right into the real world, they soon discovered they were typecast for life. They couldn't leave their characters behind because they *were* the characters. Which suited the producers down to the ground too. They took great delight in seeing old cast members slide into oblivion, or panto, because it frightened all the others into staying put where they could be killed off at the show's convenience whenever the ratings demanded another major ratings-grabbing tragedy.

In the end, it had taken Jason over two weeks to get Emma into bed which pissed him off no end. 'Have you ever done it in a Porsche?' he asked her after a five-minute snog in the street outside her B&B. He didn't like taking girls back to his place, because it was always hard getting rid of them in the morning. He had to leave for the studio around seven and he didn't like the thought of them going through all his stuff. The Porsche line had never failed. Until now.

'You need your beauty sleep,' Emma told him as she got out of the car, 'or you'll look terrible in the morning.'

The next day she caught the train back to London and found he'd already sent her two text messages. She was flattered and amazed that he wanted to go out with her when she was still a nobody and he'd had his photo in *Heat* twice. Even better than that – Chris Moyles had taken the piss out of him once on his radio show which meant he'd arrived. Somewhere. If not at fame exactly then somewhere quite close that looked a bit like fame. She expected Jason to go out with one of the other girls on the show but he said they were all bitches. 'They're really up themselves – not like you,' he told her.

One of the things Jason really liked about Emma was that she actually looked up to him and thought that what he did was brilliant and not just a stopgap until something came up in *EastEnders* or he could launch his singing career. Obviously, he had to go out with a model or an actress – how would it look if he went out with a civilian? – but he didn't want to go out with someone who was a bigger star than he was. So he sympathised with Emma when she lost audition after audition but never admitted, even to himself, that he was kind of relieved.

All the actresses on *Shelby Square* had gone to stage school, or drama school, or been in some artsy-fartsy youth theatre group, and he was convinced that they looked down their perfect noses at him because *Shelby Square* was the only acting job he'd ever done. Plus, he was a little bit dyslexic which made learning his scripts every week a kind of torture. Whenever he fluffed his dialogue, the others rolled their eyes as though he was the only one who ever got his lines mixed up. And the more they rolled their eyes, and the more sarcastic they became, the more his lines flew out of his head.

Secretly too, he resented the fact that the female stars of *Shelby Square* got all the attention – the spreads in the lads' mags, the invitations to nightclub openings and film premieres. The one time Jason flew out to Ibiza to do some fashion shots for a Sunday tabloid, the producer suspended him for a week. OK, so maybe he should have asked the press officer about it first, but she would only have said 'no'. And then, when he tried to persuade some of his co-stars to go on strike to show their support, they just laughed. Cowards – the lot of them. Even his mum turned around and said, 'Well what did you expect? You know they read the papers.' His own mum!

Emma was the only one who was on his side. 'It's not fair,' she said. 'They should treat you with more respect. You're practically the star of that show.'

Jason agreed with her. His surname, Cairns, came third on the alphabetical cast list at the end of each episode – almost at the top. But the show's producers didn't see it that way at all. As far as they were concerned, *Shelby Square* didn't have stars.

The show *was* the star and the cast were merely kindling, tossed on from time to time to keep it burning.

Now Emma sat on Jason's sofa and waited while he rewound the previous evening's episode of *Shelby Square*. Some actors hated seeing themselves on screen but Jason watched every show. He said it was the only way to learn because the directors gave you no feedback at all. They were hired to direct half a dozen episodes and most of them took a kind of pride in the fact that they'd never even seen the series before they arrived. They liked to think were too posh and busy to watch afternoon soaps but they took the money all the same.

'It was a good one yesterday,' Jason told Emma, snuggling closer to her.

'Why – what happens?'

'Ssh – it's starting.'

Emma wasn't allowed to talk while the show was on and she dunked her digestive biscuit into her mug of tea as quietly as she could. The first five minutes were just boring comedy scenes with the older cast members bickering about a proposed car-boot sale. Jason could scarcely conceal his impatience.

'They should fire all of this lot. Who's interested in any of them?' he tutted.

'Oh I think they're funny—' began Emma, who didn't like to think of anybody losing their job, but he shushed her again when Alicia came on screen. Alicia owned the boutique and was played by Nicole Lloyd – a blonde actress who strenuously denied having had a boob job four months ago despite the fact that when she'd returned after a week's holiday the wardrobe department had discovered that all her tops were suddenly two sizes too small for her. She said she'd been working out.

Today Alicia was wearing a lot of fake tan and a lime-green chiffon blouse that tied just under her bust. She was having a hard time because somebody had broken into her boutique and stolen all of her designs for next season. The shop had been ransacked and Troy was helping her clear up. She didn't know yet that Troy was also the thief.

'If there's anything else I can do . . .' he told her. 'Do you need money?'

Jason hit the pause button and leaned towards the TV so he could inspect his close-up. He liked what he saw. 'Looking good, boy!' he told himself and hit play again.

'No, Troy, but thanks,' Alicia was whispering bravely. 'You're a real friend.'

Emma got up to get some more biscuits. There was never any food in Jason's house because he always ate out.

'You should watch this,' Jason yelled after her. 'You might learn something.'

'I'll only be a second,' she said.

'Well hurry, because the good bit's coming up.'

Jason fast-forwarded through the ads and through the second car-boot sale scene which wasn't any funnier than the first one. Emma dunked her digestive too long and it broke in half. She was trying to fish it out of her mug when Troy and Alicia came back on screen again.

Alicia was locking up. 'Thank you, Troy. I really don't know what I would have done without you.'

'Any time you need me, Alicia – you know I'm right next door.'

Alicia frowned. 'I don't get it. Why are you being so nice to me? After that fight we had over my lease – I thought you wanted me out of here.'

'Alicia, that's not what I want. Shall I show you what I do want?'

Before Alicia could answer, Troy wrapped his arms around her and kissed her.

'Oh my God!' squealed Emma. 'I didn't know Troy fancied Alicia!'

'Sshh!' said Jason, not taking his eyes off the screen. Troy and Alicia were still kissing passionately and Emma watched appalled.

57

'You never told me you were going to kiss her!' she protested. 'Why didn't you say anything? You must have recorded that weeks ago.'

Jason shrugged, still staring at the TV. 'It's confidential. You know we're not allowed to give away plot lines.'

'That's never stopped you before! Look – you're still kissing her! I don't believe it! Was that your *tongue*?'

'Emma, don't go off on one. We're only acting. It's a stage kiss.'

The *Shelby Square* theme music started then and the credits whizzed past too fast to read anyone's name.

'Well it looked like a proper kiss to me,' sulked Emma. 'You looked like you were really enjoying yourself.'

'Don't be an idiot. How could I enjoy that? We're in that tiny shop set under all those lights, the camera's about four feet away from us, the microphone's hanging over our heads, we've got twenty crew just standing around staring. It's not enjoyable at all. It's humiliating, as it goes.'

'Really?' Emma had never thought of it like that. 'That's awful.'

'Nobody enjoys doing scenes like that,' Jason explained, 'but it's the job. And we have to make it look real because that's what we're paid for. So the last thing I need is you getting jealous or giving me a hard time.' He kissed her to show that there was nothing for her to get jealous about. 'You know I'd never be interested in someone like her when I've got you – don't you?'

Emma nodded. 'I know, Jason. I'm sorry. It just came as a surprise, that's all, seeing you kissing someone else. Anyway,' she smiled, smacking him playfully. 'You should be glad I'm jealous. If I wasn't jealous it would mean I didn't care. You just wait – one day I'll have to do a screen kiss like that and then you can see how *you* like it.'

'Yeah, one day.' Jason jumped up. 'Come on, it's nearly eleven o'clock. Hadn't you better start getting ready?'

The only thing Emma was ready for was falling asleep on the

sofa. She'd sort of hoped that just this once Jason would forget about going out. 'Oh, do we have to go out tonight? I've been on my feet all day.'

Jason looked at her in amazement. 'Of course we have to. You can't stay in on a Saturday night. What's the matter with you?'

Emma smiled. 'Nothing. I guess it's just been one of those weeks.'

eight

Liz unlocked the door to her pristine flat, with the blank oatmeal walls and the matching Jasper Morrison suede sofas and the emptiness hit her like a slap in the face. She paused in the doorway as she did every night and thought, 'This is it. This is my life.'

In the movie version of her life she would have been given a cat – a demanding tabby curling around her ankles – but Ben was allergic to cats and she'd been keeping her life perfect, hermetically sealed in readiness for the moment when he would eventually come back to her. So there was no cat. Just the mocking hum of silence. She closed the door.

She poured herself a glass of wine, switched on the TV, and tried to remember what her life used to be like. Whenever she tried to picture the time before she'd met Ben, it was like watching a film. That girl who was in control of her life, who could still laugh at stupid jokes, who could even laugh at herself, couldn't really be her. It was just an actress who looked like her. An actress who could never understand what it was like to have your soul ripped apart by someone you loved.

When Ben had left to catch his night flight to Mauritius, a part of the old Liz had disappeared with him. And it was a new Liz who had watched the taxi drive away in the rain, walked back inside the empty flat, laid out every photo she had of Ben on her bed, then sat down and started sketching the preliminary design for her wedding dress.

'I'll think about it,' Ben had told her, and the new Liz had dug her claws into those words and held on like a drowning cat. He hadn't said he didn't want to marry her, he'd said: *'I'll think about it.'*

While Ben was away, she phoned him three or four times a week, listening sympathetically to his tales of monsoons and the box of filters that had been mysteriously stolen from the locked camera truck. But she didn't tell him that she was continuing to plan their wedding. She ordered travel brochures and pored over the specifications of every five-star hotel in Mauritius, rejecting out of hand any that decorated their rooms with turquoise-and-salmon-coloured parrot motifs. Did an ocean-front suite mean it would be right on the beach with sand drifting in through the open shutters and across the slate floors? She read that the east coast could be windy but the beach was magnificent. And October would be the perfect month, she discovered, after the rains had vanished and before the Christmas hordes and sweltering heat arrived.

She booked five rooms for herself and Ben, their parents and a couple of friends − although she hadn't actually invited anybody, or even told them. She'd leave that until the last minute, by which time she was sure that Ben would be missing her so much, he'd propose to her himself. He'd be sorry that he hadn't said yes straight away, but he'd make up for it. In the meantime, she reminded herself, he was thinking about it and how could he reach any conclusion other than that they were twin souls who belonged together? The old Liz warned her to face up to reality, but the new Liz didn't listen to her much these days.

She delegated as much of her workload as she could to her assistants and at the weekends, instead of driving backwards and forwards to and from her empty flat in London, she stayed in her bed-and-breakfast in Chipping Norton, and made her wedding dress − ivory silk, cut on the bias with long sleeves and a plunging back. After a month without Ben she was starting to feel positively virginal.

One of the actors kept insisting on giving her 'neck rubs' which was standard film-set foreplay. He was a pretty boy American who'd been cast to suck up to the US market, even though his fake upper-class English accent foundered somewhere in the middle of the Irish Sea. The old Liz would have added him to her collection without a second thought, but the new Liz discovered that she enjoyed disappointing him even more than she would have enjoyed shagging him – and it avoided all that egginess on set the next morning when she'd have to tie his stock and slide him into his riding boots.

'You're very sweet, but I'm engaged,' she told him one evening when his usual polite 'Thanks for everything, see you tomorrow' kiss turned into more of a grope. She couldn't wait to see Ben again. Celibacy was OK in small doses, but the novelty was fast wearing off.

Her wedding dress was complete and she had to stop herself from constantly trying it on to admire her reflection or it would be ruined before the big day. But she couldn't resist wearing it that night for luck when she rang Ben. She hoped he'd know by now exactly what date his film would be finishing, so she could finalise the date of their wedding. The hotel, who'd been so charming a few weeks ago, were now politely hassling her for deposits. She smiled as she imagined how surprised Ben would be when he found out she'd organised the whole thing. All he'd have to do was turn up.

'Look, the thing is,' he said, 'I've been thinking that I don't want to come straight back to England just yet.'

This was perfect. 'I don't blame you,' Liz agreed. 'The weather here has been terrible. I was thinking that when my job finishes I could fly out to Mauritius so we could have a holiday together.'

Ben was quiet for what seemed like ages.

'What's the matter?' asked Liz finally. 'Don't you want me to come out?'

'No, no. It's not that. It's just that, well I've made friends with a couple of Australian guys on the crew and I thought I might go on to Australia afterwards and pick up some work there. We're halfway to Oz already, you see. And I've always wanted to do the backpacking thing. See the Barrier Reef. Ayers Rock. All that.'

Now it was Liz's turn to be quiet. 'Oh. You never mentioned that before. Wanting to go backpacking around Australia.' Her words sounded sharp and brittle.

'Didn't I? Well, I didn't think I'd get the chance, I guess.'

'How long were you planning to be away?'

'I don't know. It depends on what sort of work I can get out there – and I haven't had a real holiday in over a year.'

'You seem to have it all worked out,' said Liz, wondering when he would get around to asking her to go with him.

'You're not mad, are you?'

'Mad? No. Of course not. But where does that leave me?'

'I don't know, Liz. I don't want to make any promises to you.'

'What do you mean?'

'Well, I've been thinking. Maybe it would be best if we just cooled off for a while.'

'Cooled off? What are you talking about? I haven't seen you in two months! How can we cool off any more than that?'

'Liz,' he said and tried to sound gentle, 'I think you want something I can't give you.'

'That's not true!' insisted Liz. 'Just tell me – when are you coming home?'

'To London? I honestly don't know. And that feels right. I'm not like you, Liz. I'm not ready to settle down yet. Maybe it would be for the best if we split up for a while.'

Liz started to sob – quietly at first, then enormous gulps that shook her whole body.

'But I've planned the whole thing.' She started to choke. 'We could get married on the beach.'

There was a silence on the other end of the phone. Liz couldn't see Ben, but she knew he was screwing up his eyes the way he did when he was watching the football and Chelsea were losing.

'Ben? Ben? What's the matter?' Liz wept. 'I thought you loved me.'

'I do love you,' said Ben eventually. 'But I don't think I'm *in love* with you.'

Her doctor prescribed Prozac because Liz was unable to speak without crying. She didn't eat for five days and her stomach was flatter than it had ever been in her life – making a mockery of the abdominal crunches and double-leg lifts she had once performed religiously every morning.

The date that Ben was due to finish in Mauritius came and went but Ben didn't come home and there was no word from him at all. Not even a postcard of the Opera House. Liz lay sobbing on the kitchen floor for hours, thinking there was no reason for her to ever get up. All her life she'd believed that if you wanted something badly enough and you worked hard enough, then you could make it happen. Otherwise what was the point? What was the point of anything?

In her whole life she'd never been dumped. Ever since she was fourteen, she'd been the one who called the shots in relationships – it was her decision when they would start and her decision when they would end. She excelled in the art of never letting go of one boy until she had a replacement warming up on the subs bench. More often than not they overlapped slightly which was even better. Relationships were like a game. A game she always won. And then Ben had come along and she'd fallen in love. There were times before, she realised, when she'd thought she'd been in love, but not like this. When she looked into Ben's eyes, she knew that their souls had been lovers in a past life – in all their past lives – and were destined to seek each other out for all eternity. He was the missing piece to her puzzle and if she couldn't make it work with Ben, then how could she make it work with anyone?

She was afraid she was losing her mind and consulted a psychotherapist in Hampstead, where she sat in silence in a cold blue room, waiting for the woman to ask her a single question. When her fifty minutes were up, she wrote out a cheque for sixty-five pounds and didn't make another appointment.

The old Liz used to laugh at people who read their horoscopes but the new Liz consulted fortune-tellers and mediums and finally a woman called Fionnula who conducted astrological readings from her kitchen in Muswell Hill and told her she was experiencing her Saturn Return. Saturn was returning to the exact degree in the heavens where it had been when she was born and was forcing her to grow up and learn from experience.

'It happens to everybody around the age of twenty-eight. It represents a great opportunity,' Fionnula explained. 'One chapter closing and another one beginning. In your case, Saturn is returning to the Seventh House in Pisces.'

'What does that mean?' Liz wondered.

'Relationships,' said Fionnula. 'But it should all sort itself out by the time you're thirty-two.'

Liz went home and cried herself into oblivion. Her friends were attentive at first but soon grew weary of Liz's desperate phone-calls late at night when all she could talk about was Ben. They began to avoid her as though getting dumped might be contagious. When a make-up girl called Suzi invited her over for drinks one evening, Liz was so grateful for human company she went, even though she considered Suzi to be a bit of a flake.

There were about twenty people in Suzi's living room, sitting cross-legged on the floor, clutching small brown beads and chanting in a language she didn't recognise that sounded like the nasal drone of wasps. It went on for an hour while Liz sat in the adjoining dining room eating all the olives in morose silence, wondering if Suzi would notice if she just left. Then each of them stood up and reported on how their lives had improved since their last meeting.

'I've been arguing less with my daughter.'

'We've had an offer for our house.'

'I got a B in my acupuncture exam.'

'I'm still not smoking.'

'I've got a second interview for that record company job.'

'I lost another two pounds and on Wednesday I ran for twenty minutes.'

'I won fifty pounds on a Scratch card.'

Each announcement was greeted with applause, then they all hugged one another and Suzi opened the wine and two bags of Kettle chips.

'Well. What did you think?' she asked Liz. Her eyes were shining with missionary zeal.

'I don't know. What was it?'

'I should have told you, but I didn't want to freak you out. We're Buddhists,' Suzi explained.

'You mean like the religion? Then why did you clap the guy who won fifty quid?'

'Well, you can chant for whatever you want to. Sonia's chanting for world peace. Colin's chanting to get rich.'

'And it works?'

'Try it,' said Suzi, and she handed her a blue paperback book. 'Once you've heard the words "Nam-Myoho-Renge-Kyo", the seed's already been planted in your mind. If you chant with your whole heart, you'll awaken yourself to Buddhahood.'

Liz took the book home and threw it onto the bed. She wasn't interested in Buddhahood or world peace – what was the point, if she couldn't have Ben? And then she realised the answer was so obvious. The game wasn't over at all. She mustn't give up. All she had to do was get Ben back. And now the universe had given her a sign. She opened the book and started reading and for six years she'd been chanting the magic words over and over, just waiting for the day when her wish would come true.

nine

A few miles away in Covent Garden, Emma was witnessing a miracle.

'It was fine yesterday and then I wake up this morning and it's grown practically two inches overnight. I mean, look at it!' The woman with the magically growing bob lifted up a long strand of ash-blonde frizz for Emma to inspect.

'I'm sure Michael will be able to sort it out,' she promised. 'Is this water all right for you?'

'Emma, come here when you've finished that, I've got something to show you!'

Vicky, the salon receptionist, had a very mysterious and excited expression on her face. 'Look at that!' she whispered and pointed to the name pencilled in for a cut with Michael at four o'clock: H. Grant. Vicky raised her eyebrows. 'I took the call myself.'

'Oh my God! Was it really him?' Michael had a couple of B-list clients, but Hugh Grant?

'Well, I didn't speak to him directly,' said Vicky. 'It was one of his assistants—'

'Oh, yeah, of course.'

'—but she said Michael came highly recommended.'

'Oh Vicky, can I shampoo him? Oh please. Can I?' Emma begged.

Vicky's eyes shifted from side to side to make sure no one else was listening. 'Leave it to me,' she whispered conspiratorially. 'But you've got to promise to keep it a secret. They don't want everyone making a big fuss.'

'I promise I won't breathe a word!' Emma skipped back to her towel folding, her heart racing with excitement. It was like a dream! Hugh Grant coming here! What on earth would she say to him? She'd just drop it casually into the conversation that she was an actress too. He'd understand what it was like to be out of work, wouldn't he? He can't always have been a big star and he had such a kind face. Maybe he was making a movie right now and could put in a word for her and she'd get a little part in it. Nothing big, obviously, but even an extra in a crowd scene would be wonderful. But what if he really liked her and got her a part with lines and everything? Maybe she'd be in a scene with him – with Hugh Grant! They'd be up there on the screen together and she'd take her mum to the pictures to see it and she'd be so proud of her and maybe Hugh would offer to take them both out to dinner – nowhere posh, perhaps some nice country pub somewhere – and he'd make her mum laugh and they'd probably all end up being really good friends and they'd send each other Christmas cards every year and Mum could invite him up for Sunday lunch and she'd do her special Yorkshire pudding dessert with the golden syrup. He'd love that . . .

'Emma, what's up? You've been folding that towel for ten minutes. Are you all right?'

Emma jumped. 'Sorry, Michael. I was just thinking.'

'Well, if you're not doing anything, I need you to wash out some highlights for me.'

'Sure, Michael,' and she gave him a huge smile and winked to let him know that she knew all about his VIP client but that his secret was safe. She'd have to nip out at lunchtime and buy a new top. She couldn't let Hugh Grant see her in this old thing, could she?

Meanwhile, in Soho, the day was not going well.

'Do you want the good news or the bad news?' asked Angela.

'The bad news,' said Ben.

'OK. The bad news is there is no good news.'

'I don't believe this,' said Ben, jumping out of his chair in agitation. 'We're talking about an industry with the highest unemployment rate in the country.'

'It's not like I'm not trying,' said Angela.

'I could throw a stone out this window right now and hit an actress.' Ben stared morosely out into Dean Street and hoped that the answer to his prayers would materialise on the pavement. He tried to open the window, forgetting that it was sealed shut and had to content himself with tossing a hole-punch up and down in his hand for dramatic effect.

'Why don't you just give the part to Sophie Randall and cast someone else as Roxanne?' suggested Patrick irritably. Seen one actress, seen 'em all, as far as he was concerned.

'That's an excellent idea,' said Angela, 'except for three things.'

'Which are?'

'Sophie Randall is only available for one day and we'd need our Jasmine for most of the six weeks,' explained Jamie, the first AD. 'We've already had to change our schedule to fit in with Sophie's modelling bookings.'

'OK, that's one reason,' said Patrick.

'Two. Sophie's five foot eleven,' Angela reminded him, 'and Danny Parker's only five foot nine. We can only use Sophie as Roxanne because it's one scene and she's lying down.'

'So he stands on a box. What's the third reason?'

'Sophie can't act,' Ben explained.

'Ah, Jesus. This is ridiculous,' said Patrick. 'We saw eight girls for Jasmine. What happened to all of them?'

'Rachel Midwinter won't do it for the money,' said Angela. She shot a very pointed look at Patrick.

'Can't we offer her more?' asked Ben. 'Rachel would be great.'

'Only if you economise by making the band a three-piece instead of a four-piece as I keep suggesting,' said Patrick. 'Nobody will ever see the drummer, I promise you.'

'He's got four pages of dialogue,' Ben pointed out. 'And he wrote all the music.'

'You're too late anyway,' said Angela. 'Rachel's just signed up for the new Matt Damon thing.' She carried on down her list. 'Melanie can't drive and won't learn. Some kind of past-life phobia apparently.'

'So?' demanded Patrick.

'I don't want to use a double for the driving scenes,' Ben explained. 'She didn't look right anyway – too beefy.'

'So,' said Angela, 'that just leaves Kimberley, Kate and Erin who did the whole audition in a whisper.'

'We hated Erin,' Patrick remembered.

'What about the girls you saw for the part of Roxanne?' suggested Jamie.

'Exactly!' said Patrick, seeing an opportunity to slash the budget. 'Who says Jasmine needs to be a big name? Get someone nobody's heard of and we can pay them peanuts.'

'Would that mean I can have my crane shots back?' asked Ben.

Patrick sighed. 'You could have a crane for one day. If you must.'

'We didn't like any of them,' said Angela. 'Not enough to play Jasmine.'

'What about that Scottish girl?' said Ben.

'Which Scottish girl?' said Angela.

'I can't remember her name. The one we liked. Cute face.'

'Oh that one,' said Patrick. 'But she wasn't Scottish.'

'No, she had a funny little face, didn't she?' said Angela. She flipped through all the casting forms and shook her head. 'I think I know who you mean, but I can't find her.' She sorted through her folder again and looked under her chair trying to work out where it could have gone. 'Her form's just disappeared.'

'Well, that's very helpful, isn't it?' said Patrick who had tossed Emma's CV into a bin in Greek Street. 'Let me just remind you how this works. We have a certain number of what we call "Parts" to fill and your job is to find actors to fill them. It's not rocket science. All we ask is that you don't lose the little bits of paper with the actors' names on them.'

'Oh fuck off, Patrick,' said Angela. 'It's OK, Ben. I'll have her agent's details on my computer.'

'Well, good,' said Patrick uncomfortably. He watched Angela's large rear end waddle back to her desk and immediately changed the subject.

It was ten minutes to four and the afternoon had gone more slowly than seemed humanly possible, as though the salon had slipped into a time warp. Lunchtime felt like weeks ago.

'Nice top,' said Donna when Emma had dashed back in wearing a new psychedelic shirt. 'Were you wearing those trousers this morning?'

'Yes,' Emma fibbed, and could feel the blush creeping up her neck. 'I mean, no, not really. I spilt some tint on the ones I was wearing and I already had these in my bag.'

She looked down and remembered that she was holding a large carrier bag from Miss Sixty containing the black skirt and T-shirt she'd been wearing when she arrived at work that morning. 'I'm going out later,' she muttered guiltily and dashed off to the staff room to avoid further interrogation. The £52 credit-card bill pricked at her conscience but she reminded herself it was an investment.

All afternoon her eyes had been fixed on the pavement outside the salon's huge glass frontage. How would Hugh Grant get here? On foot? Surely not. He'd be in a taxi, or maybe one of those stretch limos she was always seeing around town with tinted windows. Michael said they were all just hen parties, but she'd seen them in the afternoon too. Why shouldn't Hugh Grant be in one of them on his way to get a hair cut? Michael didn't seem nervous at all about having to cut such famous hair. Look at him, chatting away as though this was just an ordinary day like any other. Emma had swept the floor about twenty times since lunch – she'd polished all the basins and taps and made sure all the seats were dry and there was no tint splashed around that might get on Hugh's clothes and ruin his day.

She was blow-drying a girl called Annie, but her attention was fixed on a half-empty coffee cup and a plastic biscuit wrapper on the work-station nearest the door. Donna hadn't cleared away the used tint bowl either – it was still there on the trolley and Hugh Grant was going to be arriving any minute. What if he came in and the first thing he saw was an untidy station? He might throw a luvvie strop and walk straight out and then she'd never get to shampoo his hair and she'd never get to talk to him and he'd never put her in his movie.

'Excuse me,' she said to Annie, 'I just have to go tidy something up.' She ran to clear away the mess, resting the coffee cup and the biscuit wrapper on top of the tint trolley for speed. She was wheeling it as quickly as she could back into the storeroom when she heard Vicky call out: 'Michael, your four o'clock's arrived!'

Emma spun around expectantly and as she did so, the cup lurched off the trolley spilling cold black coffee all over her brand new trousers. But the only person standing at the front desk was a small boy and his mother.

'Emma, you know Bev Grant don't you?' said Vicky sweetly. 'This is her son, Harry.'

Emma could hear raucous laughter start to break out all around the salon. Even Pan, the quiet Thai stylist who only ever spoke in a whisper, was doubled over his client practically crying.

'What's so funny?' asked Michael – the only one who hadn't been in on the prank.

'Nothing,' said Emma, realising that she'd been set up yet again. She wiped the coffee off her new trousers and tried very hard to join in the laughter. 'Good joke,' she said to Vicky. 'Come on, Harry, let's go find you a gown.'

The girls loved winding her up. They weren't being mean,

Emma reminded herself. On her very first Saturday when she was still at drama school, they'd told her that the best way to get tint off her hands was to wash them in white wine. So at closing time, she'd dutifully trotted off to the nearest off-licence and returned with the cheapest bottle of Bulgarian white she could find – it was coming out of her first day's wages after all, and she hadn't even been paid. The girls were already waiting with a corkscrew and four glasses.

'Cheers!' they chorused. 'You're officially a hairdresser now.' Come to think of it, when Emma remembered all the people who worked at the salon then, she was the only one – apart from Michael, of course – who was still there, six years later.

'Why did everyone laugh when I came in?' asked Harry as she scrubbed his hair.

'They weren't laughing at you,' she assured him. 'They were laughing at me because I spilled some coffee on my trousers.'

'Oh,' said Harry, more than satisfied by this explanation.

'So, have you got the day off from school today?' said Emma to change the subject.

'No, I'm not going to school this week. I've got a tutor.'

'Why's that? Aren't you very well?'

'No, because of the show.'

'The show?'

'*Les Miserables*,' Harry chirped. 'I'm playing Gavroche. I start next week.'

'Congratulations,' said Emma, and felt rather sick. Her career had just been totally eclipsed by an eight-year-old boy with sticky-up hair.

Harry, it transpired, had already been in *The King And I* and a TV adaptation of *Nicholas Nickleby*. 'I'm good at urchins,' he explained and obligingly demonstrated his cheeky, yet heart-rending ragamuffin face.

'That's great!' said Emma and wondered whether it might actually be worth asking this H. Grant to put in a good word for her after all. She was very relieved when Michael swooped in to take over.

'Emma, there's a phone call for you!' Vicky called out. She was holding up the shop phone but Emma was suspicious. She'd been caught out once today already and didn't want to be made a fool of twice.

'Emma, can you just hurry up and take it?' barked Vicky impatiently. 'You're tying up the salon phone.'

'Who is it this time?' Emma asked, wary. 'George Clooney wanting a mullet?'

'No, an Irene somebody.'

Emma grabbed the phone still convinced that it was Donna or one of the other girls pretending to be her agent. 'Hello? Irene? What are you calling me on this number for?'

'Well, your mobile's switched off as usual and I got tired of leaving messages.' It certainly *sounded* like Irene – her voice always made Emma picture candy-pink nail varnish and a gold handbag to match her packet of B&H. '*Brighton Rocks* want to see you again.'

'You're kidding!' Emma remembered Patrick's cruel laugh and knew it had to be a wind-up.

'Tomorrow, twelve o'clock.'

'But they're giving it to someone called Sophie.'

'No, it's for a different part. They want you to read for Jasmine. They're biking the script over to you this afternoon.'

'Irene, I can't.' She simply couldn't face Patrick again. She'd die of embarrassment.

'What – don't tell me you've had a better offer!'

Emma wanted to tell Irene what had happened – but standing in the middle of the salon wasn't the right place to do it. 'I don't think I want to do the film any more. I don't like them very much,' she explained weakly.

'Jesus! I'm not asking you to adopt them – just do the damn movie! What's got into you? I thought you'd be excited.' She could hear Irene lighting a fag and inhaling.

'Can't you ring them back and tell them I've changed my mind?'

'I don't think you understand.' Irene began speaking very

slowly and clearly. 'They want to see you for the female lead. Do you know what that means?'

Emma tried to say 'Yes', but the only sound that came out was a strangled squeak. She knew exactly what that meant. She'd finally be able to look eight-year-old Harry Grant in the eye.

'Twelve o'clock,' repeated Irene. 'And remember, there are only two ways you can fuck this audition up: the moment you walk through the door, and the moment you open your mouth. Break a leg!'

When Emma got home, a fat brown envelope was propped up against her front door waiting for her. Either Chris was out, or he'd slept through the sound of the doorbell, which was more likely. She carried the package inside nervously as though it was an unexploded bomb, and propped it up on the sofa where she could keep an eye on it while she boiled the kettle. She sipped her tea, opened the electricity bill, and checked the answering machine, all the while pretending to ignore the package that had the potential to change her life. She managed to keep up this façade of coolness for all of ten minutes before ripping open the sellotape with her teeth and pouncing on the script for *Brighton Rocks* and the accompanying handwritten note from the director which read: 'Hope you enjoy the script. Looking forward to seeing you tomorrow. Best wishes, Ben.'

When she'd auditioned for the part of Roxanne, she'd been given just one page from the script and a three-paragraph out-line about a band called Push, an evil club promoter called Larry Turpin, some stolen emeralds and a quarter of a million pounds in foreign currency. Now here was the whole story – all 110 pages of it. On the bottom of page 17, Jasmine appears for the first time, arriving at the nightclub where she works and then a few pages later in Scene 21, she walks through the crowds and pauses for a moment to watch the band performing on stage. The script described Jasmine as 'a heart-stopping mixture of sauciness and innocence'.

Emma read on, flicking through the pages greedily, her eyes widening in excitement when she got to Scene 148, where Jasmine saves Eddie's life when he's about to be shot by Turpin, and Scene 97, which read: 'Eddie and Jasmine collapse onto the sand and kiss passionately.'

By the time she'd reached the end of the script she wanted the part of Jasmine more than she'd ever wanted anything in her whole life.

ten

At quarter past twelve the next morning, Emma was sitting on a hard wooden chair in Ben's office, her eyes wandering across the ten-by-eight black-and-whites of the other cast members that were pinned to the walls around her.

'We're just waiting on Patrick,' Ben explained. 'He won't be long.' They'd already seen Erin, Kimberley and Kate, and Ben had spent nearly an hour with Erin – twice as long as he had with the other two, because he knew he wasn't going to offer her the part and he felt sorry for her. With each new reading Ben and Angela had discovered another aspect of Jasmine's character and now they knew exactly what they were looking for. Jasmine was street-smart, a girl who used her sexuality as a weapon, cunning and slightly superior to everything going on around her. He hoped that Emma would be all of those things.

'Did you get a chance to read the script?' he asked.

'Oh yes, all the way through – twice. It's brilliant!' Emma gushed. She'd been awake most of the night getting to know Jasmine and getting into her skin. How would Jasmine stand, how would Jasmine sit? Was she a hot-blooded minx or a cool customer? How much did she fancy Eddie when they first met? Did she smile much? Was she clever? Where did she go to school? Was she a happy person? She wanted to know Jasmine inside out and somehow at the same time be fresh and spontaneous at her reading today. The hardest thing of all, she discovered, was sitting in this room and just acting normal.

'And Jasmine's wonderful,' she went on. 'I love her, I mean, she's brave and she's clever and she doesn't take any crap from anyone, does she?'

'And is that what you're like?' asked Ben hopefully.

'Oh God, no! I wish I was!' gasped Emma and then, seeing the identical frowns of concern on Angela's and Ben's faces, she realised that this was probably the completely wrong answer. 'I mean, yeah, a little bit. A lot. Probably.'

'Now, unfortunately we seem to have mislaid your CV,' said Angela. 'I don't suppose you brought another one with you?'

'No – I'm so sorry!'

'Never mind. Can you just remind us what you've been doing recently?'

'Hairdressing,' Emma blurted out without thinking, and then immediately wished she hadn't.

'I'm sorry. I don't know that,' said Angela looking up from her notepad. 'Is that a play or a feature film?'

Emma looked from Angela to Ben and saw in their faces that the last thing they wanted to hear from their possible leading lady was that she had spent the last three years sweeping up split ends. She gulped. Her whole future was riding on what came out of her mouth next. If she told them the truth, whatever she did in the audition wouldn't matter. They would never take her seriously and she would spend the rest of her acting career lying on a *Holby City* gurney covered in fake blood. She remembered the advice Michael had given her: Just lie. No one's ever going to know. She took a deep breath.

'A feature,' she smiled, and from the way Angela and Ben immediately nodded happily she could tell she'd finally said the right thing. Gosh, she thought, lying is really easy.

'Who was the director on that?' asked Ben.

'Michael Ridgway,' said Emma quickly, knowing that her boss wouldn't mind getting credit for a film that didn't exist. 'Do you know him?'

'No – but his name sounds familiar.' Ben nodded thoughtfully, following the first rule of film-making which is never admit to not knowing anything. 'What is it – a comedy?'

'Oh yeah, it's a lot of laughs,' agreed Emma. 'But it was very hard work.'

'Of course,' agreed Ben. 'And when's that coming out?'

'Soon. I think.'

'Who else was in it?' asked Angela, and Emma confidently reeled off the names of everyone else at the salon, which Angela duly jotted down.

'So a lot of new faces, then?'

'Yes, you could say that.'

'That's very encouraging,' said Angela. 'No big names at all?'

'Do you know Pan Chatnopakun?' said Emma, naming the quiet Thai stylist. It was the biggest name she could think of.

Angela shook her head.

'He's very popular in Thailand,' Emma explained.

'And what were you doing before that?' asked Angela.

'Well I did a play called *Yellow Pages* at the Man In The Moon and all the usual TV stuff – *The Bill*, *Holby City*. Nothing very impressive, I'm afraid.'

Angela and Ben smiled, warming to Emma's modesty.

'Oh,' she added recklessly, 'and *Titanic* of course.'

'What was that like?'

'Cold and wet!'

Angela and Ben laughed. Emma felt like the king of the world.

And then Patrick walked in.

Emma's smile froze as Patrick flopped onto the brown velvet sofa beside Ben. He looked her up and down without a trace of embarrassment or shame.

'So . . . Emma Buckley, Emma Buckley,' he repeated as though her name reminded him of something. 'Good of you to make time to see us again. I should warn you – we can't pay much.'

'That's OK,' whispered Emma, and Angela and Ben glared at Patrick in disbelief.

'I don't really think that's appropriate,' Angela hissed.

'Yeah, steady on, Patrick,' said Ben. 'Emma hasn't even had a chance to read for us yet.'

'Oh right,' said Patrick. 'So she might turn out to be no good.'

Angela made a disapproving choking sound.

'Don't take any notice of Patrick,' said Ben. He felt suddenly very protective towards Emma. 'That's just his warped sense of humour.'

Patrick pressed his lips together in a fleshy smile that made Emma think of a fat lizard. She wondered whether Patrick had told Ben about their meeting at Soho House and decided that he probably hadn't. Although he might have done. She couldn't make up her mind.

'Why don't we start off with Scene 40 where Jasmine tries to warn Eddie off,' Ben suggested, 'and then we can do a little improvisation?'

'OK. Fine,' said Emma. 'Is it OK if I read it?' Last night she'd memorised the entire part but every single word had gone out of her head the moment Patrick walked into the room.

Patrick flipped through his script. 'I thought we'd cut Scene 40,' he interrupted.

Ben ignored him and stood up. Emma stood too, her hands shaking so much her script pages rattled loudly.

'Where did you get that?' she asked, glaring at the imaginary guitar case in Ben's hand.

'He gave it back to us.'

'Just like that?'

'Yeah, just like that. He said he was sorry, said he'd over-reacted, and he gave us all our gear back.'

'You broke into his office, didn't you?'

'No.'

'Don't lie to me, Eddie. I heard you. I heard you in there.' Out of the corner of her eye she could see Patrick blowing smoke rings at her.

'Yeah well, he nicked all our gear.'

'You've got to put it back.' Last night, rehearsing on her

own, she'd put real anger into that line. Now, with Patrick watching her, it came out as fear. She held on to the edge of the table so no one would see how much her hands were shaking.

'Leave it out! We're not going back in there again!'

'Eddie, you've got to put it all back. Tonight! You have no idea how much trouble you're in!' Emma aimed for rage and only made it as far as concern. It was all going to pieces.

'What are you talking about?'

'Let me show you,' said Emma, and she grabbed the imaginary guitar case from Ben and mimed unzipping it.

'And that's when the severed limbs fall out,' explained Ben.

'Thank you. That was very nice,' said Angela.

'Let's try the scene where Turpin holds Jasmine at gunpoint, shall we?' suggested Ben. He hated reading in like this, but Patrick wasn't prepared to pay for any of the other actors to be there, so he didn't have much choice.

Emma took a sip of water and tried to get back in touch with the Jasmine that she'd worked on last night. Jasmine was tough, she was fearless, but she felt as though the rug had been pulled out from under her. Everything was coming out all wrong. On her line, 'Why don't you go ahead and shoot me, then?', instead of sounding as cold as steel, she looked at the stapler Ben was pointing at her and laughed because she would have welcomed being put out of her misery at that moment. She wasn't surprised when Ben asked her to run through the same scene twice again, once very calmly as though she wasn't scared at all and the second time to show real fear. She could see Angela scribbling lots of things on her clipboard and wished she could just go home.

'Shall we try a little improvisation?' suggested Ben. 'Let's say Eddie's late meeting Jasmine for a date.'

'A date?' scoffed Patrick. 'Who the fuck goes on dates?'

Ben pretended not to hear him. 'OK?' he asked Emma.

Emma remembered all the times she'd sat around waiting for Jason and how she could never get angry with him because she knew it was his work that made him late. It wasn't his fault. And then there were all the times when she'd worry about him in that stupid Porsche driving too fast, and always on his mobile phone.

'Where the hell have you been?' she demanded and slammed her fists into Ben's chest. Ben was taken aback. He hated doing improv and knew he was really bad at it.

'Sorry, sorry, I've been working,' he said. 'I lost track of time.' How many times had he used that line in real life? he wondered.

'Do you have any idea how worried I've been about you?'

'Oh Jasmine—'

'I've called the police, I've called the hospitals! I thought Turpin had hurt you! I didn't know what had happened to you! I thought you were dead!' To her astonishment – maybe it was because she knew she'd screwed up yet another audition, and was destined to be rejected yet again – Emma could feel tears starting to prick her eyes. She hit Ben in the chest again, more weakly this time. 'I've had enough of this,' she said. 'It's doing my head in. I can't live like this any more.'

For some reason, watching Emma fight back the tears, it seemed very important to Ben at that second that Jasmine should forgive Eddie. He grabbed her wrist and forced her to look at him. 'Marry me?' he asked.

Emma was taken off guard. It was the last thing she'd been expecting. The only answer she could think of was, 'OK.'

'Oh, very touching,' said Patrick breaking into slow, sarcastic applause.

Ben let go of Emma's wrist.

'Sorry for hitting you,' she mumbled as she sat down again. 'I didn't hurt you, did I?'

'No, I'll live.'

Angela switched off the video camera. 'There's just one other thing I wanted to ask,' she said. 'You can drive, can't you?'

'Oh yes.'

'Manual or automatic?'

'Both.' She could drive a tractor too, but she didn't suppose they'd be interested in that.

'Well, that all seems very good,' said Ben.

'Yes,' said Patrick. 'Now all we need to do is see what you look like naked.'

'I beg your pardon?'

'You know there's nudity involved, don't you?'

'No, I didn't. Irene never—'

'So if you could just undress for us, please.'

Emma looked from Patrick to Ben to Angela to see if he was joking. She'd never been asked to do anything like this before.

'You don't have a problem with nudity, do you?' asked Angela.

'No, of course not, it's just—' She wanted to say that it seemed a bit weird getting undressed in the middle of somebody's office. She could see everybody else in the production office through the window.

'Oh yes, of course,' said Angela and got up to close the blinds.

Emma pulled her new psychedelic top off over her head and as she lowered her arms she saw Patrick leering at her white lace bra.

'Well they're nothing to write home about, are they?' he offered. 'What are you, 32A?'

'34B,' Emma murmured. 'It's a perfectly normal size.' Why else would M&S always sell out of her bra size first? She unzipped her new trousers, wishing that she'd worn sensible knickers and not her white, three-to-a-pack thongs. Why hadn't Irene warned her?

'What happened to your knees?' asked Patrick as she stepped out of her trousers, and Emma remembered the grazes she'd got the other night falling down the stairs of this very building.

'I fell over,' she blushed.

'Too much to drink?' suggested Patrick pleasantly.

'Could you turn around for us please?' said Angela and Emma shuffled around in a buttock-clenching circle so they could all see what she looked like from the back. If it's possible for a bottom to blush, she knew that's what hers would be doing. Why, oh why, she wondered again, had she worn a thong?

'And the rest,' said Patrick.

'Patrick, I don't think that's really necessary, do you?' said Angela.

'Well I don't want any nasty surprises.' He turned to Angela, talking across Emma as though she wasn't there. 'You see, a lot of them these days have mini-tit jobs – little party tits that still look natural.'

'Patrick, you are a veritable mine of unnecessary information,' Angela told him.

But Patrick had already turned back to await Emma's grand finale. 'Or she might have Manchester United tattooed across her chest,' he suggested.

Emma knew that Patrick couldn't have cared less if she'd had a bikini wax in the shape of David Beckham; he was just trying to teach her a lesson for the other night. If she'd shagged Patrick right there on the bar in the middle of Soho House it could not possibly have been any worse than this. Come on, don't be a baby, she told herself sternly. Actresses get their kit off all the time. Look at Halle Berry. And Nicole Kidman. And Kate Winslet is forever taking her knickers off. Even Judi Dench – well, maybe not Judi Dench. She took a deep breath and reached around to unhook her bra.

'It's OK, Emma, that'll do,' Ben stopped her. 'I think we've all seen enough, haven't we?'

'Speak for yourself,' said Patrick crossly.

'Thank you, Emma, you can get dressed now,' said Ben, and she shot him a grateful smile and started pulling her clothes back on as fast as she could.

'Oh, I nearly forgot,' said Angela as though nothing out of the ordinary had just happened. 'What about roller-blading? That roller-blading scene hasn't been cut yet, has it, Ben?'

Emma had never skated in her life, but she wasn't going to lose the part now. She remembered Irene's advice, 'Never admit to not being able to do anything. You can always learn. 'Yes, I can roller-blade,' she said. She'd put her top on inside out but there was no way she was going to change it now.

'Can you cook?' asked Patrick.

'A little. Why? Would I have to cook in this?'

'No, but it's always good to have a trade to fall back on.'

'Well, that all seems fine,' said Angela.

'Yes. Thank you for coming in, Emma,' said Ben. 'We'll let you know very soon. In the next couple of days.'

Emma stood up and shook hands with everyone and let Angela and Ben walk her out of the office. She got as far as the front door when she realised that in her hurry to escape she'd left her bag on the floor by her chair.

'I'd forget my head if it wasn't screwed on,' she said and went back to Ben's office to retrieve it. She found Patrick kneeling in front of her chair.

'You forgot your bag,' he explained and quickly stood up to hand it to her.

'You know,' said Emma to Donna later that night, 'if I didn't know better, I could have sworn he was sniffing the seat.'

eleven

Liz banged the bell with her hand again and tapped her foot. She could see the fat receptionist in the little office back there eating a Mars Bar and she was convinced the woman was deliberately ignoring her.

Pete, the gaffer and two other crew she didn't recognise had already made themselves at home in the downstairs bar with pints of the local bitter as though they didn't have a care in the world. Which, she thought enviously, they probably didn't.

'Hello? Hello!' she called for the third time. What a nasty navy-blue uniform they make their staff wear here, Liz thought, and taking her Polaroid camera out of her bag, she snatched a photograph of the receptionist for future reference. It would come in handy the next time she had to design a costume for frumpy reception staff in a down-at-heel seaside hotel.

The flash made the receptionist suddenly look up as though she'd only just realised Liz was there. She pushed her glasses back up her nose and came out to the front desk – none too quickly, Liz noted.

'I'm sorry – I've been trying to send a fax,' she said and Liz detected a South African accent – or possibly Zimbabwean. 'How can I help you?'

'There's a problem with my room. I'm meant to have a sea view,' Liz explained, trying to be as charming as possible. Thank goodness she'd had the sense to check that her room was OK before carting all her luggage upstairs.

The receptionist cast a vague look at the registration book

and at the keys hanging on a large wooden board behind her. 'I'm sorry, but all our sea-view rooms have been booked.'

'Yes. And one of them was booked by me. Liz Thorne.'

'I'm very sorry, but we don't have any more available at the moment. You can try again tomorrow after some of the other guests check out.'

'What do you mean – *try* again tomorrow? Are they checking out of sea-view rooms or not?'

The receptionist, whose name-tag revealed that she was called Belinda, glanced at her registration book again. 'They might be,' she suggested helpfully.

Liz pressed her teeth tightly together to stop herself from losing her temper. Why did this always happen every single time she left London? Was it something in the water? 'Right, well, Belinda. I wonder if you could possibly do me a huge favour? Do you think you could reserve a sea-view room for me so that when the next person checks out I can have their room?'

'Certainly. No problem,' said Belinda. 'What was your name?'

'Elizabeth Thorne,' said Liz slowly, with a heroic display of patience. 'And could you tell me what room Ben Lincoln is in, please?'

All the film personnel were listed on a separate sheet and Belinda ran her finger down the list of names. 'He's in 324. But I don't think he's arrived yet.'

'You don't *think* he's arrived, or he definitely hasn't?'

'I'm not sure. I can try phoning his room for you.'

'That's OK. Don't worry.'

As she waited for the lift, she waved to Pete through the glass doors of the bar and he lifted his glass in solemn salute. The two men sitting with him turned their heads to see who he was looking at and Liz enjoyed watching the interest register in their eyes the way it always did. That's why, Liz thought, looking at the Polaroid developing in her hand you'll never catch me wearing a size sixteen navy-blue suit with a matching navy-blue blouse. She gave them all a lazy smile and pushed the button for the lift again. Too bad, boys, you're out of luck, she thought. I've got other plans.

The yellow light above the lift showed that it was still on the fourth floor. Liz groaned and wondered what kind of cheap-skate film company would book into a hotel with only one lift – and no porter to help her with her bags. When the lift eventually arrived, she propped the doors open with one of her suitcases while she went back to reception to drag over the first of her gigantic costume bags.

'Here! I help you!' A young girl with dirty-blonde hair and an Eastern European accent grabbed the other handle of the striped plastic carrier and helped Liz slide it towards the lift. She was wearing a shapeless navy-blue tunic that could only be a uniform.

'You hold the lift and I will bring these,' she told Liz, pointing to the rest of the bags.

Well, she's certainly strong, thought Liz as she watched the girl drag over Liz's four other bags. I expect she's going to want a tip.

'You are with the film?' the girl asked when she'd brought the last bag over.

'Yes, that's right,' said Liz and reluctantly opened her purse to look for some change.

'No, no, is not necessary,' the girl insisted, embarrassed by the suggestion she was only helping Liz for financial gain. 'I am happy to help you. We are so excited you are here. I would love to be in film so much. You need peoples?'

'I shouldn't think so,' said Liz, putting her purse away.

'My name is Magda. I am chamber maid here. I would love to do anything.'

'That's fantastic, Magda, I'll keep you in mind,' said Liz and pressed the button for the third floor.

When she got to her room, there was no point in unpacking so she dragged her four large suitcases over near the window where they'd be out of the way. Her dress for the welcome party tonight was already hanging in the wardrobe in a separate garment bag and her toiletries – everything she could possibly need for the next six weeks – were all in the large plastic container that always followed her on location. She arranged them in order of height on the narrow tiled ledge, applied her favourite Dermalogica vitamin masque, lit a cigarette, and as she took off her old nail varnish, she began to chant softly under her breath.

He should have taken the A3. Ben didn't drive through south London very often and he'd never realised before that there was quite so much of it. It was only fifty miles from London to Brighton and he'd thought he'd be able to do it in an hour. On the A–Z this had looked like the most direct route, but he'd left Ladbroke Grove at three, and two hours later he was still in Streatham. It felt like he'd been in Streatham for ever. The welcome party was going to start at eight and at this rate he'd never make it. He'd been stuck at the same set of traffic lights now for fifteen minutes.

Most of the cast were arriving this evening and staying overnight for the read-through tomorrow. Patrick had foamed at the mouth at the expense of all the train fares and hotel bills, but Ben had put his foot down because his star, Danny Parker, had been in the recording studio until yesterday.

'This is the only chance I'm going to get for any kind of rehearsal,' he reminded Patrick, who pretended not to understand why he needed any rehearsal time at all.

Patrick had utter contempt for the acting profession which he claimed was an unavoidable occupational hazard associated with producing any of the performing arts. He had no time for luvvies and was likely to become hysterical if he heard an actor referring to 'his craft'. 'They can practise in make-up,' he said. 'That's two hours rehearsal time every morning.'

Ben pretended not to hear him. When he'd floated the idea of a welcome party, Patrick had had an eppy. 'Party? Party?' he demanded, hopping from foot to foot. 'I know you've never directed a film before, but even you must have noticed it's traditional to have the party *after you've wrapped?*'

So Ben said he'd pay for it out of his own pocket, which made Patrick look like a tight bastard, and after much dramatic flourishing of a pocket calculator, Patrick reluctantly agreed to split the cost. But Ben wasn't allowed to call it a party. 'It's welcome drinks,' Patrick insisted. 'No – make that welcome *drink.*' What it was, Ben thought, was emotional blackmail – his way of saying thank you in advance to his crew, who were all working at a fraction of their usual rate. Apart from Pete and his electricians, of course. The sparks prided themselves on being impossible to haggle with.

'We haven't got very much money,' Ben had explained when he'd rung Pete who he desperately hoped would be his gaffer.

'Oh dear, that's very unfortunate,' Pete had tutted sympathetically. 'You shouldn't be making a film, then, should you?' and put the phone down. Ben had had no option but to call him again and offer him the full whack.

At least he was getting Emma Buckley cheap. He and Angela had been so certain about the qualities they'd been looking for in Jasmine, and then Emma Buckley had walked in with none of those qualities and surprised them all. A shame she was a complete unknown – but maybe they could use that to their advantage.

After the audition Ben, Patrick and Angela had, for once, been in complete agreement: they were going to cast Kimberley Day as Jasmine. She wasn't as big a name as Zoe Langridge, but Angela said she'd been outstanding in that Trollope adaptation on TV (Ben hadn't liked to show his ignorance by asking whether it was Joanna Trollope or Anthony Trollope). And then Kimberley had said she hoped it wouldn't matter, but they did know she'd be five months pregnant by the end of the shoot, didn't they? Ben imagined endless scenes of Jasmine running through the streets of Brighton hiding her bump behind a large black shoulder bag, and having to shoot all of her scenes from the neck up only, and so, by a process of elimination, the part was Emma's.

Emma had brought Jasmine to life in a way that he'd never imagined her. The Jasmine she'd discovered wasn't some ball-breaking hussy. Emma's Jasmine was a girl who didn't have an unkind thought in her head. She was totally lacking in guile or cunning; the kind of girl you want to scoop up in your arms and let nothing bad happen to. And best of all, with the money he'd saved by casting Emma, he'd be able to afford the crane shot he desperately wanted. He'd been mulling it over in his mind all the way from London. The possibilities, he realised, were enormous.

Now at the top of the queue ahead of him, three cars trickled through the intersection before the lights changed back to red. At this rate he wouldn't make Brighton until morning.

Emma leaned her head against the train window as the countryside flashed past. The script lay open in her lap but she was too excited to concentrate on learning her lines. Ever since the audition, her life had been a blur. The call had come from Irene the very next morning.

'Congratulations! You got it!' But as Emma screamed for joy, Irene added, 'But I don't think you should take it.'

'What?'

'The money they're offering is an insult. I've told them to double it.'

Emma panicked. 'Irene, no, call them back. Please. The money doesn't matter. I don't care about the money. I'll do it for free – apart from your commission, I mean,' she added hastily as she heard Irene start to splutter. 'Oh please call them back before they give it to someone else.'

'You're setting a very dangerous precedent,' Irene warned her. 'You can't let people walk all over you like that. I don't think they're going to be paying Ronald Gasch or Danny Parker the Equity minimum, do you?' but she called them back, grumbling all the while, and now here Emma was on the train to Brighton and her very first proper film role.

She wasn't sure if Irene would be furious or proud if she ever found out that Emma had only got the part because she'd lied about being in a film that didn't even exist. And *Titanic* – she'd almost forgotten about that. That was the trouble with telling lies – you had to remember them and Emma knew she was too scatty to keep track of things like that.

She'd made up her mind to confess everything to Ben tonight. She'd tell him she'd been so desperate to get the part she didn't want him to think she'd been out of work for months. She was sure he'd see the funny side – wouldn't he?

Jason hadn't been nearly as excited as she thought he would have been about her big break and she was touched to think he was going to miss her that much while she was away in Brighton. She had the uncontrollable urge to call him again, even though she'd already spoken to him twice that day and sent him three text messages. She took out her mobile once again.

'Hello!' she chirped when he answered. 'Have you finished for today then?'

'Yeah. I just had one scene after lunch.'

'Ohhh' she wailed, screwing her face up. 'I could have come to Sheffield this morning and we could have had the whole weekend together.' It took the shine off her excitement knowing that she could have spent some quality time with Jason. 'What are you going to do all weekend without me? I know – why don't you come up to Brighton? Down to Brighton, I mean.'

'I'd love to, but I can't. I'm on standby for tomorrow, remember? And you'll be hanging out with *Danny Parker*.' Jason pronounced the name of Emma's co-star as though it was a particularly inferior brand of toilet cleaner. Jason had been unaware of any irony when he'd told Emma it was outrageous that the star of *Brighton Rocks* wasn't even a proper actor – just a stupid pop star. There weren't many actors that Jason could safely look down on from his own shaky toe-hold but Danny Parker was one of them.

'It's ridiculous, isn't it?' Emma agreed sympathetically. 'I'm sure they've only cast him because every girl in the country fancies him.' It turned out to be completely the wrong thing to say.

'Every girl in the country?' Jason fumed. 'I suppose you fancy him and all, do you?'

'No of course I don't,' she fibbed. She did think Danny Parker was quite good-looking, but she hated it when Jason got jealous like this because it was so irrational. And unnecessary. Fancying a pop star wasn't like fancying someone in real life.

'You said every girl in the country!'

'Well I meant every girl except me.'

'Yeah, but you bought all his CDs.'

'Not all of them. Just the last two. I like the music.'

'So you don't think he's good-looking?'

'He's not half as good-looking as you,' and she knew that was the right thing to say.

'Hang on a sec.' Jason moved the phone away from his lips and Emma heard him say, 'That's great. And can you bring us another beer, please?'

'Where are you?' she asked.

'The café around the corner. Look, my food's just arrived. Can I call you later?'

'Yeah, course. You're not still jealous, are you?'

'Of Danny Parker? Of course I'm not jealous of that runt.'

'Oh good. I miss you, Jason.'

'I miss you too. Good luck!'

'I love you,' said Emma and turned her attention back to her script and the scene where she kisses Danny Parker.

He had to hand it to Patrick for keeping overheads low, thought Ben. When it came to the hotel, every expense had been spared.

His room looked like it had been decorated by a leprechaun. The carpet was green, the bedspread was green, and when he opened the matching green and pink curtains, he found that instead of a balcony, his windows opened out on to scaffolding. If he looked down he could see the back door of the kitchens and if he looked straight ahead he could almost reach out and touch the window of the hotel next door.

The bathroom was avocado, complemented by a crusted seam of limescale that ran downhill from all the taps and when Ben inspected the bath he found a large yellow toenail clipping lying in the middle of the tub. He tore off a piece of toilet paper to pick it up with, and shivered as it made a tiny scratching noise against the plastic. He threw it the bin feeling a little sick. Thank goodness he'd asked for a room with a shower. Or, as it turned out, a shower attachment over the bath. He turned on the taps and stepped into the water and leapt out again as he was hit by an icy blast of cold water. He turned the dial all the way around to the hottest setting and waited patiently for the water to heat up. And waited. Eventually, after a little experimentation, he discovered that the shower had just two basic settings: boil alive, or, if he moved the dial the merest millimetre to the left, freeze to death. There was no middle ground, no setting that equated to anything he recognised as 'warm' or 'relaxing'. Nothing he could withstand for longer than five seconds. He gave up and ran a bath, but after the alien toenail incident he couldn't quite face lying down in it. So, instead, he stood up and scooped the water over his body as best he could.

Seeing Liz again, he thought, had turned out nowhere near as bad as he'd expected. And to think that all this time he'd been afraid she'd bear him a grudge.

He'd been so stunned by her proposal of marriage that he hadn't handled it very well at all and he still didn't feel very good about that. He'd never meant to hurt her. But to be fair, it had come completely out of the blue. Liz had never seemed the kind of girl who was into marriage and children – in fact, completely the opposite. What had been so brilliant about their relationship was the way Liz had been almost freakishly independent and expected him to be the same. 'I can't be doing with drippy men,' she'd warned him once when he'd made the mistake of buying her flowers for no reason.

Even after he moved in with her, she made a point of never referring to it as 'living together' and often reminded him that it was her flat and he was merely a visitor. He didn't even rate a mention on her answering-machine message.

And he never knew for certain, because they never sat down and talked about their relationship – which was another thing he liked about it – but he did suspect that she had other guys lurking in the background. She was always mentioning men she'd been working with, or parties she'd been to while he'd been away, and although she never actually came out and said that she'd got off with someone else, he always thought she dropped these little hints so that he'd know exactly where he stood.

And she must have suspected that he wasn't always completely faithful to her, mustn't she? He didn't make a habit of screwing around, but there was that one girl on that commercial he did in Rejkyavik, and, well, these things just happen, don't they? It's not as though he went looking for it or anything. Women just seemed to find him attractive. And besides, everyone knows that sex on location doesn't count. Nothing they did when they were apart counted. As long as they were happy when they were together, that was what mattered, wasn't it? And since most of the time they did share together was spent in Liz's king-size bed, Ben didn't really have much cause for complaint. The way it looked to him, sex was the whole point of their relationship and Liz had never given him any reason to think otherwise. Had she ever told him she loved him? He honestly couldn't remember.

So when she'd said, 'Marry me', Ben was lost. The first thought that had popped into his head was that there were so many women in the world and he'd hardly fucked any of them.

How could he possibly get married? And then, when he was still reeling from the shock of her proposal, she'd announced that she wanted his children. Liz! Who didn't eat bread in case it made her stomach stick out!

'I'm only twenty five years old,' he'd thought. 'Six years ago, I was still a teenager. I'm not ready to be a dad!'

Liz wasn't the only one who had a plan, but in Ben's plan, his career came first and marriage and kids came later – much, much later. How, he reasoned, could he concentrate on becoming a top-flight director if he was distracted by all that family stuff? How could he just pack up and go wherever in the world his work took him – Outer Mongolia, Cochabamba – if he had to worry about little Charlie's grazed knee? How could he write his Oscar-winning screenplay with Pokémon or whatever it was blaring in the background? He knew plenty of people in this business who had kids, and good luck to them, but that wasn't the way he wanted to do it. He was only twenty-five. He was still entitled to be selfish. It was his right.

And so he had stared at Liz – this new maternal, dreaming-of-a-white-wedding Liz who he didn't recognise one little bit – and every molecule in his body had climbed onto the starting blocks and prepared to sprint for the door. But he didn't have the guts to simply tell her, 'No', because he could tell that was so not the answer Liz wanted to hear. So he'd lied and told her he'd think about it. He didn't have any experience in turning down marriage proposals and consequently he didn't have any kind of ready-made speech prepared, but he was sure that was the kindest thing to do. He'd be away in Mauritius for three months and there was just an outside chance that by the time he came home, Liz would have forgotten the whole thing.

He couldn't help but be excited by the thought of being a free man in a foreign country. Mauritius was going to be a big adventure and he was secretly relieved that Liz wasn't going to be working out there with him. Naturally, he promised that he'd let her know if the costume designer quit or got sick but they both knew that wasn't going to happen.

In fact, the more he thought about it, the less sure he was that there was any kind of future together for him and Liz at all. It felt like they'd run their course and he was certain that if they had some time apart, she'd see that too. By the time he packed his bags he already knew that he wasn't going to be coming back to Liz's flat when the film ended and he'd managed to convince himself that Liz would see this was the best thing to do. But he'd kissed her goodbye when the taxi came and told her he'd see her in twelve weeks and he'd think about what she'd said. He'd felt a little guilty as the taxi drove away, but Liz had looked so happy as she waved him goodbye. She was a big girl. She was going to be just fine.

After Mauritius, he'd gone on to Australia and tried not to think about that last phone call when he told her he wasn't coming home. With twelve thousand miles between them it was easy to put it out of his mind and pretend it had never happened. He'd been so busy, he hadn't given it another thought. He'd started by directing a couple of pop promos on the cheap, and eighteen months later he'd come back to London with a tan and a hefty show-reel. He'd managed to avoid Liz since then, and as long as he kept out of her way while they were shooting, there was no reason why that whole messy business should ever be mentioned again.

Plus, she'd taught him a valuable lesson: all the girls he'd gone out with since Liz – and there had been a gratifyingly steady stream of them – all got the speech very early on about how his career was the most important thing to him and how, if they didn't like that, then they should get out now. He wasn't promising them anything and they weren't to get any crazy ideas in their heads about marriage and babies. He wasn't going to let himself be put on the spot like that again.

Now he fantasised about the moment later that night when he'd walk into the party and an excited murmur would spread through the room as people would nudge each other and whisper: 'That's the director!'

He had no idea how much beer and wine fifty-eight people could drink. He hoped it wasn't very much.

twelve

At the same moment as Flick, Patrick and Piers were sharing three neatly chopped lines of coke on the formica counter in the ladies loo, just a little further along the corridor, in the men's toilets, Ronald Gasch found the cotton wool he'd put in his pocket at the hotel and fluffed it out into two neat plugs which he inserted delicately into each ear. Why did these establishments insist on playing their music so loudly, he wondered. How was one supposed to think? He turned his head from side to side to inspect his reflection in the mirror and pushed the left-hand wad a little more emphatically into his ear canal so that it was no longer visible.

He wouldn't stay long tonight. Had his star really plummeted so low that he was now forced to find amusement in a tapas bar? Besides, he had a profound disliking of gatherings where he was the oldest person in the room. Lately, it seemed, he was being invited to a disturbing number of them. It was quite outrageous, really, because he wasn't that old. Sixty-two isn't old. The problem was that everyone else was getting younger. When had that happened? he wondered.

The director was a mere boy, younger than his own son. Ronald owned shoes that were older than Ben Lincoln. And as for that upstart who called himself a producer! Ronald knew they'd hired him for his name, so that his fame and reputation would lend credibility to their pathetic little endeavour, but he knew full well that neither of those two amateurs had the faintest idea what he was famous for. Had they seen his Hamlet? Had they seen his Titus Andronicus? Had they fuck.

However. He straightened his tie, relaxed his shoulders down and back, encouraging his ribcage to expand and his spine to lengthen, so that he was drawn up to his full height of five feet ten inches. He decided that it must be an effect of the fluorescent lighting that was making the pockets under his eyes look as though somebody had sellotaped two walnuts to his cheeks. The important thing, he reminded himself, was to be seen to make an effort and to *blend in* so that he wasn't mistaken for somebody's grandfather.

A burst of salsa rhythms swept in through the cushioning of cotton wool as the door opened and a tall black man in a yellow T-shirt and baggy trousers sauntered in. As the bar was otherwise closed for their private party, Ronald knew he must be one of the crew and extended his hand in greeting. 'How do you do,' he said. 'I'm Ronald Gasch.'

The other man chuckled and shook his hand energetically. 'Yeah, man, I know you are. I love that voice. I'm Tex, the sound recordist. I'm really looking forward to working with you!'

'I'm very pleased to meet you, Tex,' replied Ronald and left him to pee in privacy. Always the voice, he reflected gloomily as he walked back out to the sound and fury. Is that all I've become? Nothing more than a perfectly modulated collection of sound waves? Age had rendered him invisible. How he longed for someone to tell him, 'I love your acting', or 'I love your body', or, 'I love your face', but no – it was always the fucking voice.

As he hesitated in the doorway that led out to the bar, he almost stumbled over Emma who was hovering alone on the party's fringes, hoping to catch a glimpse of Danny Parker and simultaneously trying to keep out of Patrick's way.

She'd been surprised to see Patrick here tonight. She didn't really know what producers did, but she'd rather hoped that it involved sitting in an office in Soho and not being down here in

Brighton where she'd have to worry about bumping into him every day. Was she the only one who noticed that leering sarcastic smile he wore every time he saw her? She still had no way of knowing whether or not Ben knew about their meeting in Soho House. It also occurred to her that if Patrick had her home phone number he must have her CV and would know she'd never been in *Titanic* or anything else. But he couldn't have told Ben she'd lied about her experience or she wouldn't be here now. She'd tell Ben the truth tonight – the first chance she got.

Ronald Gasch took one look at Emma and decided she was probably one of the make-up girls. He'd discovered it was always as well to get on their good side early on or they were inclined to sit around gossiping and painting their nails while your false sideburns came unglued. Once again, he stuck out his hand and offered his standard greeting that implied, with such modesty, that even though he was the fourth greatest Shakespearean actor of his generation, no one could possibly be expected to know who he was. 'Hello, my dear. I'm Ronald Gasch.'

'Oh, hi. Nice to meet you. I'm Emma.'

She was a pretty little thing, he thought, but he was having trouble hearing her through the cotton wool. 'And what do you do?' he enquired.

'I'm playing Jasmine.'

Ronald thought he couldn't have heard her correctly, because Zoe Langridge would be playing Jasmine. Miss Langridge was the only other member of the cast whose work he knew and although her previous roles had all been fluff, they were commercially successful, critically acclaimed fluff and he had only reluctantly agreed to do the film in the first place after he had learned that she was doing it too. The rest of the cast were all nobodies as far as he was concerned; one of them had been in a pop group, apparently, and one of the others, so he was told, played somebody or other in a TV series that he never watched on principle.

'I'm sorry, I didn't quite catch what you said,' he told her.

Emma leaned over and repeated, in a louder voice: 'I'm playing Jasmine.' She couldn't help noticing that he had cotton wool sticking out of his right ear.

'You mean you'll be her stand-in,' he corrected her kindly.

Emma shook her head. 'No. I'm Jasmine.'

The fatherly smile vanished from Ronald's face. 'But that's impossible,' he boomed. 'Zoe Langridge is playing Jasmine!'

Before Emma could reply, they were almost trampled by Flick, Patrick and Piers rushing from the toilets with an air of unnatural, giddy urgency.

'Ah, Patrick,' said Ronald, grabbing the producer's sleeve to prevent his escape, 'precisely the man I need to speak to.' He would clear up this Zoe Langridge business right now once and for all.

Patrick wasn't listening because not twenty feet away was the terrifying spectacle of the entire make-up department – Saskia, Bex and Tracey – being served with *cocktails*. He'd made it absolutely crystal clear that the deal was for beer, soft-drinks and house wine only and he was consumed by the urgent need to make sure they paid for these drinks out of their own pockets. He didn't pause in his emergency dash to the bar, and was only barely aware that Ronald was being dragged along in his wake, still clinging, limpet-like, to his jacket.

Emma was aghast. How could she possibly take over from Zoe Langridge? What right did she have? Zoe Langridge was a huge star and a brilliant actress. She was one of Emma's idols. Emma understood suddenly that she would never have been offered the part in a million years if Ben had known she was a complete newcomer. He'd hit the roof if he ever found out the truth. He'd sack her on the spot before she even started. What on earth was she to do? If she left the party now, she could slip back to her hotel unnoticed and be on the train back to London before anyone even realised she was gone. She'd phone Ben, tell him she was sick and couldn't do the film. They'd have to get somebody else. It was the only honourable thing to do. That was when Flick noticed Emma standing all on her own and looking, she thought, a bit lost.

'Hi, it's Emma, isn't it? We met in the production office – remember? I'm Flick.'

'Oh, hi,' replied Emma distractedly.

'Do you know everybody here?' asked Flick.

'No, I don't know anyone,' Emma admitted.

'Come on – I'll introduce you.' She linked her arm through Emma's and led her into a throng around the bar where in a matter of seconds she had said 'hello' to Josephine, the production designer; Georgina, the third AD; Jamie, the first; Billy, the boom swinger; Damien, the grip; Will, the focus puller, the two riggers Bradley and Shane; Phil, the standby props; and Harvey and Arthur who were playing Lucky Louie and Buster.

'You won't remember all their names,' said Flick, and Emma just nodded, completely dazed. She had already forgotten what Flick's name was and spent the rest of the night calling her Fiona.

'So, do you need a DJ for your film?' the boy at the mixing desk asked Liz. 'Cos, like, you know I've been on TV before, right? That Newsroom South East, they come down here one time and I was like interviewed about salsa and everything, innit?'

'Really? Well, that's not really my department, I'm afraid,' said Liz, without taking her eyes off the door. 'You should really speak to Angela, the casting director.'

'What is it you do, then?' the boy persisted. His name was Paolo and he was desperate to be in the movies. He was too good-looking not to be up there on the screen with Tom Cruise and Brad Pitt. He'd positioned the spotlight over his booth so that any big-shot producers here tonight couldn't fail to see him up there, giving it his best moves and his fattest tunes. People always told him he looked like that Antonio Banderas – only younger. He was a people person and the punters loved him – especially the women. Maybe later, when he packed up, he'd shag this woman he was talking to right now, unless that Angela turned out to be better-looking.

'I design the costumes,' Liz told him.

'Right! Clothes, issit?'

Liz ignored him because coming through the front door were Hugo, the director of photography, followed by Ryan, the camera operator. And Ben. Liz caught her breath as the three of them headed straight to the bar. Their timing was terrible because her assistant Orlando was already on his way back from the bar with Liz's glass of wine. She'd have to stay put for the moment.

Liz and Orlando went back for ever, right back to when he was still called Barry. She always preferred to work with gay men because they made her laugh and didn't present her with any competition. And Orlando's bitchiness was on such a monumental scale that he made Liz seem almost saint-like by comparison.

Tonight Liz's radar was on full alert, automatically taking stock of every female working on the film and calculating the threat potential each of them posed. Unfortunately, no woman, however old or unfortunate-looking she may be, ever rated zero because Liz knew that where men were concerned, you couldn't be too careful.

On this scale, Josephine the production designer would ordinarily rate seven, but as she was going out with Jamie, the first AD, this was reduced to a four. Georgina, the third AD, was a seven – higher than she deserved with her long body and short legs, but her score had been bumped up because she was always on set and therefore right under Ben's nose. Flick, who was up for anything, and all of twenty-six, was a potential nine. The fact that for some inexplicable reason she seemed to have set her cap for Patrick, reduced this to a more manageable eight. Poppy in the art department was way too pretty for Liz's liking but she was married – not that that counted for anything – but in Poppy's case but she was besottedly, barely-back-from-honeymoon married and rated a seven. Vanessa, the production manager – mid-thirties, married (though Liz couldn't imagine to whom) with a rather tiresome martyr complex – was a two, as was Janet the accountant, not only because of her slightly squinty eyes but because Liz knew Ben could never fall in love with someone who cross-examined him about every petrol receipt. Directors and accountants were astrologically incompatible. Like bison and halibut. Stacey, the continuity supervisor, was also only a two. Even though she was thirty-one, slim, with delicate elfin features, and even though she sat next to Ben at the monitor, had his ear constantly and probably knew more about directing than he ever would, she was, thank God, gay. But she still got two points because there were men – and Ben may well be one of them, for all Liz knew – who would see this not as an obstacle, but a challenge.

As ever, the main threat would come from the combined onslaught of the make-up department who were all in their twenties and together resembled a Britney Spears box-set. Liz had worked with them before and knew that even though the rest of the crew might be wearing waterproof trousers, four layers of fleece, rough terrain boots, and technical jackets designed to withstand blizzard conditions, Saskia, Bex and Tracey – known affectionately to male crew throughout the country as The Daft Tarts – were always dressed to go clubbing. Saskia's naturally black hair had been unnaturally straightened and lacquered, Bex wore her blonde hair up in a twist decorated with lots of sparkly clips and Tracey's hair had gone back from blonde to brunette, and fell just past her shoulders. Annoyingly, the fact that all three of them were quite phenomenally, frighteningly stupid, only added to their attractiveness from a male point of view, and coming in a pack of three increased their fantasy potential exponentially. Their one saving grace was that Liz knew from her dedicated yet surreptitious monitoring of Ben's career that he had worked with The Daft Tarts many times before and had never made a serious move on any of them. Accordingly, they were all nines.

Orlando took one look at Paolo's glossy mocha complexion

and dreamy brown eyes and handed Liz her drink with a theatrically slack jaw and raised eyebrows. 'Thank you for keeping him warm, dear. I'll take over from here. I knew those merengue lessons wouldn't be wasted. By the way, don't look now but You Know Who has just arrived.'

'So?' Liz pretended she had absolutely no interest in Ben Lincoln.

'Oh, darling,' sighed Orlando. 'This is me you're talking to, remember?'

Orlando remembered everything. It was Orlando who had pinned up the hem on Liz's wedding dress and Orlando who'd picked up the pieces after she found out that she wasn't going to get to wear it. At first he'd been sympathetic because Orlando had had his heart broken so often he used to joke that Wedgwood had discontinued the pattern. But then his sympathy had turned to concern and then to anxiety as, instead of pulling herself together, Liz had fallen further and further apart.

The nose job was the first sign. Liz used to have a tiny bump on the bridge of her nose and after Ben dumped her, she'd become obsessed with having it straightened. Because she didn't have medical insurance, she had it done as a day case to save the cost of an overnight bed, and it was Orlando who'd picked her up from the Cromwell Hospital in Earls Court a few hours after the anaesthetic had worn off. He'd taken one look at the blood-stained strips of gauze poking out of her nostrils and promptly fainted. When her plaster nose cone came off a week later, Orlando couldn't even tell the difference.

And then she'd got really weird, so that even something as simple as lunch was liable to push her over the edge. Once, when they were working at Ealing Studios, the production manager had found her collapsed in a heap in Pret A Manger because she couldn't find anything to eat that didn't contain carbohydrates, fats or sugar. The production manager put her in a taxi and sent her home. 'Even the salade niçoise has got potatoes in it,' she was reported to have sobbed.

Gradually, Orlando started to lose patience with her and his anxiety turned to irritation. Liz had always been a control freak but now she was just plain scary.

'It's not normal to pine for someone for longer than you went out with them in the first place,' he told her. 'I think you need professional help. Some kind of counselling.'

But it was getting harder and harder to reason with Liz. Before she'd got mixed up with Ben, she'd been a great laugh and it pained him to see the tight-lipped, miserable shell she'd become. He was afraid she'd turn into some dried-up old Miss Havisham, sitting at home in her wedding dress and cobwebs. And now she'd taken a job on Ben's film and he was expected to believe that she was over him. If she wasn't still in love with Ben, then why, Orlando wanted to know, had she signed a deal that paid them a third of their usual rate?

But maybe, he thought to himself, there would be other compensations, and he sidled over to the DJ booth to ask Paolo where he was from. He hoped it was Cuba because he'd been on holiday there just the year before and would be able to impress him with his local knowledge of all the best hotels.

Over at the bar, Ben was necking a bottle of Sol. He'd clocked Liz standing over by the DJ booth in the far corner of the room almost the moment he came through the door, but it was so dark and crowded he'd been able to let his eyes sweep blankly past her and straight to the bar. Now that people had started dancing, they were providing good cover so that he could carry on pretending not to see her.

'So anyway,' Hugo was telling Ben and Ryan, 'there we were, heading through the jungle up this mountain, the three of us, and the fucking jeep with its poxy little lawnmower engine can't hack it—'

'Ronald! So glad you could make it,' Ben cut in as Ronald Gasch strode over to him, this time dragging Patrick with him.

Hugo nodded briefly at Ronald and didn't even pause for

breath. He couldn't stand anyone interrupting his stories. 'So anyway,' he continued in a slightly louder voice, 'old Abdul gets clever, doesn't he, and thinks he can reverse back down . . .'

Ronald waited patiently for Hugo to finish, silently seething with fury. He'd got no joy from Patrick about what had become of Zoe Langridge – just a lot of wide-boy producer double-talk. At least Ben would give him a straight answer.

'. . . and we hadn't gone more than four feet when the back wheel of the jeep rolls straight into this gully at the side of the track. The whole fucking mountain's only made of limestone, isn't it? And there we are – me and Ewan McGregor – buried up to the wheel arch. Miles from fucking anywhere.'

'Hi guys,' said Flick, who was still making the rounds with Emma and blithely unaware of the fact that Hugo had not yet delivered his punchline. 'Do you all know Emma? Emma – this is Ryan, he's the camera operator, and Hugo, the DP. Ben and Patrick you know already, don't you? And this is Roland Gasch.'

'Ronald,' Ronald corrected her quietly.

'Oh yeah, sorry, mate. Anyway guys,' Flick continued unabashed, 'this is Emma who's playing Jasmine.'

Meanwhile, Paolo the DJ was insulted because people were leaving the dance floor. He always took it personally when people didn't get into his mixes and tonight, with all these film producers here, he had to impress them with what an ace DJ he was. Consequently, he had reluctantly given into Orlando's request for 'Livin' La Vida Loca' – the only vaguely Latin tune Orlando could put a name to apart from the Macarena, which he would rather die than admit to liking – at least until he got to know Paolo a whole heap better.

'Hey, Patrick, don't just stand there like a stunned mullet,' said Flick, grabbing his hand. 'Come and dance with me.'

Patrick wasn't one of life's dancers but he was desperate to get away from bloody Ronald Gasch and he let Flick lead him onto the dance floor. The moment she was free from Flick's friendly arm-lock, Emma looked around for the exit.

'So, what have you been doing?' Ryan asked her, not because he was particularly interested in the excrutiatingly self-obsessed minutiae of another wannabe's career, but because it would be a relief to hear something other than the sound of Hugo's voice for a few minutes. He'd heard the Ewan McGregor-in-a-jeep story three times already.

With Ben standing right next to her, Emma was forced to repeat her lie. 'Have you heard of a film called *Hairdressing*?' she ventured reluctantly.

Ryan shook his head, 'No', and Emma didn't elaborate. She saw Ben was being cornered by Ronald Gasch.

'Ben, I wondered if I might have a word with you?' Ronald began. But Liz, spotting a clear path across the almost empty dance floor, had also chosen this exact moment to make her move on Ben and was now walking over to the bar on the pretext of getting another round of drinks. Ben could see her now, out of the corner of his eye, heading straight for him. Like a shark, he thought. He was trapped. The last thing he wanted to do was get chatting with Liz about old times, but there was no escape. He couldn't even get to the toilets without walking straight into her path. So he did the only thing he could. 'Want to dance?' he asked Emma. And without waiting for an answer he grabbed her hand and led her quickly to the far side of the dance floor safely out of Liz's way.

'Can you salsa?' he asked Emma, turning them both around so that his back was to the bar and he wouldn't have to look at Liz.

'A little. I'm not very good,' she admitted. She'd been to a salsa class with the girls at the salon twice but stopped going because she'd been partnered by a very short man who stank of cigarettes so badly she had to dance with her head turned sideways. That had kind of killed the romance of salsa for her. 'Can you?'

'Not really,' said Ben, 'but I'll have a go.' Pilar, his Spanish ex, had tried to teach him a couple of times, but had grown impatient with his lack of rhythm. He put his arm around

Emma's waist and counted the beats under his breath to get them started.

'Sorry!' said Emma as she trod on his foot. 'I thought you were going left!' She kept her eyes on her toes and tried to think of the best way to break it to Ben that she'd never been in a film before. She had to tell him tonight before it was too late for him to find someone else.

The Daft Tarts were dancing together, slowly, so they wouldn't spill their banana daquiris, Patrick was letting Flick lead, and over at the bar, Ronald Gasch was furious. All he wanted was a straight answer from the producer or the director and they'd both walked off and ignored him. That was it, he thought. He pushed through the dancers and planted himself in front of Ben and Emma so that they had no choice but to stop dancing.

'Goodnight,' he told them both firmly.

'Oh, you don't have to go so soon, do you?' asked Ben. 'It's still early.'

'I came tonight hoping to meet Zoe Langridge, but it seems I am to be disappointed,' Ronald replied with a sarcastic edge in his voice. 'As for you, my dear,' and he turned now to Emma, 'I look forward to the read-through tomorrow and hearing exactly how you will be approaching the role. I have not had the pleasure of seeing any of your work before.' Then he turned and stormed off back to the hotel to phone his agent.

Ben seemed not the slightest bit bothered and carried on dancing – or rather, stepping from side to side and backwards and forwards, sometimes accidentally coinciding with the beat, but most often missing it by miles and not caring because he was starting to enjoy himself.

'Don't let Ron get to you,' he said to Emma. 'I think he's just pissed off because nobody told him officially that the cast had changed.'

This was Emma's opportunity. 'Ben, I don't think I can step into Zoe Langridge's part just like that,' she said. She still didn't have the nerve to look him in the eye and addressed her speech to one of his shirt buttons. 'I don't have nearly enough experience.'

'Don't worry about that,' Ben assured her. 'You're going to be great. I can feel it.'

'But Zoe Langridge is a huge star. I'm a nobody. If I'd known I only got this part because she dropped out—'

'Yeah, I'm sorry about that. Maybe I should have told you. But it's professional etiquette, isn't it? You never say who's turned a part down, do you? I mean, for all Zoe Langridge knows, she might not have been our first choice, either.'

'Wasn't she?' asked Emma, looking up at Ben for the first time.

'Well, as a matter of fact she was,' Ben admitted and was caught off guard by the intensity of Emma's blue eyes. She really did look fabulous with the light behind her. He moved his hand a fraction higher up her waist. 'But the point is, she might not have been.'

'So, I shouldn't worry that I was your second choice?' Perhaps it wasn't as bad as she thought.

Ben remembered that his second choice had actually been Kimberley Day and tried to spin Emma around so that she wouldn't see his guilty expression. But he didn't lift his arm high enough and smacked her in the head.

Emma saw the look on his face and knew what it meant. 'Do you mean to say I wasn't even your *second* choice?' she asked, and dropped his hand in horror.

Ben knew what insecure, neurotic sugar-mice actresses were, apt to dissolve at the slightest thing. 'Look,' he said hastily, 'the point is you're going to be fantastic and that's all that matters.' He grabbed her hand again and tried to pick up the rhythm.

'But if I changed my mind, you could just move on down the list and find somebody else, couldn't you?' Emma asked. They'd danced around now so that the front door was only a few yards away. If she hurried she could be back in London by midnight.

Ben put it down to first-night nerves. 'Bad luck,' he smiled and fought the sudden impulse to stroke her hair. 'You've signed your contract and we start shooting the day after tomorrow. I'm afraid you're stuck with us!' He meant this to be light-hearted and reassuring, but Emma didn't laugh and looked more alarmed than relieved.

Emma decided to give it one last shot. She had to let Ben know she was a complete fraud. 'It's just that I'm really scared I'm going to let you down,' she said. 'You know, I've never had such a big part before.' It was as close as she dared get to a full confession, but Ben just smiled.

'God, is that all you're worried about?' he laughed. 'How do you think I feel? I've never directed a film before! If anyone's going to bollocks things up, it's going to be me!'

He'd never admitted to anyone before how terrified he was about the next six weeks, and in a desperate burst of fake confidence, he lifted his arm to spin Emma around again. As they ended the turn facing each other and in time with the music, they both burst out laughing in surprise. Maybe, Emma thought, everything was going to be all right after all.

'Can I buy you a free drink?' said a voice beside Liz. She turned her head to see the tall man who'd been in the hotel bar earlier with Pete.

'No. Thanks,' she said, and turned her eyes back to the dance-floor. Who was that girl Ben was dancing with? She thought she'd safely accounted for all the cast and crew.

'I'm Tex,' he introduced himself, taking the lime out of the neck of his beer bottle. 'You're Liz, aren't you? We did a commercial together a couple of years ago.'

'Did we?'

'Yeah. A studio in Fulham. Mobile phones, I think it was.'

'Really? I can't remember,' said Liz, not really listening. She watched Ben and this other girl with their heads bent together, staring down at their feet with fierce concentration. Ricky Martin had ended but instead of coming back to the bar, they had carried on dancing.

'Do you want to dance?' Tex asked.

'No!' Liz almost snapped. 'Sorry. No, it's not really my kind of music.'

'Nah, me neither. Sure you wouldn't like a drink? You seem a little tense.' Christ, Liz thought, this guy just doesn't know when to give up. Perhaps, after all, Tex could be useful to her. 'So, Tex, have you worked with Ben before?'

Tex shook his head. Good, Liz thought. That meant he wouldn't know about her and Ben.

'What about you?' Tex asked.

'A couple of times. Ages ago,' she said casually. 'Do you know many people here?'

'A few.'

'Oh good, I'm terrible with names,' she told him. 'You see that girl dancing with Ben? I know I've worked with her before, but I can't remember her name.'

'You mean the girl playing Jasmine? Her name's Emma, I think. Flick introduced me to her before.'

'Emma! Of course, that's it!' said Liz as though it had been on the tip of her tongue all the time. 'I knew it began with an E.'

Now she wondered why she hadn't taken more trouble to check out Zoe Langridge's replacement in the flesh. The last-minute costume fitting she'd arranged with Emma in London had been cancelled because Danny Parker had kept her hanging around until 2 a.m. at a recording studio in Oxfordshire and then refused to try on anything without his personal stylist present. So she had spoken to Emma for just five minutes on the phone, just long enough to get an idea of her measurements and colouring and to satisfy herself that the costumes she'd already chosen for Zoe Langridge could be made to work with only minor alterations. On the phone, Emma had seemed slight and insignificant, almost irrelevant to Liz's overall plan, but now she could see that she'd completely underestimated the threat she posed.

Now Liz mentally amended her calculations to include Emma. Age: Younger than Liz. Build: Slim enough. Prettiness: A bit natural for Liz's tastes, but some men go for that scrubbed fresh look. Proximity to Ben: Maximum. Relationship status: Unknown. Liz was taking no chances. She marked Emma down as a Ten.

thirteen

The sun snaked through the gap between the heavy green curtains, straight into Liz's eyes. Years of early mornings had instilled in her the discipline of getting out of bed the moment she woke up because it didn't get any easier lying there thinking about it. Liz didn't go in for snooze buttons or five minutes more because that was only putting off the inevitable. Automatically then, she threw back the covers and leaned over to switch off her alarm clock, which wasn't due to ring for another six minutes. And as she did so, she couldn't help admiring the perfectly rounded ebony buttocks in the bed beside her where Tex had kicked off the sheet.

If Ben wanted to ignore her and pretend she didn't even exist, then she was prepared to work even harder to get his attention. The old Liz would have loved a fling with Tex. The new Liz felt dead inside and could only go through the motions, trying to remember the time when sex had been fun.

She took the phone into the bathroom and closed the door so she wouldn't wake him. First, she dialled Ben's room number, and when she heard him pick up the phone, she hung up immediately. Then, she rang Emma's room – she'd found out her room number from the receptionist last night after the party. She breathed a sigh of relief when she heard a girl's sleepy voice say, 'Hello?' Well, that was something. At least they were both in their own rooms.

Last night had not gone at all the way she had planned, she thought, as she stepped into the shower. After they come off the dance floor, Emma had joined Ben at the bar with the rest of the cast who monopolised him for the whole evening. Ben had spoken to Liz just once when she'd gone to get a drink, standing right next to him so that he couldn't pretend not to see her.

'Hi, having a good time?' he'd asked her with forced jollity and just for a moment she'd wondered why she bothered. She despised his cowardice. Why couldn't he just talk to her normally? Why did he have to hide from her? Why was he so afraid to admit that what they'd had together had been perfect? But then as he brushed past her, he'd got close enough for her to breathe in the scent of him, that faint warm musky smell that reawakened a thousand memories and her resolve returned. She would have him back. She would.

'I'm having a great time, thanks,' she'd told him and walked off, carrying a glass of wine and a beer for Tex to let Ben know that she wasn't letting the grass grow under her feet. She spent the rest of the night laughing loudly at Tex's jokes, but watching Ben until he left the bar with Hugo just before midnight.

Instead of following him, Liz stayed to keep an eye on Emma until the bar closed at one o'clock and all the stragglers stumbled out into the street. Paolo said he could get them in free at Concorde 2, so Danny Parker and the other three boys who were playing the band members, The Daft Tarts, Emma, Flick and Orlando, of course, had gone with him. Liz couldn't see any point in going to a club with a bunch of actors if Ben wasn't going to be there so she went back to the hotel with Tex. She thought sex would make her feel better, but she couldn't get rid of the picture in her head of Emma and Ben dancing together and the way salsa dictated that he hold her right hand in his left, and rest his other hand on her waist to guide her. Tex had seen the tears in her eyes and mistaken it for passion.

'Hello? Hello?' Emma heard a click as whoever was on the

other end of the line hung up. She turned the bedside clock to look at the time and saw that it was only a quarter to seven. Perhaps the hotel had been asked to give everyone an alarm call after last night's party. The read-through wasn't scheduled to start until ten and it seemed a little early to be waking people up, but maybe that's what it was like in the film world. She rolled over and closed her eyes. Just five more minutes, she thought and fell asleep again almost at once.

Overhead, the seagulls wheeled and cried as Ben walked out the front door of the hotel and jogged across the road to the seafront. The sky was already a clear milky blue and although the morning air was chilly and fresh, it was going to be a beautiful day. For a moment, Ben envied the seagulls whose only responsibility for the day was to find some breakfast and then hang out by the beach chasing other seagulls. His mind was already racing with all the problems he needed to sort out.

After the read-through he'd apologise to Ronald Gasch for the fact that no one had told him about Zoe Langridge dropping out. Trust Patrick to land him in it like that. Angela had offered to ring Ronald herself and explain the situation, but Patrick had told her it would be better coming from the producer – as indeed it would have been if he'd had the guts to actually do it. It was typical of Patrick to bury his head in the sand like that and just hope the problem would go away. Like the way you're dealing with the Liz problem? said a guilty little voice in his head, but Ben chose to ignore it – the same way he was managing to ignore Liz.

He jogged on slowly, down past the gaily painted beach huts where the first roller-bladers of the day were already circling. He hoped Emma was going to be OK at the read-through and that Ronald hadn't rattled her too much. After he'd lost Zoe Langridge, he'd worked out a way that the part of Jasmine could be cut right back anyway if necessary. But after last night's chat with Emma, he knew that his instincts about her had been right and that she'd give the part a whole new complexion. Sweet and vulnerable — that's what Jasmine needed to be. Zoe Langridge was a terrific little actress but there was no way in the world you could describe her as sweet and vulnerable. In her last three films she'd played a stripper, a crack whore and a murderer. In fact, as Ben turned and jogged back towards the hotel, the thought suddenly occurred to him that Zoe Langridge had always been completely wrong for Jasmine. But they'd been so preoccupied with trying to secure a big-name actress for the role, they'd completely overlooked that. Perhaps Emma was exactly what he needed. Perhaps everything was going to be fine.

'Am I the first?' As Ronald Gasch entered the large function room, the only other person already there was Flick, who was putting a copy of the latest revised version of the script in front of each chair.

'Oh, morning, Ronald,' she greeted him cheerfully. 'Did you sleep well?'

'No. I'm afraid I had a very restless night. There is a door in the corridor right outside my room that was banging all night. Each time somebody walked past, the door slammed behind them and woke me up.'

'Oh no, that's terrible!' Flick sympathised. 'I'll have a word with the hotel this morning and see if I can get you moved to somewhere quieter.'

'Oh, would you, my dear?' He gripped her arm gratefully with both hands and stared up into her uncomplicated young face. At last. Somebody on this godforsaken production who was prepared to look after him properly.

'Yeah, sure,' she laughed. 'No worries.'

There was a tinkle of china as a trolley bearing jugs of tea and coffee was wheeled in through the door.

'Oh terrific. You can just leave that over there for now, thanks,' she told the porter. 'And we've ordered water and orange juice as well. Is that coming?'

The porter apologised and promised to return with the missing items immediately.

'Still and sparkling, please!' Flick called after him.

Ronald helped himself to a coffee, sat down and took out his reading glasses from his inside top pocket so he could go through the new script quietly before everyone else arrived. Occasionally he allowed himself a secret glance up at Flick who was neatly laying out the cups around the large oval table. Each time she stretched forward, her shirt rode up and the sunlight caught the tiny silver jewel glittering in her taut, brown tummy. He felt older than God.

Ben came in, saw Ronald sitting alone at the table and wavered over whether or not it would look rude if he left a gap between them. On the one hand, the table was almost empty so he could sit wherever he wanted and it would look like he was respecting Ronald's space. On the other hand, he was the director and Ronald was his biggest star and he knew that meant they were supposed to have some kind of a rapport. He didn't really want to sit next to him, but it would probably make things worse if he didn't. He decided to bite the bullet and go for the hearty approach.

'Morning, Ronald,' he said, taking the seat beside him. 'Sleep well?'

'It's curious how everyone seems so concerned by my sleeping patterns this morning,' replied Ronald, looking up from his script pages. 'As a matter of fact—'

But Ben never found out what the fact was because Alex Wylie, who was playing Sam, burst into the room with a hyperactively loud cry of, 'Benny! My man!' and began elaborately shaking his fingers to make them snap. 'Hey, is this it, then?' he said, grabbing up his new script and flipping the pages. 'Wicked! How you doin' there, Ronald?' and sat down beside him.

Stacey, the continuity supervisor, arrived, shot them all a quick, 'Morning!' and sat down at the far end of the table in the middle – giving them all plenty of personal space, Ben noticed.

She took out two stopwatches, her pens and pencils, and began skimming the new script looking for Ben's alterations.

Meanwhile, in the breakfast room on the ground floor, Emma was regretting ordering the scrambled eggs. They'd taken fifteen minutes to arrive and it now looked as though they'd spent every one of those fifteen minutes cooking because they were the consistency of scrambled brick. When she poked them with her fork they didn't move. And she still didn't have any toast.

'Excuse me!' she called after the waitress. 'Could I have some toast, please?' But the woman disappeared into the kitchen without giving any sign that she'd heard her.

Emma looked at her watch. It was already a quarter to ten and there was no time to order anything else. The dining room was almost empty.

'Here. Would you like some of mine?' The girl at the table beside her leaned across and passed over a stainless steel toast rack with four slices of cold, flabby hotel toast wedged inside. 'I don't do carbohydrates.'

'Oh, thanks very much. That's really kind of you,' said Emma, helping herself to two slices. 'I'm really running late this morning. Are you with the film too?'

'Yes. You're Emma, aren't you?' said the girl. 'I'm Liz – the costume designer. We spoke on the phone.'

'Oh, hi! Nice to meet you, finally. I'm supposed to see you this afternoon for a fitting, aren't I?' Emma was carelessly smearing butter all over her toast and Liz watched her aghast. White bread, butter, and now – *marmalade*? Either this was some new high-fat, high-carbohydrate diet that Liz hadn't heard of, or, the more likely explanation, she decided with satisfaction as she sipped her black coffee, was that Emma was bulimic.

'Yes, I hope you'll like what I've picked out for you.'

'I'm sure I will,' said Emma trying to talk through a mouthful of toast, taking a sip of tea and brushing the crumbs off her T-shirt all at the same time. 'Gosh, I'm so late! Do you know where the King George Suite is?'

Liz stood up, and smoothed down her skirt. 'Yes, you can come with me if you like. I'll be back in a minute. I just need to go to the ladies.'

Emma nodded gratefully, because her mouth was now too full to speak. Some people can't eat when they're nervous, but Emma was exactly the opposite. Tea and toast were her tranquilisers of choice. She was glad now that Ben had persuaded her to stay. She'd come so close to telling him the truth last night but she'd lost her nerve at the last minute. She didn't want to lie to him because he'd been so kind to her. He must have known she was feeling a bit lost and it was so thoughtful of him to dance with her like that and make her feel welcome.

Even though it was only a read-through of the script this morning, it would be her first public performance and now it was more important than ever that she prove to Ben and to everybody else that she was worthy of his trust. And she also needed to prove to herself that whatever talent she had hadn't all been bleached and trimmed and shampooed right out of her. She spread some more marmalade on the last corner of toast and chewed it with silent desperation.

In the ladies, Liz washed her hands thoroughly, took her toothbrush out of her bag, cleaned her teeth, brushed her hair, twisting it up into a careless fan, expertly secured by a large clip and reapplied her lip gloss. Perfect.

When she returned to the dining room, she gave a friendly little wave to Emma who jumped to her feet, still clutching her second slice of toast.

'I'm sure I recognise you from somewhere, but I can't remember what. What have you done before?' Liz asked her in a gossipy, girlie sort of voice as they walked up to the first floor.

'Have you heard of a film called *Hairdressing*?' asked Emma wishing that she didn't have to carry on with this stupid lie.

'No.' Liz folded her arms as she walked so that Emma wouldn't leave jammy fingerprints on her Marc Jacobs cardigan.

She waited for Emma to tell her more about *Hairdressing*, but all Emma said was, 'I really need to go and wash my hands.' Liz looked at her watch. 'There's no time, it's practically ten now. Ben can't stand people being late.'

'I feel really sticky,' said Emma, wishing now that she'd got up when the phone rang instead of having a lie-in.

'Don't worry, you look fine. It's only a read-through.' Liz led the way down the corridor and pushed open the door to the King George Suite. They were almost the last to arrive and everyone was comparing hangovers and helping themselves to coffee. Tex had saved a seat beside him for Liz and he looked disappointed when she sat opposite him instead, diagonally across the table from Ben.

Ben noticed Emma hovering uncertainly in the doorway, not sure where to put herself. 'Emma, why don't you sit down here next to Danny?' he said. 'How are you this morning?'

'Good thanks,' she said, but her voice came out in a whisper as she took her seat and picked up the script in front of her. She turned to Danny with a shy smile and tried not to stare at his hair which had been bleached white and dyed blue at the tips. She'd been longing to speak to him last night at the party, and then afterwards when they went to the club, but she'd been so in awe of him, all she'd managed to get out was a squeaked, 'Hello!'

Ben leaned towards her across the table. 'You won't have seen this before,' he explained. 'This is the shooting script and there are a few dialogue changes for you. I'll go through it with you later if there's anything you want to talk about.'

Patrick came bustling in with his mobile phone pressed to his ear, and glaring tetchily into the middle distance. He poured himself a coffee with his free hand and continued his conversation in the middle of the room, oblivious to the curious sea of faces around him. 'No – not four thousand feet. Forty thousand! That's what it says on the purchase order and that's what I've paid for. What am I supposed to do with four thousand feet?' He sipped his coffee crossly just waiting for another excuse to lose his temper. 'No, Vanessa – it's your problem. You sort it out. That's what I'm paying you for. You're the one who signed the delivery note and you're the one who'll have to drive back to Hemel Hempstead to pick it up yourself if you can't sort it out.'

He held the phone away from his ear and looked at it in distaste as Vanessa let fly with a stream of abuse. 'Vanessa? Vanessa?' he wheedled gently. 'Now don't be like that. You know you don't know what any of those words mean. Now just pour yourself a nice big glass of vodka and DO YOUR FUCK-ING JOB.' He snapped the phone back into his pocket and looked around the room with a cheery smile.

'Morning, everybody!' he beamed, his phone call with Vanessa having gone immediately out of his head.

Ben looked around the table. 'Right. I think we're all here. Thank you all for coming this morning. I know we have very little time before we start shooting tomorrow, and in an ideal world I would have liked to have given you some more rehearsal time. But I know I've got a fantastic cast and crew and that we're going to do some great work together. So perhaps what we should do first of all is just go around the table and everyone can introduce themselves. My name is Ben Lincoln and I'm the director. I also wrote the script, so I hope you can all read my typing.'

There was a barely audible ripple of polite laughter. Ben turned to his right and it was Ronald's turn. 'My name is Ronald Gasch,' he announced solemnly, enjoying the way his voice sounded like the rumble of distant thunder, 'and I shall be playing Larry Turpin, known to his friends and enemies alike as Dick.' He gave a humble little bow of his head.

And around the table they went. When Danny Parker got to his feet there was a splatter of ironic applause because he needed no introduction. Even with his new hair-do, there couldn't have been anyone in the room – apart, perhaps, from Ronald Gasch – who didn't recognise Danny from his many appearances on *Top of the Pops* and MTV or who hadn't followed his hell-raising exploits in the tabloids. He was classic pin-up material with freakishly blue eyes, cheekbones you could slice tomatoes with, and this morning he was wearing a black V-necked vest that showed off his sunbed tan.

When his boy-band had imploded last year amid law-suits, sackings and financial investigations, Danny had fled to Los Angeles to find himself and work on a solo album. He rented a house in the Hollywood Hills where he could see deer, raccoons and skunk from his floor-to-ceiling windows. And because YunGuns had never cracked America, he spent hours happily cruising the aisles of supermarkets, revelling in his new-found anonymity. He told his manager he wanted to stay in LA for ever and announced his intention to take up American citizenship. He got up and sang in karaoke bars, anticipating the same hysterical acclaim that had always greeted him on tour, but when his heartfelt rendition of 'Flashdance' was met with silence, he took to carrying around a copy of the YunGuns unauthorised biography to show shop-keepers and cab-drivers. 'I played Wembley Arena,' he'd tell them and would become incensed when they'd pretend to have never heard of the place.

One day he came home and found a scorpion on his kitchen table which was the last straw. He gave up the lease and flew home to the UK where he gave several interviews about how he'd been forced out of the States by the menace of gun culture. Since then, he'd been dividing his time between parties, buying houses, and fitful attempts at song-writing, interspersed with prolonged stays in a private clinic for exhaustion and frequent trips to a tattoo parlour in the Finchley Road to have a large scorpion etched into his thigh – one inch at a time due to his genetically low pain threshold. The solo album was still pending release due to unspecified 'personality clashes' with no less than three separate producers.

When journalists seemed sceptical about his ability to make the leap from singing to acting, he was quick to remind them that he'd been an actor long before becoming a singer. Hadn't he played the Artful Dodger on stage when he was only twelve? All summer, he'd been having drama coaching from a woman in Highgate who favoured the Stanislavsky Method and he'd already flown back to LA for meetings with agents.

Ben thought once again how lucky he was that Danny had chosen this to be his first feature film, and Emma, remembering that she was going to get to snog Danny Parker, had to take a sip of water to calm her nerves. Just wait till the girls at the salon heard about this!

'Right, then,' Ben said. 'That's all our principal cast except for Sophie Randall who'll be playing Roxanne and can't be here today,' – he was interrupted by elaborate groans of disappointment from all the men around the table – 'so I'll be reading in for her. And I'll also be reading in for our Malaysian gentlemen – Mr Ho, Mr Yo and Mr Wong.' They hadn't actually been cast yet, but there was no need for everybody else to know that. 'I can't do the Chinese, obviously, so I'll read the translation. There are only minor changes from the scripts you were sent last week – the main change is that scene 97 now takes place in Jasmine's flat instead of on the beach. Scenes 57 and 59 have been cut. There are two new scenes – 90A and 108A – and various dialogue changes. So, if everybody's ready, we might as well get cracking.'

At the other end of the table, Stacey, the continuity supervisor, picked up her two stopwatches in readiness and Ben began to read.

'Scene 1. Exterior. Brighton Seafront – Day. It's daybreak and the road is empty except for a light blue Vespa—'

'Does it have to be a Vespa?' interrupted Danny.

Stacey clicked off her stopwatches.

'Sorry?' asked Ben.

'Does it have to be a Vespa? It's just that I think Eddie's the sort of guy who'd ride an Aprilia.'

'Well, I suppose it could be an Aprilia.' Ben turned to Josephine. 'Have you finalised the scooters yet?'

'I think Poppy's already done the purchase order.'

'But we could change it, yeah?' said Danny.

'I suppose so.'

'Cool.' Danny crossed 'Vespa' out of his script and wrote in 'Aprilia'. 'Aprilia Habana,' he told Josephine. 'Make sure it's the 125. I don't want one of those poxy 50cc jobbies.'

Ben continued reading. 'It's daybreak and the road is empty except for a light-blue *Aprilia*,' he glanced up at Danny for confirmation, 'being ridden by Eddie – a good-looking man in his mid-twenties. As he comes closer, we see he has a guitar bag strapped to his back and as he passes the pier, a bunch of twenty pound notes fly out of the bag and are caught by the wind. The camera tilts up to follow these notes as they dance against the blue sky and we hear Eddie's voice-over.'

'We weren't in it for the money,' read Danny. 'We were in it for the music. But when half a million quid falls out the sky and straight into your lap, what ya gonna do? Like Ollie said, you can buy a lot of Pot Noodle with half a million quid. We had big plans for that money. The only trouble was – so did a lot of other people.'

'Scene 2. Exterior. Brighton Seafront – Day.' Ben read. 'The camera tilts down from the sky to find a scruffily dressed band busking on the pier. The singer and lead guitarist is Eddie, the boy on the scooter. Around him are Jackson on rhythm guitar, Sam on bass and Ollie on drums. A passer-by tosses ten pence into the open guitar case on the pavement in front of them and they all acknowledge it gratefully.'

'Cheers, guv!' read Alex, who was playing Sam. He had a light-brown quiff, blue eyes, and a cheeky Essex way about him. Perfect casting, thought Ben who'd first spotted Alex in a commercial for oven chips.

Emma relaxed a little because, apart from one line, 'Evening, Douggie!' when Jasmine arrives for work, she didn't have any proper dialogue until Scene 30, when she meets Eddie in the nightclub cloakroom. She watched Ben following the dialogue he had written, nodding enthusiastically at the way Ronald made Dick Turpin sound so wonderfully sinister and marvelling at the way Luke, who was playing Ollie, the drummer, was so deadpan that every time he opened his mouth, the whole room cracked up. It must be brilliant, Emma thought, to hear words you'd written coming alive like that. Uh oh, Scene 30 coming up.

'Scene 30,' read Ben. 'Interior. Nightclub cloakroom – Night. Jasmine, the cloakroom girl, is counting her tips when Eddie runs in and leaps over the counter.'

'Hey! Where do you think you're going?' read Emma in a shocked and angry voice that came out a little louder than she'd meant it to. She'd noticed that Danny had been reading his lines in a monotone, so maybe that was the way to do it.

'Eddie takes cover inside a large fake-fur coat,' read Ben.

'Oi!' protested Emma, taking her performance down a couple of notches. 'You're not allowed back here!'

'Eddie says nothing but sticks his head out of the coat just long enough for her to see that he is the singer she was watching on her break,' Ben continued. 'Turpin and his two goons run down the corridor and lean across the cloakroom counter.'

'Have you seen anyone come past here?' boomed Ronald, fixing Emma with a genuinely flinty stare.

'No. No one,' said Emma innocently, not having to fake the note of alarm in her voice. Ronald Gasch made her feel like something he'd found stuck to his shoe.

'Turpin and his goons run off and Jasmine tackles Eddie.'

'What the bloody hell do you think you're playing at?' Emma challenged him. She was starting to enjoy herself.

'Thanks,' said Danny. 'Thanks for not giving me away.'

'Why's Turpin after you?'

'I guess he's not a fan of our music.'

'I can't say I blame him. That set you did tonight was complete pants.'

'Oh great. Everyone's a critic. If they'd let us do a proper soundcheck like they were supposed to—'

'Don't tell me – you'd sound just like Robbie Williams.'

'Jackson and Ollie run in and find Eddie wearing a fur coat and arguing with Jasmine,' read Ben.

'Hey, Eddie. Come on! We gotta get out of here!' said Giles. At twenty-nine, he was the oldest of the four with spiky dark-blond hair and green eyes.

'Nice coat,' said Luke, and everyone burst out laughing.

'I had no idea that was a funny line,' laughed Ben. 'How do you do that, Luke?'

'I dunno. I think I get it off me mum,' said Luke solemnly and everyone laughed again.

Except Liz. She'd been watching Emma during that short scene, or more accurately, she'd been watching Ben watching Emma. Instead of following the words on the page, he'd been watching her as she sat with her head bent in concentration over her script. And he was smiling at her. It was the kind of smile people wear when they spot genuine Art Deco at a car boot sale. The kind of smile you see on teachers when a child who's been scraping along at the bottom of the class unexpectedly calculates pi to thirteen places. The kind of smile gardeners wear when they see the first crocuses breaking through the brittle winter earth. Ben looked like he'd discovered something wonderful he hadn't been expecting to find. Something delicate he wanted to protect and nurture. He probably didn't even realise he was doing it, thought Liz. He probably wouldn't even be conscious of the way his lips were stretched taut as though the smile inside him was fighting to get out, or the way the skin around his eyes crinkled into a dozen spidery creases. He had no idea, had he?

For the next ninety minutes as the arc of Ben's story soared and dipped and rose again, Liz studied the way that Ben watched Emma. Each time it came to one of her scenes she could see him practically willing her to say the lines the way he heard them in his head and as they turned the pages, she'd look up at him for reassurance and he'd flash her a smile of encouragement.

A weaker woman than Liz might have read the signs and

backed away. A woman without Liz's self-discipline and iron will backed by years – *years!* – of careful preparation might have given up. But Liz sat around that table on that sunny Sunday morning watching Ben take the first unmistakable steps on the path to falling in love with Emma and it only made her resolve even stronger.

fourteen

The read-through ended in a free for all, with Ben using toy cars to demonstrate the car chase and Luke and Alex providing the sound-effects as Jasmine, Eddie and the boys drove off into the sunset all squashed into Jasmine's old Saab – or rather Patrick's Saab – an ancient dusty-red model called Butch which he was hiring out to the production for the going market rate.

Emma felt the same rush of exhilaration as Jasmine did at having pulled it off. To think that just last night she'd been on the verge of leaving the film and running away to London! Whatever could she have been thinking? This was the best script she'd ever read. These were the best actors she'd ever worked with and the film was going to be brilliant.

She didn't hear Ronald Gasch mutter a weary, 'God help us all,' as he closed his script and tucked his reading glasses back into his inside pocket.

'Band rehearsals will be in here after lunch for everyone who needs to be there!' announced Jamie, the First AD.

Emma had been trying to think of something to say to Danny and it suddenly came to her. 'Did you write the music for this?' she asked.

'No,' he said bluntly, and got up to go back to his room, leaving her sitting there like a lemon.

'Luke wrote it all,' explained Giles. 'He's the only one who can actually play. Me and Alex and Danny are just going to be miming.'

'What's it like? Is it pop – like YunGuns?' Emma asked, and the boys laughed as though she'd made a very good joke.'

'It's Skate Metal,' Luke told her.

'Oh. Great,' said Emma and wondered what that was.

'Nice work, everyone,' Ben told the boys and then turned to Emma. 'I was very pleased with that,' he said. 'Just a little more energy and you'll be there.'

'Oh right,' said Emma quickly. 'Well, I wasn't giving it a hundred per cent because it was just a read-through.' She wished now that she'd stuck to her original plan to come out with both guns blazing.

'Yeah, good idea. Keep a little something in reserve. We're all going for a quick drink before band rehearsals. Want to come?'

'I'd love to, but I've got a costume fitting.' She smiled at Liz, who was pulling faces at Tex.

'Of course,' said Ben. 'I suppose I'd better get along to that too.' He really wanted to buy Emma a drink and get to know her a little better but now he saw Liz materialise at her side. 'I'll see you in about half an hour, then,' he said, addressing the first half of the sentence to Liz before he lost his nerve and turned to Emma. It was only the second time he'd spoken to Liz since they'd arrived in Brighton.

'We'll be in my room – 309,' Liz told him. Just down the corridor from you, she thought, as she steered Emma away.

'Was I OK?' Emma whispered once they got out the door.

'You were wonderful,' Liz assured her.

'Really? You're not just saying that? I mean it was only a read-through. It'll be different when we do it for real. More energy and that.'

'Honestly, you were great,' said Liz automatically. She'd spent all her working life plumping up actors' fragile egos and she was sick to the back teeth of it. You were wonderful. You were extraordinary. You were brilliant. You look amazing on camera. You're totally photogenic. Your performance moved me to tears. You were so funny. It was so *real*. That dress looks stunning on you. Your skin is like porcelain. Your smile could charm the birds from the trees. Your voice is like music. Your talent is astounding. You have no faults. You are without a doubt the most perfect human being I have ever encountered and I feel humbled just breathing the same air as you do. That's what they wanted her to say.

God, she hated actors. What a pathetic bunch of babies they were. Paid ten times as much as everyone else for one tenth of the work. They don't even fetch their own cups of tea – they expect one of the runners to get it for them. They have a driver to pick them up from their hotel and take them home again at night so they don't have to sully their delicate little minds with distractions like traffic or map-reading. Another runner stands in the lunch queue for them so they don't have to rub up against any ordinary people. On set, there are chairs for them to sit down on. When it rains, flunkeys appear with umbrellas so they don't get wet and when the sun comes out, there are more umbrellas to shelter under so their precious little heads don't get hot. If they have to carry a bag, or a gun, or a newspaper, the props people will personally put these into their correct hands because actors can't possibly be expected to tell their right from left.

And they're the ones who get all the credit. Nobody ever went to see a movie because the costumes were historically accurate, or because it was beautifully lit, or the scenery was well-built. All Joe Public ever cares about is the actors. Look at Sam Mendes. Gets the Best Director Oscar for his very first film, but what's he *really* famous for? Shagging Kate Winslet.

'You were brilliant,' she told Emma. 'So real.'

'Thanks,' said Emma and immediately felt much better.

Liz's room was still piled high with suitcases and striped plastic carrier bags because the wardrobe trailer wouldn't be arriving until later that afternoon. Emma walked in and bounced up and down on Liz's bed.

'Isn't this exciting?' she gushed. 'I can't wait till tomorrow.'

Liz had already bought most of Jasmine's costumes before Zoe Langridge had pulled out. Fortunately, Emma and Zoe were both a size 10, but Liz had been doing some quick thinking since last night and the clothes she was laying out on the bed now weren't the darling Miu Miu or Matthew Williamson pieces she'd splashed out on for Zoe, but the cheap stuff she'd bought for some of the club extras.

'Now, the thing about Jasmine,' Liz was saying, 'is that I see her as a bit of a rebel, so she's not going to wear something just because it's fashionable. She's more of an individual, so she's likely to go for something a bit quirky – maybe vintage. Don't you think?'

'Yeah, and she works in the cloakroom of a nightclub, so she's going to be broke,' agreed Emma, remembering her own student days living on Marmite sandwiches with no butter. 'She'd probably be a bit studenty and grungey. She'd get stuff at markets and Oxfam and places like that!'

'Exactly!' said Liz, marvelling that it was going to be much easier persuading Emma than she had dared hoped. 'Like this jumper, for instance.' She held up a cheap knitted jumper in pink, yellow and orange stripes.

'Oh, that's so Jasmine!' said Emma excitedly. 'Can I try it on?' She pulled the jumper on over her T-shirt, and turned to Liz with her hair plastered over her face.

'Look,' she laughed. 'It's perfect!'

'Not bad,' said Liz, straightening the shoulder seams and approving of the way the jumper made Emma look totally asexual – like a fourteen-year-old boy. She'd expected to have a battle on her hands and was prepared to compromise by throwing in a few more flattering outfits as well if she had to. But it looked like Emma was going to swallow the bait, hook, line and sinker. 'I thought this would be a good look for daytime. With jeans, of course.'

'Oh yeah – Jasmine would never wear skirts, would she? She's one of the lads.'

Liz almost felt a twinge of regret, thinking of the divinely floaty summer dresses packed away in the bag marked 'Jasmine', but she pressed on. 'You can't go wrong with jeans.'

'Levis?'

'Definitely. But not the twisted ones.'

'No, far too trendy,' agreed Emma. 'I think I'm a 28-inch waist.'

'I've got just the thing,' said Liz. She dug around in another bag to find the two pairs of battered old 501s that she'd got for Alex when he was busking. They'd fit Emma and she'd give Alex those Evisu denims he'd been badgering her for. 'Try these on,' she told Emma. 'They should be your size.'

She watched Emma unzip her suede skirt and let it drop to the floor, revealing tiny white lace knickers and taut, slim legs. Liz hoped there'd be a scar or premature varicose veins or dimpled flesh or a bikini line of black fur stretching all the way to Emma's knees, but she was unmarked, unblemished, with all the carelessness of youth.

'They're a bit long,' said Liz, tugging the hems until they almost obscured Emma's dainty little toes.

'Yeah, but that's good,' said Emma as she buttoned up the fly. 'I like long jeans. We can rip the seams at the bottom a little. What about shoes?'

'Well, you've got to do a lot of running, so heels are out,' said Liz pushing every last shred of professional integrity and artistic sensibility to the back of her mind. She could forget about the BAFTA for this job, that was for sure.

'Jasmine would never wear heels, anyway, would she?' agreed Emma. This was so great, she thought. She was getting into character now and starting to think like Jasmine. She wished she'd worn this jumper to the read through. Liz was brilliant.

'Trainers,' they both said at once.

'Adidas gazelles,' added Liz more precisely. She couldn't help herself. 'Very rock 'n' roll.'

There was a knock on the door and Liz caught her breath when she opened it to see Ben standing in the hall.

'I decided to skip the pub,' he said. 'Thought I'd be more use here.'

'What do you think?' asked Emma, giving Ben an excited twirl. 'With Adidas gazelles.'

Ben looked confused. 'What's this for?' he asked Liz. 'I thought you were going for a funky look for Jasmine.'

'This is very funky,' said Liz confidently.

'I love it,' enthused Emma. 'It just feels right. Really comfortable. Like I could take on anybody.' She aimed a high kick at the wardrobe door. 'Ha! Take that, Turpin!'

'This is just for day, anyway,' said Liz smoothly. 'Let me show you her uniform for the nightclub.

'Sit down! Sit down!' said Emma.

'No, I'm fine,' said Ben and leaned against the wall, rather than take a step closer to Liz's bed.

Liz held up a plain navy-blue shirt from Gap. She'd bought several of these in various sizes for the extras who'd be playing the nightclub bar staff. She'd planned to put Zoe Langridge in a strappy pink sequinned top but Ben need never know that. Navy-blue, as the hotel receptionist had so superbly demonstrated, was the most sexless colour in the world. 'And black jeans for work,' Liz continued, holding up a pair of black Warehouse trousers.

Ben looked doubtful.

'Here, I'll try them on,' said Emma, jumping up. 'Can I use your bathroom?' She ran into the adjoining room and closed the door leaving Liz and Ben alone for the first time. Ben thought he could feel the air getting heavier.

'I thought the read-through went very well this morning,' said Liz. She knew this was precisely what Ben would want to hear.

'Thanks. Me too.' Ben sounded relieved, but he wished that Liz was doing the fittings somewhere else, somewhere a little less intimate. Like the M25.

'The wardrobe trailer's arriving later on,' she said and Ben was struck by the disturbing notion that Liz was able to read his thoughts. 'I'll be glad to get all this stuff out of my room and have a bit of space.'

'Yeah, I expect you will,' agreed Ben.

Emma came out of the bathroom looking a bit doubtful. 'This top's a size fourteen. Do you think it's a bit big on me?'

Liz noted the way the shoulder seams were sliding off Emma's narrow frame and the way the shirt itself hung shapelessly around her.

'No,' she said. 'That's the way it's meant to look.' She tucked it into the black trousers to see whether this made it better or worse. She pulled at the fabric so that it puffed out Emma's waist, revealing nothing of her figure at all. 'There. That's perfect. You see, this is meant to be a uniform so we don't want to make the mistake of making it look too feminine.'

'No. You're right,' said Emma, looking at her reflection in Liz's full-length mirror and pulling the fabric out even more until it swamped her. 'It's not something Jasmine chose to wear herself, is it? It's what she's been forced to wear. So she *should* look uncomfortable in it.'

'I don't know,' said Ben cautiously, not exactly sure why the navy-blue shirt felt all wrong to him – apart from the very obvious fact that it was completely horrible.

'No, that's it!' Emma was suddenly stuck by inspiration. 'It's Turpin's club and he's the baddie, so this shirt *shouldn't* fit her! It should look like she doesn't belong with all these other people. Liz, you're brilliant! Isn't she brilliant, Ben?'

They both looked at Ben expectantly and what could he do but agree? 'Yeah. She's pretty clever, all right,' he said.

'Will I have to do camera tests?' Emma asked in a serious voice. She'd picked up the phrase from an interview she'd read with Sharon Stone or Julia Roberts – she couldn't remember. She wasn't sure exactly what it meant but it sounded like a professional sort of comment to throw in at this point.

Liz laughed and Ben just looked uncomfortable.

'We don't really have the budget for that, I'm afraid,' he shrugged.

'Oh,' said Emma. He must think she was a right little prima donna.

'Now. The love scene,' said Liz, swiftly changing the subject. 'A very different look again. She's left the club and is walking home when she gets beaten up by Turpin's thugs, so she's going to be cold and exhausted when Eddie finally rescues her.' She held up another hanger for Ben's approval. 'What do you think?'

Ben looked at the garment for a long time, considering his reply. It wasn't at all what he'd been expecting. 'It's an anorak,' he said finally.

'Actually,' said Liz, 'it's a parka.'

'Come on, Liz,' protested Ben. 'It's supposed to be a love scene. I was expecting something a little racier.'

'The military look is very in at the moment,' said Liz calmly. She knew she was running the risk of Ben thinking she was a terrible costume designer, but she also knew that where fashion was concerned, Ben, like most men, would be easily bamboozled. 'Khaki, big furry hood. I think it's wonderful.'

The last thing in the world Ben wanted to do was to get into an argument with Liz. He didn't even want to talk to her if he could avoid it. 'I just think—' he began weakly, and wondered what made him think he was going to be able to direct a film when he couldn't even win an argument about a coat.

'Ben, be realistic,' said Liz patiently. 'This is a long scene for Emma – and it's a night shoot. It makes sense to put her in a costume that going to be warm and comfortable while we're shooting.'

'But couldn't she wear something a little more glamorous?'

'Jasmine's left the club, it's late, she's walking home – what's she supposed to be wearing? Crotchless knickers and thigh-high boots?' Liz didn't think for one minute that she was going to be able to pull this one off, but she had to give it a go. She'd play up the realism and comfort angle, although in her entire career, realism and comfort had never before entered into the equation. She'd put the entire cast in boob tubes and G-strings for a night shoot at the North Pole if she felt like it.

'But does it have to be an anorak?' Ben asked wishing he was somewhere else. 'I mean, couldn't it be a normal coat or a jacket – or – or something?'

'Liz's right,' said Emma unexpectedly. 'That whole scene where Jasmine's in danger, it's such a cliché. I mean,' she added hastily as she remembered that Ben had written it, 'it *could* be such a cliché. I hate films where the girl's being chased and she's running away from the bad guys in six-inch heels and a red leather mini-skirt – it's so unbelievable. The whole point about Jasmine is that she's not like that. She's a poor student, struggling to pay off her loan with this crappy job in a nightclub.'

Is she? thought Ben. There was nothing in his script about that.

'She doesn't dress to get noticed,' Emma went on, grabbing the anorak from Liz and putting it on over the shirt and trousers. 'She doesn't want to draw attention to herself. Of course she'd wear an army parka. It probably belonged to one of her brothers and he gave it to her when she went away to college and now she wears it all the time because it smells of home and stops her feeling so lonely.'

Liz and Ben stared at Emma in astonishment. Liz thought she had never heard such a load of actressy bollocks in her whole life.

Ben looked at her, dwarfed by the dark-green coat, saw the way the heavy sleeves hung down over her hands and imagined how he would run the scene. How Eddie would find Jasmine lying hurt in the factory yard and wrap the giant parka around her to keep her warm like an injured sparrow, and then when he got her inside, where it was safe, he'd take it off her shoulders, and the two of them would lie on it like a blanket while he unbuttoned that ugly, navy-blue shirt and threw it into the open fire . . .

'Ben?'

'Ben? What do you think?' asked Emma.

Ben blinked and looked into Emma's hopeful blue eyes.

'The anorak's great,' he said. 'I love it.'

*

Later, after Ben had left for the band rehearsal, Emma sat on Liz's bed drinking Evian from her mini-bar straight out of the bottle and chattering so excitedly that Liz was afraid she'd never get rid of her.

'How did you become a costume designer? It must be fantastic working with clothes. Can you sew as well? You must have the most amazing wardrobe. I bet you get to go shopping all the time. Have you ever done one of those big Jane Austen numbers where everyone wears petticoats and bodices and crinolines and things? I'd love to be in something like that. Who's the most famous person you've worked with?' Liz patiently answered all her questions while she continued to hang and label all the individual pieces of Jasmine's costume right down to the grips she would wear in her hair and the more Emma wittered on – 'Ooh, do you have to put little tags on everything?' – the more Liz got the distinct impression there was something about Emma Buckley that didn't quite add up.

'So – do you have a boyfriend?' asked Liz, and breathed a silent sigh of relief when Emma nodded.

'Yeah,' she beamed, hugging her knees into her chest with girlie pride. 'His name's Jason Cairns – do you know him?'

The name rang a bell. 'Is he an actor?' asked Liz.

'He's terribly good. Much, much more talented than me. He's going to be massive, I just know it. Do you want to see his picture?' She rummaged in her bag until she found her phone and showed Liz the photo stuck on the back.

Liz recognised him immediately. 'He's in that soap, isn't he?'

Emma nodded proudly.

'How long have you been going out?'

'Nearly a year.'

Liz was pleased. This was all very good news. It meant that Emma was less likely to be on the pull, but she couldn't afford to be complacent because that wouldn't stop Ben from making a move on her. The fact that Emma was unavailable would only make her more desirable – not less.

'So, have you worked with Ben before?' Liz asked casually.

'No, never. What about you?'

'A few times.' Liz played her cards close to her chest.

'What's he like to work with?' asked Emma.

'Well, he likes to be left on his own. He doesn't like people chatting to him and distracting him when he's trying to work.'

'Is he quite serious, then?'

Liz was thoughtful for a moment, remembering the time they'd got stoned watching a French movie on TV and Ben had become hysterical at the way a group of nuns kept running across the screen. She thought he was having a heart attack because he was laughing so hard there were tears pouring down his face and he couldn't breathe.

'Yes, I'd say so. He's not really one for joking around. My advice is to keep out of his way as much as possible and just let him get on with the job. I think he'd really appreciate that.'

'Right. Right. Thanks for the tip. You don't mind me asking you all this stuff, do you?'

'Of course not.'

'Only, all the lads seem quite pally already and it's nice to have another girl around for moral support. I didn't realise until this morning that the rest of the cast were all boys.'

'Any time,' said Liz. She looked at her watch. It was gone two and Ronald was late for his second fitting. 'Excuse me a sec,' she said to Emma while she rang his room. She was surprised when a woman's voice answered and even more surprised when this woman claimed to have never heard of Ronald Gasch. Liz rang the front desk in some confusion and got Belinda the South African receptionist again.

'Mr Gasch has just changed rooms this morning,' Belinda explained. 'He's now in 401. He wanted a sea-view.'

Liz nearly exploded. 'But I gave you my name last night and asked you to let me know if a sea-view room became available.'

'Did you?' asked Belinda. 'What was your name?'

'Elizabeth Thorne,' said Liz slowly and clearly.

'Oh yes, I can see it here now in my list. Well, we don't have any other sea-view rooms available at the moment I'm afraid.'

'No, of course you don't,' Liz sighed with sarcastic sweetness. 'What room did you say Ronald Gasch was in?'

'401.'

Liz hung up without saying thank you. 'I'm surrounded by idiots,' she muttered grimly.

'Did you want a sea-view room?' asked Emma.

'Yeah, I told them last night. They were meant to ring me if anything came up, but they gave it to that –' Liz was about to spit out the word 'actor' but stopped herself in time '– that *man* instead.'

'You can swap with me if you like. It's a bit noisy, though, because you're overlooking the main road. And there's no shower. I was going to ask them if I could change.'

'It's a sea-view?' Liz was amazed. Nobody gives up a sea-view.

Emma nodded. 'You can have it, if you like.'

'Really?'

'Room 302. It'll only take me five minutes to get my things out. I haven't got nearly as much as you!'

Liz couldn't believe anyone would be so generous. There had to be a catch. 'Thanks. Thanks a lot.'

'Well,' Emma smiled as she jumped off the bed, 'we girls have got to stick together, haven't we?'

fifteen

At five minutes to eight on Monday morning, Ben walked into the empty Mongo Club with his third polystyrene cup of coffee in one hand, his script pages in the other and his lucky red-and-beige baseball cap on his head. He was closely followed by Hugo, his DoP, who was moaning about last night's football to Jamie, and Stacey who'd suddenly remembered that she'd left her Nurofen back at the hotel.

Enjoy this moment while it lasts, Ben thought to himself. Five minutes before the official start of principal photography and for the first and possibly the last time, he was still on schedule. Not even the rain could hurt him today because, by a stroke of luck, or what he liked to think of as genius, all of his scenes were inside. The gods were obviously smiling on him.

'We'll start looking towards the stage, and do a couple of passes on the band,' he started to say to Hugo when he heard Georgina, the third AD's voice come over Jamie's radio.

'Luke's fallen over,' it said.

Hugo stopped talking about football to ask, 'Which one's Luke?'

'Ollie, the drummer,' said Stacey.

'Fallen over how?' said Jamie into his radio. He turned away from Ben as if this would somehow shield him from the news.

'He slipped coming out of the make-up bus – the stairs were wet,' Georgina replied.

'Is he OK?'

'He thinks he's broken his arm.'

'Copy that,' said Jamie briskly. 'Find the nurse. I'm on my way over. It's probably nothing,' he added to Ben, not very convincingly. 'But I'd better check it out.'

Ben nodded blankly and sat down on the stage where the art department were setting up Push's band equipment. It was 8 a.m. on Day One and his film was already going down the toilet.

'Oh, you poor baby.'

'Can you move your fingers?'

'Do you want a cup of tea?'

The Daft Tarts were huddled around their patient in the make-up chair. Bex was gently massaging Luke's shaved head.

'Dunnit feel lovely and soft?' she was saying to no one in particular.

Tracey was holding his good hand and absentmindedly shoving back his cuticles with an orange stick and Saskia, who was head of department, had given herself the added responsibility of supporting Luke's injured arm until Kim, the unit nurse, arrived.

Saskia couldn't believe her luck at having an exciting medical emergency happen literally on her own doorstep. And on the very first day too. Her only regret was that it wasn't Danny who'd fallen over. Not that she wanted to see him get hurt or anything like that – but that really would have been a story to dine out on. Luke was OK, but he was the funny fat one; he wasn't in Danny's league. She'd shooed everyone else away to give their patient room but let Giles, Danny and Alex stay to give Luke moral support. Four boys to us three girls – it was a nice ratio, she thought. It meant Bex and Tracey would at least get a choice between the other three. Then Kim arrived and arranged an ice pack for Luke to rest his arm on while Saskia wondered whether, when she married Danny, it would be classier to sell the wedding pictures to *OK!* or *Hello!*

Unaware of the drama taking place a few yards away from her,

Emma sat on the dining bus finishing off her fried breakfast and trying to get a signal on her mobile. A combination of nerves, excitement, missing Jason, and a vague terror that she would somehow screw up and ruin the entire movie had given her an enormous appetite. She was desperate for some moral support before her first day. She'd left two messages for Jason yesterday, calling from the phone in her hotel room, and he'd finally called her back at ten o'clock just as she was falling asleep. She'd woken up just long enough to murmur, 'I miss you,' and he'd promised to call her in the morning. Except he couldn't because she couldn't get a signal. They were only in Brighton, for heaven's sake. Why wasn't it working? Everyone else's phones were working. She must be on the wrong network.

She looked up as Orlando stuck his head through the open door like a stern schoolmistress.

'Miss Buckley – there you are, you naughty thing,' he scolded her. 'We thought we'd lost you. Leave that sausage alone and report to wardrobe this instant!'

Emma put her mobile back in her bag and licked the fried egg off her lips. It was pouring with rain and Orlando shrieked as they ran through the puddles to the wardrobe trailer under the shelter of his huge red-and-white golfing umbrella. He was wearing pink trousers with an orange belt, a white zip-up shirt with a pink collar, all topped off with a sage-green jacket. Emma thought he looked fab.

'It wasn't a sausage, it was a mushroom,' she explained, but Orlando had other things on his mind.

'There you are!' said Liz. 'Where've you been?'

'Oh it's all going off out there,' he reported. 'Luke's arm is definitely broken and they've taken him to casualty. Saskia says he'll probably have to stay in hospital for a week.'

'Broken!' said Emma. 'What happened?'

'Well—' said Orlando, delighted to find somebody who didn't know the story so that he could tell them all about it. But Liz interrupted him.

'How's Ben taking it?' she asked. She didn't care whether Luke was on a life-support machine. All she cared about was that an opportunity had come up for her to show Ben some solidarity. She'd been so busy with the band this morning, she'd missed him at breakfast and was desperate for any excuse to go on set.

'I haven't even seen Ben,' said Orlando. 'He must be going spare.'

'Yes. You're right. I should go and see if I can help,' said Liz. 'Look after Emma, will you?' She tossed Orlando the polythene bag and hanger containing Emma's shirt and trousers, grabbed an umbrella and ran out of the trailer.

'I can radio him,' said Orlando, holding up their walkie-talkie, but Liz was already out the door and didn't stop.

'She's very dedicated,' said Emma. 'What happened to Luke?'

Orlando pulled the curtain across so that Emma could change and told her the whole story as he had heard it from Saskia. 'Of course, some people are saying he was pushed – but nobody can prove it.'

'That's awful,' said Emma, pulling the curtain back.

Orlando took one look at her in the navy-blue blouse and black trousers and pulled a face.

'Ooh, you look ghastly,' he said, and started tucking her blouse in tighter. 'Look at this – the neck is absolutely swimming on you.'

'It's meant to,' Emma explained. 'Jasmine's not meant to look glamorous. She's meant to look like she doesn't fit in at the club. We talked about it.'

'Well, excuse me, but you don't look like you fit into the human race in that thing. Liz must have put the wrong blouse on the hanger by mistake. She's got twenty of them for all the nightclub uniforms. Off!'

Emma looked at him in confusion.

'Take it off,' he repeated. 'I'm not sending you out looking like Olive from *On the Buses*. I do have my reputation to think of, you know.'

145

Emma unbuttoned the shirt and handed it to him. He looked at the label in disgust.

'Fourteen! See, I told you it was a mistake!' He rifled through the rails until he found the same shirt in a smaller size. 'Here you are, madam – size ten – and even that's probably going to be too big.'

He dressed Emma in the shirt, and buttoned it up, pursing his lips.

'Such a nasty colour,' he muttered, shaking his head. He undid another button at the top and pulled the neckline this way and that. He stood back and studied her. 'Turn around,' he said, making a circular movement with his finger.

Emma made a hesitant twirl and he sighed. 'Come here.'

He undid the cuffs, rolled them back twice, and fastened the buttons again. Then he stood back and studied her. 'It's still gruesome,' he announced, 'but with a bit of cleavage and a three-quarter sleeve you can just about cut it, I suppose.'

Emma turned to look at herself in the full-length mirror. 'It does look better, doesn't it?' she agreed.

'Choccie?' offered Orlando. He passed her his jumbo box of Quality Street and began jotting down all her costume details in his folder.

'We can't shoot it,' said Ben. 'It's impossible.'

'You have to shoot it,' said Patrick. 'You've got seventy-five extras waiting next door in the bar, and I'm not paying for them all to come back when he's better. How bad is he, anyway?'

'He's broken his radius and his ulna,' said Tim the runner.

Everyone looked at him blankly.

'His wrist,' Tim explained.

Hugo stared at him accusingly. 'And I suppose you're a doctor, then, are you?'

'No, a medical student,' said Tim, which only seemed to make Hugo more angry. Tim had been in the film business for exactly three hours and he wished everybody would stop looking at him like it was all his fault when all he'd done was drive Luke to the hospital. He'd only got this job in the first place because Angela the casting lady was his auntie and he wasn't even getting paid – just three meals a day, petrol money and his accommodation.

'You can't buy experience like this,' Patrick had told him. 'So if you don't want to do it, I've got fifty other kids I can call right now. They probably eat less than you as well.'

'Where's Luke now?' asked Ben.

'Still at the hospital. The nurse is there with him,' said Tim.

'Did they specifically say he wasn't allowed to play drums?' demanded Patrick.

'No – I don't think so,' said Tim.

'Well, there you go.'

'Patrick, don't be an arse, he's got a broken wrist,' said Ben.

'Well that bloke in Def Leppard only had one arm and you didn't hear him complaining, did you?'

Jamie came over with what he hoped was good news. 'Hugo says he's lit, the camera's up and we're awaiting your instructions,' he said genially.

Ben looked at his watch. It was already half past ten. Giles and Alex were sitting on the stage trying to play the *Magic Roundabout* theme on bass and electric guitar. Danny was drumming his heels on the back of the stage and doing bicep curls with a sandbag that was supposed to be stopping one of the lights from toppling over.

'Oh Jesus,' said Ben. 'I don't know.'

'You could shoot it all in close-up on Danny,' suggested Jamie.

'Terrible idea,' said Ben. 'But thanks.'

'Why don't you just write Luke out completely?' said Patrick. 'I told you right from the start to make Push a three-piece.'

Ben rubbed his hands over his face in desperation. 'I can't write him out now – it's too late. I wouldn't know where to begin.'

'Why don't you use a double for the wide shots?' suggested

Stacey. 'It's so dark at the back, you'd probably get away with it.' No one seemed to hear her so she shut up again and carried on labelling the scene numbers in her script folder.

'Luke's the funny one,' said Ben, still with his hands over his eyes. 'I can't write him out now.'

'What else can we shoot in here today?' asked Hugo. 'Can we do the office scene with the money?'

'The office set isn't dressed,' said Jamie.

'What about the cloakroom scene? Can we do that?'

'There are no extras in the cloakroom scene,' said Patrick. 'You've got to shoot them today because I promise you, you're not getting them again.'

'Won't the insurance cover it?' asked Jamie. 'If we have to run over?'

'We've scheduled everything around Danny's availability,' Ben reminded him. 'We can't run over because we lose him on August the 24th.'

'Well, you know what?' said Hugo with the smug air of a magician pulling a rabbit out of a hat. 'We're shooting the band so wide, you could use a double for Luke and no one would even notice.'

Stacey rolled her eyes and said nothing.

Ben took his head out of his hands as though he'd seen the light at the end of the tunnel. 'Any of our extras got shaved heads?'

'And can any of them play the drums?' asked Jamie.

'Well, they only have to mime,' Ben pointed out.

'I could show them what to do, if you like,' piped up Tim. 'I used to play a bit.'

Everyone turned and stared at Tim, who blushed all the way to his neatly gelled roots.

'I think it's about time you got a haircut, don't you?' said Patrick.

As Tim drove back to Unit Base, Liz was telling Gary, the minibus driver, to park on the wrong side of the road so she wouldn't get her suede mules splashed crossing the street to the Mongo Club. She checked her teeth in the make-up mirror on the back of the passenger sun-visor and popped a Tic Tac in her mouth just in case she had coffee breath.

'Wait right here!' she barked, and opened the umbrella out of the door before sliding out of the minibus and running inside.

She left her wet umbrella propped up just inside the foyer then walked as calmly as she could out to the main dance floor where they were setting up. She could see Ben talking to Jamie and Hugo and felt her stomach turn somersaults. He hadn't shaved and the just-got-out-of-bed look suited him.

'Ben,' she said stepping in between him and Jamie. 'Is there anything I can do to help? About Luke, I mean.' She remembered to rotate her shoulders to make her arms look thinner and draw attention to the way her breasts pressed against her soft brown suede jacket.

'I've been trying to get you on the radio,' said Jamie. 'Where were you?'

'Well, I'm here now,' she said curtly, annoyed at his tone of voice. Who did he think he was anyway, telling her off in front of Ben? Had he been nominated for a BAFTA? No, he damn well hadn't.

'It's OK, Liz,' said Ben. 'We're going to use the runner as a double. He's on his way back to make-up now to have his head shaved. He's taller than Luke, but do what you can with the wardrobe. We've just spoken to Orlando and he said he'd sort it out.'

'Oh, did he?' said Liz, the wind taken out of her sails ever so slightly. How dare Orlando save the day without her? 'Well, that does seem like the best thing to do. I'll find him a hat or sunglasses as well in case you need to disguise him more. Maybe pad him out a bit.'

'That's a very good idea, Liz. Thank you,' said Ben.

'That's what I'm here for, Ben,' she smiled. Now that she had him, she didn't want to let go, and she waited for him to say something else but he didn't.

'Not the way you want your first morning to go, is it?' she prompted sympathetically.

'You can say that again,' he agreed. 'I could have been in deep shit.'

'Oh, you would have found a way around it,' she smiled. 'I have great faith in you.'

'Thanks, Liz. I need some encouragement right now.' He looked over his shoulder. 'I think we're going to do a run through now – I'd better . . .'

'Yes, you'd better,' she agreed. She wondered if she'd gone too far. Had she been too friendly? She didn't want to panic him. She saw Tex wheeling his recording equipment into place and decided that this was probably a good time to go and speak to him. She leaned over to rub Tex's back and waited for Ben to stop talking to Hugo long enough to notice. Liz knew that the best way to get Ben's attention was to remind him that other men found her desirable. Wasn't that what she had done all the time they were living together? Always dropping hints about the other men who were after her – all of them totally imaginary, of course – but it stopped Ben taking her for granted.

'That's magic,' said Tex. 'Can you do that a bit lower?'

But Ben had turned away again and Liz dropped her arm abruptly. 'Not now, Tex. Can I borrow your radio?'

He handed her his radio and she rewarded him with a dazzling, Tic-Tac flavoured smile. 'Liz to Orlando,' she said, and waited for the crackle of his reply. 'Orlando, listen, I'm on set now and they're going to do a run through. The weather's terrible and there's no point in me traipsing all the way back there. With all these extras as well, I think you're going to need me on set with you today, don't you? I've spoken to Ben and he's told me about the plan to get the runner to double for Luke. He was still in costume when they took him to hospital, wasn't he? There are doubles for all his clothes on the rails, but if it doesn't fit, steal what you can from the other boys. They're all just in jeans and T-shirts anyway. Don't use any of Danny's stuff, obviously, oh and there should be a pair of Oakley sunglasses in Giles's pile – can you send those on set with him? We haven't got any hats with us, have we? . . . No, I didn't think so . . . OK. See you in a bit.' She gave the radio back to Tex.

'What are you doing tonight?' he asked. 'Do you fancy Thai food? I passed this place this morning that I liked the look of.'

'Oh, Tex, I've just had breakfast, I can't think about dinner right now.' She was looking over the top of his head, watching Ben talk to Hugo and felt a sudden surge of pride. Her little boy was all grown up – he was a director now. He'd got what he wanted and now it was her turn.

The background artists were shepherded in and Jamie explained to them that they'd be filming two different songs. For the first number they'd have to stand around and look bored as though the band were terrible.

'And then the second number is meant to be happening on a different night so we'll be moving you all around, and if you remembered to bring a change of clothing, like we asked, you'll need to put that on. And the second time, we want you all to act like they're the best band in the world. Got that?'

All the extras grunted a half-hearted 'yeah'. The foreign language students explained to their friends whose English was not so good that they were about to see the best band in the world. Georgina started making her way through the crowd, as diplomatically as she could, culling all the ones who'd got the dress-code wrong and had turned up either looking as though they'd come for a job interview or as though they were going to perform in the circus. For no apparent reason, two Italian girls had spent a very happy morning in the toilets covering themselves in silver body paint. She'd expected Ben to kick up a stink about it, but thanks to Luke's broken wrist he was too preoccupied to care what the extras were wearing.

Tim got a big round of applause from the crew when he slunk back in, rubbing his newly shorn head and blushing profusely. Ben scrunched up his eyes, peered at Tim through his eyelids, and decided that in the dark, sitting down, they might just get away with it.

Liz rushed over and pretended to be straightening the neck of Tim's T-shirt. 'He looks pretty good, doesn't he?' she said to Ben as though she had personally brought about this transformation, then quickly added, 'Nice work, Orlando', as her assistant came to join them.

Tim hopped up on the stage, sat behind the drum kit, rolled out a neat paradiddle and went scarlet when he saw so many people staring back at him.

Georgina came running over to Liz in a state of agitation. 'Liz, do you still need the minibus? We need Gary to bring Emma to the set, but he says he's been waiting outside here for you for three-quarters of an hour. Is it OK if I send him back?'

'Oh, the stupid man,' tutted Liz. She'd completely forgotten all about the sodding minibus. 'What's he talking about? I never told him to wait. I told him to go straight back.' She glanced at Ben, raised her eyebrows and shrugged off all responsibility.

'Ah, bollocks, we need Emma now,' said Ben crossly. 'I need her to walk through this shot.'

'It's OK,' said Orlando. 'She came in the car with me and Tim. Billy's just putting a radio mic on her.'

They all turned to see Tex's assistant Billy on the other side of the room rummaging down the front of Emma's shirt trying to attach a mic. 'She doesn't need it, Billy,' Ben shouted over. She hasn't got any dialogue in this scene.'

Billy, a quiet, unflappable boy who naturally followed the path of least resistance, retrieved his battery pack from the back of Emma's trousers. She giggled as she unfurled the long mic cable out of her blouse and gave it back to him.

'Still, you can't blame the boy for trying, can you?' said Jamie in Ben's ear and Ben laughed for the first time that morning.

Liz narrowed her eyes as they all watched Emma readjust her clothing, and suddenly noticed that the sleeves on Emma's shirt didn't reach her wrists. And why had she left three buttons unfastened at the top? She hurried over to repair the damage, but even from across the room she could see that Emma's top wasn't billowing in the way that she'd intended it to. In fact, she could see quite clearly now that it wasn't even the same shirt.

'What's happened to your top?' she demanded, tugging at the material. 'This isn't yours.'

'Orlando gave it to me,' said Emma. 'He said the other one didn't fit.'

'Final checks, please,' called Jamie, and Liz panicked because that meant that they were about to start shooting.

'Of course it didn't fit!' she hissed at Emma. 'That was the whole point. Remember? Oh fuck. I'm going to have to go back and get the other one.' She pulled down the back of the collar and looked inside. 'This is a size ten! For God's sake!'

'I think it looks OK,' said Emma helpfully.

'Well it's not OK,' said Liz. She marched over to Jamie, doing some furious mental calculations. Five minutes to get back to the wardrobe truck, maybe ten. Five minutes back, if the traffic's not too bad. Two minutes to change.

'Jamie,' she said, in a tone of voice that would brook no argument. 'There's a problem with Emma's costume. I have to change it. If somebody can send over the right shirt it'll take no more than ten minutes.'

'Liz, it's ten past eleven and we haven't even turned over,' said Jamie wearily. 'I can't give you ten minutes. What's the matter with what she's wearing?'

'It's the wrong shirt,' insisted Liz. 'If I can borrow your radio, I'll have Dominic send it over. It really won't take a minute.'

'Now what's the problem?' asked Ben, whose radar had picked up the fuss.

'It's Emma's shirt,' said Liz evenly, trying not to get hysterical. 'It's not the one I picked out for her. I have to change it. It really won't take a minute.'

'Isn't that the shirt you showed me?'

'It's similar – but it's not the right one.'

'Well, have you got the right one here?'

'No – but I can tell Dominic exactly where it is –'

'Liz, forget it,' said Ben. 'We can't wait. The shirt looks fine. All she's going to do is walk through shot. Honestly.'

'I'm only trying to do my job.'

'I appreciate that, and thanks, but really, don't worry about it.' And he walked away before she could persuade him. She was going to murder Orlando. It wasn't the shot she cared about. It was the thought of Emma standing around all day under Ben's nose looking even the tiniest bit attractive.

She walked quickly back over to Tex. 'Radio,' she demanded, holding her hand out. She'd call the second AD who was back at base.

'Dominic, come in? . . . Dominic, it's Liz. I need you to send a shirt over for Emma. It's one of the long-sleeved navy-blue shirts hanging up in the wardrobe truck. But make sure you send a size fourteen. Have you got that? Size fourteen. As quickly as you can.'

Up on the stage, Jamie clapped his hands for attention. 'OK, people. We've got a lot to do this morning.'

Down in the middle of the small crowd of punters, one of the silver Italian girls winked at him but he recovered his composure just in time to say, 'Turn over!'

Ben closed his eyes for a second. 'Please God,' he whispered. 'Please don't let this be shit.' His film had started.

sixteen

Liz looked at her watch in anger. She'd thought she'd only have to put up with Emma for the morning, but at this rate, her scene was going to spill over into the afternoon as well. Just who did Orlando think he was going over her head like that and changing costumes? How dare he suggest that she didn't know what she was doing?

The size-fourteen shirt had arrived a full thirty-four minutes after she'd asked Dominic to send it over, and she'd dragged Emma away for a few seconds to change. But just as they were about to go for a take, Stacey took one look at the baggy shirt with the neck buttoned up and the sleeves pulled down and came running over.

'What are you doing? You can't change her now,' she protested. 'We've already seen her in the other shirt. It won't match the wide shot.'

'Oh, nobody's going to notice,' said Liz crossly. 'It's so dark, nobody's going to be able to tell what she's wearing anyway.'

'Then what difference does it make?' demanded Stacey. 'Change her back.' Liz glared at Stacey, but Stacey didn't even blink.

'Cat fight!' she heard one of the riggers shout, and out of the corner of her eye she saw Ben coming towards them.

'Oh, God, all right, then,' Liz muttered, and dragged Emma back to the ladies toilet to change her back into the size ten. First Jamie had had a go at her in front of Ben and now Stacey. It was all too much, she thought.

Finally she heard Will call, 'Checking the gate!' which meant that another set-up had finally been completed. Thank God. If she had to listen to this raggedy band recording one more time with Luke deliberately drumming out of time she was going to scream.

'Is that a wrap on Emma?' she asked, rushing over to Jamie.

'No, we've got one last shot before lunch, but you've got about ten minutes while we set up. Go get yourself a cup of tea and have a rest,' he told Emma.

Rest? thought Liz as she and Emma walked over to the tea table. What did Emma need a rest for? All she'd done for the last hour was walk through the crowd, stop, look towards the stage for a few seconds and then walk on. Talk about money for old rope. But then she realised that Emma was no longer standing beside her. She'd spotted Ben and Hugo reviewing the footage on the video playback and couldn't resist going over to take a look at her film debut.

'How are you getting on?' asked Stacey kindly, pulling up a chair for her.

'I'm loving it!' Emma confessed. 'It's so exciting and everybody's so friendly. It's like being part of this huge wonderful family.'

'Yes, it's always like that at first,' said Stacey wearily. 'It's like watching fruit rot.'

'What do you mean?'

'Oh, it's always the same on location. Everyone's so sweet and agreeable to start with and it's all one big happy family. But you take a bunch of seemingly normal people away from home, lock them up together, and after a couple of weeks something evil starts to happen to them. It's like *Big Brother* without the chickens.'

Just then the playback kicked into life and Emma watched herself walk through the crowded nightclub.

'Oh wow,' she gasped. 'It looks just like a movie!'

'Well, that was the intention,' said Ben. He tried to sound

stern so the others wouldn't see how pleased he was that Emma was flirting with him so openly.

Emma was sure she'd offended him. 'No, I mean,' she explained, 'from where I was standing everything looked like a complete mess, but you put that frame around it and it looks like a film. It's amazing.'

Ben looked puzzled and Emma suddenly remembered what Liz had said about him not having any time to chat. 'Well, I'm just going to get some tea,' she said getting up. 'It looks great,' she added.

Stacey watched her go. 'Are you planning to do a close-up on Jasmine watching the band while we're here?' she asked.

'Why? Do you think I should?' asked Ben.

Stacey shrugged. 'Can't hurt,' she said mildly, which Ben understood to mean he'd be mad not to. He watched Emma walk away – even in that awful shirt she was spectacularly cute – and then he noticed Stacey looking at him and laughing.

'What?' he demanded defensively.

'Nothing,' Stacey laughed. 'I think it's sweet. Really.'

It was a huge relief when Jamie finally called lunch at quarter to two.

Emma jumped into the first minibus with wardrobe and make-up and took out her mobile to try Jason for the fifth time that day.

'Oh, this is hopeless,' she sighed. 'I can never get a signal.'

'Here, try mine, if you like,' offered Liz, and handed Emma her phone.

Emma's face fell as she got his answering service. 'Hi, Jason – it's me. We've just stopped for lunch and it's going really well. I'll try you again later, I guess . . .' she hesitated, not sure what to say. 'Well, bye,' she finished weakly. 'Miss you.' He must be working,' she explained to Liz. Then a new and troubling thought occurred to Emma.

'This is terrible! If he's working and I'm working, we're never going to be able to speak to each other. I've been so excited about getting this part I never even thought about that before.'

'Well, it must have been like this on your last film as well, mustn't it?' asked Liz and Emma realised she'd been caught out.

'Oh yeah,' she said quickly. 'But that was in London.'

Liz pressed her head against the window and watched the sea scroll past. 'Still, you'll be going home on your days off, won't you?' she said, praying that Emma would say yes. Keeping track of her on set was going to be bad enough – keeping her out of Ben's way on Sundays was more work than she'd bargained for.

'There's no point,' said Emma. 'By the time I got to Sheffield I'd just have to turn around and come straight back again. But Jason's coming down here in a couple of weeks because he has four days off in a row. You've got to meet him.'

'I can't wait,' said Liz as the minibus pulled in alongside the wardrobe truck. Liz slid back the heavy side door and noticed that it had finally stopped raining.

She queued up for lunch and felt the familiar panic of wondering if there would be anything she could actually eat. Steve, the red-headed chef, had catered a film she'd worked on the year before and she knew he had a butter fetish. She ordered a chicken breast with all the sauce scraped off, spinach and broccoli.

'No potatoes, Liz?' asked Steve hopefully. He'd had a bit of a crush on Liz on their last film and had spent a fruitless winter trying to tempt her with his puddings and pasta sauces. She was the only girl who'd ever held out against his steamed chocolate roulade for an entire shoot. 'Dauphinoise – made them myself.'

Liz examined the creamy, starchy gloop disdainfully. 'No. Not for me, thanks.'

'You're not still dieting? I don't know why you bother. You've got an amazing figure.'

Liz took her plate. 'And did it ever occur to you, Steve, that those two things might somehow be related?'

Tex was sitting with Orlando and they'd saved her a seat.

'What are you two doing tonight?' Orlando asked Tex. Liz was annoyed at his use of the words 'you two'. Just because she'd slept with Tex – once – didn't make them an item. Although, she realised, it would suit her plans nicely to carry on sleeping with Tex until she had Ben's undivided attention. But it was really none of Orlando's business, and how on earth did he know about it anyway? She was furious to see that Hugo, Ryan and Ben had decided to sit with Emma. She strained to hear what they could be talking about that was so amusing.

'So, how long have you been going out with this Jason, then?' Hugo was asking Emma.

'Oh ages! Nearly a year,' said Emma proudly. She'd been making a real effort not to talk about Jason – the girls at the salon always told her off because she could never shut up about him – but Ryan had seen the photo on the back of her mobile phone and it had all come out.

'A year's not bad going for this business,' said Ryan.

'Did you meet on a film?' asked Ben.

'Oh no! It was on *Shelby Square.*'

Ben realised it should have occurred to him that Emma would already have a boyfriend, but that probably wouldn't prove too much of an obstacle, he thought. 'I didn't know you'd done *Shelby Square,*' he remarked.

'Well, it was just a small part,' said Emma.

'He's a good-looking boy, isn't he?' said Hugo, holding up Jason's photo to Ben. 'We could have done with him in the film as well.' And Ben could only agree.

'OK, everybody, stand by for a rehearsal,' Jamie called out an hour later when everyone had drifted back from lunch. Stacey and Georgina moved among the extras, shifting them back into their original positions.

'You have to be in the same place you were before lunch,' Georgina explained slowly to a group of Croatian girls. 'Is This Where You Were Before?' They looked at her blankly.

'No, they were on the other side,' said Stacey. 'Second row from the front. The one in the green T-shirt was on the end.'

'OK,' said Jamie. 'Now as you can see, the band aren't here, but we want you to look at the stage as though they were here. Look at the instruments – don't look at the camera. Have you got that? Don't look at the camera.'

Finally hearing a word they understood, all the extras immediately looked straight into the camera.

Ben explained to Emma that the camera would be tracking across the crowd and then settling on a close-up of her looking at the band. 'Just do exactly what you did before,' he said. 'Walk, stop on your mark, look at where Danny was for a couple of seconds, and then walk on. OK?'

Emma widened her eyes to show that she understood. She couldn't speak, or even nod, because Bex was brushing on more lipstick and Orlando's hands on the back of her neck were adjusting the collar of her shirt. Emma's heart was pounding with nerves and excitement. Thank God she didn't have any dialogue.

'You might want to shift your weight a bit onto your back foot,' Ben whispered to her. 'When you can feel the light on your face, you'll know you're in the right spot.' She smiled at him gratefully. She'd learned more about film-acting in one morning than she had in three years of drama school. In her final year, an actress Emma had never heard of before – or since, come to think of it – had come in to teach them about acting techniques for film and TV. Emma would never forget the look of horror on the woman's face when she'd seen the latest batch of competition about to graduate. Her main piece of advice, or at least the only bit Emma could remember, had been: 'All the hanging around is unbelievably boring, so make sure you always take a good book with you.'

'No, DON'T look at the camera!' Jamie was yelling in exasperation. Some of the crowd were waving at the lens, unaware that the camera wasn't running yet. 'Look at ME!' He waved his hands over his head. 'Georgina, get up here. Go stand at the microphone where Danny was.'

Reluctantly, Georgina clambered on stage and picked up Danny's guitar.

'Now. Everybody – look at me and Georgina! Don't look at the camera! And remember to look bored! OK! Good luck everybody, and turn over!'

Half an hour later, when the minibus dropped the boys back at the Mongo Club to shoot their second number, Liz looked around for Emma and saw her sitting with Ben and Stacey at the monitor. What was she still doing here? She went straight up to Jamie to ask what was going on.

'Scene 81. Push perform and the crowd go wild,' he told her.

'So that means Emma's wrapped for the day, does it? And I can take her back to change?'

Jamie double-checked his schedule. 'Yes, she knows she's wrapped. I think she's just talking to Stacey.'

Liz smiled. Talking to Stacey, my arse, she thought grimly. She was flirting with Ben – just look at the way she was staring at him with those big doll eyes of hers as though he was the most fascinating human being she'd ever encountered. Well, she'd soon put a stop to that, she thought, as she walked over to where Emma was sitting.

'Do you want to come back now and get changed out of your costume?' she asked, taking care not to look at either Ben or Stacey.

'Oh sorry, yes. I completely forgot,' Emma said, jumping up. 'You want these clothes back, don't you?' She followed Liz out of the club, and then turned back to Stacey and Ben. 'Bye, then! See you tomorrow!' She saw Liz's horrified expression. 'Don't worry,' she whispered. 'I remembered what you said and I'm not getting in Ben's way. I asked him and he said he doesn't mind me sitting with them at all.'

'Well that's great, then,' said Liz, and hustled Emma away before she could do any more damage.

Later that night, after they'd wrapped and the band had changed and been driven back to the hotel, Liz and Orlando were alone in the wardrobe bus for the first time.

'So, what are we all doing tonight?' asked Orlando. 'Hotel bar, or do you want to try that tapas place again?'

Liz ignored the question. 'What the hell do you think you were playing at before?' she hissed.

'Excuse me?'

'Emma's shirt. Why did you change it?'

'The one you'd left out for her didn't fit – it was really baggy.'

'I know,' said Liz, turning to face him. 'It was supposed to be baggy.'

'Well don't get your knickers in a bunch. It was only a poxy shirt. This film's going straight to video, anyway.' He put on his jacket and carefully adjusted the collar.

'Orlando, you are missing the point. You don't over-rule my designs. Ever.'

'Designs?' Orlando laughed. 'Those shirts came from Gap. Get over yourself, dearie.'

Orlando had worked with Liz on eleven different jobs and this wasn't the first time he'd laughed at her. But it was the first time Liz had sensed he was actually making fun of her.

She picked up the closest object to hand and threw it at his head. 'Don't you *ever* fucking laugh at me!' she screamed.

Orlando stared at her, his mouth an O of disbelief and indignation as his jumbo box of Quality Street hit him in the jaw, and strawberry creams and hazelnut triangles ricocheted off the walls.

Ben was buying the drinks downstairs in the hotel bar. 'Nice work this morning, boys,' Ben told the band. 'You really looked the business.'

'What do you think's going to happen to Luke?' asked Alex. 'Is he going to be off the picture?'

'I don't think it'll come to that,' said Ben, but Dominic had been on the phone all afternoon, changing the schedule for Day Two, and getting some of the other actors to come down to Brighton a day early. They'd do the scene where Turpin cuts off a bloke's fingers with a pair of hedge-trimmers. He was quite looking forward to that.

'Maybe we should call him,' suggested Giles. 'See how he's doing.'

Ben felt guilty that he'd been so wrapped up in work that he hadn't thought to call the hospital and speak to Luke himself. Flick had sent flowers on behalf of the office but it wasn't the same thing.

'Ben, I've got a question,' said Danny.

'About Luke?'

'No, it's just this bit in the script here.' He read aloud: 'Above Danny's mantelpiece is a pin-board decorated with club flyers, concert-ticket stubs and snapshots of some of his many ex-girlfriends.'

'Right. That's the flashback.'

'Well, who are they – these ex-girlfriends?'

'Oh, that's just a bit of a visual clue to your character – you know that Eddie's a popular guy. A bit of a babe magnet, I guess.'

Danny nodded. 'Yeah, I know that. But who are they? Who are the girls in the photos?'

Ben was stumped. 'I don't know. The art department will have found some photos to stick on there. I mean, it doesn't really matter. Nobody's going to see those photos up close. They're just set-dressing.'

'So I should speak to the art department?'

'Yeah, sure, Danny, whatever you like.'

'Eddie.'

'Sorry?'

'Can you call me Eddie? It helps me to stay in character.'

'OK – Eddie. If you think it will help.' And a little dribble of lager ran down Ben's chin.

'Well, that's it. She's completely fucking lost it,' fumed Orlando.

'Oh man, that's like completely out of order,' agreed Paolo.

Orlando hadn't intended to go to the tapas bar again after Saturday night, but somehow he had found himself walking past the orange and blue awning on Sunday night and it had seemed the most natural thing in the world to just wander in, order a glass of Rioja, and sit down at the back table by the DJ booth. And now here he was again on Monday night sitting in the same corner opposite Paolo with his Dairy Milk complexion and caterpillar eyebrows. They were, he thought with a little shiver, practically going steady. His fantasy of a free holiday to Latin America staying with Paolo's picturesque relatives in their colour-supplement village had rather bitten the dust when he discovered that Paolo was not from Cuba or Belize but had been born in Haywards Heath. However, Orlando was of pragmatic nature, and this fantasy had been quickly replaced by a vision of two weeks of sun, sea and sodomy in Ibiza.

'I've got a good mind to resign,' said Orlando, shouting to be heard over the music. 'I turned down two other jobs to work with Liz, you know. I don't have to put up with this bollocks.'

'That's right. You should!' Paolo shouted back, hoping of course that he wouldn't resign – because how then was he supposed to get a part in this movie? He thought Orlando was too pretty – on the whole he preferred men who were a bit rough around the edges but, like Orlando, he was a pragmatist and took his opportunities wherever he could find them. Not for nothing had he earned the nickname Catflap for his willingness to swing both ways.

'I won't stand for having chocolates thrown at me,' Orlando announced. 'It's so not on.'

'You tell her,' cooed Paolo and got up to change the record.

The revolving platform in the centre of the small circular table in the Thai Orchid sent plates of deep-fried courgette and Pak Choi, green chicken curry, Pad Thai noodles, spicy fish cakes, chicken satay and steamed pomfret in plum sauce turning slowly under Liz's nose like a fat-fuelled merry-go-round. How, she wondered, could oriental people be so skinny when they deep fried all their vegetables in batter?

'Do you think we've ordered too much?' asked Tex.

'Not for three of us,' said Emma, dipping a fishcake into peanut sauce before it could spin away again.

'So you don't eat meat, but you do eat fish,' Liz said to Emma. 'Don't you feel like a bit of a hypocrite?'

'Sometimes,' Emma admitted. 'But I don't feel emotionally attached to fish. I've never met any of them socially.'

'And I suppose you know a lot of chickens, do you?' asked Liz.

Emma told them about the farm. 'When I was little and the lambs went away to be slaughtered, Dad would say they were all having such a nice time on holiday they didn't want to come home,' she explained. 'It was ages before I found out what all the Sunday roasts and the chops I'd been eating were actually made out of.'

Tex put down his chicken satay untouched.

'It must have been terribly boring for you on set today,' said Liz. She could hardly bear to look at Emma but had been forced to bring her out to dinner to keep her out of Ben's way in the hotel bar. 'I've never seen real actors – you know, I mean experienced actors – just hanging around on set like that.'

'Oh, but I didn't find it boring at all,' said Emma, completely missing the implied insult that she wasn't a proper actor. 'It was so interesting seeing what everybody does – watching Ben, watching the other actors, watching the lights and everything. I mean,' she corrected herself, 'it's always so interesting.'

'Did you manage to speak to Jason?' Liz asked, to get Emma off the subject of Ben.

Emma rolled her eyes. 'I've left him two more messages. But he's not home and his phone's turned off. I think he's avoiding me!' she laughed.

'Jason's an actor,' Liz explained to Tex.

'Oh, well, you better watch out – you know what actors are like,' he laughed and then stopped when he saw the stricken look on Emma's face. 'It's all right. I'm only joking. Don't mind me.' He filled his mouth with noodles to stop himself putting his foot in it.

Liz decided to risk a fish cake and cut it suspiciously in half. 'I don't know how you can eat so much and not put on any weight,' she said, looking at the mound of noodles on Emma's plate. 'I'd be the size of a house if I ate half of that.'

'It'll probably catch up with me when I'm thirty,' smiled Emma, 'and I'll suddenly explode into this great bloater.' She laughed, safe in the knowledge that this was not likely to happen and Liz winced at the reminder that she would never see thirty again.

Tex leaned closer to Liz and casually nuzzled her ear. 'Don't worry,' he whispered so that Emma couldn't hear. 'I'll give you a good workout later.'

Liz forced a smile and casually wiped away the residue of oil he'd left in her hair.

'No, but seriously,' she said to Emma. 'Do you have some kind of eating disorder?'

Emma looked up, a little surprised. 'No.'

'Because, you know, If you have, that's OK. A lot of actresses are chuckers. It's very fashionable. If you're going to go throw up afterwards, you can tell us, you know. We're your friends.'

'Liz,' said Tex. 'Leave her alone.'

'I'm just concerned about her,' said Liz.

'Honestly, Liz, I haven't got an eating disorder, I promise.

It's sweet of you to worry about me, but you really don't have to.' And, to prove her point, she scooped up the last piece of baby corn that Tex had had his eye on and munched it down.

A few streets away in a small, family-run Italian restaurant, Ronald Gasch morosely inspected the various soggy layers of his lasagne and wondered whether it would be the cheese that would eventually clog his arteries and stop his heart from beating, or the ground beef that would turn him into a drooling, gibbering vegetable.

'I can't see how Luke can possibly continue with a broken leg,' he sighed hopefully. 'I expect we shall all be sent home tomorrow.'

Flick shook her head. 'No, you've got it wrong. It was only his wrist. He'll be fine. Who told you it was his leg?'

'I was speaking to the young lady on the reception desk at the hotel and she told me one of the electricians had told her. He saw it all. Apparently there was a fight and Luke was pushed downstairs.'

'No, I'm sure that's not right. He just slipped.'

'Well, he claims he saw the whole thing. I'll be very surprised if this film continues.' Ronald had been on productions that had shut down overnight. The money the financial backers had promised would fail to materialise and everyone would be out of work. Thankfully, now he didn't need the money. What was he to spend it on? His house was paid for. He had no more need of clothes. In fact, it would be a huge relief if the film collapsed around his ears and he could return to the quiet and familiarity of his own home, away from all these terrifying twenty-five year olds who he didn't understand. He'd been twenty-five once himself – he'd considered himself rather racy – but he had been nothing like them. In one generation the human race had evolved into a new species he no longer recognised.

'Don't worry,' said Flick. 'I'm sure the film's not going to fold. Even if Luke had broken his leg, Patrick would find a way to stick it back together somehow.' She rather regretted asking Ronald to join her for dinner instead of waiting for Patrick like she'd planned. But after work, she'd gone downstairs to the bar and there was Ronald reading the *Daily Telegraph* and looking very lonely and out of place sitting there all on his own. He reminded her a little of her grandad and she just knew that he would end up eating a solitary supper if she didn't ask him to come out with her. It almost broke her heart thinking about it. Old people got to her like that every time. She thought of her own grandparents back in Australia, playing bowls in their white uniforms and eating home-made fruit cake, and she promised herself once again that she'd only stay in England for one more year before going home.

From a distance of twelve thousand miles, London had glittered to her seductively, promising culture and creativity on every street corner. Flick wanted to be a producer and she'd imagined coming to London and taking the film world by storm, learning from the wealth of experience and talent she was sure she would find there. Instead, she'd been sucked into the chaos of a Patrick McKay production – a world of low budgets, inept planning, shoddy scripts and disastrous people skills. But she'd decided, perversely perhaps, to stick by Patrick. If she couldn't learn from the greats, she would learn from his mistakes.

'Anyway,' she asked Ronald, 'did you have a nice day off today?'

'No it was terribly dull. I should have gone back to London.'

'Is that where your family are?' Flick asked and then immediately wished she hadn't.

'My wife is dead,' said Ronald bluntly. 'My daughter lives in Canada. And my two sons are far too busy with their own careers to come and visit their decrepit old father.'

'Well, at least it's nice to get some fresh air, isn't it?' said Flick. She wished Patrick would hurry up. It was nearly nine o'clock.

'It might have been had it stopped raining,' said Ronald. 'There wasn't much fresh air to be had in my hotel room.'

'Oh dear,' said Flick, and started to laugh, despite herself. 'You do need cheering up, don't you?'

seventeen

Luke had sustained a Colles' fracture, an injury common in skateboarders which Luke had ironically managed to avoid in fifteen years of riding half-pipes, rails and vert ramps. He arrived on set with his arm in a bulky, but lightweight bright-blue plaster cast and assured everybody that, thanks to the morphine and industrial-strength analgesics he'd been given at the hospital, he was in absolutely no pain whatsoever. The same could not be said for Ben – Luke's arm was already giving him the most enormous headache.

'We can only shoot him from the waist-up,' Hugo complained.

'Or camouflage it,' said Ben.

'With what? Get the art department to drape a bit of ivy around it?'

'I'll ask Liz,' said Ben. 'She'll think of something. She's very resourceful.'

So Luke was packed off to wardrobe where Liz quickly worked out which of Luke's jackets were wide enough to fit over his cast. She had hardly any long-sleeved shirts because the band were mostly wearing T-shirts, so as soon as everyone was dressed and the shops were open, she'd send Orlando to see what he could rustle up. She couldn't believe she was expected to cope with a wardrobe department of just two because Patrick was such a tight-wad. Even make-up got three – but then, the combined IQ of the Daft Tarts barely made it into double figures.

'Leave it to me, Ben,' she'd promised, letting him see how calmly she coped with any crisis.

'I just hope my arm will be OK on the boat on Sunday,' said Luke.

Liz was unpicking the seam of a corduroy jacket so that Luke would be able to pull it down over his knuckles. She'd missed breakfast again, but it was a chance for her to prove how indispensable she was. Whatever would Ben do without her? 'What boat?' she asked.

'A friend of Giles's dad has got a yacht at Brighton marina. He's taking us all out sailing.'

'That'll be nice for you,' said Liz. 'Are all you boys going?'

'Yeah, and Emma and Ben and Patrick. I'm not sure whether Ronald and that lot are going to come as well. They're invited, but I think they're going home.'

Liz froze with the unpicker in her hand. Emma and Ben on a yacht together? Not if she had anything to do with it. 'So it's sort of like a director and cast outing?' she said icily.

'Yeah, I guess. Giles has organised it all.'

'How very jolly,' said Liz and ripped the material in two.

It was their last day in the Mongo Club and Tim was helping the caterers set up the tea urn on the street outside. Two teenage girls, one large, one small, and both wearing identical white mini-skirts, came to see what was going on.

'What's all this for?' the little one asked Tim. She looked all of fifteen and was pushing a pram containing a red-cheeked baby with snot streaming from its nose. There were crumbs clinging to the snot that might once have been crisps.

'We're making a film,' he told her rather proudly. Dominic had given Tim his own walkie-talkie and a fluorescent yellow jacket and he was already starting to feel like part of the crew. At lunchtime he was going to see if he could buy a Leatherman army knife like the camera boys had.

'For the telly?'

'No, it's a feature. For the cinema.'

'Oh yeah, what's it called?' challenged the plumper of the two. Stretched across her barrel-like bosom was a T-shirt proclaiming 'Babe With Brains'.

'*Brighton Rocks*,' said Tim.

The girls looked at each other scornfully. 'Never heard of it!' said the little one and they carried on their way.

Ben was trying to eat a bowl of cornflakes in the face of an endless stream of questions.

'Ben, have you got a minute?' This time it was Poppy from the art department.

'Sure what's up?'

Poppy handed him half a dozen colour photographs. They looked like her holiday snaps.

'Very nice,' said Ben. 'What am I meant to be looking at exactly?'

'Well, these are the photos we were going to put on Eddie's pin-board – you know, for his ex-girlfriends.'

'Yeah, these will be fine.' Ben handed them back to her.

'But Danny says he doesn't like them. He said he didn't think they looked like the sort of girls Eddie would go out with.'

'What?'

'He said he wants to choose the girls himself. He's got a whole bunch of model cards and he wants us to call in some girls for a casting.'

'What's he going on about? We're not going to pay for models!'

'Well, that's what I thought, but I thought I'd better check with you.'

'Tell him no models – period. And whatever you do, don't let Patrick hear about this.'

'OK. Thanks, Ben.'

Then it was Ronald Gasch who had another suggestion about the script.

'Now, Ben. Do I really have to say this line here? "I'm not a man you want to get on the wrong side of"? Couldn't I just do it with a look?'

'Of course, Ronald, if that's what you'd be more comfortable with', and Ronald went away, scrawling through his script with a black biro. Ben couldn't bear anyone criticising his script because it just reminded him how mediocre it was. He'd meant to write a brilliant script, he truly had. That had always been his sincere intention, but it had turned out to be a lot harder than he ever imagined. Just writing a bad script had almost finished him off. And now, to top it all, his cornflakes had gone soggy.

It had come as a surprise to Emma to discover that they were shooting the film out of order. She'd never really thought about it before, but she'd imagined that it would be done like a play: they'd start at the beginning of the film on Scene 1 and carry on through until the end, to Scene 163. But it wasn't like that at all. Today they were filming scenes 30, 57, 43, 25, and part of 82. Nobody else seemed to think this was out of the ordinary and Emma didn't like to show her inexperience by asking.

She wandered around the cloakroom and examined the coats that Liz had borrowed from some charity shops in Worthing. She swivelled the red leather stool, read the flyers sticky-taped to the walls, and fiddled with the plate on the counter filled with fifty-pence pieces.

'What shall I be doing at first?' she asked Ben. 'Just hanging up coats?'

Phil, the stand-by props man, quietly stepped in and pushed the plate of coins two inches back to the left where it had started.

'That's a good point,' Ben replied, looking around. 'Where are our cloakroom extras?'

A couple of girls in ripped jeans shuffled forward.

'Am I giving them their coats or taking them?' asked Emma.

Ben thought for a minute. 'The band have played, it's the end of the night. You're giving them back to them.'

Emma nodded. Phil showed her the denim jacket and the

fake fur coat that she'd be handing over. There was so much to remember before she'd even spoken a word.

'Should I say anything to them when I give them their coats back?' she asked. 'There's nothing in the script.'

'Yeah, "There you go", or something like that. I'll leave it up to you,' said Ben.

'Flashing!' announced Liz, and Emma turned to look at the camera as Liz shot off a quick Polaroid and tucked it into her pocket.

Danny, who was sitting down in the corridor, yawned ostentatiously. He'd been at Escape with Alex till three in the morning, making friends with the local talent and he hadn't been to bed. His new platinum-blond hair was ace because nobody recognised him.

'Sorry, Danny, I mean Eddie – are we keeping you up?' asked Ben pleasantly.

'Just waiting to get on with it,' Danny sulked. 'All this coat bullshit is wasting time.' He'd preferred shooting Monday's scenes because the camera was on him all the time – like it was on his pop videos.

'Right, well, we're ready now,' said Ben. 'Are you ready, Eddie?'

'I've been ready for a fucking month,' said Danny, and slouched off to his starting position.

'Is this Method Acting?' Stacey whispered to Ben, 'Or is Danny a pain in the arse in real life?'

'I'm sure it's just Method,' Ben whispered back. He'd promised himself that he was going to try not to lose his rag on this shoot; he was definitely going to hold out longer than ten past nine on Day Three.

'Quiet everywhere for a camera rehearsal,' called Jamie. 'And action.'

He gave the two girls a little shove as their cue to step in. Emma gave them their coats and as they stepped away, she sat down on the stool, drummed her fingers on the counter, and waited for Danny to rush in. And waited.

After about ten seconds, Danny came running full pelt down the corridor, lifted up the hatch and sent the plate of coins flying.

'Oi!' cried Emma. 'Where the hell do you think you're going? You're not allowed back here!'

Danny ignored her and climbed in between two long overcoats and hid as Ronald, Harvey and Arthur ran in.

'You seen anyone come down here?' barked Ronald.

'No, no one,' said Emma, looking guiltily at the coins scattered all over the floor.

'Cut!' yelled Ben and Emma kneeled down and helped Phil pick up the strewn fifty-pence pieces. Ben and Hugo went into a huddle. Emma could see them frowning and nodding.

'It slows it right down,' whispered Hugo. 'You lose all the momentum if he just slips in there like that.'

'Ben,' said Ronald, walking back down the corridor, 'if there are coins are all over the floor, I'm going to know something's wrong. I can't pretend not to see them.'

Ben held up his hand. 'I hear what you're saying, Ronald. Don't worry. On the day, there won't be any coins on the floor. Let's look at that one more time at half-speed. Eddie, this time can you leap over the counter the way we talked about?'

'I was trying something different,' said Danny.

'Yes, I know. But can we just have a look at it the way we discussed? Please?'

Danny shrugged. 'Yeah. Whatever.'

'Oh and try not to look at the camera.'

'Why not?'

Ben was stumped. 'Well – you just don't.' Did Danny really know nothing?

'Would it help if I moved out of your way?' Emma suggested shyly to Danny but he couldn't have heard her, because he was walking back to his first position. She was completely in awe of doing her first scene with Danny, and all morning she'd been trying to think of something to say that would let him know she was a huge fan, but obviously, not an anorak.

In the meantime, there was the second walk-through. Danny attempted to leap over the counter but he had to sit on it and swing his legs over the side.

'He looks like a girl,' groaned Hugo.

Ben glared at him and reminded himself of all the reasons why it would be a bad idea to lose his patience with Danny.

At nine-thirty, Tim was dispatched to Argos to buy a mini trampoline to give Danny an extra bounce to launch him over the counter. 'I'll show you how to use it, shall I?' Tim offered.

'Now if we're careful, and keep this clean,' said Phil, 'we can probably return it and get our money back.'

Danny curled his lip. 'Oh yeah, like that's my problem,' he muttered. He could have made two pop videos by now and he wouldn't have had to memorise any stupid dialogue. Videos were better because all you had to do was lip-sync and you could look straight into the camera. How was anyone going to see his face if he turned away? Tim took off his shoes, ran up to the trampoline, stepped on it once, took the weight on his hands and swung his legs neatly over the counter.

'See? Nothing to it,' he said encouragingly. 'It's just like the vaulting horse at school.'

'I didn't go to your school,' said Danny and began deliberately rubbing the sole of his boot on the edge of the red nylon fabric, leaving a small but definite black scuff mark.

Danny looked no more convincing leaping over the counter with the trampoline than he had done without it. After each clumsy attempt, he had to have a sip of water and a sit down before he was ready to go again. On Take 9, he bounced in the wrong direction and knocked over Billy the Boom. Then on Take 12, the only time he got over the top without stumbling or getting stuck halfway, Emma was so surprised, she completely forgot to say her line.

'I'm sorry, Ben,' she said. 'I didn't expect him to make it.'

'That's OK, Emma' said Ben. 'Neither did anyone else. Let's go again.'

After each take they had to wait at least a minute while

Saskia re-dusted Danny's face with powder and Bex ran her fingers carefully through his hair to rearrange his spikes.

'Is this really necessary?' sighed Jamie as the morning ticked away. 'I notice that nobody's bothering to check Emma's make-up.'

'Emma's not running about,' said Saskia sternly and patiently teased apart two of Danny's eyelashes that had somehow got crossed. She had to stand right up close to him so that she could see what she was doing and when Danny opened his eyes she was rewarded with the seductive smile he'd used on the video for 'Can't Take These Lies'. Bex glared at her.

By Take 17, Ronald Gasch, waiting for his cue that never came, had already completed the *Telegraph* crossword and Ben was ready to admit defeat.

'We're going to have to move on,' Jamie whispered to him, showing him his watch.

'Get wardrobe to send over another pair of Danny's jeans,' said Ben. 'We'll get Tim to double for him and shoot him from the waist down.'

'Or we could just shoot Danny.'

'Don't tempt me.'

'Enjoying yourself?' asked Hugo, ignoring the sign that said 'No drinks on set' and drinking his third black coffee of the day.

'Oh yeah, it's great fun,' replied Emma. 'Can I ask you something, though?'

'Of course.' He liked the way Emma fixed him with her wide blue eyes as though he was the most fascinating man she'd ever met.

'Where does the film go?' she asked.

'We're sending it tonight to a lab in Soho.'

'No, but I mean, where's it going now?'

Hugo frowned. 'What do you mean?'

'I mean,' she said, looking around the club, 'isn't there some room with loads of screens and buttons and things?' *Shelby Square* was shot on three cameras and once when she'd gone to visit Jason in the studio, the floor manager had let her have a quick peek into the gallery upstairs where there was a bank of video screens and the P.A. calling out, 'On Three next!' and 'On Two next!' It was all terribly professional.

Hugo realised she must be thinking of TV and was about to explain to Emma that the film just lived in the camera. Ben's monitor was about as flashy as it got.

But Liz, who'd been listening, winked at him. 'It's OK, Hugo, I know what she means.' She pointed to a nondescript black door at the rear of the upstairs balcony. 'See that up there?'

Emma nodded.

'That's the door to the control room,' Liz explained. 'But don't disturb them up there – they're all terribly busy.'

Emma smiled. 'Oh right! Because I wondered, you know? I couldn't see anything. Thanks a lot.'

'No problem,' said Liz.

'OK, we'll pick it up from Turpin's entrance! And action!'

'You seen anyone come past here?' Ronald Gasch narrowed his eyes at Emma so menacingly that she was almost shocked into pointing at Danny's hiding place. But that would have been a very short film.

'No. No one,' she said, and counted to three after they'd gone.

'What the hell do you think you're doing?' she raged, pulling the coats apart.

'Thanks for not giving me away,' said Danny in his customary languid murmur.

'Why's Turpin after you?'

'I guess he's not a fan of our music.'

'I don't blame him. You sounded shite.'

'Well, if they'd let us do a proper soundcheck—'

'Don't tell me – you'd sound just like Kylie Minogue.'

'Hey, Eddie. Let's get out of here!' Alex lifted the hatch carefully to save Danny from having to jump out again.

'Nice coat.'

'And cut!'

There was a burst of weary applause, as the first shot of the day was finally completed. On her continuity sheet Stacey drew a neat circle around Take 18 Pickup and in the column labelled 'Notes' she wrote: 'Thank God!'

'Sorry, I said "Kylie Minogue" – I don't know why,' said Emma. 'I've had her song in my head all morning. Do you want me to do it again?'

'No, Kylie's funnier,' Ben told her. 'There's no time anyway.'

They shot the three-shot of Turpin and his heavies next, then a close-up on Turpin. Then the two-shot of Luke and Alex and their close-ups which all went with only the usual minor hitches. They shot Tim's legs leaping over the counter which he did in one take and everyone clapped loudly.

Danny went into a sulk and stomped off to have a cigarette outside. He'd switched to Camels now, the same brand that Eddie smoked. He returned five minutes later, having left his jacket out by the tea urn and Orlando broke his own personal best sprint time to get it back.

While they were shooting Danny's close-ups, Emma stood beside the camera feeding Danny his lines and giving him an eyeline.

'Can you get him to stop whispering?' Tex asked Ben. 'I'm barely getting a level on him.'

After nine takes, Danny still sounded like he was half asleep, but it was already five past one and Jamie was insisting that they had to move on to Emma's close-up. Reluctantly Ben agreed. There wasn't much point doing another take anyway because Danny's performance was getting steadily worse instead of better.

As they tweaked the lights, Emma grabbed her chance. All morning she'd been thinking of what she could say to Danny to break the ice and she'd finally come up with the perfect thing.

'Danny,' she said shyly, 'I just wanted to say I thought "Back in Your Eyes" was a great song.'

Danny stopped and looked at her as though he was seeing her for the first time. 'It was crap,' he said. 'They were all crap.' Then he took out his mobile phone and stalked off.

'Don't go far, Danny,' Jamie called. 'We'll be ready to go in five minutes. We're already lit.'

Danny turned. 'It's lunchtime,' he said.

'We're breaking a little late to get the scene completed,' explained Jamie. 'Could you hang on for another ten minutes and read in for Emma's close-up?'

'It's lunchtime,' said Danny again and walked out. When they'd shot the YunGuns videos, he wasn't expected to hang around while the camera was on someone else. They could sod that.

'I'll read in for Danny,' offered Stacey.

'That won't be necessary. I'll read in,' announced Ronald. He'd stayed to watch out of a morbid fascination and been appalled at what he'd seen and heard. How was it possible that Danny Parker had become highly successful when it was clear that he had absolutely no talent whatsoever? He refused to call it acting. He'd show everyone how these lines should be spoken.

Emma had no idea that Danny had just committed a professional foul by not staying to read his lines with her and was positive she'd offended him somehow by saying she liked his songs. It felt amazing acting opposite Ronald Gasch, though – he put much more feeling into it than Danny did. Perhaps now was her chance to make peace with Ronald by paying him a compliment. After all, it wasn't her fault that Zoe Langridge had dropped out.

'That was really good,' she told him when they'd finished the scene. 'You did that even better than Danny.'

Ronald Gasch drew himself up to his full height and glared at her. Even his hair seemed to get taller.

'Young lady,' he said carefully, 'if I had ever dreamed that one day I would find my name mentioned in the same breath as that snivelling simpleton I would have cut out my own tongue with a bread-knife. Good day.'

He flounced off, and Emma fancied she could see an imaginary cloak being flung around his shoulders. When, she wondered, would she learn to just keep her big mouth shut?

*

The caterers had done a Chinese theme for lunch or possibly a Thai theme – it was so difficult to tell under all the oil, thought Liz. There were noodles, and squares of sesame toast, bowls of prawn crackers and pretty green vegetables with leaves like floppy rabbits' ears. Liz took some plain salad and a few of the prawns that were wrapped in pastry which could be easily peeled away and took her plate to the wardrobe truck. She had to work through lunch, repairing the sleeve of Luke's corduroy jacket for the next day. Ben was in his trailer watching rushes and there was no point going to sit with Tex if Ben wasn't there to witness it. He was being maddeningly slow about noticing her affair. Too busy, she thought blackly, watching what Emma was getting up to.

Orlando had found a corduroy remnant in a local fabric store and now she cut a triangle of material to make a vent. She threaded the thick needle and unpeeled another prawn from its pastry casing. It still tasted greasy and Liz pushed her plate aside and wiped her fingers clean. She pinned the two pieces of fabric together and, as she began to painstakingly hand-stitch them into place, she looked up out of the window for a moment to see Emma walking back to the buffet table for seconds. That girl could certainly put her food away, thought Liz, with a growing sense of injustice. She must have hollow legs.

Liz watched Emma take two more prawns from the table, swill them in the chilli dipping sauce and eat them whole. It wasn't very smart leaving the prawns out there in the sun like that, thought Liz, and she paused with her needle in mid-air, staring into space as a new, rather marvellous plan began to take shape in her mind.

Emma wasn't really hungry, but she'd had to escape from Giles and Alex who were starting to ask too many awkward questions. They weren't trying to catch her out, but all anybody ever talked about, she was beginning to realise, were the other jobs they'd done and other people they'd worked with.

181

'Have you ever worked with Ray Winstone?' they'd ask and she'd pretend to think about it for a while, scrolling through an imaginary CV in her head before deciding finally, 'No, I don't think I ever have.' And then she'd politely listen to their Ray Winstone anecdote or their Jimmy Nesbitt story or a piece of gossip about another actress she greatly admired who'd had a sound man fired because she thought her radio mic made her look fat. Emma didn't have any stories like this to tell and sooner or later she knew she was going to get found out as a complete beginner.

'Who's the worst director you've ever worked with?' Alex had asked her just this morning and she'd managed to get away with a mysterious, 'Oh, I couldn't possibly say.' Perhaps she'd get brownie points for not being a gossip. She scanned the buffet table absentmindedly and decided that the safest thing was to sit with Hugo in future. He liked the sound of his own voice so much, he didn't really expect anyone else to say anything.

Lunchtime was nearly over when Liz finally finished the jacket and walked up the steps to the caterer's serving hatch.

Steve wiped his hands on a tea-towel and rushed to serve her. 'Liz! Don't tell me you're going to have dessert!'

'Mmm. I was thinking about it,' replied Liz.

'We've got a lovely pecan pie. I made it myself this morning.'

'Well, I'd better have some of that, then.'

Steve looked overcome with pride as though the Pope himself had come to tea.

'Cream?' he asked.

'Just a touch. 'I really don't know how you do it,' said Liz, casting her eye around the tiny stainless steel box where Steve and the other two chefs worked. 'How do you manage to turn out such amazing feasts for sixty people every day from this tiny kitchen? It's just incredible.'

Steve tore off a piece of kitchen towel and wiped the lip of the bowl before handing Liz her pudding. 'It's nothing,' he said modestly, but all his freckles seemed to join together as he blushed.

'Those prawns today were fantastic,' Liz continued. 'I could eat them every day.'

'We can do them again if you like.'

'Oh Steve, I wouldn't want you to go to any bother.'

'No, really, it's no bother. We can do them again tomorrow.'

'How about Saturday?' said Liz. 'As a special treat for the end of the week. That'd really be something to look forward to.'

'Saturday it is.' Steve took down the large red book which contained their daily menu planner, turned to the page marked Saturday and wrote: 'Prawns.' His menus had been planned for weeks in advance, but for Liz nothing was too much trouble.

'In pastry,' said Liz.

'Prawn wraps,' wrote Steve.

'And if you're free Saturday night, perhaps we could go for a drink?' Liz suggested. That was a nice touch, she thought to herself. The icing on the cake. As Steve turned back to his work-top, she tossed the uneaten pecan pie into the bin.

In the afternoon, they had all the scenes in Turpin's office to get through: the band breaking in to steal their instruments, the band breaking in again to put their instruments back, Turpin unlocking the safe in his office and taking out a copy of the *Racing Post*, Turpin paying the band after their first gig and handing them each a £5 note, and Emma hiding in Turpin's cupboard.

There was no dialogue in Emma's scene but she was worried about it all the same. Jasmine had to sneak into Turpin's office looking for his mobile phone. When she hears footsteps, she hides in a cupboard, scrolls through the numbers in his phone book, and writes a telephone number on the back of her hand. She puts the phone back into the pocket of Turpin's jacket which is hanging in the cupboard, just before Turpin's men find her. There wasn't a lot to remember but she wasn't great in small spaces – ever since her brothers had shut her in one of the feed bins as a joke.

It was a tall grey metal cabinet like a gym locker, with a shelf at the same height as Emma's head, so she had to crouch down and hold her breath as she pulled the door in towards her. Phil Props had attached a piece of string to the inside of the door so she could pull it shut behind her.

'Try not to let it rattle so much,' Ben called out, wishing they'd thought to get a wooden cupboard instead.

On Action, Emma crept quickly into Turpin's office, and started rummaging through the papers on his desk, trying to ignore the boom mic that was dangling over her head, the camera sliding across the track just a few feet away from her, the huddle around the monitor, and Jamie, who kept checking his watch every five minutes.

Emma looked for Turpin's jacket and pretended to notice the tall cupboard. She opened it and put her hand in the jacket pocket, feeling for the phone just as Harvey and Arthur who were playing Lucky Louie and Buster began to run down the corridor. Emma leapt into the cupboard and pulled it closed behind her. She could hear Harvey and Arthur coming into the office and willed them to hurry up and find her. What was taking them so long? Even though she could see light through the three angled slits in the metal cabinet, she was afraid there wouldn't be enough oxygen and she'd suffocate. Then Harvey pulled the door open and the camera snaked around just in time to capture her look of terror at being caught red-handed.

'Nice one, Emma,' said Ben, but he couldn't stop because his bladder had been bursting for over half an hour. He made a mental note to congratulate make-up on their good job. The sweat on Emma's face looked almost real.

'Oh, Jason, it was horrible,' said Emma when she phoned him later that night. She'd discovered that the only place she could get a signal on her phone was right down by the beach. 'They shut me up in this tiny cupboard and I thought I wasn't going to be able to breathe.'

'Was it as small as your bedroom?' Jason joked.

'Smaller! Much smaller!' but then she started to laugh. Jason always knew just the right thing to say to cheer her up. 'It was awful though.'

'Well, think how good it will look in the film,' he reminded her.

'Oh, I almost forgot. I showed the director your photo and you know what he said? He said he should have cast you in the film as well.'

'What? Instead of *Danny Parker*?'

Emma had a terrible thought. Jason had always been the successful one and she suddenly worried that she'd leap-frogged over him in one bound. Was one low-budget film better than a whole TV series? She had a nasty feeling it might be.

'Maybe Ben will put you in his next film,' she suggested. She didn't want Jason to get despondent all on his own in Sheffield. 'Wouldn't it be great if we could do a film together?'

'What's he like anyway, this director?'

'Oh, he's really nice. He's been giving me loads of advice. And he never loses his temper.'

'They're all like that at the start,' said Jason cynically. 'You just wait a couple of days.'

That's what Stacey had said, Emma remembered, but she couldn't imagine Ben losing his temper. He was always so nice to her. So encouraging and helpful. 'Well, you'll meet him for yourself next week. I can't wait till you get here. You'll love it. It's really sunny, and there's the sea and all these cute little antique shops in the Lanes. Do you know what I'm doing right this second? I'm walking on the beach.'

'That's right. Rub it in. Do you know what I'm doing right now? Trying to learn my lines for tomorrow.'

'I wish I was there to help you.'

'I do too. I've got pages and pages this week.'

'Well, that's good, isn't it?' Now it was Emma's turn to cheer Jason up. Ever since the suspension incident – which got more press coverage than the offending photo shoot he'd done in the first place – Jason had been living in constant fear of opening his script pages and finding out that Troy was 'Moving to Manchester' which was the usual destination for all the characters who were written out of *Shelby Square* – apart, obviously, from the ones who were murdered, run over, burned to a crisp in suspicious nightclub infernos, electrocuted by faulty household appliances, drowned in gravel pits, crushed by falling masonry or otherwise sacked.

'I suppose,' Jason agreed but all Emma heard was crackle.

'Oh damn, you're breaking up!' She waved her mobile over her head trying to get the signal back. 'Can you hear me, Jason?' she shouted into the phone. 'I'll call you tomorrow. I love you!'

She didn't hear Jason say he loved her too, but she knew it anyway.

eighteen

Steve was flushed and sweaty as he scooped fried eggs, baked beans, sausage, mushroom and black pudding onto white china plates and handed them out to the hungry mob. Breakfast times were murder. He'd been up since four and the damp pools under his arms were about to join the little rivers of perspiration flowing down his back to form one giant ocean of sweat.

'Morning, Steve,' Liz called out and waved her orange at him playfully.

Steve wasn't used to being singled out for Liz's attentions. 'I've got your prawns today,' he shouted back.

'Oh Steve, you're a complete star!' said Liz. 'I'll see you at lunchtime.'

Liz had spent another restless night. Tex's body, curved around her as he slept, gave off a radiant heat, so that she woke up bathed in sweat.

She'd put on a robe and lifted the chiffon scarf from her bronze Buddha statue on the window ledge. Then she'd lit two sticks of incense, sat down cross-legged in front of her make-shift shrine, and began to chant under her breath: 'Nam-Myoho-Renge-Kyo, Nam-Myoho-Renge-Kyo,' softly, so as not to wake up Tex. In her right hand she held the Polaroid of Ben that she'd taken on set the day before when he'd been discussing the cloakroom scene with Emma. She'd tried to keep Emma out of the frame altogether but her left shoulder and part of her head had crept in. Fortunately she'd managed to cut around her. It wasn't the most flattering photo of Ben – the camera had flashed just as he turned away and he had one hand on his forehead, smoothing back his hair. It didn't compare with the photos in the album at the bottom of her suitcase, but it was the first photo she'd taken of him since they split up and she focused all her concentration on it as she chanted, willing Ben to come back to her. Tex had snored on, oblivious. When he woke up ten minutes later, she quickly blew out the incense, hid the photo, covered the Buddha with the chiffon scarf and went to take a bath.

'You don't have to stop on my account,' said Tex. 'I like the sound of it.' Tex had been impressed the first time he'd come to Liz's room and seen the Buddha. He liked that Liz had a spiritual side and respected her for it. Liz didn't tell him that becoming a Buddhist was merely a means to an end. She didn't tell him she would have become a Young Conservative if she'd thought it would help get Ben back.

'Hey, don't I even get a kiss?' Tex called after her as Liz sailed out to catch the first minibus, the door banging shut behind her. Tex just laughed. He'd grown up with a house full of fiery women and until he left home he hadn't realised it was even possible for a door to close without being slammed. His three sisters and his mother Elsa who had raised them single-handed and put the fear of God into them would have welcomed Liz into the family as one of their own.

On the make-up bus, the Daft Tarts were pissed off because they'd all gone to The Honey Club the night before and Danny and Alex had left with a couple of girls they'd met at the bar. It was just rude, that's what it was, going off with outsiders like that. It showed no respect. So they were being especially nice to Giles this morning to punish them.

'Yours looked a right dirty little bitch,' grinned Alex appreciatively. 'She had such a nice little arse and then these massive tits like, like –' Alex groped in the air for an appropriate metaphor and failed to find a word he liked. 'Well, they were fucking special, anyway.'

'There, you're finished,' said Bex, wiping the hair gel off her hands. The minute her back was turned, Danny leaned towards the mirror and started spiking up his hair with his fingers.

'Don't do that,' she told him off. 'I've just finished. You do this every morning!'

'Yeah, because you never do it right,' said Danny. 'They should be paying me not you.' He was getting seriously pissed off now with being blond because nobody recognised him. He could walk down the street, he could go into a club – and nothing. No screaming, no fainting, nothing. 'By the way, which one of you girls would like to be my ex-girlfriend?'

'Your *ex*-girlfriend?' said Tracey.

'In the movie. Who wants to be in the film?'

Saskia was desperate to be in the film. She usually managed to get a small walk-on spot on most of her jobs. 'Maybe,' she purred. 'What would we have to do?'

'Well, I'm auditioning girls to play my ex-girlfriends. Be in the King George Suite tonight at eight-thirty.'

'Jesus Christ,' muttered Hugo. 'Who do you have to sleep with to get off this movie?' It was their first day in the empty flat they were using for the band's squat and people were literally falling over each other as they tried to set up for the first two scenes in the bathroom. The previous owner had very inconsiderately died before doing his spring cleaning and the whole flat smelled of damp dog. Now Hugo had been bitten by a flea.

'I hate shooting in these poxy little flats,' he moaned as he climbed over Kevin who was laying cables in the doorway. 'Why aren't we doing this in a studio?'

Danny made Poppy, who'd been promoted to Stand-by Art Director, scrub the bath twice with disinfectant before he'd get in it.

'On second thoughts,' he said when he saw that all Poppy's efforts hadn't made any difference to the suspicious yellow stain running down the middle of the tub, 'you'd better give me a bin-liner to sit on as well.' Danny was wearing swimming trunks because he'd only be seen from the waist up and he didn't want to catch any old man germs.

'And what's this meant to be?' he asked when Phil handed him a bar of amber-coloured soap.'

'It's meant to be soap.'

'Nah. Eddie wouldn't use this. It's girl's soap.' And so Poppy was sent to the corner shop to buy a packet of Imperial Leather which Danny said would be Eddie's preferred brand.

'Now Eddie,' said Ben. 'It's late. You're scared. You've spent the whole day dodging Turpin's men—'

'So why am I having a bath? If I was scared, I'd be moving around, pacing about.'

'Yes, except you're hot and sweaty as well,' said Ben as patiently as he could, 'and exhausted. You need to relax and think of a plan. So you're lying in the bath, and that's when you notice the hole in the wall where one of the tiles is missing.'

'What if I was walking around the bathroom? I could notice it then.'

'That's a very good idea,' said Ben diplomatically. 'But as we're set up now for this shot, why don't we do *in* the bath first and then if there's time, we can try it that way as well.'

'Where's he going to walk to in this bathroom?' muttered Ryan who was having to perch on the window-sill with one foot on the cistern to look into the eyepiece. He felt something bite his leg but if he reached down to scratch it, the camera would fall into the bath.

Finally, after much agonising over lighting, the temperature of Danny's bath water, and the fact that there was nowhere for Billy the Boom to stand where he wouldn't cast a shadow on the white tiles, they were as ready as they were going to be. Ben who was crouched uncomfortably out on the landing with the monitor resting on his knees, called 'Action' and Danny leaned back and stared moodily at his bar of Imperial Leather, sliding it slowly around in his hands as the film rolled expensively on.

Things got worse in Scene 118 where the whole band and Jasmine are in the bathroom at the same time. The boys are trying to re-tile the bathroom wall and Jasmine is reading out the instructions from a DIY book. As if on cue, the minute they were about to turn over, thumping drum and bass started pounding out of the flat next door, making the walls vibrate.

Tex took off his headphones and shook his head. 'Impossible,' he said. 'I won't be able to get any usable sound over this.'

Jamie took £10 out of his wallet and handed it to Tim. 'Go next door and ask him to stop – just for fifteen minutes while we get this shot.'

Ben's knees creaked as he got painfully to his feet to give his actors some notes.

'Giles, is there something you can be doing? Maybe reading the packet of adhesive?' He sat down on the edge of the bath and rubbed his back. 'I'm getting too old for this,' he complained.

Emma gave his back an exploratory prod. 'What have you been doing? Your neck is like concrete!' she told him and automatically began to massage his shoulders – one of the useful skills she'd picked up at the hairdressing salon.

'OK, forget the film everybody,' Ben sighed. 'It's be-nice-to-the-director time.' He closed his eyes in grateful submission, thinking he could fall asleep right there. So he didn't see Liz come into the bathroom to check on the costumes and find him leaning back with a blissful smile on his face as Emma worked her fingertips into the knots in his neck and shoulders.

'That feels fantastic,' Liz heard him murmur. 'You could do this professionally, you know.'

Liz's eyes flashed and she turned and walked out, more determined than ever to kill off this budding romance before it was too late.

Fifteen minutes later, when the music hadn't stopped and Tim still hadn't returned, the others didn't know whether to be impatient or concerned.

'Do you think he's OK?' asked Georgina, looking out the window. 'Maybe we should go and look for him.'

'Where's Piers?' asked Hugo. 'He's locations, it should be his job to sort it out.'

Piers's whereabouts were a constant mystery to the rest of the crew. They saw him at breakfast when he'd let them into the premises and he could usually be counted on to turn up for lunch. Then when they wrapped, he'd appear to lock up, but for the rest of the day he was maddeningly elusive. It was Hugo's theory that he nipped back to the hotel in the afternoons for a nap.

'He's a DJ,' said Tim, when he eventually came back. 'He says he's rehearsing his set for tonight and if you want him to stop it'll cost you fifty quid.'

'Chancers!' Hugo fumed. 'The second they see a film crew in the street they all start mowing their lawns because they know there'll be money in it for them to make them stop. Pay him. It's not worth even arguing about.'

Jamie took out another twenty and had to borrow a tenner from Georgina to make it up. Tim took the money and wondered how they could afford to pay the bloke next door fifty quid for a few minutes' silence when they couldn't afford to pay him a penny for the entire film. Perhaps, instead of looking for a runner's job next summer, he'd be better off following film units around with a ghetto blaster and demanding cash. He'd make a fortune.

When silence descended once again, the cast took up their positions in the bath, Giles quietly reading the instructions on the tub of tile adhesive, Luke gently drumming on the side of the bath with the spirit level in his good hand, Danny trying to comb his hair with the plastic adhesive spreader and Alex pressing the first tile into place against a nailed wooden batten.

'I hate this fucking shot,' said Hugo just to boost everyone's morale. Ryan's leg had now gone completely to sleep.

'And action!'

Emma started to read aloud from the DIY manual: 'If the tiles don't have spacer lugs, use plastic tile spacers between them. Alternatively, place a matchstick between adjacent tiles.'

'Didn't we see The Spacer Lugs at Glastonbury last year?' said Luke, and then Ben heard the surreal sound of the theme from Star Wars. For a brief second, he thought it was a sign from his god, George Lucas, but then he realised it was a mobile phone. Everyone groaned and there were a few laughs as well as people wondered who the poor bastard was. It said on the call sheet that anyone whose mobile rang on set would be fined ten pounds. Danny dropped the adhesive spreader and leaned out of the bath to pick up his phone from the floor beside him.

'And cut!' yelled Jamie.

'Oh hi,' said Danny. 'No, no, that's cool . . . we haven't really started yet . . .' He sat down on the bath and held up his finger to Jamie to say, 'One second. Don't bother me right now.' 'Right . . . right . . . Are they talking money? Well am I free then? . . . Yeah . . . Send it down here and I'll take a look at it . . . But let them know I'm interested.'

'Un-be-lievable,' sighed Hugo.

'It'd probably be a good idea if you left your mobile in your trailer,' Jamie suggested diplomatically. 'Then you wouldn't have to worry about remembering to turn it off.'

'It was my agent,' said Danny, as if that explained everything. 'It was important.' So no point asking him for the ten quid then, thought Jamie.

'You know what you should have done?' Hugo said to Ben when they finally broke for lunch. 'You should have had them find a hole in the kitchen wall instead. There's plenty of room in the kitchen.'

'Great. Thanks for the suggestion,' said Ben, gritting his teeth. 'Pity you didn't think of that a month ago when we came here on the recce.'

Emma went back to the wardrobe truck with Liz to change. 'Well that's me done for the day. I think I might go shopping.'

'But you're going to stay for lunch, aren't you?' asked Liz, trying not to show how important it was that Emma didn't leave.

'I don't know. I had quite a big breakfast this morning.'

'Well, yes, you say that now, but in a couple of hours you'll be hungry again and you'll end up snacking on junk food. That's not good for you.'

'No, you're right.' Emma found it touching that other people took such an interest in her well-being.

'You've got to stick to regular mealtimes or your blood sugar levels will be all over the place.'

'I know.'

'Besides, they've got those prawns again that they had the other day.'

That settled it. Emma was staying for lunch. She got changed and went to join the long queue at the catering van.

'Save me a seat on the bus,' Liz told her.

When Emma had gone, Liz opened the drawer under the counter and took out a small object carefully coccooned in bubble-wrap, then tenderly unwrapped it and placed it in the pocket of her cardigan.

She joined the lunch queue that crawled up to the serving hatch, keeping a watchful eye on the dish of prawns that was laid out on the buffet table. She hoped Steve had made enough. She didn't want them to run out before she got there and grew alarmed when she saw Hugo greedily helping himself to six. That was so typical. By the time the queue had reached the buffet table, there were only two left. She reached out to take them at the very same moment as Giles.

'You have them,' he insisted politely, and Liz silently thanked Giles's mother for turning out such a nicely mannered young man. She placed the two prawns on the edge of her plate with the tails facing outward and piled a mixture of salad leaves next to them. But she'd need more food than this to pull it off.

Reluctantly, she looked at the hot meal menu: Noodles with chicken and cashew nuts, sweet and sour pork or stir-fried rice and vegetables.

She ordered the stir-fry, which made Steve's day. There was

a strange smell coming from the kitchen which Liz correctly identified as Aramis.

'Are we still on for that drink later?' he asked piling her plate with twice the portion allowed.

'Oh Steve, I'm so sorry, I'm not going to be able to make it. Something's come up.' She ignored Steve's disappointment and as she stepped down from the counter, she slipped her hand into her pocket. Life was like a game of chess, she mused, and it was time to bring out her prawn.

She was pleased to see that thanks to its pastry overcoat, her leftover prawn from Wednesday's lunch still looked identical to the ones she had just put on her plate. She placed it gently on the bed of lettuce so there would be absolutely no mistake. Emma had saved her a seat at the table with Alex and Luke.

'It's going to be a blinder,' said Alex, referring to the boat trip. 'The weather report for tomorrow is sun, sun and more fucking sun.'

'I'm going to buy a new bikini this afternoon,' Emma piped up. 'I don't think my old one's good enough for a yacht.'

'Let me be the judge of that, sweetheart,' said Alex.

'I'm so excited. I've never been on a boat before,' admitted Emma, 'apart from the ferry to the Isle of Wight with the school once.'

Meanwhile, Liz was reacquainting herself with deep-fried pastry – a taste she also connected with school. What a disgusting concept. It was like fried glue. She chewed each mouthful grimly and then started on the stir-fry which was swimming in cheap peanut oil; a lifetime of healthy eating habits wiped out in just a few mouthfuls. She could already feel her large intestine starting to swell up from shock. It had better be worth it, she thought and was pleased to see that Emma had already made short work of her prawns.

Liz put down her fork and sighed ostentatiously. 'That's it! I'm completely full,' she declared, and was surprised to realise that it was probably the first time in years she'd uttered those words and actually meant them. 'Would you like my last prawn, Emma? I couldn't eat another bite.'

'I'll have it, if you don't want it,' said Alex reaching out to take it, but Liz moved her plate away just in time.

'Don't be so greedy!' she said and smacked his hand teasingly. 'You've still got two left!'

'Well, if no one else wants it,' said Emma, and picked up the last prawn lying on its little lettuce pillow. She dipped it in the pool of chilli sauce on the side of her plate and slid it into her mouth. It wasn't as crunchy as the others, she noticed, but she decided that must be because it had been sitting on Liz's salad.

Liz watched Emma's jaws rhythmically crushing the three-day-old prawn and all its pastry lining into tiny digestible fragments and held her breath until the subtle rolling wave of peristalsis indicated that the pulpy mass had begun its long and eventful journey down Emma's oesophagus and into her digestive tract.

Liz clapped her hands once in satisfaction. 'Now,' she asked, 'who's for coffee?'

The band were back in the squat after lunch, racing to get three scenes completed. First up was the scene in the living room where they sit around eating cold baked beans on toast and moaning about their lack of cash. In another scene, Ollie waters a rubber plant and moves it lovingly around the flat to a spot where it will get the most light. And while they were doing all of that, the art department was working flat out to finish the tiling job to a more or less professional standard. The final scene of the day was another shot of Eddie in the bath, this time looking very pleased with himself as he admires the new tile-work.

'Should have done it in the kitchen,' said Hugo again and Ben resolved to cross Hugo off his Christmas-card list.

Meanwhile, Emma's search for the ultimate bikini continued until, at half past five, she was suddenly overcome by a giant wave of nausea. Her skin felt cold and clammy, but her forehead was beaded with sweat. And as she stepped out into the fresh air of East Street all these sensations were over-ridden by the urgent need to find a toilet within the next ten seconds. She ran into the coffee shop across the road, not even stopping to ask the waitress if she could use their loo, but barging in, mumbling, 'Sorry, excuse me!' and following the signs to the ladies where she bolted the door in relief and didn't emerge until just before six when the owner came to ask if she was all right because they wanted to lock up.

When Liz got back to the hotel at half past seven, Belinda handed her a large package.

'This came for you today. All the way from America. Anything exciting?'

'Just books,' said Liz, and carried the white cardboard box covered in official US Customs and Express Mail stickers up to her room. Buddhism was OK up to a point, but in an emergency, you couldn't put all your eggs in one basket. You had to have a back-up.

She hung the Do Not Disturb sign on her door, made sure it was locked, and snipped the sticky tape from around the edges of the package.

Immediately, the sweet perfume of the contents filled the room. She unfolded the white tissue paper, and untied the gold raffia that sealed the plastic bag inside. She placed the individual items on the bed around her, examining each one with excited curiosity: a small bag of herbs that looked like fine chaff, tiny cones of black incense, a red candle, a mixture of sand and fine flecks of glitter, two vials of oil, a long twisted silver nail, and most thrillingly of all, a wax effigy of a woman about nine inches high.

It was amazing, thought Liz, what you could buy on the Internet these days.

'What's this meeting about exactly?' asked Stacey. She'd spread her paperwork out on the table in the King George Suite and was totting up her new estimated running time for the film.

'I dunno,' said Georgina. 'Poppy just said she wanted us all here. Something about the art department.'

'Well, where's everybody else?' asked Flick.

'They better turn up soon,' said Georgina. 'I'm driving home to Kent tonight.'

A girl none of them had ever seen before, with long dark hair and a 36D bust that threatened to escape at any minute from a zip-fronted white top, was sitting on the opposite side of the room licking her lips self-consciously.

Danny and the Daft Tarts all arrived together, giggling and drinking champagne out of wine glasses, followed by Poppy with her digital camera.

'Is this the lot?' Danny demanded. 'Is this the best you could come up with?'

'You said everyone else was too old,' Poppy reminded him.

The girl in the white top leapt up and kissed him hello.

'Oh hi, doll,' he greeted her. He'd forgotten that he'd told her to come here tonight and he certainly didn't remember her name. Was it Kelly? Or Claire?

Billy was sitting in the corner eating a packet of crisps. 'What are you doing here?' Danny asked.

Billy looked blank. 'I heard there was a meeting.'

'Girls only,' said Danny, and held the door open for Billy to leave.

'Danny, what's this about, exactly?' asked Georgina, starting to get impatient. 'It's been a long day.'

'We need to do some photos of Danny's ex-girlfriends,' said Poppy. 'For set-dressing.'

'So I've got a few questions for you, before I decide who it's going to be,' said Danny.

'Oh, Jesus Christ,' muttered Georgina and started putting on her jacket. 'I haven't got time for this.'

'She's not really stacked enough anyway,' Danny told Poppy.

'Now, Flick,' he continued, 'if you'd been going out with Eddie, what sorts of things would you have liked doing together?'

Flick tried not to laugh. 'I don't know. Going to see films, clubbing, going to the beach, eating out. The usual.'

'And what size are you?'

'What size? I'm a 12.'

'No, your bra size.'

'34C. Why do you need to know that?'

'And why do you think you and Eddie would have split up?'

'Musical differences?' suggested Flick.

Danny nodded approvingly. 'Can I see you walk up and down please?'

'Sorry?'

'Walk up and down for me.'

Flick stood up and walked across the carpet and back again, watched jealously by Saskia, Bex and Tracey, who were trying to think of their own answers to Danny's questions.

'OK. Now what about you, Stacey?' Danny asked. 'If you were going out with Eddie, what sorts of things would you have liked doing with him?'

Stacey carried on ruling tram-lines through her script. She didn't look up. 'Hmm, lets see. Bondage, S&M, torture, flagellation, ritual piercings – the usual.'

Danny swallowed hard. 'And why do you think you and Eddie would have broken up?'

'Gee, I dunno, Danny.' Stacey smiled and closed her folder. 'Maybe because I'm a dyke?' She gathered up her things and left the room, shaking her head.

Danny blinked and tried not to show his surprise. 'Well, it'll be just this lot then,' he told Poppy, indicating Flick, the Daft Tarts and the girl in the white top. Was it Kathy?

'And you. I suppose you can be in it as well.'

Liz opened the voodoo instruction booklet. 'This is white magick,' said a large disclaimer on the first page. 'Do not attempt to bring harm upon another person or you will find the magick will turn against you.'

'Yeah, yeah,' said Liz. 'Whatever', and she turned to page three which explained how to lay out her altar. There were strange symbols to cut out and each day she would have to leave some chocolate and a glass of brandy for the voodoo spirits at a road junction. Liz had a quick look in her mini-bar and hoped the spirits would be happy with miniatures. Using the twisted nail, she carved her own name carefully into the red candle and scratched nine lines across its length, dividing the candle into nine days.

Next, she turned her attention to the wax doll, carefully anointing it with oil, prior to its baptism. Taking up the twisted nail again, she cut the name Emma into the wax and scored it with nine horizontal slashes. The doll's waxy breasts and buttocks were more pronounced than Emma's but she was sure it would serve its purpose. Then, as the instructions suggested, she visualised Emma and Ben with a wide ocean between them that they would never be able to cross. She smiled to herself, happy to be in control of her destiny once again. This was a very good plan.

'Such a shame you had to miss the boat trip,' said Liz the next morning. She was sitting in the armchair beside Emma's bed, pouring her some lukewarm water from the teapot. She held the cup up to Emma's lips 'Sip this,' she told her. 'You don't want to dehydrate.'

'Oh Liz, what's the use? It's only going to come back up again in five minutes.'

Emma had spent all Saturday night and most of Sunday morning rushing to the toilet, never entirely sure which end of her body was going to give way next. But she sipped the water anyway, grateful that Liz had given up her day off to look after her. The nurse had given her anti-diarrhoea tablets and lozenges to suck that would stop her throwing up, but she

200

preferred to get whatever was poisoning her out of her body as quickly as possible.

'There's no way I could go on a boat today,' moaned Emma. She imagined flushing the toilet on the boat and killing all the marine life on the South Coast. It was too disgusting to think about. 'But it's lucky, isn't it, that this happened on my day off and not when I'm supposed to be working?'

'Isn't it lucky?' Liz agreed, and mopped Emma's brow with a cool damp cloth. She'd timed Emma's food poisoning perfectly. Just serious enough to keep her away from Ben, but not enough to disrupt his movie. After all, she didn't want to sabotage his career − that would be counter-productive. By the time she finally became Mrs Ben Lincoln she wanted him to be hugely successful.

'Kim said I might be OK to carry on filming tomorrow.'

'Well, don't worry about that now. The film can wait. The important thing is to get you better.'

'Thanks, Liz,' Emma mumbled. 'I don't know where I'd be if it wasn't for you.'

Prancing about in a bikini on a yacht with Ben, is where you'd be, thought Liz. But she just smiled and patted Emma's hand. 'Don't mention it,' she said. 'That's what friends are for.'

Flick had taken pity on Ronald Gasch yet again and took him out for dinner on Sunday evening. She couldn't understand why he'd turned down Giles's offer of a boat trip and preferred to mooch around the hotel all day reading the papers.

'Would you like to see the dessert menu?' asked the waiter.

'No, thank you,' said Ronald. 'What about you, Flick? Would you like pudding, or coffee?' Flick, he thought. What a ridiculous name. What kind of parent would christen a child Flick? What was it short for? Felicity, he supposed.

'Not for me. Just the bill, please,' she told the waiter, and Ronald wondered whether she would let him pay for the whole meal or would embarrass him by insisting on going Dutch. Another terrible expression which he loathed.

But when the bill came and he picked it up, Flick just said, 'Thanks. My treat next time', and smiled as he signed the credit-card slip.

'Fancy a walk back along the front?' she asked as they left the restaurant.

Ronald was in no mood for an outing, but he let himself be led along the narrow street that led down to the sea, across the main road and onto the promenade. He started to walk in the direction of the hotel, but Flick kept walking towards the beach.

'Come on, it's a lovely evening. Let's just look at the sea before we go back.' She sat on the wall, swinging her legs over the side. Flick needed to be near the sea, the way other people needed air to breathe. When she had arrived in Brighton a week ago, and Patrick had shown her the beach, she'd laughed for half an hour. 'Call that a beach?' she'd snorted. 'What are all these stones doing here?' On the beaches at home she could walk for hours in either direction before running out of white sand. And in the evening, she'd watch the sun turn the sky blood-red as it was squashed down into the sea. She'd endured two English winters, but she'd never been as homesick as she was that summer watching people stumble over Brighton's brown and grey pebbles under the delusion that they were having a good time.

Not quite so nimbly, Ronald sat down beside her. He remembered that he and Marianne had spent the day in Brighton once, shortly after they were married. He tried to remember the reason they'd come, but it was more than forty years ago.

Flick noticed his troubled expression and knew what she had to do. 'Now Ronald,' she said, suddenly serious. 'You don't seem very happy, and I think I might be able to help you.'

Ronald didn't know whether to be flattered or afraid. He had grown accustomed over the years to women offering him their bodies – he knew it was his fame that attracted them rather than his face – but it was many, many years since he had been propositioned by a girl quite so young as Flick. Even if his body was willing, his vanity would never allow his own sagging flesh to stand up to such stern, youthful scrutiny. Since Marianne's death there had been no one.

'My dear, that's very flattering,' he said gently. 'But I'm old enough to be your grandfather.'

'How old are you?' she asked.

'I'm sixty-two,' he told her truthfully. It wasn't old. But Marianne had been just fifty-seven when she died and that was no age at all. 'And you are?'

'Twenty-six. I think my granddad's seventy-something. I've only got one. The other one's dead.'

Ronald wondered whether he was meant to find this information reassuring and then he saw Flick holding out her hand to him. Young women today were really quite amazingly forward. Did she expect him to hold it or kiss it? he wondered. And then he noticed a small white tablet cupped in her palm. It looked like an aspirin.

'Do you have a headache?' he asked.

'It's Ecstasy,' she told him. 'Do you know what that is?'

'Of course I know what that is,' he told her. His *Telegraph* was full of Ecstasy stories – usually accompanied by a picture of a teenager hooked up to a life-support machine and another photograph of them smiling and well and passing all their exams before they had slipped into the drug's evil clutches. Teenagers took Ecstasy, went to discotheques and either danced themselves to death, or became junkies and prostitutes, selling their bodies to pay for smack and crack cocaine. It was a well known fact. 'I know all about Ecstasy,' he said again.

'Have you ever tried it?'

'Of course I haven't,' he said, shocked and angry that she would even suggest such a thing. 'Do you take me for a fool?' Cognac was his drug, occasionally Scotch, and he enjoyed a good claret or burgundy. But he preferred Hine – the same brand as Winston Churchill. Since Marianne had died, he had got into the habit of drinking four or five glasses each evening, before slipping into an uncomfortable, restless sleep that ended with a false, alcohol-induced dawn at precisely 4 a.m. But without the cognac, he couldn't get to sleep at all.

'It would probably kill me,' he reprimanded her, and his subconscious added, *and what a blessed relief that would be.*

For a second, Ronald stared at the small white pill and realised that he didn't much want to live anyway. What was he doing, just going through the motions of life? With no one to love or love him, his existence had become a joyless trudge through a living hell. The only reason he was still alive was that he was too much of a coward to kill himself. He wouldn't know how to get hold of a gun, hanging terrified him, slashing his wrists was too slow – imagine lying slumped on the bathroom floor watching your own blood spill out – and overdoses were by no means foolproof. What if he were found and rushed to hospital to have his stomach pumped? The newspapers would be full of his shame – he had seen it happen. But he wasn't just afraid of suicide, he was more afraid of everyone – his fans, his fellow actors, complete strangers – knowing he had taken his own life. What an ignominious footnote that would be to a glorious career. The church might even refuse to bury him in sacred ground.

And so, instead, he watched for symptoms – the lump, or discharge, or shortness of breath that would inevitably take him into a respectable grave. The obituaries would be reverential and gushing. On News at Ten, colleagues would testify to the bravery with which he had fought this last battle – taking his final curtain call with dignity and a smile. There would be a retrospective series of his work on BBC2 and Radio 4 and the memorial service at All Souls would be standing room only as the theatre world wept profusely and publicly for its lost son. Was that really so much to ask?

Ronald continued to stare at the tablet in Flick's hand. One tablet could hardly constitute a suicide bid, could it? Accidental death – that's what the coroner's report would say.

'Will you tell them I thought it was aspirin?' he asked Flick and put the tablet into his mouth.

nineteen

'Good morning!' said Belinda cheerily as Ben handed over his room key. 'You've got a lovely day for it.'

Ben wondered how Belinda always managed to look so wide awake when she must get up even earlier than he did and was still on reception when they finished filming. He wondered if she was a twin.

Yesterday's boat trip had started out as a relaxing, if rather uneventful, jaunt but when they reached the turning point just past Shoreham, Danny and Alex had chucked him overboard as he had suspected they would. As he bobbed back up to the surface he tried to take it all in good spirits but the water was beyond freezing and he shivered and squelched all the way back to the marina. Patrick who'd spent the trip lolling in the sun and catching up on back issues of *Variety*, *Screen International* and the *Hollywood Reporter*, issued a stern warning that if so much as one drop of saltwater touched his body they would all be fired and he would personally see to it that they would never work again. Nobody had the bottle to find out whether he was joking.

When they got back, Ben had taken the boys and the four-man yacht crew out for a drink and then crashed out early at around half past ten. But, then, just like every other night, he'd been woken up by the telephone in his room, just after midnight. As always there was nobody there – or rather, whoever was calling him wasn't speaking. He'd had enough of this stupid game.

'Liz, is that you?' he demanded. 'Please stop calling me. I have to sleep.'

He was sure he could hear somebody breathing on the other end and then the line went dead.

'Belinda,' he asked now. 'Is there any way of tracing a call that's been made from another room in the hotel?'

'Do you want to make a phone call?' Belinda picked up the black phone off the reception desk and put it on top of the counter for him.

'No. Somebody's been making anonymous phone calls to my room and I'm pretty sure they're coming from inside the hotel. Is there any way I can find out what room a call has come from?'

'I don't think so,' said Belinda, 'unless they came through the switchboard. Did they come through the switchboard?'

'I don't think so. I don't know.'

'Well, have you tried asking the person calling you what room they're in?'

'No,' said Ben wearily. 'I haven't. Perhaps I'll do that. Thanks for the advice.'

'My pleasure,' smiled Belinda helpfully.

He walked out to the front of the hotel and waited for the minibus. Hugo was yawning widely in the early morning sun.

'You look how I feel,' Hugo told him.

'Rough night?'

'Yeah, some idiot phoned my room and woke me up just after midnight and it took me hours to get back to sleep after that.'

'Me too,' said Ryan. 'My phone went twice – once at eleven and once at twelve. I'll kill them if I ever find out who it was.'

'Wasn't anybody there?' asked Ben.

Ryan shook his head. 'Somebody playing a practical joke, I suppose. Don't think much of their sense of humour.'

Now Ben didn't know what to think. Why would Liz ring Hugo and Ryan? Maybe it wasn't Liz after all. He had to stop being so paranoid.

206

Ben was still mulling this over as he poured himself a coffee at Unit Base. A squeal of brakes announced Patrick's arrival as his Saab squeezed into the narrow gap between the lighting truck and the fence. He marched over to Ben with a face like thunder.

'Your front tyre's looking a bit flat,' Ben told him.

'Sod that!' roared Patrick as he searched his pockets for his cigarette lighter. 'I've just spent half the night at the police station. More of your bloody actors causing grief.'

Ben looked around the car park in alarm. He'd just spoken to Alex and he'd seen Giles and Luke wandering about. 'Not Danny!' he groaned.

'No. Not Danny,' said Patrick. 'Ronald bloody Gasch! The police picked him up at three o'clock this morning walking down the main street of Brighton stark bollock naked. They're doing him for indecent exposure.'

'Where is he now?'

'Back at the hotel. Sleeping it off. Feeling very sorry for himself, I hope.'

Ronald Gasch could barely summon the strength to open his eyes. His jaws ached, his bowels ached and he'd lost one of his favourite suits – although he had found a shoe. Not his own, he realised now as he lay in bed and stared at the offending slipper lying on his carpet. It wasn't even leather. But it wasn't true to say that he felt sorry for himself, because never, in all his sixty-two years, had he felt more glad to be alive.

Whatever had happened to him last night was a kind of miracle. He'd been sitting on the seafront with Flick, looking out to sea and waiting to die, when he had suddenly been filled with a sense of peace he'd never known before. His eyes seemed to grow accustomed to the dark, and the image came into his head of this same spot the first time he'd visited Brighton with his wife Marianne. Now he remembered why they had come here. Her younger sister Audrey, who lived in Hove, was emigrating to Canada and they'd come down on the train to say goodbye to her. They'd walked down to the sea licking ice-cream cones – one scoop of vanilla and one scoop of strawberry ripple in a double cone. Marianne was wearing a blue-and-white striped dress with a full skirt and a nipped-in waist and her hair was longer then, pushed back from her face in dark, rolling waves. She never left the house without her lipstick. Audrey's husband David had taken a photograph of Audrey and Marianne sitting on the biscuit-coloured pebbles. 'I'll send you a copy,' he'd said, but it had never arrived. Now, as Ronald stared into the darkness, he could still see the two sisters sitting there together, laughing as the waves rolled in behind them and shouting at David to hurry up before they got wet. That was the last time Audrey and Marianne had ever seen each other.

He was clutching the blue railing that ran along the sea wall and now he began to stroke it, marvelling at the sensation of the metal under his fingers. He imagined he could feel every layer of paint that had been applied over the years, here it had chipped, there the paint had been applied too thickly and had dripped a little. He could feel the imprints of the thousands of other hands that had come into contact with this spot. A living history, right there in the paint. And then Ronald had remembered something else. The night six years earlier when he had first seen the two sisters queuing up outside the theatre as he hurried to the stage door and how it was Audrey, in the green cardigan, who had caught his eye with her mane of red hair and brilliant blue eyes; Audrey who caught his eye, but Marianne who he married.

'How could I have forgotten that?' he said aloud, his voice cracking with wonder. 'I was too afraid to speak to Audrey so I married her sister.'

Flick didn't know what he was talking about but he knew she understood. He took hold of her hands and began stroking her arm. The rope lights strung along the pier sparkled on the sea. It was so beautiful he could hardly bear to look at it.

'Can I hug you?' he asked Flick, and she laughed and put her arms around him.

'Now I don't want you to think you love me or anything stupid like that,' she told him, 'This is just the E that's making you feel like this, OK?'

'I know,' he said.

She led him onto the pier where he was dazzled by neon lights, and the chimes and blasts of arcade games seemed to herald his arrival into a new world. He stared for a long time at a glass case filled with small red-and-white striped plush tigers. His palms pressed against the cool smoothness of the window and he longed to reach in and touch them. On another stall, giant tropical fish hung above his head and Ronald marvelled at a world that contained so much colour. Why had he never seen it before? They walked down to the end of the pier, past karaoke bars and doughnut stalls to the fairground rides and Flick jumped into the empty car of a waltzer that was about to start up.

'I was always so afraid,' Ronald confessed as he climbed in beside her, 'but I can see now, there's nothing to be afraid of at all, is there?'

'Safe as houses, mate,' replied the tattooed man who took their tickets and he clicked the metal bar down firmly over their laps.

While Ben had been swimming the channel and Ronald had been experiencing oneness with the universe, Jamie, Dominic and Piers had spent their day off ripping up Monday's schedule and starting again. They were supposed to be shooting outside the DIY store this afternoon, but because Emma was sick they had to find a day's worth of scenes that didn't include her. Phone calls were made, agents were got out of bed, knees were grovelled on and the two Chinese actors who'd been booked for the following day were told to get down to Brighton ASAP because the scene in the pub was being brought forward.

When they shot the street scene where Sam and Ollie phone all the Wongs in the East Sussex directory, Liz stayed in the wardrobe truck deliberately keeping out of Ben's way. She'd been a bit rattled by the way he'd seemed to just know that she was the one calling his room. She'd known it was risky, but she couldn't get to sleep at night without hearing his voice. She'd wait until Tex fell asleep, then rest the phone on the pillow beside her and listen to Ben's voice saying, 'Hello? Hello? Who is this?'

Fortunately, she'd been prepared for the possibility that Ben would suspect her, which was why she'd taken the precaution of phoning Hugo and Patrick and Ryan as well. That way if Ben ever compared notes with them, as she was sure he would, he'd be thrown off the scent. Maybe he'd think it was just some kind of electrical fault. A couple of times she'd even phoned Janet the accountant and she could tell by the way Janet said, 'Who *is* this?' in a musical, girlish voice that she was secretly thrilled by the possibility that she might have a secret admirer. Liz breathed into the mouthpiece for two minutes before she got tired of Janet saying flirtatiously, 'I know you're there', and hung up. 'Stupid cow,' she said to herself. But obviously, her efforts to avoid detection would have to be stepped up. And if Ben ever found out that it was Liz who'd deliberately caused Emma's food poisoning . . . She shuddered and reminded herself that there was no way he ever could find out.

Just after eleven o'clock, the unit were on the move again to shoot a key scene. The band are in the pub playing pool and Jackson overhears Mr Ho and Mr Yo – as Ben had rather unimaginatively christened them – talking about a racehorse that's guaranteed to win. The men are talking freely in Cantonese because they don't know that Jackson spent six years living in Hong Kong where his dad was in the diplomatic service and Jackson doesn't know that Mr Ho and Mr Yo are part of a Malaysian gambling syndicate.

Patrick had barely calmed down over the Ronald Gasch fiasco, when he found something else to send his blood pressure soaring.

'What do you mean, they're not closing the pub?' he said to

Piers. 'How are we supposed to shoot in here with all this racket going on?'

'They're closing the back bar for us,' Piers explained. 'But the front bar's staying open. They said they don't want to turn away their regulars. We'll just have to ask them to keep the noise down.'

'It's a Monday morning, for fuck's sake,' screamed Patrick. 'It's not Happy Hour at the Club Med! How many customers are they going to turn away?'

Patrick cast his eye over the ruddy-cheeked, watery-eyed specimens who appeared to be glued on to their bar stools like some nightmarish version of *Blind Date*. Will it be contestant number one, who smells of pee and is only wearing one sock? Will it be contestant number two with the pubic hair growing out of his ears and the egg and sauce decoration on his vest? Or will it be contestant number three who says, 'If you pick me, I'll focking fock fock the lot of yez'?

They stared at Patrick and Patrick stared at them.

'Well, get them to at least turn the jukebox off,' said Patrick at last. It was true, he thought sadly. Piers really couldn't organise a piss-up in a brewery.

Ben's main concern was that the audience would wonder why Luke's turn to play never came. But if he held his arm down by his side, the pool table was the perfect height to hide his plaster cast.

He got a bit carried away shooting endless cutaways of coloured balls sliding into the pockets, but they were still more or less on schedule at four o'clock when a man with a large wart in the middle of his forehead decided that it was time to get on his feet and start singing 'Danny Boy' in a surprisingly steady and powerful tenor voice.

'They must have recognised me,' said Danny, pleased.

'Get in there and tell them to keep it down, will you, Tim?' said Jamie.

Tim hesitantly approached the man with the wart, who sang with his shoulders thrown back and his eyes squeezed shut while Tim's nervous 'Excuse me's bounced off him like corn-flakes off a rhinoceros.

'So what is it you're all doing back there?' asked the man who smelled of pee.

'We're making a film.'

'A fillum? For the television now, is it?'

'No, it's a feature. For the cinema. It's called *Brighton Rocks*.'

The man shook his head sadly. 'Ah no,' he sighed. 'I've never seen that.'

That evening, after Liz got back to the hotel, she ran across the road to the statue of the angel which stood at the Hove crossroads with her arms outstretched to the sky. She took out the previous day's offerings to the voodoo spirits – a miniature of brandy and a Ferrero Rocher chocolate that she'd been carrying around in her bag all day – and left them at the angel's base. She was pleased to see that the voodoo spirits, or more likely a tramp, had carried away her offering from the day before which she took as a sign that her spell was being heard. Just as well, because those disgusting herbs she had to burn were making her room smell of cheap toilet cleaner.

At the hotel, she took the lift straight up to the third floor without stopping first at the bar where she knew she was bound to bump into Tex. He had become alarmingly devoted to her and was still blithely unaware that even though she slept with him every night, in her overall battle plan to win back Ben, he was merely cannon-fodder. As she passed her old room 309, she heard the TV was on and decided to knock.

Emma came to the door in her checked blue pyjamas, looking pale and a little unsteady on her feet but pleased to see Liz.

'How are you feeling?' Liz asked.

'Oh much better. Just a bit wobbly when I try to walk around. I haven't been sick at all today, though.'

'Oh I'm so glad. I've been worried about you all day. Is there anything I can get you?'

'No, I'm fine. Ben came by a few minutes ago to see how I was and he's ordered me some soup.'

'Really?' said Liz, her face hardening into a mask. 'How very thoughtful of him.'

'And look – he sent me these as well.' Emma opened the door wider so that Liz could admire the enormous bunch of white lilies standing in a bucket in the corner of her room. 'Aren't they lovely?'

'Beautiful,' said Liz evenly. 'Arum lilies are my favourite.' And Ben wouldn't have known an arum from his elbow before he met me, she thought bitterly. 'I expect he got somebody in the office to send them. He's been very busy today.'

'Oh I forgot to ask – how did it go?'

'The filming? Well, they managed to work around you. Patrick was furious of course and we had no end of problems in the pub because of the schedule being changed, but that's not your fault, so don't blame yourself. Don't even think about it.'

'Oh. OK. I won't,' Emma replied, but as she closed the door she could think of nothing else and climbed back into bed feeling the huge weight of responsibility for messing up the film pressing down on her. No wonder Ben had been so sweet and concerned about her getting better – he couldn't afford to have his film thrown into chaos for another day.

Liz went to her room and immediately pulled the large white box containing her spell kit out from the wardrobe where it was safely hidden away each night. She'd been hoping she was just being paranoid about Emma and Ben but the flowers confirmed it. And ordering her soup! How pathetic! Furiously, she flung out the white sheet and began slapping the incense, voodoo symbols and offerings angrily into place. She sprinkled some of the herbs onto the altar, then put the two candles into position and lit them. Emma's head and neck had already been burned away and she watched with satisfaction as her shoulders and breasts began to melt. It would not be long before Emma was out of her life for good. If only, she thought, there was

213

some way to magically stop Ben suspecting her of making the phone calls.

And at that moment, in the corridor, she heard the voice of the Polish chambermaid and a plan dropped into her head, fully formed. Hurriedly, she blew out the candles, picked up the corners of the white sheet so that all of the voodoo paraphernalia was rolled inside, and hid the entire bundle in the wardrobe again. She opened the door and looked down the corridor just in time to see Magda handing Emma a tray with her bowl of soup on it.

'Magda!' she called out, and was amazed that she could suddenly remember the girl's name. 'Have you got a minute?' Emma's door closed and Magda came to find out what Liz wanted.

'You're just the person I need to see,' Liz told her. 'You know how you said you wanted to be in the film?'

'Yes, I'd love to be in film!' Magda said eagerly.

'Well, we need to record a telephone call. All our equipment is set up in one of the other hotel rooms, but we need somebody to call the number so that the phone will ring. Do you think you can do that?'

'Of course! That is easy!'

Liz wrote down a number on a post-it note and handed it to Magda. 'Now, you'll hear the phone ringing at the other end, but when the phone is answered don't say anything.' She spoke slowly and clearly so that Magda wouldn't be confused.

'I don't say anything?'

'That's right. You have to be absolutely quiet or otherwise the recording will be ruined. Do you understand?'

'I understand. I don't say anything.'

'And then you wait for ten seconds and then you hang up.'

'I hang up,' Magda repeated, keen to get it right.

'Your English is very good,' Liz complimented her.

'Thank you. I call now?'

'No. I have to go there and let them know. Wait three minutes and then call.'

'Three minutes. OK. I have my watch.'

'And then after you've hung up, I want you to call the same number again and do exactly the same thing. Just in case we don't get a good recording the first time.'

Magda nodded, beginning to understand the way the film business worked. 'I understand!'

Liz fished around in the plastic bags, picked out some bras, and on her way out the door, she held up her right hand to Magda with three fingers outstretched. 'Three minutes,' she told her. 'And when you've done it, wait here.'

'OK, Liz!' Magda was used to the film people's unusual requests. Only last week, the producer, Patrick, had asked her if he could have the slivers of used soap that she collected from other people's rooms. At first she hadn't understood and had brought him half a dozen packets of soap from the store room, still wrapped in their red paper. And so he'd had to explain it again. He wanted used soap – it was for set dressing he said – and he gave her a list of room numbers that she was to collect it from. Liz's room was one of them and so was Emma's and the make-up girls' and Poppy's and Flick's. They were all girl's rooms, in fact, apart from Ben's and Danny Parker's. So she collected them all in a wicker basket and Patrick gave her £10 each day.

Liz walked down the corridor and knocked on Ben's door. She was pretty sure that he would still be in his room, because he always liked to have a post-mortem with Patrick and Jamie at the end of the day. Otherwise her plan would be useless. But she was in luck. Ben opened the door almost immediately and she could see Patrick sitting on Ben's bed with his laptop and surrounded by papers. There was an open bottle of red wine on the desk and two glasses had been poured.

'Join us for a drink?' Patrick offered.

'Oh, thanks, but I don't want to disturb you,' she said assuming her most businesslike tone. 'I just wanted to get your opinion on these bras for Sophie Randall.'

Ben glanced at them briefly. He seemed to be in a hurry to get back to his schedule.

'Can I give you a decision when I see what they look like on her?'

Perhaps she'd mistimed it. Maybe three minutes was too long. Ben was going to close the door and her plan would be wasted.

'Of course,' she said. 'But I thought you'd like to have a look at them first.' She handed Ben the first one – a cheap, pretty bra made of flesh-coloured gauze and embroidered with red flowers. He rubbed the fabric thoughtfully between his fingers and Liz knew that she had his undivided attention.

'It's got no underwiring, but it would give you maximum nipple action,' she explained. 'If that's what you're after.'

'Mmm,' said Ben thoughtfully as the phone by his bed started ringing.

'Excuse me a minute,' said Ben.

'Of course,' smiled Liz and breathed a sigh of relief.

'Hello?' Ben was saying. 'Hello? Oh, for fuck's sake!' He slammed the phone down and Liz put on her most concerned face.

'Who was that?' she enquired.

'I dunno,' said Ben. 'Some nutter. It happens all the time.'

'Perhaps it was a Wong number,' joked Patrick stupidly.

'Now there's this balconette,' Liz carried on as if nothing had happened, 'and I've got this in red, light-blue, black and cream.'

Before Ben could voice an opinion, the phone rang again.

Attagirl, Magda, thought Liz.

'Jesus Christ!' shouted Ben, and picked up the phone, absentmindedly stroking the cream balconette bra. 'Who is it?' he demanded. 'Nobody? OK, then fuck off then!'

Liz pulled a face. 'Maybe it's some kind of electrical fault,' she suggested. 'Or kids. Playing around. I read about a cat once that dialled Australia.'

'Yeah maybe,' said Ben, but now he was confused. It obviously wasn't Liz making these anonymous phone calls, so then who was it?

'So which do you prefer?' Liz asked.

'Look, can this wait?' Ben handed the bra back to her. 'Patrick's talking to Sophie's agent.'

'We want her to do the scene topless,' Patrick chipped in.

'Really?' said Liz. 'Oh well, in that case, there's no point bothering with these now then, is there? Have a good night.' She went back to her room, mission triumphantly accomplished, her perfect alibi established, and thinking about the way Ben's fingers had rubbed against the lacy fabric.

'Well done. That was absolutely perfect!' she congratulated Magda. 'But you mustn't tell anyone that you've done this.'

Magda was crestfallen. She wanted to tell everyone that she'd been in a movie.

'Why not?'

'Because you're not in the union. Do you understand "union"?'

Magda nodded.

'Of course you do, you're Polish. Well, you'd be in the most awful trouble if anyone found out we'd employed you. That's why I'm paying you in cash.' Liz took a £20 note out of her purse and gave it to Magda. 'Tell nobody — not even the other people on the film. Do you understand?'

'I understand.' Patrick's soap was a secret too. She was good at keeping secrets.

'Good.' Liz was sure she could rely on Magda. She was smart and terrified.

'Can I tell my parents?' Magda asked.

'Where do they live?'

'In Poland.'

Liz thought about it and decided that the probability of her deception getting all the way from Poland back to Ben's ears in Brighton was low enough to risk. 'OK. You can tell your parents.'

Magda looked so happy, Liz was afraid she might kiss her. She hustled her out of the room as quickly as she could so that she could put on the bra with the rose embroidery and feel the second-hand imprint of Ben's fingers close to her heart.

twenty

As Danny queued impatiently for his full English breakfast, he spotted Stacey walking towards him, looking ridiculously hot in an Indian print singlet top with no bra and tight black clam-diggers. She hadn't even shaved under her arms and he was tormented and affronted by the tiny black tufts that peeked out each time she moved her arms. Now was his chance to put that stuck-up dyke in her place. He nudged Alex in the ribs. 'Watch this.'

'Hey Stacey,' he called out. 'Do you know the difference between a lesbian and a letterbox?'

Stacey smiled. 'Yes, I do, thanks,' she said sweetly and carried on walking.

Alex thumped Danny hard. 'Crashed and burned, mate, crashed and burned!' he laughed.

The first shot on Tuesday's call sheet couldn't have been simpler. The camera was set up on the pavement right outside the hotel to shoot Jasmine waiting on the seafront. Eddie would drive up on his scooter, Jasmine would hop on the back, and they'd drive off. But by eight-thirty when they were ready to start shooting, a persistently annoying drizzle had started to fall and Ben, Hugo, Pete and Jamie stood in the hotel bar peering doubtfully out the window.

'What do you reckon? Shall we do Turpin's scene first?'

'This is going to blow over,' said Hugo confidently. 'Give it twenty minutes. The forecast said sunny spells.' But he was pulling on his waterproof trousers as he spoke.

Emma and Danny were all made-up and ready to roll, sitting in the bar drinking tea and reading the papers.

'What'll happen if it doesn't stop raining?' asked Emma.

'I guess we get wet,' said Danny sarcastically.

'No, I don't want to shoot your scene in the rain,' said Ben. 'It's meant to look like a picture postcard, not a warning to shipping. How are you feeling today anyway, Emma?'

'Oh I'm much better,' she told him. 'And thank you again for the flowers. I told Jason that you'd sent me white lilies and he said that on *Shelby Square* when you're sick, they just shoot all your scenes from behind.'

Ben realised that he was starting to get a little sick himself of the way Emma managed to bring Jason into every conversation. 'Well, if you need to rest at any time,' he said, 'just let me know – I don't want you to be overdoing it.'

After half an hour when the rain showed no sign of easing up – it had got heavier, if anything – Ben decided to cut his losses and shoot Turpin's scene first. He needed three shots – one long-shot of Turpin on the seafront making a call on his mobile where he was sure he wouldn't be overheard, a medium close-up of Turpin on the phone and a close-up of the phone showing the name he was dialling. Ben felt a little twinge of guilt about asking Ronald Gasch to work in the rain – it seemed a bit disrespectful – but he didn't have much choice.

'Let the bastard drown,' was Patrick's professional opinion.

Orlando held a large, striped umbrella over Ronald's head while Will measured his focuses and made a discreet chalk mark on the pavement at the spot where Ronald should stop.

'And how are you today?' asked Ronald genially. 'Are you having a nice time in Brighton?'

Will was taken aback. 'Yes, thanks,' he stammered. It was the first time since the film had started that Ronald had spoken to him. It was the first time that he'd ever seen him smile.

Phil handed Ronald his mobile phone with the names and

numbers already programmed in, Ryan took up a camera position over Ronald's shoulder, and Hugo stepped in to take a light reading.

'What's that exposure like, guvnor?' asked Phil innocently.

Hugo consulted his light meter. 'Positively indecent!' he announced loudly. The pair of them had been working on this gag ever since they'd found out about Ronald Gasch's arrest and everybody laughed.

Ronald just smiled. He hadn't stopped thinking about that night and how exhilarated he had felt. Being bundled into a police van, having his fingerprints taken, and knowing he would have to go to court in a few months time and have his name dragged through the mud – none of that mattered because Marianne had sent him a sign.

He'd been overcome by a desire to go skinny-dipping, but he'd left his clothes too close to the water's edge and they must have been washed away, because when he came out he couldn't find them again.

And then, as he tried to make his way back to the hotel, he'd found it waiting for him. At the feet of a towering angel, her mighty stone wings lifted skywards, there it was – a tiny bottle of Hine, his favourite brandy, and a single chocolate wrapped in gold. He'd known at once it was a gift from Marianne – a message to let him know that she was still with him, that she forgave him for not being able to save her, and telling him that life was for living. She wanted him to be happy and what message could be more wonderful than that? He'd tried to explain all that to the policewoman who arrested him, but she hadn't seemed at all interested.

By the time they were ready to shoot, the rain was chucking it down. Orlando whipped away Ronald's umbrella and waterproof jacket at the last moment. On 'Action', Ronald walked swiftly along the front, stopping at the precise spot where Will had made his mark, even though the rain had washed the chalk away. He reached into his pocket, scrolled through the numbers on his mobile phone, had a brief conversation with the party on the other end and then he put the phone back into his pocket and smiled. The rain was running down his face and neck, into the back of his jacket and then Ronald Gasch did an extraordinary thing. He lifted up his arms, raised his face to the heavens and he laughed.

Nobody watching him said a word. It was ten seconds before Ben remembered he was supposed to call cut. 'Check the gate,' he told Will.

'Move in for the close-up?' asked Jamie.

'No need,' said Ben. 'That's the shot. That was fucking A.'

The rain carried on all morning so they took the camera up to the top floor of the hotel and shot some general views of Brighton In The Rain out of a bedroom window. Ben knew he'd probably never use these shots, but with no interior locations he could move to, he was screwed. Then typically, the moment they sat down for lunch, it stopped raining.

Ben hardly spoke through lunch because he was having nightmares about the next scene. Two of his actors on a scooter, on a main road, and Danny driving? He could hardly bear to look.

'For obvious reasons, I only want to do this once,' he said to Ryan, when they eventually assembled outside. 'So take as much rehearsal time as you need.'

To Ben's surprise, Danny was completely at home on the scooter. He rode up, stopped, Emma put on her helmet, hopped on the back, and he rode off again, exactly the way Ben wanted him to. The only problem was that the camera missed the whole thing because a large white lorry drove past, blocking the view at the crucial moment. They'd recce'd this location weeks ago and nobody had considered how busy this road would be at the height of summer.

'We'll have to hold the traffic,' said Ben, and Georgina and Flick were despatched with walkie talkies to the pedestrian crossings in either direction to turn the traffic lights red.

It called for split-second timing but the gods seemed to be smiling on them. The traffic came to a halt, Danny rode up and Emma climbed on, just as two girls wheeling suitcases walked right in front of the camera.

'Who was stopping pedestrians?' Ben wanted to know.

'Georgina was from that side,' Jamie explained, 'but she's gone to do the traffic lights.'

'Well put somebody else on it! I don't want anybody walking across this shot!'

'I'll do it,' offered Billy, who didn't have any boom duties.

Saskia fluffed up Emma's hair, which was getting squashed by the motorcycle helmet, Danny drove out of shot, and Georgina and Flick pressed the pedestrian crossing buttons simultaneously, ignoring the furious motorists whose journeys were being delayed.

As Danny began his approach, Tim stopped two Japanese girls who giggled and covered their faces with their hands when they saw the camera. And then, crossing the road from the beach and coming towards him, Tim saw a jogger – a middle-aged man with a sweatband around his balding head, lycra shorts, and a body that was one long dogged sinew.

'Sorry, do you mind,' Tim whispered, 'we're making a film—'

'Sod you,' said the jogger. He'd had a disastrous marathon that year, being struck down by diarrhoea just as he turned towards Canary Wharf, and he was determined that nothing was going to get in the way of his training schedule this year – not rain, not snow, not bleeding toe-nails, and certainly not some jumped-up little twerp with a two-way radio. He kept on running.

Tim could see Danny approaching the spot where Emma waited. He could see the jogger approaching the camera. He could see his film career ending as suddenly as it had begun. So he did the only thing he could – he ran after the jogger, launched himself at his back and rugby-tackled him to the ground.

'Cut!' yelled Ben, and then turned to see Tim staggering

wildly into the hotel's ornamental shrubs as the jogger got to his feet and punched him in the nose.

Patrick sighed wearily as he took out his mobile phone to phone his solicitor. Perhaps he'd get a bulk discount for taking on an indecent exposure and an assault charge at the same time.

'Well considering the weather, today didn't go too badly at all,' said Hugo as they all got into the minibus that night.

'But it must rain all the time when you're making films,' said Emma, quite forgetting that she was supposed to have made a couple of films herself. 'What do you do if it rains so much you can't shoot at all?'

'Ah, well,' said Hugo, 'what you do then, is get in an animator and you do all those missing scenes as cartoons using the actors' voiceovers.'

'No!' Emma sounded amazed.

'Oh yeah, it happens all the time,' said Phil. 'You know *Who Framed Roger Rabbit?* That was supposed to be all live action, but they had terrible storms in L.A. so they had to do half of it with animation. It was just a stroke of luck they'd shot all Bob Hoskins's scenes before the weather got really bad.'

Ben could see Hugo preparing to launch into another story – perhaps about how *Bambi* was the result of flash floods – and shook his head at him. It wasn't fair the way they always wound Emma up like that.

'They're pulling your leg,' he told her, and he was surprised when she just laughed.

'Oh I know that,' she whispered back, 'but I didn't want to hurt their feelings.' And she gave Ben the smile that he'd seen the first time she walked into audition for him – the smile that made him feel like he was the only man in the room – a smile that implied that under that sweet, kittenish exterior was a young woman just longing to be corrupted. Did she use that smile for everybody, he wondered now, or was it just for him? He realised that he badly wanted to find out. He had a feeling there was more to Miss Emma Buckley than he'd realised.

*

When Liz got back to her room that night, she found a sheet of blue paper had been shoved under the door bearing a photo-copied message: 'Welcome drink tonight for Sophie Randall, Blanch House, 8 p.m. Ben.'

Liz decided she'd wear the black dress she'd bought for Zoe Langridge. It would be such a shame to waste it and it had the desired effect when she walked into Blanch House an hour and a half later and felt all eyes turn towards her. Annoyingly, they all immediately turned back again towards Sophie Randall who was wearing shiny jeans, a gold top with a plunging neckline and no bra. The boys in the band had formed a semi-circle around her and Sophie was giving the impression of being fascinated by their self-important chatter, although Liz could tell immediately from the faraway glaze in her eyes that she was as high as a kite.

It only took Liz's radar another second to discern that, apart from Sophie, she was the only girl in their party. Ronald, Harry and Arthur, in fact all the cast, were there – with one notable exception. Emma was nowhere to be seen. And neither was Tex. In fact, where were the rest of the crew? Was she, God forbid, unfashionably early? She sat down on the end of the sofa beside Patrick and poured herself a glass of wine from the open bottle on the table.

'What are you doing here?' he asked – rather rudely, Liz thought.

'I was invited,' she said.

'Really? Ben said it was cast only. He must have made an exception in your case.'

'And yours, I see,' she pointed out.

But Ben was also looking at her with a slightly puzzled expression and Liz realised at once what must have happened. Whoever had slipped the invitation under her door couldn't have known that she and Emma had switched rooms. Well, she was here now and she was damned if she was going to slink out with her tail between her legs. She'd always believed that attack was the best form of defence, so she marched straight over to Ben who was talking to Harvey and Arthur, and waved her invitation under his nose as proof that she wasn't gate-crashing.

'One of your half-wit production elves delivered this to my room by mistake,' she told him crossly. 'If I'd known it was cast only I wouldn't have wasted my time. I'm just going to have one drink and go.'

Ben felt awkward. He'd gradually come to realise that all his worries about working with Liz had been a huge overreaction on his part. She'd been doing a fantastic job with the costumes even though she was hugely overstretched with just Orlando to help her, and she'd never once shown any sign that she still held a grudge about the way he'd ended their relationship. He felt a little foolish now for imagining that she might still have feelings for him, and for suspecting her of making those anonymous phonecalls. 'Well you're here now,' he said generously. 'You're more than welcome to stay.'

'Really? Oh well, you've twisted my arm.'

She saw Ben's eyes flicker towards the door and wondered if he was waiting for Emma to arrive. She smiled to herself, knowing that he'd be very disappointed if he was, because Emma was probably already tucked up in bed with slices of cucumbers on her eyes.

'So I see Sophie Randall's made quite a hit with our boys,' she observed. 'What's she like?'

Ben rolled his eyes. 'A nightmare. A complete space cadet. I gave her some additional dialogue for her scene tomorrow, but I don't think she had the faintest idea what I was talking about.'

'Oh, she'll be fine,' said Liz soothingly and was relieved that, despite appearances, she wouldn't have any serious competition from Sophie where Ben was concerned. 'After all,' Liz continued with growing confidence. 'She can't be any worse than that guy with the moustache, can she?'

'What guy with the moustache?' Ben looked blank.

'You remember,' Liz prompted. 'That commercial we did for pasta sauces? All he had to do was stir the saucepan, look at his dog and then look at the saucepan again.'

'Oh my God, yeah, you're right.' Ben shook his head and laughed at the memory. 'What a disaster. I mean, we can look back and laugh about it now – but at the time . . .' Suddenly he remembered that had been the shoot where he'd bunked off with Liz at lunchtime to have sex in one of the empty offices downstairs and they'd got locked in the stairwell because they didn't know the security pin code to get back in. It was half an hour before anyone heard them knocking.

'Yeah, we can look back and laugh now,' agreed Liz, feeling a dizzy electrical charge as her arm brushed against Ben's for an instant. 'Can you feel it too?' she wanted to ask him. 'Do you know how much I miss you? Do you know how much I still want you? Can't we try again?' but all that would have to wait. The time still wasn't right and she had long ago learned how to be patient.

'How long did Moustache Man take to get that right?' Ben was still wondering. 'Two hours, was it? He made Danny Parker look like Robert De Niro.' The words were out before he could take them back.

'Ooh, Ben! I can't believe what I'm hearing,' Liz teased him. 'Don't tell me your big star is turning out to be a bit of a dis-appointment?'

Ben lowered his voice. 'Truthfully? He's doing my head in. He whispers. He never knows any of his lines. If he hits his mark, it's purely by accident. His attitude stinks and I'm beginning to suspect that he doesn't actually have any talent at all. You know he insists on being called Eddie, don't you?'

Liz was delighted to see that she'd earned Ben's trust enough to be taken into his confidence. All her hard work and white magic were starting to pay off.

'Patrick was right,' Ben continued. 'I should have made the band a three-piece – and written Danny Parker out.'

Liz laughed and Ben excused himself, saying he needed to make a phonecall.

'Of course,' said Liz, feeling pleased with what she'd accomplished. She'd made him laugh. She'd made him remember. She'd made him confide in her. The seed had been planted. She saw Sophie slide off her barstool and sashay over to the ladies so she joined the boys at the bar. Giles's and Luke's faces were screwed up as though they were deep in concentration.

'Hi, boys,' Liz greeted them. 'What's up?'

'It was her, wasn't it?' said Luke, watching Sophie walk across the bar.

'What was her?' asked Liz.

'Sophie Randall,' explained Giles, fanning his face. 'She farted.'

Ben stepped outside into the street and called the hotel on his mobile. It was already ten o'clock. Where on earth was Emma? He suddenly realised that she was the only person he wanted to see tonight.

'Could you put me through to Emma Buckley's room?' he asked.

The phone rang and rang and there was no answer – not surprisingly because the hotel still had Emma's room number down as 302 which was now Liz's room. And Liz was in the bar, not twenty feet away from him. But Ben wasn't to know that.

'She might have gone for her walk,' the receptionist suggested. 'I usually see her go out last thing at night, but it's still a bit early for her. Do you want me to tell her you called if I see her?'

'No, it's OK.' Ben felt strangely disappointed for a second. It occurred to him that Emma might be deliberately boycotting the evening because it was in Sophie's honour. He hadn't thought Emma would be so petty, but she was an actress and he knew how touchy they could get about things like that. Perhaps, he thought as he went back inside, he should try and get Sophie and Danny together for five minutes and talk them through their scene tomorrow. But then he saw Sophie sitting on Harvey's lap, knocking back her fifth After Shock with a glassy look in her eye, and he decided against it. He pushed the door open again and started walking back towards the hotel.

twenty-one

It was one o'clock in the morning and Liz was wide awake, her ear pressed hard against the cold wall between the corridor and Ben's room. All her earlier success of the evening had been wiped out the moment she'd looked out of her window and seen Ben and Emma walking back along the seafront together.

Immediately, she'd gone out into the corridor, walking up and down so she could accidentally bump into Emma and find out what the hell she was playing at. When Emma didn't appear, she decided they must have stopped in the bar for a drink and she'd gone downstairs, rehearsing the friendly smile she'd wear when she spotted them. Except they weren't there. There was just Pete the gaffer and the two riggers Bradley and Shane at their usual table where they had succumbed once again to the lure of the hotel's steak and kidney pie rather than cut into their valuable drinking time by venturing out to a restaurant. The brown oven-proof dishes, still garnished with their forlorn sprigs of parsley had not yet been cleared away.

'Ah, the lovely Liz's come to join us at last,' beamed Pete, and he began shifting his chair to make room for her. But Liz was already heading back up the stairs. If they weren't downstairs and they weren't in Emma's room – then they must be in Ben's room.

A few steps from his door she paused, scared to go any closer because of the squeaky floorboard she knew was there. The door fit too snugly for her to tell if there was a light on in his room or not. So she pressed her head against the wall and listened. She thought she could make out voices, or could she? It could have been the TV. Then she heard a girl's laugh and recognised it at once as Emma's. Once she'd tuned in to the sound of her voice she could hear their conversation continuing as a low mumble, occasionally punctuated by giggles. It was more than she could bear. Emma had no right to be in there. Liz had worked so hard to become the kind of person Ben would fall back in love with. But what chance was she going to get with that bimbo muscling in on her act?

She stood in the corridor, listening, ready at any second to leap away and pretend she was just walking back to her room, should somebody come past and see her. But nobody did. Her ear and her cheek were numbed by the chilly plaster of the wall and still she didn't have a plan. Could she humiliate Emma by phoning Ben's room and demanding that she leave? No, she was cleverer than that. A lot cleverer. She'd think of something.

Ben was still a little surprised to see Emma in his room and even more surprised at how comfortable it felt having her there. If only she'd stop going on about her boyfriend.

He'd left Blanch House and got back to the hotel just as Emma came downstairs wrapped up to go for a walk – exactly as the receptionist had predicted.

'Want some company?' he asked. 'I was just going out for a stroll myself', and he congratulated himself on his impeccable timing. But what he hadn't expected was that the reason Emma took these walks was, as she explained to him, because she got a better reception on her mobile on the seafront than she did in the hotel. As soon as they'd crossed the road, she dialled Jason's number, and he'd had to endure five minutes of Emma telling Jason how much she missed him, and how she couldn't wait to see him again.

Ben felt rather annoyed. He'd been prepared to overlook Jason's existence in his quest to get closer to the mysterious Miss Buckley, but it was a little difficult listening to Emma gush over him like this.

'So, how's your day been?' Emma was asking and for the next five minutes, all Ben could hear was Emma's side of the conversation which consisted of the occasional 'Oh really?' and 'That's great!' and once, 'Well, that doesn't seem very fair. I'm sure he didn't mean it like that.'

Eventually, Jason's rant ended and Emma said, 'Well, I've had a lovely day. I've been getting rides on a scooter. The director's right here. Want to say hi?'

And then Ben had been forced to go through a ridiculous performance of making small-talk with Jason, who wanted to know if there would be a part for him in his next film.

'Give me a fucking break,' Ben wanted to say. 'I haven't even finished this one yet.' But he'd said he'd certainly keep him in mind and asked him, absurdly, because he couldn't think of anything else to say, what the weather was like in Sheffield before finally handing the phone back to Emma.

And then he'd had to put up with another five minutes of Emma telling Jason all over again, how much she missed him – just in case he hadn't been paying attention the first time, thought Ben bitterly – and a ridiculous few minutes where Emma kept saying 'Bye' but instead of hanging up carried on chattering. Ben was shivering now and wished he'd brought a jacket.

Finally, Emma hung up and put the phone in her pocket. 'Oh, I can't wait to see him,' she sighed and gave a little skip of excitement.

'How come you didn't come to Blanch House tonight?' Ben asked.

'What was at Blanch House?'

'I invited all the cast for a drink. Didn't you get my note?' He thought it best not to mention that the drinks were to welcome Sophie Randall.

Emma shook her head. 'Oh, I wondered where everyone was! What a shame! I've got a day off tomorrow as well, so I could have stayed up late and everything!'

'Well, you didn't miss much,' Ben admitted. 'We'll do it again another time. Shall we walk back?' He was freezing.

'OK. Do you know what I'd really love right now? A great big mug of hot chocolate!' She looked around, hoping that a café would suddenly materialise, but they'd walked in the wrong direction, away from the pier, and everywhere was in darkness.

'So it sounds like it's pretty serious with you and Jason, then?' Ben asked casually.

'Oh yeah, I think so. I know he's the one.'

'The one what?'

'The one I want to spend the rest of my life with, silly!' Emma laughed and gave his arm a playful shove.

'You're not engaged, are you?' asked Ben, alarmed.

'No, not yet,' said Emma. 'But it's only a matter of time.'

Ben sighed. Maybe he was barking up the wrong tree, after all. He changed the subject and talked about the film all the way back to the hotel. But then, as he pulled the heavy, old-fashioned lift door closed behind them, he couldn't help noticing the involuntary way her pupils widened nervously, and he chalked it up to sexual tension.

Perhaps he was still in with a chance after all. Ben knew that to get to her room, Emma would have to pass his room first, which was just around the corner from the lift. To say he'd planned it would be an exaggeration, but when they got to his door he realised this was the reason why he'd gone for a walk with her in the first place.

'Do you still fancy a hot chocolate?' he asked as he took out his key. 'Because I'm pretty sure I've got a couple of packets of Marshmallow Melts tucked away somewhere.'

Emma's face lit up at the magic word 'chocolate'. 'Oh yeah!' she said, and Ben smiled to himself. He hadn't lost his touch.

Emma immediately took charge, filling up the kettle from the bathroom tap. 'Does your shower work properly?' she called out to him.

'No,' he admitted, grabbing the dirty socks and boxer shorts off the floor and hiding them in his suitcase. 'I think the thermostat's broken.'

'Mine too!' Emma came back into the bedroom, plugged in the kettle, and inspected the state of the cups.

'I'd better wash these as well,' she told him.' I saw a TV programme once that said people who work in hotels just spit in the cups and then wipe them with their finger.'

'I wish you hadn't told me that,' said Ben.

'Have you got any washing-up liquid?'

'No.'

'I'll just use a bit of shampoo instead, then.'

Ben could hear the cups clinking in the sink and remembered that he didn't even like hot chocolate.

'Ben, why do you use shampoo for oily hair?' Emma called out.

'Um, because I've got oily hair?' he suggested.

'No you haven't. You should use normal shampoo or you'll strip all your natural oils out.' She shook the cups over the basin.

'Thanks for the tip,' he said, amused. 'Any particular brand?'

'Well, personally, I like Clairol Herbal Essences.' She leaned over towards him so that her hair fell in front of his face. 'Feel that,' she told him.

Ben stroked her hair, thinking that seducing Emma was going to be child's play. Her hair smelt deliciously of roses and chamomile and he wanted to bury his face in it. But then Emma stood up again and threw her hair back.

'See?' she said triumphantly. 'Soft, isn't it? I'll lend some.' Immediately she turned her attention to the instructions for making Marshmallow Melts. 'Now . . . do you have to add milk to this as well?' She ripped open the sachets, emptied them into the cups and poured on the hot water. 'Jason always puts Scotch in his hot chocolate, but I think that's just spoiling it, don't you?'

Ben had just remembered the Scotch in the mini-bar and had been about to suggest this himself, but he seized the chance to put Jason down. 'That's a criminal waste of hot chocolate, if you ask me,' he agreed.

'Exactly!' said Emma. She handed him a cup and bounced onto the bed beside him, the way she used to bounce on her brothers' beds when she was little. Ben reminded her a bit of her middle brother, Mark, the nice one who became a vet and used to take her to school every morning on the back of his motorbike. It felt nice to have a big brother again.

'Ooh, springy!' she giggled. 'Mine's like a rock!'

'Did you learn all about shampoo when you were doing that hairdressing film?' asked Ben. He leaned back so that his arm rested on the bed just behind her.

Emma knew that this was the moment that she should tell Ben the truth – that there was no film about hairdressing. 'Sort of,' she admitted, and began phrasing her confession in her mind. How should she start?

'Is that where you learned to do your famous head massages as well?' Ben asked.

'Actually, it was,' said Emma. 'Would you like me to give you one now?'

Ben bit his lip to stop himself from stating the obvious and replied with an equally innocent: 'Yes, please.'

Emma kneeled on the bed behind him and began gently kneading his temples and the top of his skull.

'Oh, that's fantastic,' he sighed, melting under her touch. 'I adore having my hair played with.'

Emma decided to wait until he was properly relaxed and then she'd tell him everything. She made little circles with her fingers on his forehead and could feel the tension slipping away. If she gave him a really good head massage maybe he wouldn't be angry at her for lying to him.

'So this Jason,' said Ben after a while, deciding that all he had to do was talk Emma out of her childish infatuation. 'How long did you say you've been going out with him?'

'Nearly a year,' said Emma proudly.

'But you can't get to know somebody in a year.'

'Of course you can!' Emma laughed, expertly dragging her

fingers up the back of Ben's neck. Her clients always loved it when she did that.

'Oh, that's amazing,' moaned Ben, leaning back against her. 'But you can't *know* that he's the one. What if you're wrong?'

'But I'm not wrong.'

'How do you know that?'

'Well, you just know, don't you? I mean, you must have met somebody and just known that they were the one for you.'

Ben thought about it. 'Actually,' he said, 'I don't think I have.'

'But that's terrible!' Emma gasped, forgetting all about her confession for a moment. 'Are you saying you've never been in love?'

'Oh, I've been in love, but it doesn't last. I've never had that feeling that this is it and this is the person I want to spend the rest of my life with.'

'Well, I'm sure you will one day.' Years at the salon had taught her one thing: that when people are single they always think they'll never find love again. Emma considered it an essential part of her job description to reassure them that they would. 'Just like I know I want to spend the rest of my life with Jason.'

'But how can you say that?' demanded Ben. 'There are thousands of other blokes out there you haven't been out with and you might love one of them even more.'

Emma laughed. 'I don't want to meet thousands of other blokes! One's enough for me, thanks very much.'

'But you're so young. How can you even think about settling down?'

'Well, if I took your advice and met these thousands of other blokes, I'd be ninety by the time I'd be ready to settle down. And so would they. Or dead.'

'Well, I envy you.'

'That's silly. You must have thousands of girls after you.'

'Well, not thousands . . .' he laughed modestly, pleased that Emma had noticed what a fantastic catch he was. Tall, good-looking, not badly off, devastatingly charming, silver Golf. 'Maybe hundreds.'

'And what's wrong with them? Out of all those hundreds, hasn't there even been one who's made you happy?'

'Oh, they all made me happy. Just not for very long.'

'What's the longest you've ever been out with somebody?'

'I don't know. Maybe a year. Maybe less. Sometimes a lot less. Can you do my shoulders as well?' He sighed again as Emma's hands slid underneath his collar. Any minute now, he told himself, he'd turn around and make his move.

'Well, I think it's very sad if all your life you're just going to keep going from one girl to another looking for someone who's going to make you happy all the time. Why don't you try making *them* happy for a change?'

'I just don't know if two people can be happy together.'

'Well, Jason and I are very happy.'

'Have you ever cheated on him?' If she said yes, he was definitely in.

'Of course not!' Emma scoffed at the very idea. 'I'd never cheat on him. I couldn't. I love him!'

Ben frowned. This was going to be more difficult than he thought. 'But doesn't it frighten you,' he persisted, 'the idea of getting married and never having sex with anyone else ever again?'

'No. Why should it?'

'It's just so *boring*.'

'Maybe you're not doing it right,' she laughed, and as she dug her fingers deeper into his neck he was positive she was flirting with him.

'Are you making fun of me?' he asked.

'Maybe.' Emma giggled. 'So, what are you saying? That you'll never get married?'

Ben thought about it. 'No, I will get married one day, I suppose. I mean everybody gets married, don't they? But not until I've directed my first film.'

'Congratulations. That means you've only got a month to go.'

Suddenly, Ben realised Emma was right. He'd been using his first film as a landmark, putting off everything else in his life until he'd achieved that particular goal. What was he supposed to do now? Get married? Or get a new goal? It was a disturbing thought.

Emma paused. 'Sorry, am I hurting you? You've gone very tense.'

'No, don't stop,' Ben begged. 'It feels fantastic.' He loved the way she was rolling his flesh under her fingers – but it was taking him longer than he'd anticipated to bring Emma around to his way of thinking. She hadn't even taken her shoes off yet.

'Maybe what you should do,' Emma continued, 'is find someone who you have really great sex with so it'll never get boring. If you can find someone like that.'

'I'd love to,' said Ben sincerely, thinking that now was his opportunity. And so he could have kicked himself when he heard himself add, 'There was somebody like that once.'

'And what happened to her?' asked Emma.

Ben didn't get the chance to answer because the air was suddenly rocked by a noise louder than anything they had ever heard before – a terrifying electronic roar right there with them in the room, that sounded like the world had come to an end.

'What is it?' Emma screamed, clamping her hands over her ears. 'Is it a bomb?'

'I think it's the fire alarm!' Ben yelled back. 'Let's get out of here!'

The noise followed them out into the corridor where doors were being flung open and the occupants of the hotel, in varying stages of shock and undress, were trying to follow the green signs pointing to the fire exit.

Most of them had been fast asleep when they'd been woken by the wailing of the alarm and in the dark and confusion they'd grabbed whatever clothes they could. Patrick was just in his boxer shorts and his lip was bleeding. He had leapt out of bed in fright, tripped over the waste-paper bin and fallen into the trouser press. He was clutching his laptop and a briefcase and a small wrap of coke.

'My computer!' remembered Ben, and raced back to his room to rescue it.

'Ben! No! Save yourself!' screamed Emma.

'Well I can't smell any smoke,' said Patrick as he started down the stairs. 'This had better be a big fucking fire.'

Downstairs in reception, the night porter, who was unused to dealing with humans in bulk, had been startled out of his slumber by the alarm and then confronted with the even more shocking sight of hotel guests crowding around his desk demanding information. He hadn't had any previous dealing with film crews but he disliked this lot intensely. They weren't like other guests who went through the motions of being polite. The film people demanded things – lots of things – and acted as though the staff, the hotel and the entire county of East Sussex had been put on this earth solely for their convenience, as though making their film was the only thing that could possibly matter. They acted like they owned you, even though they were paying 30 per cent less than the other hotel guests who arrived individually, in pairs, or in small, manageable family groups, and who had the decency when they were woken by a fire alarm to go out into the street and shiver quietly in their thin nylon dressing gowns and not bother anybody.

'Is it a fire?'

'Where's the fire brigade?'

'I suppose you realise we have to get up at 5 a.m., don't you?'

'Has anybody called the fire brigade?'

The film people swarmed around his desk like angry wasps. He held up his hand as though to swat them. 'There's nothing to worry about,' he announced. 'It's a false alarm. You can all go back to bed.'

'How do you know it's a false alarm? Have you called the fire brigade?'

'I've phoned the fire brigade and told them it's a false alarm and there's no need for them to come out.'

'We could all burn in our beds!'

'Why should we take your word for it?'

'I refuse to go back to my room until the fire brigade give us the all clear.'

'Ooh yeah, let's see some firemen,' squealed Tracey. She was standing with Saskia and Bex and their short satin dressing gowns in Opal Fruit shades of orange, lemon and strawberry made a mouthwatering combination.

'I can show you the light in the office that came on telling me what set off the alarm,' the porter told them. 'Somebody opened the fire door on the ground floor – that's all it was.'

There was a roar of protest from the throng at the realisation they had been cheated out of an honest-to-goodness fire.

'It was probably somebody coming in drunk,' the porter explained.

'Well, don't look at me,' protested Bradley, the rigger, seeing heads swivel accusingly in his direction. 'I was fast asleep!'

'It happens all the time,' the porter continued, but instead of making things better, this information only made the mob angrier.

'Is it really necessary for that God-awful shrieking to go off in all the rooms at one o'clock in the morning just because somebody has opened the wrong door?' demanded Patrick, angrier than Ben had ever seen him.

'You want to do a head-count, mate,' suggested Hugo. 'You've probably killed off half your guests with heart attacks.' He nodded over at two terrified old biddies who were still making their shaky way down to reception, one painful stair at a time, clinging to the banister with both hands. 'It's all right, ladies,' he called over to them. 'False alarm. Don't go breaking a hip.'

Even Liz had been surprised at how loud the fire alarm sounded in the stillness of the night.

Sometimes the best plans were the simplest ones, she thought. 'Fire Exit only,' the sign had read. 'This door is alarmed.' All it had taken from her was one gentle push.

She'd been the first one to come downstairs looking appropriately startled and had waited patiently on the corner settee, from where she was able to see Ben and Emma come down, still, thank God, wearing their street clothes. She'd obviously intervened just in the nick of time. All she had to do now was make sure they went back to their own rooms – alone – and now that everybody else was awake, that should be simple.

'So where were you tonight?' Tex asked her.

'Party,' she told him, lighting a cigarette. 'I thought you'd be there.' She didn't add that she was awfully glad that he hadn't been. She turned away, caught Emma's eye and patted the settee beside her. Emma left Ben's side and came dutifully trotting over. Tex, sensing he'd been dismissed, went outside to see if he could spot any smoke.

'Are you all right, Liz?' Emma asked sitting down. 'Wasn't that the most terrifying thing you've ever heard? I couldn't work out what it was.'

'Did it wake you up?' said Liz.

'No, I was still awake.'

'Well, we might as well go back to bed,' said Liz. 'I don't think this hotel's going to burn down tonight.' They got up and Liz went to press the button for the lift.

'Do you mind if we take the stairs?' asked Emma.

'I'm sure it's safe to use the lift now,' Liz assured her.

'Oh I know, it's just that after being shut up in the cupboard the other day, I think I'm starting to get a bit claustrophobic.'

'Really? You poor thing. How awful for you,' said Liz sympathetically. 'Did you tell Ben?'

'Oh no, it's nothing really.'

'So what were you doing awake at this hour?' Liz asked casually.

'Ben and I were having a hot chocolate.'

'Oh how sweet! How are you two getting along?'

'Really well. He's not at all what I expected a director to be like.'

'He's not like James Cameron, then?'

'James who?'

'James Cameron. Angela told me you'd worked on *Titanic*.'

Emma blushed. She really couldn't keep up the pretence any longer. They were alone now on the third floor landing. 'Listen, I might as well tell you the truth. I was never in *Titanic*.'

Liz paused. She wanted to make sure there was no mistake. 'But I thought Angela said—'

'I know. I lied. At the audition. I knew I wouldn't get the part if they thought this was my first film.'

'But it's not your first film. What about that other thing – *Hairdressing*?'

Emma shrugged.

'You mean you weren't in that either?' asked Liz.

'There's no such film,' Emma admitted. 'I made it up.'

'No!' gasped Liz, amazed that this priceless nugget of information had just fallen right into her lap. 'Well, good for you!'

'You don't think I'm awful?'

'Oh God no! Most actors would sell their own grandmothers to get a break. Who cares about a tiny white lie?'

'You won't tell anyone, will you?' begged Emma. 'I was trying to tell Ben tonight, but then the fire alarm went off and I didn't get a chance. I'd hate him to hear it from anyone else.'

'Darling, my lips are sealed.'

Emma breathed a sigh of relief. 'Gosh, I'm so glad I told you. I've been carrying this secret around with me for weeks and it's been killing me. I feel so much better now.'

'Well, I'm glad. 'Don't you give it another thought.' They were outside Emma's door. 'Sleep tight!' She kissed Emma on the cheek.

'Night, Liz.' Emma returned the kiss. 'See you tomorrow. And thanks.'

Liz waited outside Emma's room until she heard the lights being switched off and the squeak of Emma's bed, and then carried on around the corridor to her own room.

On the white sheet on the floor, she had already spread out her altar and now she used her cigarette to light the straight red candle, the incense and the remains of the wax effigy that she had been burning now for seven days. In just two more days, she thought, with satisfaction, Emma would be out of the picture.

twenty-two

By noon the next day it was all over the unit that Sophie Randall would be doing her scene that afternoon completely starkers. The great smell of testosterone hung heavy in the air.

'Well, surprise, surprise, we won't be needing these then,' said Orlando huffily, and he moved the bra and knickers they'd got in for Sophie to the end of the rack. He'd begged his friend at La Perla to let them borrow them and now he'd have to send them back with a note saying they hadn't been needed after all.

'D'you reckon it'll be pubes and everything?' asked Alex.

'Don't get excited, boys,' said Liz. She was flipping through the new issue of *Vogue*, feeling a wonderful sense of peace because Emma had the day off today. 'It'll be a closed set.'

Orlando snorted. 'I don't see why. Is there anyone left in the country who hasn't seen Sophie Randall's tits?'

Danny just looked at the floor. After Blanch House, Sophie and the four boys had gone on to a club, and they'd all ended up back in Sophie's room snorting charlie off her stomach. That was about ten minutes before Sophie had passed out and they'd stood around her bed, trying to wake her up before the fire alarm had gone off and Danny had panicked and left her there. Between them, the other three had managed to carry Sophie down to the first floor where they'd met Damien the grip on his way back up.

'Don't worry, false alarm,' he'd reassured them and, noticing Luke's broken wrist and their general air of inexperience at manhandling unconscious models, he'd slung Sophie over his shoulder in one deft move. 'Where'd you want her?' he asked.

Now, ten hours later, Sophie was standing naked by her hotel room window on the fourth floor, chatting on her mobile while Saskia topped up her all-over fake tan.

'I might get that new Maserati now,' she was saying. 'Yeah, the silver one. I told the producer if they wanted the full monty, it'd be ten grand for minge.'

A passenger being driven along the Esplanade in a white van suddenly looked up and saw Sophie standing at the window. His mouth dropped open and Sophie laughed and gave him a wave.

The house they were using for the flashback scene was half an hour's drive along the coast in Worthing. It was owned by Piers's auntie Phyllis who was eighty-two and had recently gone to live with her daughter. The house was still on the market and Auntie wouldn't mind if the art department re-painted the walls purple, red and bottle-green, because she'd never find out.

'Ten grand!' Ben was saying to Patrick as they left the house to walk over to lunch. 'I can't believe you agreed to pay that!'

'You'll thank me when you see the press we'll get,' said Patrick. 'There won't be a man in the country who won't want to see your film.'

As if to prove his point, when they got back to Unit Base, the riggers, Bradley and Shane, came over with their wallets in their hands.

'Guv, we heard you had to dosh her up big-time for this and we just wanted to make a little contribution,' said Shane solemnly, and they each handed Patrick a fiver.

Bradley patted Patrick on the shoulder and Shane gave him a kiss. 'It's days like this that make all the graft worthwhile,' Bradley told him.

'Lesson one,' said Patrick to Ben. 'You want bums on seats, you gotta give 'em tits and ass on screen.'

Ben sighed. He knew Patrick was right – sort of, but sometimes it felt like his film was being pulled away from him in directions he hadn't intended. Instinctively, he looked around for Emma in the lunch queue but then he remembered that she wasn't working today. And then he also remembered that Emma was so obsessed with Jason it was a waste of time even thinking about her. He'd tried everything last night to try and seduce her, but maybe she was one of those girls who really didn't cheat on their boyfriends. He'd heard about girls like that, but he wasn't sure he'd ever met one before. Well, if that's what she wanted, he certainly wasn't going to beg her. Onwards and upwards, he told himself.

He ordered the roast pork and all the veg and carried his tray onto the bus, looking for a seat. Liz was already at the far end with her back to him. She was sitting with Tex and Billy, and Ben realised for the first time that she seemed to sit with Tex most lunchtimes. There wasn't anything going on between them, was there? From the way Tex was smiling at Liz it certainly looked as though he wanted there to be something going on between them. Well, what did he care if there was? Liz wasn't anything to him any more. He chewed his pork but found he had no appetite for it and left most of it on his plate.

Sophie had her lunch standing up – a bottle of Martini and two fat lines of coke chopped out on the dressing table. She paced around the room growing more and more agitated, not able to sit down because of the fake tan on the back of her legs and bottom. Saskia had gone and she hated being on her own. Tim the runner had brought her a plate of salad and a Mars Bar but then he'd gone too. She wanted company and she needed more cigarettes. She picked up the remote control and flicked through the channels, desperate for entertainment, but unable to concentrate on any of the images for longer than a few seconds. She couldn't remember whether she'd finished her last pack of Silk Cut or not and she shook out the contents of her Louis Vuitton bag all over the floor looking for it. The thought suddenly struck her that she'd been mad to settle for ten grand. She should have asked for twenty. She could feel her heart racing and it excited her and scared her at the same time. What if she got so high she could never come down? Every time she closed her eyes she could see herself lying in a white coffin and her mother weeping hysterically.

'God!' she screamed. 'I need a cigarette!'

Ronald Gasch had finished his only scene of the day and had just returned to the hotel when he heard the banging. It seemed to start down the far end of the corridor and then moved gradually closer every few seconds. It must be the cleaners, he thought, and then he heard someone pummelling on his own door.

When he turned the handle he was astonished to see the tall girl he'd met the previous night. Apart from a bedspread wrapped around her shoulders, she was completely naked.

'Oh hello,' said Sophie, in genuine surprise because she'd given up on finding anyone in their rooms. She'd been trying to find her way downstairs to reception but couldn't remember the way. 'Have you got any cigarettes?' She thought the man looked vaguely familiar but she couldn't quite remember where she knew him from. It was hard, when you met so many people, to remember them all.

'Sophie!' Ronald gasped. 'What are you doing out there?' He took her arm and led her into his room, checking the corridor to make sure nobody else had seen her. 'Aren't you supposed to be filming this afternoon? Where are your clothes?'

'I'm not wearing any in this scene,' she confided. 'I'm going to buy a Maserati Spyder.' Spotting Ronald's cigarettes on the bed, she let the bedspread drop as she staggered over to them.

Ronald was in a quandary. The poor girl was obviously drunk and out of her mind. But more than that, she was extremely beautiful. She lay on his bed, inhaling deeply, not even remotely embarrassed at being naked in his presence. Ronald thought that if he'd been blessed with a body like hers, he probably wouldn't have felt embarrassed either.

'Black coffee,' he said to himself. 'That's what she needs.' He took his dressing gown from the hook on the door and spread it awkwardly over as much of her body as he could. 'Here you are, my dear,' he told her gently. 'Cover yourself up. I'll make you some coffee.'

The hotel only provided two sachets of instant powder each day, but he was reluctant to phone down for any more. He didn't want anyone to find Sophie in his room and get the wrong idea. And then he realised that Sophie might understandably be nervous about being in a strange man's room because she didn't seem to recognise him at all, even though they'd spoken at length just the previous night.

'It's all right. You're quite safe,' he told her. 'I'm Ronald Gasch. We met last night.'

Sophie had already finished her first cigarette and greedily lit a second. She tossed the dressing gown aside and held his gaze provocatively.

'So, what do you think, Ronald?' she asked, stretching out her long legs and pointing her toes. 'Would you like to fuck me?'

Ronald stared at her for a long time, unable to tear his eyes away from her extraordinary body. He knew it was wrong. He knew it was very wrong. But he also knew that he wasn't going to live forever and that he was unlikely to ever be offered such an astonishing opportunity again. He didn't waste any time.

'There's no sign of her,' said Tim. He was standing outside the hotel shouting into his mobile and looking up and down the street. 'I've tried her room. I've called her mobile. Reception say she hasn't left the hotel. She's not in the production office. She's not in the bar. She's not in the restaurant. She's not anywhere.'

'Well, she's got to be somewhere,' said Dominic.

'Are you sure she didn't already go back with make-up?' asked Tim. He wished Dominic wouldn't make it sound like it was his fault Sophie Randall had vanished off the face of the earth. 'Maybe she's on the bus having some lunch.'

'Well, I'll check here again, but for fuck's sake find her. Jamie's freaking out. She was due in make-up half an hour ago.'

'Right. Oh wait, hang on, she's here! I can see her in reception!' Thank Christ. He could see Sophie laughing loudly as she was steered out the front door by Ronald Gasch.

'We've been looking everywhere for you, Sophie,' said Tim in confusion, pulling open the back door of the minibus. 'Where've you been?'

Ronald held on to Sophie's elbow and helped her climb in. 'She was washing her hair,' Ronald explained. 'She wouldn't have been able to hear you.' That would explain why her hair was wet, he thought, and no one need ever know that after Sophie had given him the shag of his life – such suppleness, such athleticism, such unbridled animal lust – and she hadn't been bad either – he'd returned the favour by holding her head under a cold shower. Black coffee and cold showers were the only sobering-up techniques he knew. When he had taken her back to her room to dress, he'd seen the white trails of powder on the dressing table. He really ought to clean it up before the maid saw it, he'd thought, and wiped it off with his finger. He wondered what he could wipe it on and looking up, he caught his own reflection in the mirror, standing there in his suit with his white finger and a tall naked girl in the background hunting for her clothes. This didn't look his life. It looked like a scene from a particularly racy farce, he thought, with satisfaction. He popped his finger into his mouth and licked it clean. It didn't taste that bad.

Tim was about to ask Ronald why he was getting into the van with them when he'd finished for the day, but then he saw the look on Ronald's face and thought better of it. In the rear-view mirror, he saw Sophie snuggle into the crook of Ronald's arm and close her eyes, her long wet hair fanning out over his dark suit. Tim sighed. He'd probably get the blame for this as well, he thought glumly.

Georgina was standing in, or rather, lying in for Sophie so that Hugo could get on with lighting while they waited for Sophie to emerge from make-up. Danny, his hair dyed back to its original dark brown for this flashback scene, was sitting on the edge of the bed reading the script for a new film his agent had sent him that morning. Jamie, Ben and Ronald had gone into the kitchen for an urgent, hush-hush meeting.

'The bottom line is, is she going to be able to do it?' insisted Jamie.

'Stacey's in make-up with her now, running lines with her,' whispered Ben.

'How much do you think she's had to drink exactly?'

'There was an empty bottle of Martini on the floor,' said Ronald. 'But it's impossible to say whether she's had it all today. She could have had some of it last night.' He decided he wouldn't tell them about the coke. Or the sex.

'How could anyone drink a whole bottle of Martini?' asked Ben incredulously.

'Thank you for looking after her, Ronald,' said Jamie. 'You shouldn't have had to do that. She's not your responsibility.'

'It was my pleasure,' Ronald insisted smoothly and realised he wanted very much to laugh. These two had no idea what he was capable of.

'We should do the two-shot first,' Jamie suggested. 'Then at least we know we've got something in the can we can use.'

'If we're lucky,' said Ben. 'If you ever hear me trying to cast a model again, just shoot me. OK?'

Flick had managed to escape from the make-shift production office back at the hotel where Vanessa and the ADs kept her more or less chained to the photocopier and was delivering some more tapes for the video playback. Liz took advantage of the delay to go and speak to her. She was sure that Flick – so enthusiastic, so efficient and so Australian – could turn out to be very useful to her.

'Hello, stranger,' she greeted her as though they were close friends. 'Staying to watch the circus?'

'No, I can't. I've got to get back and finish tomorrow's movement order.'

'Well I'm looking forward to seeing Sophie Randall in action. Have you ever seen her in anything before?'

'No, I haven't,' Flick confessed. 'I'd never even heard of her. To tell you the truth, I've never heard of any of them before.'

'What? Not even Danny Parker?'

'Nope. I've heard of his band, I think – but they weren't huge in Oz like they were here.'

'Oh that's a shame. I worked on a film once which had a very international cast – Indian, Turkish, Mexican – all over the place, and what the director did, which I thought was really nice, was get in tapes of all the cast's previous films so that everyone could see what they'd done before.' Liz thought this was a stroke of genius. She could almost picture the scene in her head – a gaggle of swarthy thespians in colourful national costumes sitting cross-legged around a video screen and cheering with excitement as though they were watching the moon landing. It seemed almost a pity she'd made the whole thing up.

'We ought to do that here!' said Flick. 'Like a mini film festival!'

'Well, Flick, that's a brilliant idea,' said Liz admiringly. 'But who on earth would have the time to organise something like that?'

'I could do it!' said Flick. 'It'd be no trouble. There's a video store just down the road from the hotel. And I saw a copy of YunGun's video collection the other day in WH Smiths.'

Liz could see Flick getting more excited about the idea.

'We could set up the video in the hotel lounge,' she went on. 'No one ever uses it.'

'But Flick,' Liz protested mildly. 'You've got so much else on your plate. And how ever will you be able to find out what everyone has done? Ronald Gasch alone must have done a hundred films. And Luke and Giles – I have no idea what they've been in.'

'Oh that's easy,' Flick insisted. 'There's this great site on the Internet. You just type in the actor's name and it gives you a list of everything they've done. Films, TV, the lot.'

Liz's eyes widened in what she hoped was surprise. 'Really? How terribly clever! What would we do without you, Flick?'

And Liz sauntered off, confident that Flick would swear she had thought of this idea all on her own and that when Emma was eventually revealed as a liar and a fraud, there would be nothing to connect Liz to her downfall.

An hour and a half late, Sophie arrived on set oblivious to the fact that she had been holding everyone up. In fact it was safe to say she was oblivious to practically everyone and everything except the cigarette she was holding.

'Right, everybody who's not absolutely essential to this scene, please clear the set,' shouted Jamie. But before anybody could make a move, Sophie slipped off the dressing gown she was wearing and marched up to Ben.

'Where d'you want me?' she asked. Ben struggled manfully to keep looking her in the eye and not let his gaze wander south of her collarbone as he showed her where he wanted her to lie on the bed and reminded her and Danny how the scene would play out.

'Fuck it,' Alex said to Luke and Giles. 'We might as well stay here. She's not bothered.' They perched on the sideboard in the living room and craned their necks to see through the doorway to the bedroom. Bradley and Shane stood on chairs to get a better look.

'Do you think she's attractive?' said Luke.

'You're joking, aren't you?' said Bradley.

'Nah, I think she's scary.'

Billy and Tex tossed a pound coin to see who would get to hold the boom pole for Sophie's scene.

'I should do it, really,' said Billy. 'I'm the boom op.'

'Yeah, and I'm your boss. Call it.'

'Heads!'

The coin spun into the air and Tex exploded with glee as he leaned over to examine it.

'Tails! Give me that thing,' he laughed, grabbing Billy's boom pole. 'No point sending a boy to do a man's job.'

'I thought you said best of three,' protested Billy.

Ronald Gasch, listening to all of this, smiled to himself with quiet satisfaction.

'You did a good job on her,' Liz told Saskia. They were sitting behind Ben and Stacey watching the monitor. She wasn't jealous of Sophie Randall because Sophie Randall was a space cadet and a nightmare. Ben had said so himself, just last night. She stared lovingly at the back of Ben's head and wished she could stroke the dark curls on the back of his neck.

'She was half an hour late, her hair was soaking wet and she wouldn't take the cigarette out of her mouth while I was doing her make-up,' Saskia moaned. 'Look, she burned my hand!' Saskia showed Liz the tiny red mark on her thumb and Liz tutted sympathetically.

'What a lot of fuss for somebody with just one line!' said Liz.

'No, she's got three lines now,' said Stacey. 'There were dialogue changes issued yesterday.'

'Wow. Three lines,' drawled Saskia. 'You know what I heard? She's had plastic surgery to make her feet smaller.'

'Quiet! Please!' yelled Jamie. 'We can't work with all you lot yabbering like this.'

Saskia rolled her eyes. 'You'd be no good working in Marks and Sparks then, would you?' she said loudly enough for Jamie to hear and then in a whisper, 'Wanker.'

'We're going to shoot the rehearsal!' called Jamie and Saskia bustled in with her make-up bag for a final primping. Sophie was lying on her stomach and Saskia carefully arranged her hair so that it fell down in front of her shoulders and covered her breasts.

'No, Sas!' Patrick shouted impatiently. 'Other side!' He gestured with his hands to show that he wanted Sophie's hair to fall down her back and nodded patronisingly when Saskia reluctantly carried out his wishes. 'I'm not paying ten grand to see her fucking smile,' he muttered.

As Tex hoisted his boom pole, Ben noticed the way Tex's rock-hard triceps caught the light. His red T-shirt seemed unable to contain the expanding muscles that suddenly appeared out of nowhere. Almost every time Ben saw Tex on set he'd been sitting down so he hadn't appreciated before what a massive piece of work he was. He felt an irrational twinge of something like jealousy as he realised why Liz was so obviously over him these days. It was one thing for him to have dumped Liz, quite another to find out he'd been superseded by a taller, better-looking model with arms like tree trunks and whiter teeth. Ben felt very small suddenly, like somebody had just kicked sand on his life.

'And action!'

'What's going to happen to us when you're a big star, Eddie?' said Sophie. 'Do you ever think about the future?'

'All the time, Roxanne. All the time,' said Danny. He was packing for his band's tour and had been positioned so far in the foreground of the shot that you'd never know he was two inches shorter than Sophie.

'Have you ever thought about getting married?'

'Married? I'm too young to get married. I thought we were just having fun.'

Sophie stood up and Tex frowned as his microphone picked up the involuntary intake of breath from every man in the room. 'Is that all I've been to you? Fun? I love you, Eddie! I want to spend the rest of my life with you! I want to have your children!'

'Roxanne, I'm sorry. You want something I can't give you. Maybe it would be best if we cooled off for a while.'

'But Eddie! Think how beautiful our children would be! Yours and mine! What's the matter? Don't you love me?'

There was a long pause. 'Sorry,' said Danny, breaking character and turning to face the camera. 'I've completely lost it.'

'And cut!'

'That's OK, Danny, I know it's not easy to concentrate,' said Ben.

'You can say that again,' muttered Bradley.

'I do love you, Roxanne – but I'm not *in* love with you,' prompted Stacey.

'Right, thanks,' said Danny. 'Can I get a glass of water?'

Liz needed a glass of water too. She thought she was going to be physically sick. She hadn't bothered to read the replacement script pages that Flick had distributed that morning because dialogue changes didn't make any difference to her, but she unfolded them now, and read the scene again with disbelief.

Eddie exits, closing the door behind him. Roxanne is left heartbroken. It was like watching her life flash before her eyes. Liz couldn't believe that Ben would be so unbelievably callous as to put their own break-up in his movie. Was that why she'd been hired on his film – just so she could relive the most humiliating moment of her life from three different camera angles? Was that why he'd persuaded Sophie to do this scene naked? To remind Liz of how totally vulnerable she'd made herself that day? Did he really hate her so much?

'Sophie works, doesn't she?' Stacey murmured to Ben. 'In a completely off-her-face, bunny-boiling kind of way.'

'Yeah, with any luck, people will think she's just acting,' laughed Ben.

Liz couldn't stand by and listen to any more. She flung the pages into Ben's face.

'You forgot the part where he goes backpacking and climbs Ayers Rock,' she said bitterly and stormed off set.

Stacey and Saskia looked at Ben in confusion as Alex made a beeline for Liz's empty chair.

'What was that all about?' asked Stacey.

Ben shook his head. 'I don't know,' he lied. But he did know. He'd done a stupid, cruel thing. He'd thought Liz wouldn't notice, or if she did notice that she wouldn't remember, which was even more stupid. If he remembered it as clearly as if it were yesterday, then Liz wouldn't have forgotten. Write about what you know, the screenplay experts said. Well, that was the last time he'd listen to the experts.

'He must be off his rocker,' said Giles.

'Who?' asked Ben.

'Eddie. He's got this absolute knockout babe wanting to shag him senseless for the rest of his life and he says, no thanks, love, I'm going to go off and be a failed rock star. You'd have to be out of your mind, wouldn't you?'

Stacey laughed. 'Yeah, is that a guy thing, Ben? Not being able to take yes for an answer?'

'No, you don't understand. Eddie's ambitious. He doesn't want a commitment –' Ben began, but then he stopped and realised that he was getting into precisely the same argument he'd had with Emma the night before. Was it just possible that Giles and Stacey and Emma were right and he was wrong? Maybe you would have to be out of your mind to let the perfect woman get away like that. So why was Eddie doing it? He didn't want to get tied down, just in case it turned out there was somebody even more perfect just around the corner.

'Who knows,' Giles was saying, 'if Eddie had stayed with Roxanne, he probably wouldn't have got mixed up with Turpin and be running for his life right now.'

'But would he be happy?' said Ben.

'Is he happy now?' said Stacey.

Ben thought about it. Would he be happier if he'd just said yes to Liz? There'd been lots of girls since Liz but he'd found excuses to end it with all of them as well.

'Stand by to go again!' called Jamie.

'Just waiting for a plane to go over,' said Tex.

'I mean, does Eddie think he's going to find someone better?' insisted Giles. 'Look at her! What's wrong with her?'

'It's not the girls who are the problem,' sniffed Saskia. 'It's the men.'

'Can I have a bit of hush, PLEASE!' yelled Jamie in exasperation, and Ben sat in silence, staring at Tex's mighty arms stretched over his head. Would he have let Liz slip through those giant fingers of his? Ben's imagination didn't have to work too hard to picture the two of them together. Tex looked like he knew a good thing when he saw it. Well, maybe, so did he.

Ben found Liz at the end of the day in the wardrobe trailer with Orlando, silently bagging up the costumes to be returned. He knocked nervously on the door, and waited on the second step, knowing that he owed Liz some kind of apology, but not quite able to bring himself to say it.

'Liz, we're just going to run the latest batch of rushes back at the house. I thought you might want to sit in.'

She regarded him coolly as though he was beneath contempt. 'I'll be over in a while,' she said quietly and went back to labelling the bag she was working on. If Ben thought this pathetic gesture was going to make up for humiliating her on film, he was wrong. How could she have wasted so much of her life thinking she wanted him back? He wasn't worth it. She was better than that.

'Well, you're honoured,' said Orlando, when Ben had gone. 'It's been what, nearly two weeks now, and the only people who've seen any rushes are Ben, Patrick and Hugo. It's outrageous, really, the lack of courtesy this lot show to other departments.'

'I've a good mind not to go,' said Liz. If Ben expected her to be grateful, he was wrong. But she was already collecting her bag and jacket. 'Don't wait for me,' she told Orlando. 'Lock up when you're done. I'll get a cab back or something.' It was the longest conversation she'd had with Orlando in days.

Patrick and Hugo looked up in surprise as the living-room door opened and Liz walked in. Typically, she thought, they hadn't waited for her and the VHS was already running. Hugo and Ben were eating fish and chips out of the paper on their laps and Patrick had a kebab.

'I thought Liz should have a look at the scenes we shot of Luke,' explained Ben. 'Make sure she's happy with his arm.'

'Oh right,' agreed Hugo. Patrick looked at Ben out of the corner of his eye but kept his thoughts to himself. The three of them were sitting on the sofa in front of the TV and Hugo moved over to make room so that Liz could sit down too. But she sat down in an armchair behind them, deliberately putting as much space between herself and Ben as she could. She regretted it immediately because the armchair was the old-fashioned straight-backed kind with high arms that seemed to tip forwards and made it impossible for Liz to sit comfortably, however much she twisted about.

'Would you like a chip?' offered Hugo.

'No, thank you.' As if she cared what Luke's hand looked like, she thought, lighting a cigarette. She watched the scenes flicker past, the same boring action over and over again. Luke stands up. Luke sits down. Luke walks around the table. For half an hour she watched, her interest waning with every minute. Ben and Hugo's excited commentary was getting on her nerves. She inspected her split ends and searched in her bag for a pair of nail scissors. Her first impulse not to come at all had been right. It was already half past eight. What was she doing here? she wondered. Other people had jobs where they got up in the morning, went to work and came home at a normal hour. They ate dinner with their families, they saw their friends, they stayed out late if they wanted to and didn't have to get up at six o'clock the next morning. They didn't spend their spare time sitting in a stranger's living room watching the same bad silent movie over and over again.

It suddenly struck Liz that she actually hated her job. She used to love it so much, but now it felt like an anchor around her neck weighing her down. Why was she still doing it? When she was just starting out she used to think that everything would be great once she got more experience and started getting bigger films. But bigger films just meant bigger bullshit. And big or small, most of the films she worked on were utter garbage. Would the world be a better place just because *Brighton Rocks* was in it? Of course not. If every film she had ever made had never existed in the first place, it wouldn't have made a blind bit of difference. The only reason she was doing it now was for the money, which was good – it was brilliant, in fact – but it wasn't enough. She wanted a life. She wanted eight hours sleep. She wanted a family. She wanted love – not fish and chips with people she had utter contempt for.

'And that's your lot,' said Hugo as the VHS finally came to an end. Liz heaved a sigh of relief.

Ben scrunched up the fish-and-chip wrappings and went into the kitchen to look for a bin bag. 'What did you think, Liz?' he asked.

'Fantastic,' she replied but he couldn't tell if she really meant it or not. 'I'm sure Josephine and Saskia would have liked to see them too. But I guess there wasn't enough space for them in here,' she said, looking pointedly around the vast, empty room.

'Do you need a lift back to Brighton, Liz?' asked Patrick.

'Oh no, Patrick,' she smiled sarcastically. 'It's only eleven miles, I can walk.'

'Cor, what's got into you, Liz?' asked Hugo.

'Nothing,' Patrick told him. 'That's her problem.'

Liz shot him a filthy look. 'Actually, my sex life is perfectly healthy,' she corrected him. 'Unlike some people I could mention.'

Worthing at a quarter to nine was like a ghost town. Liz didn't fancy her chances of finding a taxi at this time of night so she sulkily followed the others to Patrick's car which was parked around the corner. Hugo, on account of his long legs, commandeered the front passenger seat and Liz squeezed into the back beside Ben, sliding as far away from him as she could. She wouldn't speak to him all the way home, she decided. That would show him.

She didn't need Ben Lincoln and his pathetic film. In fact, she didn't need films at all. What she needed was a new plan and it came to her in flash as they turned into the deserted high street and passed a darkened store called Selina's with two manne- quins in the window modelling monstrous frocks for the fashionably challenged. That was it! She'd open a shop – selling her own designs – accountable to no one but herself. She'd speak to Orlando tomorrow and see if he was interested in coming in with her. She'd be a star in her own right – the toast of London Fashion Week – not some overworked, unappre- ciated lackey running around after a spoilt brat director who wouldn't know his arse from his Armani. That'd show Ben. Then he'd be sorry. Oh yes, then he'd be sorry.

They were on the coast road now, travelling towards Brighton and a light rain started to fall as they drove through Shoreham. Liz watched the sky darkening over the sea and she could see Ben's face reflected in her window. All those years she'd wasted waiting for Ben to come back to her and then he puts their break-up in his film. How dare he, she thought. How *dare* he?

Hugo had put on the new Red Hot Chili Peppers CD and was trying to find the track he liked.

'Which is the button to go backwards?' he asked, mystified by the controls on Patrick's ancient in-car sound system.

Patrick leaned over to show him and that's when Liz heard the bang. She sat up in time to see Patrick tugging at the steering wheel as the car veered sharply to the right and into the oncoming lane of traffic. There were headlights coming straight towards them.

'I can't turn it! I can't turn it!' Patrick was yelling and Liz knew they were all about to die. There were no seatbelts in the back of Patrick's car and she closed her eyes and waited for the moment of collision. Without thinking, she threw her arms around Ben and buried her face in his neck.

'Ben, I love you!' she whispered desperately. 'I love you!' She could feel the car spinning.

'Jesus Christ!' Hugo screamed.

All those years she'd wasted, but she'd be together with Ben at the end. His arms were wrapped tightly around her and their faces were pressed tightly together.

'Hold on!' cried Patrick and then they felt another bang. It flung them from their seats, but the impact was side-on and when the car stopped moving, Liz realised she was still alive.

She opened her eyes, pushed back her hair, and tried to work out where she was.

'It's OK,' said Patrick. 'We've hit a boat.'

The car had come to rest on the wrong side of the road. There were no obstacles in a hundred yard radius, except for the yacht on its cradle, which Patrick's car had ploughed into as if drawn by a magnet.

Ben opened his passenger door and he and Liz clambered out. Liz's legs were shaking so much, they buckled underneath her when she tried to stand.

'Are you OK?' Ben asked, sitting on the grass beside her and putting his arm around her.

'I think so,' she said. Her teeth were chattering. 'How about you?'

'I'm fine.' He rubbed his cheek. 'I think I hit my face on the front seat, but I'm OK. What happened?'

'Looks like a tyre blew out,' said Hugo, kicking Butch's front wheel. He punched some numbers into his mobile. 'Anyone need an ambulance?' he asked. Ben and Liz shook their heads.

Patrick was so upset, inspecting the damage, that all he could say was the word, 'Fuck,' over and over again.

'It's a miracle we weren't all killed,' said Hugo, shining his pocket torch to see exactly what kind of boat it was they'd hit. He was already formulating the anecdote he would be telling everyone at breakfast the next day.

In the dark, Ben took Liz's hand and squeezed it and didn't let go and she knew that was the greatest miracle of all.

When the taxi dropped them at the hotel, they didn't speak until they got into Ben's room. As the door closed behind them, Ben grabbed her like a drowning man clings to a raft.

'Oh Liz, oh Liz, oh Liz,' he said over and over again as he kissed her, and his fingers hurried to undress her. 'I haven't got any condoms,' he confessed. 'Are you still on the Pill?'

'Yes,' said Liz, and thought that Ben need never know she had stopped taking the Pill over five years ago and switched to a cap. Tonight she had been convinced she was about to die and she needed to do something life-affirming. She wanted to get pregnant tonight. She wanted to have Ben's baby.

Her legs would no longer support her and she tumbled back on to the bed, pulling Ben down with her. Maybe she was really dead, she thought, as she felt Ben's hands on her skin for the first time in six years. Was it really possible to want something so much for so long and then to finally get your wish? Could life really be so kind? Ben kicked off his shoes and wriggled out of his jeans. Had she and Ben both been killed? she asked herself. She ran her hands down his back, over the sweet curves of his buttocks and buried her fingers into the curls of fur between his thighs. Every inch of Ben's body was still as familiar to her as her own. She pulled off his shirt and gasped with pleasure to feel the warmth of his chest against her breasts again. The way their bodies fitted together so perfectly felt like coming home. Was this heaven? she asked herself, and she knew that it was.

twenty-three

'Oh Christ!' Ben flung back the bedclothes and launched himself out of bed. 'Liz! Get up. It's half past seven!'

Liz opened her eyes slowly. She'd been having the most delicious dream. 'What happened to the alarm?' she asked drowsily, but as her foot touched the floor, she felt something hard and round beneath her toe. Ben's alarm clock had been knocked onto the floor during the night and the battery which had fallen out was now lying nestled in her gauze bra with the rose embroidery.

She found her knickers rolled up in the bedspread and tried to get dressed. Her arms ached from the effort of doing up her bra-strap and a fist-sized bruise was starting to appear on the side of her ribs. Ben's mobile was ringing. He came running out of the bathroom to answer it, still brushing his teeth.

'Yeah. Yeah. Don't worry about sending the minibus back for me. I'll take my own car today. We can park in the grounds, can't we? Yeah, I'm leaving now. Save me some breakfast, will you?'

'Your face is swollen,' Liz told him and touched his cheek.

'I know. It hurts like hell. Are you OK?'

'Yeah. Just a little achy. Like I spent the night in a tumble-drier.'

'I know. I feel like someone's been throwing rocks at me.'

He looked at her as though he might say something else but changed his mind. There was a silence and then, 'Can you be ready if I meet you downstairs in ten minutes?'

'Sure.' She pulled on her dress. She could only find one shoe and ran barefoot down the corridor to her own room where she rubbed cleanser into her face, cleaned her teeth and grabbed a clean pair of knickers. She pulled a skirt out of the wardrobe, and winced as she squirmed into a T-shirt. Dragging a brush through her hair felt like bench-pressing two hundred pounds. She pinned up her hair, stepped into the pair of sandals closest to the door and grabbed her make-up bag for essential repairs later when she had more time.

Ben's silver Golf was already waiting when she came running out. He leaned over and opened the door for her and she climbed in, marvelling that what seemed so natural this morning would have been impossible just a day before. Ben looked over his shoulder and nipped out into the traffic. It was nearly five to eight and the location was a good twenty minute drive out of town. Liz's mind was spinning with all the things she wanted to say to Ben, but where to begin? Neither of them spoke until they'd passed the Pavilion.

'I like your car,' she said eventually, stroking the leather upholstery. 'When did you get it?'

'Last year. July sometime. I was going to get the GTi, but they talked me into the Turbo.'

'It's very nice,' she said, and an awkward silence fell again. She'd waited six years. She could wait a few minutes longer.

'Sorry for making you late this morning,' said Ben.

'Well, it's Patrick's fault anyway for nearly killing us last night.'

'That's true. I can't believe nobody was hurt.'

'Are you sure you're OK?'

'I think so.'

'So what happens now?' asked Liz.

'About what?'

'About this. About us.' It was the word she hadn't dared to speak for six years. Had hardly dared to think it. Just a few hours ago there had been no 'Us'. Now, here they were.

'I don't know. What do you want to happen?'

'Ben, you know what I want to happen,' Liz turned to Ben, and told him what was finally in her heart. The time for playing games was over. 'Do I really have to spell it out for you? Last night we both could have been killed. Maybe this is a sign that we're meant to have another chance.'

Ben turned off onto the slip-road leading to the location. He pulled the car over to the side of the road.

'What?' asked Liz. 'Do you want me to get out here and walk? Is that it?'

'Don't be daft.' Ben leaned over and kissed her. 'It's just that I won't be able to do that in front of everyone when we get there. Our secret. Remember?'

How could Liz forget the game they used to play whenever they worked together – ignoring each other on set and pretending to be professional and then sneaking away for secret, frenzied embraces whenever they got the chance.

He kissed her again to show he really meant it and it was as though she was waking up from a bad dream. Yesterday afternoon it had seemed impossible that she would ever again be sitting in Ben's car, that Ben's hand would be moving up between her thighs, that his tongue would be inside her mouth – yesterday afternoon the world had been an altogether different place.

Ben drove on again, up the long drive leading into the park, and Liz rested her hand on the inside of his leg the way she always used to when he was driving and the years seemed to just roll away.

'My God, Liz! Are you OK?' gasped Orlando. 'I heard all about the accident. You shouldn't be here, should you?' What he really wanted to ask her was why he'd just seen her getting out of Ben's car at the end of the driveway and then limping the two hundred yards to Unit Base while Ben drove on without her. But for the moment he decided to keep this information to himself.

Liz tried to run up the stairs of the wardrobe truck the way she did fifty times a day, and winced on every step. Every one of her bones felt as though it had been subtly shifted just a millimetre out of its usual place and the cumulative effect wasn't at all pleasant. It was a shock to hear the word 'accident' because already it seemed like something that had happened days, or even weeks ago, relegated to a place of no importance by the earth-shattering event that had taken place later that night.

'I'm fine,' she replied dreamily. Everything felt quite unreal. 'Fine' didn't even come close. She looked at the day's call sheet taped to the wall and struggled to make head or tail of the simple information it contained. Scene 54: Jasmine visits the band in secret. Scene 130: Turpin's goons discover the band's hideout. The words meant nothing to her.

'Everything's under control here,' Orlando told her, picking up the iron again. 'The boys are already in make-up. And they're going to be ages lighting, by the looks of it. Why don't you take it easy and I'll make you a cappuccino?'

Liz scarcely heard him because she was having a flashback to the moment when Ben had cried out her name as his fingers dug into her breasts.

'How were the rushes?' he asked as he scooped out two measures of coffee.

'The rushes?' She'd forgotten all about them. 'Oh, yeah, they were good.'

Tex woke her out of her day dream as he leapt up the stairs. 'Liz, are you all right? Hugo said you were in a car crash. What happened? I brought you a cup of tea.'

Oh God, Tex. She'd forgotten all about him too. What was she supposed to do with him now? She took the polystyrene cup he offered and pretended to be very busy studying the call sheet.

'Thanks, Tex, but I'm not hurt and I haven't got time to talk right this second. I'm really up against it this morning.'

Tex nodded. 'Well if you're sure you're all right. I was worried about you.' He stroked her arm protectively. 'Come and find me later, OK?'

'OK,' Liz lied. Tex kissed her on the cheek and went back downstairs. Liz waited until he was out of sight and then emptied the cup of tea out the doorway so that it spilt on the grass. She didn't want anything else to touch her lips and wash away the taste of Ben's kiss.

Orlando watched all this in silence and recognised the signs. If Liz was crazy enough to get involved with Ben again, this time he wasn't going to be around to pick up the pieces when it all blew up in her face. It was Tex he was really worried about. He was running after her like a love-sick pup and he was about to get dumped on the roadside. Orlando sighed. Why were all the good men straight? He couldn't wait until this job was over and he'd never have to work with Liz again. He looked out of his smudged window at the cows grazing in the distance and was cheered by the fact that this was the nicest location they'd been in for a while.

They were shooting in a derelict stately home set in acres of parkland and Unit Base had an air of a picnic about it. As the morning wore on and the day got hotter, everybody made the most of their free time while they waited for the set to be lit, by sunbathing or playing frisbee.

It was Damien, the grip, who started the game. 'So go on, Saskia, if you had to shag one of the cast or crew, who would it be?'

'Only one?' scoffed Orlando. 'Is there anyone left on this film you haven't slept with, Saskia?'

Saskia gave Orlando a playful kick. 'You know that's not true,' she simpered, happy at being the focus of everyone's attention. 'I've been an absolute saint.' She looked around the faces of all the men lolling on the grass, wondering which one she should flatter. The person she really wanted to sleep with was Danny of course, but she couldn't very well say so with him sitting right there, could she? 'I think Alex,' she said eventually, hoping this would get Danny's attention, but Danny carried on reading the script for his next job. Tracey scowled at Saskia. She'd had her heart set on Alex for weeks.

267

'OK, so what about you, Alex?' Damien continued. 'Who would you sleep with?'

'Sophie Randall,' said Alex without a moment's hesitation and Saskia and Tracey both fumed silently behind their stuck-on smiles.

'She doesn't count because she finished yesterday,' Bex pointed out.

'Yeah, but I've still got the hard-on,' said Alex, unabashed.

'What about you, Billy?' asked Damien.

'Do I have to say?' Billy was embarrassed.

'Yes, of course you have to say!' Damien ordered. 'My game. My rules.'

'Tracey,' mumbled Billy and everyone cheered, except Tracey. As if she'd sleep with the boom swinger. Or any of the crew. She only ever slept with the talent. Everybody knew that.

'Bad luck there, I'm afraid,' said Damien. 'Tracey only fucks above the line, don't you, darling?'

'Absolutely,' said Tracey, only too happy to put Billy in the picture. Honestly, the nerve of some people.

'Georgina?'

'Forget it, I'm not playing,' said Georgina shaking her head. 'Too dangerous.'

'You can't get out of it,' said Damien.

'Well too bad, I don't fancy any of you.'

'What about you, Emma?' asked Damien.

'Me? Oh I'm spoken for – you know that,' laughed Emma.

'Yeah, but if you had to,' Damien insisted. 'If there was a gun pointed at your head and you had to have sex with one of us lot, who would it be?'

'Well, you obviously, Damien,' replied Emma diplomatically.

'Well that seems fair,' said Damien, quite satisfied with this result, then ducked as he was nearly decapitated by a frisbee.

'Sorry, guys,' Tex apologised as he ran in to scoop it up.

'What about you, Tex?' asked Orlando. 'If you had to sleep with one of the cast or crew, who would it be?'

Liz glared at him.

'Oh, I wouldn't like to say,' said Tex bashfully. 'A gentleman would never say. But she knows who she is.' He shot a furtive glance in Liz's direction and she looked away in annoyance. She hoped he wasn't going to make a scene when he found out about her and Ben. Couldn't he just dissolve quietly into the background? She got to her feet with some difficulty and went back to the wardrobe trailer, hoping he wouldn't follow her.

'Well I think this is a terrible game,' tutted Saskia who could stand it no longer. 'Doesn't anyone want to shag me?'

'Come here, darling,' said Damien, and wrestled her to the ground, rolling on top of her and trying to chew her ear.

Saskia pretended to struggle but she was giggling too much and discovered that she quite enjoyed it.

Inside the house, in what Ben supposed had once been the ballroom, he watched Hugo, Pete and Kevin set up the lights and tried to put his finger on the reason why he felt so agitated. That sick, empty feeling in the pit of his stomach must be because of the car accident, he concluded. Kim, the unit nurse, had rubbed some arnica cream on the bruise on his face and given him a glass of water containing a few drops of Rescue Remedy which he was supposed to sip throughout the day. 'It's very good for shock,' she explained. But half an hour ago he'd given it all to Patrick after he got off the phone from his car insurance company looking very white. Butch had been towed away from the scene late last night and it was up to the insurance company now to decide whether she was worth saving or whether it would be cheaper to put her out of her misery.

'How can they write her off?' Patrick was saying. 'She's been with me for twenty years.' Ben had never seen him like this. He was so upset, he hadn't even mentioned the fact that he'd put Ben and Liz into a cab on their own back to the hotel.

'It's OK, she's a tough old girl, she'll pull through,' Ben reassured him.

Last night with Liz had been just like old times and part of him was already looking forward to a repeat performance tonight. And that was good, wasn't it? Wasn't that what he wanted? He'd made up his mind that he'd been crazy to let Liz get away from him before, so he ought to be pleased that he was getting this second chance. And he was, he really was. Liz was fabulous. She'd always been fabulous. There was no reason to be scared of her. She wasn't the enemy, she was on his side. He tried to think positive as Jamie called everyone inside for a camera rehearsal.

At lunchtime, Liz took her tray to a sunny patch of grass far enough away from the rest of group to ensure privacy. Despite what Ben had said that morning about keeping their relationship a secret, she still hoped he'd come and have lunch with her. They'd wasted so much time apart, every hour was precious now, so she could barely hide her frustration when she saw Tex coming to join her.

'Why didn't you get the salmon?' he asked as he inspected her plate. 'It looks really good today.'

'Tex, I don't have to have the fish every day,' Liz sighed in exasperation. 'I just felt like salad, all right?' She methodically sliced her tomato into tiny cubes although she had no appetite.

Tex cut off a square of his salmon and held it out on the end of his fork. 'Try a bit.'

'No.'

'Go on, it's delicious.'

'Tex, I don't want your stupid fish, all right?' and Tex put his fork down, feeling rather foolish.

'You're probably still feeling a bit shaken up,' he suggested. 'After the accident, I mean. You still haven't told me what happened.'

'I don't know. I wasn't driving. Why don't you ask Patrick?' She could see Ben over by the bus getting a knife and fork. There was no way he'd come over now with Tex in the way.

'I did ask Patrick. He said a tyre blew out and you crashed into a boat.'

Liz opened the latest issue of *Dazed and Confused.* She hoped Tex would get the hint. She wasn't ready to deal with this right now.

'Liz?'

'What?'

'I said, Patrick said a tyre blew out and you crashed into a boat.'

'Great. So now you know as much as I do.' She flipped over another page without looking up.

Tex put down his plate and frowned. 'Liz, why won't you ever let anybody just be kind to you? I know you always act like you're so tough you can look after yourself, but there are people who care about you. I care about you. I want to help.'

'Oh, for God's sake, Tex, can't I just eat my lunch in peace?' Liz pushed aside her untouched salad and lay down on the grass, as far away from Tex as she could get. She closed her eyes and immediately her mind filled with thoughts of Ben.

Her spell complete, that night Liz buried the remaining candle stubs and matches under the pebbles on the beach where no one would ever find them and, to thank the spirits who had helped her, she left one last miniature of brandy at the foot of the angel along with the rest of the box of Ferrero Rocher.

As if by magic, Liz could feel everything in her life starting to return to its proper shape. Wheels were turning and cogs sliding back into position. Planets that had been temporarily knocked off course were resuming their correct alignment.

Each night, she'd let herself into Ben's room, taking care there were no prying eyes to see her. She gave up her sea view without a second thought because she preferred to be woken by the sound of his snoring, rather than the squawking of seagulls, and if Tex knocked on her door and got no answer, he was an adult and free to draw his own conclusions.

Each morning when she woke, Liz would feel desolate for just a moment because the feverish love-making she remembered was surely just a dream, and then she'd open her eyes and see Ben lying beside her and her heart would be filled with a kind of stunned fulfilment.

'I don't know what I was so afraid of,' he told her one night, exactly a week after they'd got back together. 'I was never able to commit to anybody — not just you — I mean anybody. I thought it was because I was just looking for the right person, but maybe I'd already found the right person and I just didn't know it.'

'Maybe,' said Liz and she could see he'd got that look in his eye again.

These days they took care to move the alarm clock well out of harm's way.

twenty-four

The film's newest cast member was unhappy.

'Why do I have to wear this?' protested Paolo. 'Green's not my colour, man.'

'I thought you wanted to be in this movie,' Orlando scolded him. ' "Oh, Orlando, put me in your movie, put me in your movie!" Isn't that all I've been hearing for the last two weeks? Well, I've got you a part in the movie, so show a little gratitude.'

'I'm not wearing these green trousers,' Paolo insisted.

'Fine,' snapped Orlando and pursed his lips. 'Take them off. I'll find somebody else to do it.' He leaned out of the truck and called to Bradley the rigger who was walking past.

'Bradley, darling, do you want to play the shop assistant in this scene? Our actress isn't up to the job.'

Paolo fingered the name badge on the lapel of his green shirt. It said 'Paolo'. 'Hey, I didn't say I wouldn't do it,' he backtracked. 'I just wish you'd find me a better colour.'

Ben needed four shots in the DIY store – a tracking shot past the ends of the aisles to find Jasmine and the band asking a shop assistant for directions, then a tighter group shot and a couple of close-ups as Jackson chooses some bathroom tiles, adhesive and a bag of grout. And they had to get it all done before the store opened at ten. It was all to set up the ingenious plan for hiding the emeralds. At least it had seemed ingenious, Ben thought, when he'd written this scene over a year ago.

Now it seemed slightly idiotic – the sort of plan an eleven-year-old boy might come up with. Was there time for him to come up with a new plan that somehow required his five actors to be in a DIY superstore? Could he totally rewrite the ending of his movie in the next ten minutes? The answer was no. He was stuck with the tiles. It's going to be brilliant, he told himself, and he glanced over at Liz for moral support. Don't panic.

'Look, he's done it again,' moaned Bex, pointing down the aisle at Danny preening his hair. She'd told Ben it was just asking for trouble starting this shot in the aisle with all the bathroom mirrors in it. 'I go and do his hair and then the minute I come back here, he starts messing about with it.' She folded her arms crossly over the heavy make-up bag slung over her shoulder.

'Do you need to get in there and fix it?' asked Jamie.

'Nah, sod him. There's no point.' Bex sat down on her folding stool and started buffing her nails.

'And action!'

Damien pushed the camera dolly slowly along the track until it reached the aisle where the actors were. His timing was spot-on. Ben held his breath, staring at the image on the monitor, willing it to be good. Paolo was feeling very self-conscious in his green shirt and trousers and when he saw the camera drift into view, he instinctively looked straight into the lens and smoothed back his hair.

'And cut! Don't look at the camera!' called out Ben.

'Oh yeah, yeah!' Paolo giggled, blissfully unaware that he'd wasted the most precious commodity known to man – a film crew's time.

Damien ostentatiously rolled the dolly back to its starting position and Ben looked nervously at his watch. On Take 2, he watched in mounting disbelief as Paolo extended his entire arm and swivelled his hips in the direction of the grout aisle.

'Jamie, tell him this is not *Grease* and he's not fucking John Travolta! He's pointing to bathroom tiles, for Christ's sake. Where did we find this clown?' he whispered to Stacey.

'That's Paolo – Orlando's boyfriend,' said Liz in his ear. She had no qualms about laying the blame squarely at Orlando's door. It served him right for his outrageous lack of loyalty.

Paolo, who was getting the standard £64.50 and had taken last night off from DJ-ing, was extremely miffed that Ben hadn't appreciated the bit of flair he'd added to his rather mundane part. Consequently, on Take 3 he pointed to the aisle in the manner of a very disgruntled and disenchanted employee – which was precisely the attitude that Ben was after.

'Cut!'

'Printing Take 3,' announced Stacey.

'And moving on!'

With less than an hour to go, they were set up for Danny's close-up. He only had one line of dialogue and he couldn't possibly screw it up.

Oh, but he could.

'Danny, can you say the line: "Better get the lot", rather than "Better get all of them"?' asked Ben. He kept forgetting to call him 'Eddie', but he asked as sweetly as he could.

'What's the difference?'

'I don't know – I just think it sounds funnier the way it was written. Humour me, OK?' The trouble was that nothing Danny said sounded funny. He was like a bell jar sucking the oxygen out of every scene and killing it stone dead. Ben knew he should have given that line to Luke, but Danny was supposed to be the star and he had to have some dialogue sometimes.

They were about to go for a third take when there was loud pop and the aisle went dark.

'Five minutes, sir, we've blown a lamp,' said Pete. 'Kevin, fetch another 5K.'

'Running all the way!'

Ben checked his watch nervously and Stacey began ruling up the script on her lap and copying out her continuity notes. If she didn't keep on top of her paperwork as she went along she could kiss goodbye to lunchtime. In an ideal world, she thought, they'd take two hours to set up every shot. They couldn't break enough lamps for Stacey's liking.

And then they heard it.

'He's a fucking useless director if you ask me,' Danny was saying. 'Does anybody even know what this scene is supposed to be about?'

Ben froze as he listened to Danny's voice in his headphones. Stacey still had her cans on too and she caught his eye and bit her lip. Was Danny really so dense he didn't realise that as long as he had his radio mic on, they could hear every word he said?

Tex looked over at Ben, embarrassed.

'What difference does it make whether I say the words his way or my way?' Danny went on. 'He shouldn't employ actors if he's not prepared to respect their ideas.'

Ben bristled but said nothing. Danny didn't have any ideas. The lazy little git just never bothered to learn his lines.

'This is the last time I'm working for a first-time director,' Danny was saying. 'I'm fed up with all these fucking amateurs.'

The lamp flickered back into life and Ben let Danny say the line whichever way he wanted.

'That was brilliant, Danny,' Ben told him. 'Absolutely perfect. Why don't you go for an early lunch while I knock off these other shots?'

Danny didn't need to be asked twice. 'Later guys,' he muttered and sauntered out.

The moment Danny had gone they set up for an unscheduled close-up on Luke.

'Tell you what, Luke,' Ben called out, casually. 'Why don't you say Danny's line as well? Just to give you something to do.'

Luke said the line exactly the way it was written and added the extra ingredient of struck-by-lightning comedy timing that not even the greatest screenwriter in the world could provide.

'Print that one,' Ben whispered to Stacey, and without needing to be told, she turned back to the continuity sheet with Danny's close-up on it and beside each take she wrote the letters: 'NG' which stood for No Good. It was going to be fun, she thought, as she packed up her folder to see how little of Danny they could get away with putting into the final edit.

By the time Liz was ready to go to the next location, the first minibus had left and the only unit car by the front door was Tex and Billy's little white sound van.

'Liz, hop in, I'll give you a lift.'

She was torn between not wanting to get into a discussion with Tex about why she'd been avoiding him and walking a hundred yards in her new heels across the car park to where the second minibus was parked. She knew she should wear trainers on set like everybody else, but she had standards to maintain.

'Oh what the hell,' she thought, and climbed into the front seat next to Billy.

'Have I done something to upset you?' asked Tex.

'No.'

'Well why are you avoiding me?'

'I'm not avoiding you. I'm just busy and tired. I haven't got the energy to go out every night after work.'

'I called your room last night and you weren't there.'

'Really? What time was that?'

'Around ten.'

'I must have been in the bath.'

'Me and Billy are staying in Brighton this Sunday. Do you want to hang out with us?'

'I'm probably going to have to go shopping.' The van pulled up into the DIY store car park where their base had been set up. 'Well, thanks for the lift,' said Liz and jumped out.

'Reckon she's blowing you out, mate,' said Billy watching her walk across the car park towards Ben's trailer.

'I reckon you're right,' Tex agreed and tried not to let on how much it hurt.

They finished at sunset outside a Chinese takeaway for a scene starring Luke, Alex and the shop's real owners, the Tan family, playing themselves. Luke and Alex ask the boy behind the counter if he knows a man called Mr Wong. The Tans find this pretty funny at first, but then Mrs Tan decides they're taking the piss. Tim and Flick had been press-ganged into being extras in the takeaway and self-consciously pretended to study the laminated menu while Mrs Tan abused the boys in sarcastic Mandarin.

Ben loved the way the green neon signs reflected in their faces and Mrs Tan was a real find – he'd have to find something else for her to do in the movie. Maybe in his next film he'd use all real people instead of actors – he knew Patrick would approve.

'Ben, have you got a minute?' Flick asked as everyone was packing up to go home.

'What's the problem?'

'Oh no problem,' Flick assured him. 'It's just that I had an idea for a video night – showing films that the cast have been in before.'

Ben nodded. He didn't have time to worry about Flick's extra-curricular activities.

'And?'

'Well, I just wondered, did you ever see that film Emma was in before? Only I've looked her up on the Internet and I can't find any record of her in anything. Was it like a student film or something?'

Ben stopped. He'd meant to try and get hold of a copy of Emma's film, but there hadn't been time. 'No. I never saw it. But I think it's still in post-production. It was something about hair.'

'*Hairdressing*,' Flick agreed. 'I checked with Angela. But I can't find it. There's no film listed called *Hairdressing*.'

'Well it's probably changed its name. That must have been its working title.'

'It should still show up,' Flick insisted.

'Well what do you expect me to do about it?' Ben said, impatient over all this fuss about nothing. It had been a long, stressful day and all he wanted now was a beer and his bed. 'Why don't you just ask Emma?'

'I wanted it to be a surprise.'

'Flick, I'm sorry. I really haven't got time for this right now. I haven't seen the film you're looking for and right now I'm trying to make another one, so if you don't mind –'

Flick stepped aside to let Ben pass and he jumped into the waiting minibus and sped off leaving Flick and Tim stranded on the pavement.

'Jeez,' said Flick. 'I only asked.'

Ben slept badly these days, Liz discovered. He'd lie awake for hours, editing and re-editing the film in his head, going over every shot and every line of dialogue, still desperately trying to think of a new ending that was better than the one he'd already written. He'd asked Jamie to change the schedule so that the end of the film would actually be shot in the last week and every morning he'd pray that inspiration would suddenly strike.

And that day there'd been more bad news – they'd lost the location where Eddie was supposed to find Jasmine after she's been beaten up by Turpin's heavies. The factory yard Piers had found was wonderfully sinister, but now the owners had decided they didn't want a film crew interfering with their night shifts.

'Maybe we should go back to the Mongo Club and shoot it there,' Ben said as he lay in the half-light, idly stroking Liz's arm. There was no use in her trying to sleep when Ben was in one of these moods. 'But I'm sick of that location,' he answered himself. 'We've shot half the damn film in that club.'

'Why don't they just lock her in the boot of the car?' Liz suggested drowsily.

'Jasmine?'

'Yeah. That way you can save yourself a location move and do it the same night as you do all the driving shots.'

'And then we don't have to beat her up!' Ben realised. He'd been fretting about that scene since day one because he knew that seeing Jasmine getting thumped by Buster and Lucky

Louie was going to unbalance the comedy mood he was going for. He was wide awake now, and already visualising the new scene in his head. 'So Eddie finds the car parked down by the seafront – or wherever – he hears her shouting to be let out and maybe she's got some bruises on her, but we don't have to see her actually getting hit. You're brilliant!'

He kissed Liz and she wrapped her legs around him, knowing what was coming next.

'Whatever would I do without you?' he wondered.

'Play your cards right and you won't have to find out.'

twenty-five

The seagulls woke her long before the alarm went off. Emma threw back the curtains and was a little disappointed to see the same old rooftops and the same old bird droppings streaking the window.

It was ten o'clock on Sunday morning and Jason would already be on his way. She wouldn't phone him – she didn't like him using his mobile while he was driving. Besides, she could enjoy missing him now knowing that he'd be with her in just a couple of hours. When he arrived, she'd take him somewhere nice by the sea for brunch. So she decided to skip the hotel toast and eggy bullets and practise her roller-blading instead. Tim had given her a couple of lessons in secret and she was now able to go forward more or less in a straight line, although stopping was still a bit hit-and-miss.

She ran downstairs in her socks, tugged on her new skates in the hotel foyer, strapped on her wrist guards and knee protectors, and then made her way cautiously out to the road, hanging on to a lamp post until the coast was clear so she wouldn't roll under a car. Having made it safely to the path, she clung to the railing and tightened the elastic band that held back her hair in a pony tail.

Down past the statue of the angel where the path got wider and the tarmac got smoother, she started to find her balance, let go of the railing and began to skate in large, wobbly circles. Overhead, the gulls kept up their running commentary while Emma rolled on, hypnotised by the grinding of her wheels, the salty taste in the air and the huge calm ocean shimmering benignly under a clear sky. Life really didn't get much better than this, she thought to herself and, buoyed up by a moment of supreme optimism, she tried to spin around, got her feet tangled up and ended in a heap on the ground just as she heard a familiar voice call out her name.

'Emma!'

She scrambled back to her hands and knees as Ben jogged towards her. He stopped and held out his hand to help her up.

'You OK?' he asked.

'Oh yeah, I'm fine,' she said, picking the crumbs of asphalt out of her shin. 'I must have hit a crack in the path or something.'

'That must have been it,' Ben agreed, although he couldn't help noticing how uniformly flat the path was in that particular spot. 'Coming back to breakfast?' He didn't have the heart to tell Emma that the roller-blading scene had been cut.

'OK.' She really fancied a cup of tea. She skated carefully along beside him back to the hotel, trying to look like she knew what she was doing.

'So. Today's the big day, then?' he asked, jogging slowly alongside her.

'Sorry?'

'Isn't Jason coming today?'

'Oh, he is. But how did you know?'

'I think everybody knows,' said Ben.

'Have I been really going on about it?'

'Just a bit.'

'Well, only because I'm so excited. I haven't seen him in three whole weeks.'

'What have you got planned?'

'Well, I'm going to take him out for brunch, and then . . .' Emma laughed, thinking that they'd probably spend the whole day in bed. Knowing Jason, they wouldn't even make it out to breakfast.

'Oh right. Well you don't have to tell me the rest,' said Ben, wishing he hadn't asked. He knew he'd drawn a blank with Emma but still, he had no desire to hear all the gory details. Then he remembered that he'd made love to Liz less than an hour ago and that what Emma got up to with her boyfriend shouldn't bother him in the slightest, one way or another.

'What about you?' asked Emma. 'I didn't expect to see anyone else up this early.'

'I've got rewrites. I'm still not happy with the ending. But I could do with spending the day in bed. Asleep, I mean.'

They'd reached the hotel and Emma unbuckled her skates and pads and followed Ben into the breakfast room in bare feet. Some of the crew were already up and Liz, Hugo, Stacey, and Kevin, one of the electricians, were sitting around the long corner table drinking coffee and reading the Sunday papers. Emma poured herself a glass of orange juice and a packet of Alpen – just to tide her over till Jason arrived, she told herself.

Liz's hackles rose when she saw Emma and Ben walk in together. An hour ago, Liz and Ben had woken up together, had a Sunday morning quickie and then he'd suddenly announced he was going for a run.

'But it's your day off,' Liz had protested.

'Exactly. It's the only day of the week when I *can* run.' He put on his shorts, not entirely sure himself why he was so eager to give up his one chance of a lie-in.

'Can't you run later?'

'Early morning is the best time to burn fat. On an empty stomach. You were the one who told me that.'

'Come back to bed. That's good exercise too.'

'I will when I get back. We can spend all day in bed, if you like.'

'Promise?'

'I promise.' He kissed her and she could smell the old sweat on the faded grey T-shirt he always wore when he ran.

She could smell it again now as he sat down across the table from her and ordered eggs, sausage, bacon and a pot of coffee.

'You could have saved yourself that run if you skipped the

fried breakfast,' she said casually as though she were offering a purely medical opinion.

'It's all protein,' Ben pointed out equally casually. He wasn't going to get into a lovers' quarrel in public with Liz. Film crews were the worst gossips in the world, but despite the odds, they'd so far managed to keep their affair off the bush telegraph. Liz had turned out to be a far superior actress to any of his actual cast. Whenever she spoke to him on set she had a good trick of never actually looking him straight in the eye, but letting her gaze wander off somewhere over his shoulder as though she were thinking about something else entirely, so that sometimes even Ben forgot they were sleeping together every night.

'It's a fabulous morning out there,' said Emma to anyone who was interested. 'I've just been roller-blading.'

'You're energetic,' said Kevin, looking up from his *News of the World*. 'What's the weather like?'

'Gorgeous. It's the most perfect day you could possibly imagine.' Emma's eye was suddenly caught by an upside-down image in Kevin's paper.

'Oh look, it's Jason!' she squealed. 'Can I see?' Without waiting for an answer, she twisted the newspaper around and her smile froze.

'What's the matter?' asked Stacey.

Emma didn't say anything. She just stared at the photo, trying to work out how the papers could have faked this image. Was somebody playing a practical joke on her? Was it April Fool's Day? It couldn't possibly be real.

'Well give it here,' said Hugo, impatiently dragging the paper away from her. 'Let us all in on the secret.'

He read the picture caption aloud: '*Shelby Square* stars Jason Cairns and Nicole Lloyd announcing their engagement this week at a party to celebrate the show's five hundredth episode.'

Still Emma couldn't speak, and carried on staring at the upside-down photo of Jason and Nicole holding hands while Nicole flashed a diamond ring for the camera.

'Is she a friend of yours, then?' asked Kevin, who wasn't the brightest spark on the block.

'Shut up, Kevin,' said Stacey.

'It's just a mistake,' said Emma and she tried to laugh, but her shoulders were trembling. 'The paper's got it all backwards. They're just getting engaged on the show – that's all it is. God! Jason's going to be so angry when he gets here and sees this.' She got up, holding on to the table to steady herself and walked as calmly as she could out of the dining room and up the stairs. She'd phone Jason and he'd explain it was all a mix-up.

It was only when she got to her room that she remembered she'd left her key at the reception desk before she went skating and she crumpled onto the carpet in the hallway because the effort of going back downstairs seemed suddenly beyond her. She was still sitting there when Ben came up the stairs to find her.

'Emma, are you all right?'

She tried to sit up straighter and attempted a laugh. 'Oh, yeah, I'm fine. I've just left my key downstairs. Every time you see me today I'm sitting on the ground.'

Liz was right behind him. There was no way she was going to leave Ben alone with Emma. If she wanted a shoulder to cry on she was going to have to find somebody else.

'Go down and get Emma's keys for her, Ben,' she told him. She sat down beside Emma and put her arm around her. 'Oh you poor thing,' she cooed.

'It's OK. It's not true,' said Emma, with forced cheeriness. Anyone overhearing their conversation would have assumed it was Emma who was trying to comfort Liz and not the other way around. 'It's just a publicity stunt for the show. Honestly, I'll murder him when he gets here for not warning me!'

'Yes, I'm sure that's all it is,' Liz agreed, and for reasons of her own she didn't suggest to Emma that it was entirely possible Jason wouldn't be coming to Brighton after all.

Emma hung the 'Do Not Disturb' sign on her door and didn't

come out. She didn't want to see anyone unless it was Jason. She redialled his mobile number and his home number one after the other but they were both picked up by his answering services.

She left four messages: 'Hi, Jason, it's quarter to eleven. It's a really lovely day here and there's the funniest thing in the paper this morning. Call me?' 'Hi, Jason, me again. It's eleven o'clock. What time are you getting here?' 'Jason, it's Emma. Please can you call me when you get this message. I have to talk to you.' 'Jason, it's half past eleven. What's going on? Where are you?'

When one o'clock came and went and Jason still hadn't arrived, she knew he wasn't coming.

Locked inside her hotel room Emma had never felt so alone in her whole life. It was stifling, even with the window open, but she was too ashamed to go outside. She realised she hadn't shut up about Jason ever since she got here and she just knew everyone would be laughing at her now behind her back.

She felt as though she didn't have a friend in the whole world. She wished she'd never met Jason. She wished she'd never done this stupid film. She wished she'd never gone to drama school. She wished she was back at the salon, washing hair and sweeping the floor where she belonged. She could be married now to some nice boy from school – she couldn't actually think of anyone in particular off the top of her head but there must have been *someone* – and they'd have two kids and live in a little flat, and money would be tight but they'd love each other, and somehow they'd muddle through and she wouldn't be moping about on one of the hottest days of the year on a pink-and-green nylon bedspread with no one who cared about her.

Eventually, she couldn't stand it a moment longer. She put on her biggest sunglasses to hide her red-rimmed eyes and decided to go out for a walk. She hoped to make it out of the hotel without having to speak to any of the others but in reception she bumped into Jamie, the first AD, who looked as embarrassed as she was.

'Are you OK?' he asked. Stacey had shown him the *News of the World* and he sincerely hoped Emma wasn't going to fall apart because then he'd have to spend the rest of his day off rejigging the week's schedule.

'Of course I'm not OK,' she shouted back. 'Why can't everyone just leave me alone?'

She turned right out of the hotel towards Hove, and started walking, with no plan or destination in mind apart from a vague superstition that if she did *something* then Jason would be more likely to ring. On and on she walked, oblivious to the cloudless cobalt sky and to the hundreds of day-trippers who'd descended on the south coast for a spot of sun-worship, as she rehearsed in her mind exactly what she'd say to Jason when she finally got hold of him. She didn't think about the heat, or the time, or how far she'd walked, or about anything at all apart from Jason and Nicole and the mobile phone in her bag which was still stubbornly refusing to ring. Four hours later, when she finally got back to the hotel, her arms and face were as pink as a stick of rock.

'Oh my Lord!' exclaimed Orlando, when he passed her on the stairs. 'Did you use ketchup instead of moisturiser this morning?'

'What do you mean?'

'You're practically fluorescent!' Orlando had spent the night with Paolo and so had missed all the revelations at breakfast.

'Good,' said Emma. And then to Orlando's horror she started to cry.

'Oh baby!' Orlando wrapped his arms around her, mortified at the way his teasing had backfired. 'No – it's a good look. Truly. Everybody loves pink – it's a fabulous colour. And with your hair you can totally carry it off.'

Emma stopped sobbing and looked up at him like a confused and tearful lobster. 'What are you talking about?' she sniffed.

'I don't know. What are you crying about?'

And so she told him all about the photo in the *News of the*

World and he took her to his room and poured her a gin and tonic from the mini-bar.

'I don't feel like drinking,' she sulked.

'This isn't alcohol – it's medicine. You've had a nasty shock and I'm the St Bernard coming up the mountain to rescue you.'

Emma took a large gulp and felt instantly better.

'Oh why are men such bastards?' she demanded, flinging herself dramatically onto the bed. 'Oh sorry, Orlando, I didn't mean you.'

She felt very hot and flushed and put this down to the gin. 'He hasn't even rung me!'

'Perhaps he's left a message in your room.'

'Well tough. Because I'm not there.'

'So you had no idea anything was wrong?'

'Of course I didn't. He was supposed to be coming to see me today. That was the last thing he said to me yesterday: "See you tomorrow." Not, "See you tomorrow in the *News of the World*." Or, "See you at my wedding." I didn't even know he *liked* her. He said they made him kiss her for the show. I can't believe he made me watch that. That's so cheap.'

'He's not a very good actor,' said Orlando. Every time a scene ends he pulls this face like he's posing for a catalogue. You must have noticed.'

'No, I haven't,' said Emma.

'And she's had her tits done, hasn't she?'

'No, I think she's been working out.'

'Oh please. Working out how much more silicon she can get inside her, you mean.'

'Do you think she's a bitch?'

'A complete bitch,' agreed Orlando.

'And Jason's a bastard.'

'A complete bastard.'

'So what am I crying about?' asked Emma, and buried her face in his white cotton duvet, thinking that she really didn't have the energy left to cry any more. Suddenly she sat up, slightly puzzled. 'How come you've got a duvet?' she asked, looking around her. 'Your room's much nicer than mine.'

'Home comforts,' he explained and Emma noticed the four large suitcases stacked in his bathroom. 'I don't do squalor.' On the side table where in Emma's room there was just a kettle, one cup and saucer, a teaspoon and a wicker tray of instant coffee sachets and UHT milk, Orlando had a cappuccino maker, a blender and a large bowl of fresh fruit.

'You have to look after yourself because no one else is going to do it for you,' he explained. He was rummaging around in a large plastic tub. 'Here,' he said, handing her a bottle of After Sun lotion. 'Slap lots of this on. And tonight, you're going to come out with us. It's Saskia's birthday and we're all going to get very, very drunk.'

'Oh I can't,' moaned Emma. 'Everybody's going to be laughing at me. I think I'll just lie here and die.'

'Emma, nobody's going to be laughing at you. We're all your friends.'

'Really?' Emma hadn't thought of it like that.

'Of course. We're on your side. We all love you. Who needs Jason Cairns when you've got all of us?'

Emma brightened up and she realised it was true. Orlando, Liz, Stacey, Ben, all the band, all the crew – they were all her friends. But still the thought of going out in public was too much.

'Oh Orlando, thank you. But I really don't want to go out.'

'Doctor's orders,' said Orlando, and topped up her glass.

'Everybody loves me,' Emma repeated to herself a little later as she staggered unsteadily down the corridor to her own room. It was only when she started to run her bath, that she understood why Orlando had given her the After Sun. Around her eyes were two white ovals where her sunglasses had been. Oh bloody hell, she thought. This is all your fault, Jason Cairns. She used the phone in her room to ring his mobile again, not expecting for one minute that he would answer.

'Listen, you complete and utter bastard shit,' she shouted at his answering service. 'Now I've got sunburn and it's ALL YOUR FAULT. I hope you and Nicole ROT IN HELL!'

After three gin and tonics, Jason's contribution to her failure to use sunscreen seemed like a far more serious crime than getting engaged to somebody else without telling her.

'What happened to you?' asked Patrick when she arrived at the restaurant with Orlando. 'You look like somebody punched you.'

'They did. Didn't you hear?' smiled Emma, feeling pleasantly anaesthetised to everything. She was glad she'd come. All these people were her friends. Wasn't that great? Who needs Jason? She gave Saskia a big birthday kiss, sat down and poured herself a glass of red wine from the open bottle on the table.

'That's a lovely top,' said Saskia.

'Thanks. Zara. Eighteen quid! I was saving it to wear for when Jason came. There's no point in wasting it, is there?'

'It shows off your tan really well.'

'Oh this isn't a tan, it's sunburn,' Emma assured her.

'How are you, Emma? Are you feeling better?' asked Stacey.

'I'm fine. I'm fantastic!' beamed Emma. 'Why wouldn't I be?' She took another swig of wine.

'Are you going to be able to cover up that redness?' Stacey whispered in Saskia's ear. 'She's been pale in all the other scenes we've shot.'

'Oh it'll be fine,' Saskia replied, offhandedly. 'We can tone it down. You'll never notice.'

'Good,' said Stacey, but she had a nightmare vision of Emma going from pink to white and back again in successive scenes like a schizophrenic chameleon.

Across the table, Liz was trying to conceal her displeasure and gripped Ben's hand tightly under the table. She'd seen the way his eyes flickered when he'd said hello to Emma. Even with a candy-floss complexion and panda eyes, this restaurant was so dark that it just read as a healthy glow. She hadn't expected

Emma to turn up at all tonight and she certainly hadn't expected her to turn up in a slashed-to-the-waist black halter-neck top. Emma had been a big enough threat when she was madly in love with Jason. The last thing in the world she wanted now was for Emma to be single. Couldn't she at least have the decency to go into relationship mourning like a normal person and stay locked up in her room out of harm's way?

'I didn't think you smoked,' Liz said, referring to the cigarette in Emma's hand.

'I don't,' said Emma and remembered why. As she lit it and took her first drag, all the blood rushed from her head. It felt horrible, but she decided it was horrible in a good way – she didn't want to have any blood in her head tonight – and took another defiant puff.

Orlando ordered a beer and went over to say hi to Paolo. 'Go easy on the wine,' he told her.

'OK,' she promised him. 'I'll just have this one glass.'

When he'd gone, Liz passed Emma her own drink to sample. 'Here, try some of this,' she said.

Emma took a sip. 'That's delicious. What is it?'

'Just fruit punch. Want some?'

'Ooh, yes please.'

Liz poured her a tall glass of Sangria from the jug on the table that was filled with chopped apple, slices of lemon, red wine, and several glasses of brandy. Emma took it gratefully. By the time the food arrived, she was flying.

'So Emma,' Danny sat down in the empty seat beside her, 'me and the lads are going on to a club after this. D'you want to come with us?'

'I'd love to! I'll show that bastard, Jason,' she announced loudly, too absorbed in her own woe to be surprised that Danny Parker was actually striking up a conversation with her. The film was already half over and apart from their scenes together, he'd never spoken more than two words to her in a row. 'How could he just get engaged without telling me?' she wailed.

'What do you want to go worrying about that loser for when you've got the four of us? Here, girl, have some of this', and he re-filled her empty glass with the cheap house red.

'But I miss him!' she said unhappily, draining half the glass in one go. 'I haven't had a snog in three whole weeks!'

'Hey, aren't you forgetting? You get to snog me this week.'

'That's right I do, don't I?' She suddenly realised that she was pouring out her heart to Danny Parker who was only the most fanciable bloke in the whole country, practically.

'I'm a bit nervous about it, if you want the God's truth,' Danny confessed with that bashful, little-boy stare she recognised from his first CD cover.

'You! Nervous? I don't believe that.'

'Yeah, well, I don't know how you kiss, do I? And the camera's going to be on me and all that and I've got to make it look like I'm the best kisser in the world. It's a bit of a mind-fuck. Aren't you nervous?'

'I hadn't really thought about it before, but when you put it like that, I suppose I am.' Emma started to get worried.

'You see the problem is that I don't fancy you,' said Danny.

'You don't?'

'No. No offence, I mean you're a nice girl and all but you haven't got the equipment I go for.'

'Oh. Right. I'm sorry.' Emma felt crestfallen. Now if their scene didn't work it would be all her fault for not living up to Danny's high standards.

'So I'm not going to be able to just snog you naturally. I'm going to have to make an effort to make it look real.'

'How do you mean?'

'Well when you kiss,' asked Danny, 'what side does your nose go on?'

'Gosh, I don't know. I never really thought about it. Is that important?'

'Yeah, course it's important. What if they say "Action" and the first thing we do is bump noses? We'll look like right tossers. You know how they rush everything on this shoot –

they're not going to hang around while we figure out how we're going to kiss.'

'I think maybe my nose goes to the right.' Emma closed her eyes and bobbed her head from side to side to see what felt most natural. 'Except, sometimes, I'm pretty sure it goes to the left!' Why hadn't they told her about this at drama school?

Danny sighed. 'See now that's going to be tricky. But you know what they do on proper films? Like in Hollywood and that?'

'No, what?' Emma was dying to know.

'They rehearse don't they? To break the ice. You go off together in a little room somewhere quiet and you have a couple of kisses to work it out. Like, say you and I had to do a scene where we had to do a waltz or something like that, well we'd rehearse that, wouldn't we? We'd get lessons and shit. Dancing, kissing, it's the same thing.'

'That's what I've been doing with the roller-blading!' Emma agreed enthusiastically. 'So when do you want to rehearse? How about tomorrow afternoon? I've got the day off.'

'How about now?'

'Now?'

Danny got up slowly, pausing as he rose to whisper in her ear so that no one else could hear. 'Meet me in the toilets,' he said, and then sauntered off towards the back of the restaurant.

Emma stared after him wondering if she'd heard him correctly. Meet me in the toilets? The very thought of rehearsing a snog with Danny Parker in the toilets was completely ridiculous. Danny Parker was one of the most famous men in all of Britain! People like Danny Parker didn't even breathe the same air that she did. She looked around the table. Everyone else was talking so loudly over the music, they had no idea what Danny had just said to her. Maybe he was right. They ought to practise a bit so they'd be sure of getting it right. And besides, wouldn't it serve Jason right if she just went and snogged Danny anyway? That was two reasons. She was already on her feet and the room was spinning.

Danny was waiting for her outside the door with the wooden plaque of a flamenco dancer on it. There were two girls they didn't know at the basin reapplying their make-up. They recognised Danny at once and shot Emma a look of unbridled envy as she followed Danny into the end cubicle and he closed the door behind them.

'Listen, Danny,' she began, but he pushed her hard against the wall.

'Have you ever done it in a toilet before?' he demanded.

'I've never even done it in Brighton before,' she confessed and then she felt Danny's cold hard tongue slide between her lips. Which way was her nose going? Definitely to the left. She wanted to tell Danny to remember to go to the right, but it was a little tricky with his tongue in her mouth.

Wow, she thought. I'm actually kissing Danny Parker! It took her a little while to realise that she wasn't enjoying it quite as much as she'd thought she would. Even though he might be the most fanciable man in Britain, it turned out she didn't fancy him after all. But perhaps she should kiss him a bit longer just to make sure. After all, she thought, she hadn't kissed anyone else apart from Jason in such a long time. She was probably just rusty. It was like driving a strange car, wasn't it? You go through the motions: mirror, signal, manoeuvre, clutch, brake, accelerator, and it eventually all falls into place.

'Perhaps I should run my fingers through your hair?' she suggested. She gave it a try and he seemed to enjoy it, because his cold fleshy lips clamped themselves more vigorously to her mouth and after thirty seconds of determined snogging, he pulled his T-shirt out of his trousers.

'Squeeze my nipples,' he told her and Emma, grateful to be given some direction, gave his right nipple a friendly tweak. Up close she realised, up *really* close, he wasn't that good looking at all. Funny that.

'Harder,' he commanded. 'Really hard.'

Emma wasn't sure how hard was really hard, so she upped her tweak to a pinch and Danny moaned and started undoing his belt. Any moment now, Emma thought, I'll start to fancy him. And she closed her eyes again so she wouldn't think about the wet toilet paper all over the floor and the fag burns on the plastic cistern.

She was caught by surprise as Danny's hand delved between her legs and inside her knickers.

'I really want to fuck you,' he whispered urgently as his trousers dropped around his knees.

'That wasn't in the script!' she squealed.

Danny took her hand and guided it inside his Calvin Kleins. 'That's OK, I'm not acting. Can't you tell?' He'd been telling the truth when he told Emma he didn't fancy her, but he'd shagged loads of birds he didn't fancy that much. Sometimes, having high standards could be a burden, but he tried not to let it cramp his style. He'd barely noticed Emma before but he approved of the top she was wearing tonight – once, when she'd leaned forward, he'd got a good look at her tits and decided she was probably worth a go. Besides, he liked doing it in toilets – the smell really got him going. He still had fond memories of the toilets on the Intercity 125 to Doncaster where a reporter from *Smash Hits* had given him a blow-job while he was taking a dump.

Emma could hear heels on the tiled floor as the door opened, and then two girls' voices. It sounded like Bex and Tracey.

'I'm not going to have sex with you,' she hissed, and took her hand out of his briefs before it could touch anything she didn't want it to. But Danny wasn't to be put off so easily. He turned her around and pinned her against the other wall, pushing himself up against her from behind so the toilet roll holder jabbed her in the stomach.

'Go on, just let me slide it in and out a couple of times,' he whispered, and meanwhile his hands reached around from behind and inside her top and suddenly, Emma found out exactly what he'd meant by 'really hard'. He took hold of each of her nipples between a thumb and thick blunt forefinger and squeezed as though he was trying to tear them right off.

'Owww!' Emma screamed silently to herself. Was he insane? Did he think that was supposed to feel *nice*? She elbowed him in the ribs to make him let go and he sat down on the toilet with a bump.

'Well, then either you go down on me, or I go down on you,' he suggested.

Emma flushed the toilet so Bex and Tracey wouldn't hear him. 'I'm not going down on you,' she whispered back.

'Well, let me go down on you then,' he said matter-of-factly.

'No. I don't want you to.' The fug of air freshener and hairspray mingled with Danny's Camel breath was starting to make her feel queasy.

'Why not? What's the problem? You don't have to do anything. You can just sit on the toilet seat.'

Emma started to giggle. Was this really how Britain's most fanciable man chatted up women? She remembered that she'd been really unhappy a little while ago, but she was having trouble remembering why. How could she have been so sad when the world was so funny?

'Is that you in there, Emma?' she heard Bex say. 'Wotchu laughing at?'

'Nothing,' she replied. 'I'll just be a minute.' She wanted to leave, but if Bex and Tracey saw her with Danny, they were bound to get the wrong idea. Danny grabbed hold of her arms and pulled her down onto her knees. His job was made easier by the fact that she could barely stand up without assistance. I'm drunk! she thought with surprise as she tumbled to the floor. Fancy that! It must be the gin and tonic.

Bex and Tracey were now discussing whether Giles was nicer than Danny, unaware that Danny was just six feet away from them, pushing Emma's head firmly down into his groin.

'Giles has got a puppy,' Bex was saying.

'Ohhhh! That's so sweet,' said Tracey.

Emma heard the music outside get louder as they opened the door to leave and then two pairs of kitten-heels walking away.

'Go on, girl, you know you want it,' Danny encouraged her. 'Suck my big YunGun!'

'Your *what?*' gasped Emma. She struggled to her feet with some difficulty and stared down at the great Danny Parker who was now sitting on the toilet seat with his trousers around his knees, pointing towards his surprisingly small pink erection like a helpful tour guide. Even in her half-cut state she realised it was time to go.

'Sorry, Danny,' she told him. 'I don't think I fancy you either', and she unlocked the door. 'Oh, by the way,' she said, suddenly remembering, 'your nose goes to the right.'

Emma paused just for a moment to straighten her top before staggering back out to the restaurant – not quite long enough to see Liz come out of the middle cubicle a few moments later, having heard everything, from the moment Danny had told Emma: 'Meet me in the toilets'.

Liz took out her lipstick and smiled at her reflection in the mirror. Sometimes, she was sure, absolutely sure, there was a God. There had to be.

twenty-six

'You should go and see him,' Liz told her. 'Get to the bottom of it.'

It was nearly midnight and Emma was lying face-down on her bed back at the hotel, pretending not to cry. The alcohol had worn off and the world no longer seemed like a hilarious party planet where pop stars wanted to cop off with you. It was a harsh, inhospitable asteroid where boyfriends stabbed you in the back and didn't return your phone calls.

'Hey,' said Liz soothingly. 'The papers have probably got it all wrong and Jason's just afraid to talk to you in case you're angry about him going to the party in the first place. You know what cowards men are.'

Emma sniffed and sat up a little.

'D'you think?' She turned to look at Liz and couldn't help noticing that at the end of the night Liz still looked fantastic and was completely sober. I wish I was more like Liz, she thought. Liz doesn't go out without sunscreen and get falling-down drunk and have fumbles in the toilet or find out she's getting dumped by reading about it in the *News of the World*. Emma wondered whether she should tell Liz what had happened with Danny, but decided not to. Not until she was sure herself exactly what had happened. We ought to rehearse, Danny had said. She groaned into her pillow so that Liz wouldn't hear her.

'Are you feeling OK?' Liz asked.

Emma nodded. She sat up and drank a little from the glass of water Liz was holding. In her darkest hour, she realised, she could always count on Liz to be there with a glass of water. A true friend.

'You've got a day off tomorrow, haven't you?' Liz persisted.

Emma nodded.

'Well, get yourself up to Sheffield and sort it out. I'll pay for your ticket, if you like. You know Jason loves you. He's only got to see you and everything will be OK.'

Emma looked at her reflection – at her puffy bloodshot eyes, sunburned cheeks, lank, drunken hair and hoped Liz was right.

The next morning, Emma sat on the train watching the familiar blur of scenery roll by and was able to pretend for a while that everything was still OK. At St Pancras, she'd bought a stack of postcards and a thick black felt-tip and was composing various notes to push under his door in case he wasn't home. 'Jason, I forgive you. We can work this out.' 'Please call me, Jason – we need to talk.' 'Jason please, please call me.' None of them were quite right and for a while as the train headed north, she told herself she wouldn't need them anyway because Jason would be waiting for her on the platform as usual. Except of course, he wasn't.

She let herself in the main door of Jason's block of serviced apartments with her spare key, just as she always did, nodding a distracted 'hello' at the small but dedicated knot of teenage *Shelby Square* anoraks who camped rain or shine on his wall outside. She hadn't phoned to say she was coming and if he wasn't here, there'd still be time to try the studio. But walking down the corridor on the second floor she was relieved to hear music coming from his flat. He'll be so surprised to see me, she told herself. And I'll forgive him and everything will be OK. She took a tiny mirror out of her handbag and checked her hair one last time before she pressed the buzzer. Her face resembled a giant strawberry but she hoped Jason would be able see past that and realise that he still loved her. A few seconds later she could hear the security chain being put on.

That's odd, she thought, Jason doesn't usually bother with the chain. And then, when the door opened, she thought for one moment that in her heartbroken confusion she must be on the wrong floor – all the doors in his building were painted an identical dove grey. Very tasteful.

'Yes, can I help you?' An eye peered out through the narrow gap. It was wearing small black-rimmed glasses and Emma thought she'd seen it somewhere before.

'Sorry, have I got the right place? Is Jason home?' Emma asked, and a second too late, she remembered where she'd seen this girl before.

'No. Hang on.' The eye rolled as though it was used to being asked this question, disappeared, and when it returned a second later, a hand came with it and shoved a postcard through the door. And then Nicole Lloyd shut the door in Emma's face, leaving her standing on the doorstep clutching a *Shelby Square* publicity still autographed: 'Best wishes, Jason Cairns.'

Liz thought about Emma a lot while she watched Ben direct endless scenes of Turpin and his heavies running from one end of Brighton to the other. She really was a Good Samaritan, she thought to herself. She hoped Emma would sort it out with Jason. She hoped she wouldn't hurry back. It was so peaceful on set without her and that stupid band hogging all Ben's attention.

After they wrapped, she dragged him out for a drink before he could waste another evening in a budget meeting with Patrick.

'It's ridiculous being cooped up inside on a glorious evening like this. You know Patrick doesn't listen to a word you say anyway. He just likes you there for company.'

'I need to find a cashpoint,' Ben told her. 'I've only got my credit card.'

'That's OK. My treat,' said Liz. She took some pound coins out of her purse and Ben went to fight his way through to the bar while Liz stretched out her legs with satisfaction. Ben was eating out of the palm of her hand these days.

She emptied her purse on the table and began to make little piles of all the ten- and twenty-pence pieces. There was more than enough here to pay for another round. She had fifty pence in copper alone. No wonder her shoulder was aching, carrying all that sharpnel around. When Ben returned with a beer and a glass of wine her heart leapt to see him walking towards her. How could she have spent six years without him? She missed him when he was out of her sight for six minutes.

'You know, I've been thinking,' she said, as she lit a cigarette. 'Maybe splitting up was the best thing that could have happened to us.'

'How do you mean?'

'Well, because now we appreciate each other,' said Liz. 'Now we know what it's like to be apart and we know that we're much better together.'

Ben admired Liz's luxurious profile and thought she might be right. What exactly had he been so afraid of? She was stunning and the sex was even better than ever. He rested his palm on the inside of her silky thigh, letting his finger wander underneath her tiny skirt. A few weeks ago, he hadn't thought it possible that he would ever desire Liz again but now he cast his eye along the seafront and wondered if there was somewhere they could do it right this second without being seen. They'd passed a photo-booth a little way back . . .

'You're not thinking about work, I hope.'

'I wasn't – but now that you've reminded me, I should really go and find Danny and Emma and go over their love scene.'

Liz snorted. 'I wouldn't worry about them. They've been doing their own rehearsals.'

'What do you mean?'

'Oh, didn't you know?' said Liz innocently. 'I caught them shagging in the toilets last night at Saskia's party.'

'Don't be ridiculous,' said Ben. 'She's only just broken up with her boyfriend.'

'What can I say?' said Liz sweetly. 'The girl's a fast worker.'

301

'No, you've got it wrong. She wouldn't shag Danny. Emma's not like that.'

'Darling, I heard them with my own ears. They were hard at it.'

'But how could she? With *Danny*?' Ben was horrified and disgusted, as Liz had known he would be.

'Well some girls go for that kind of thing,' Liz pointed out. 'That *is* why you cast him in your movie.'

'Yeah – but that was before any of us knew what he was really like. How could anyone who's ever spent more than ten minutes with Danny Parker actually fancy him? Emma's really gone down in my estimation.'

'Oh I'm sure she's gone down on a lot of things even bigger than that,' smiled Liz.

'Spare some change, please?' The young man standing by their table was wrapped in a filthy grey blanket, even though the temperature was still around twenty-six degrees. The hand he held out was dirty and covered in cuts that hadn't healed.

Liz shook her head apologetically. 'Sorry,' she said, not bothering to look at him properly. 'I haven't got any change.'

'Liz?' whispered Ben in embarrassment and nodded at the table in front of her which was covered in coins.

Liz sighed. 'Oh, for heaven's sake,' she muttered, and reluctantly handed over a small pile of five two-pence pieces.

'Wait,' said Ben, and before the boy could walk away he gave him a couple of fifties as well.

'What did you do that for?' said Liz. 'He'll only spend it on drugs or booze.'

'Well, so would you,' said Ben, and wondered what had got into him to make it come out so nasty.

The house they were using as the location for Jasmine's flat belonged to a couple called Trisha and Jeremy. They were friends of Piers's sister-in-law and were rapidly having second thoughts about letting a film crew into their home. Trisha and Jeremy had got halfway through doing the place up when their money had run out and so they'd leapt at the opportunity to get their two downstairs rooms decorated at somebody else's expense – and make some cash into the bargain. And then the art department had turned up with vile turquoise paint, and another colour that reminded Trisha of dried blood.

'We'll repaint it whatever colour you like when we've finished,' they promised her, but that would mean at least another two days of upheaval and mess with all their own furniture squashed into the children's upstairs bedroom. Yesterday, Trisha had gone to Toni and Guy to get her hair done. She'd imagined that if she hung around, they might give her a little part in the movie, but all morning people had been pushing her aside as though she was in their way. In her own house!

Right now there were two men in her front garden hanging some kind of black curtain right across the downstairs windows, trampling her newly planted lavender border and flicking their cigarette ends all over the York paving.

'Where's the toilet, love?' somebody asked her, and she pointed upstairs.

'Do you mind not going upstairs in your boots?' she called after him. 'This stair carpet is brand new. We haven't had it Scotchguarded yet.'

She was going to give Piers a piece of her mind when she could find him. Typically, he'd disappeared and now the neighbours were having a go at *her*, blaming *her* for the enormous blue truck that had woken them all at seven o'clock, reversing noisily into the coned-off parking space right outside her house.

'Oh, do mind the wallpaper!' she cried as another man wearing khaki shorts and a bulging tool belt around his waist came through the front door carrying two heavy black metal stands which clattered into the wall behind him.

'Sorry, love,' he said, giving the spot a quick rub with his suede glove. 'Was that already there?'

'No, it wasn't already there!' she retorted, examining the

damage. There was a new, definite dent in the wall and the paper had been nicked. 'You're going to have to repair this too, you know,' she said angrily. 'This wallpaper costs £59 a metre!'

The man shrugged and didn't look at her as he erected the black stand in her living room. 'Better take it up with locations,' he advised.

'I certainly will,' said Trisha, and she stormed out into the street to look for Piers, nearly colliding with Ben who was still mulling over the conversation he'd had with Liz the night before. Emma and Danny? It had to be a mistake.

In make-up, Bex was buffing Emma's nails with more force than usual because she could barely keep a lid on her jealousy that Emma was going to get to pretend to shag Danny today when so far she hadn't had a look in. She was pretty sure he'd already shagged Saskia and Tracey – although they denied it of course – Poppy in the art department, and at least three girls he'd met in a club, and it was insulting being left out like this.

Emma closed her eyes while Tracey blended the neutralising concealer all over her face and neck to disguise the sunburn. She was miles away, and Danny Parker was the last thing on her mind.

Yesterday, after Nicole Lloyd had shut the door in her face, she had stood on Jason's landing stunned, not entirely sure what had just happened.

Maybe, she'd thought, she should go to the studio and have it out with him. There was still a chance that it was all a horrible misunderstanding. Perhaps Nicole Lloyd's flat was being redecorated and she was just staying with Jason for a few days. Perhaps she was sleeping on the sofa. She opened her bag to look for her mobile. She'd try and call him one more time. He'd tell her it was all perfectly innocent. But then she noticed the postcards and the black felt-tip pen in her bag and had a better idea. She put the phone away and in letters four feet high wrote the word: 'Bastard!' on Jason's tasteful, dove-grey front door. Then she went downstairs and gave his mobile number and his home phone number to all the members of his fan club sitting on the front wall.

'You know he farts in bed, don't you?' she told them, and started walking back to the train station.

'You look dead nervous,' Tracey was telling her now. 'Is it because of your nude scene this afternoon? I'd be shitting meself if it was me.' She selected a second colour from her palette to match Emma's normal skin tone and began to colour her back in. 'Now this will stay on pretty well provided you don't rub it in.'

'Yes, Tracey,' said Emma, jolted back to reality as she remembered exactly what she was supposed to do today. Until now, she'd been so excited about being in a real film that she'd managed to push this scene to the back of her mind. She'd somehow imagined that by the time she came to do it, she'd be such an old pro that stripping off in front of a bunch of strangers would be a piece of cake. But now she'd gotten to know everybody and she realised that made it much worse. She'd had breakfast with these people every morning and now they were all going to see her bits? It would have been far easier, she realised, to get naked in front of a room full of total strangers who she'd never met and would never have to see again. What on earth had she been thinking when she agreed to do this film? Was she mad? She wondered if Tracey had a concealer in her make-up box that would make her completely invisible.

'You know some actors have a little drink before they do a sex scene to relax them,' said Tracey. 'Do you want some vodka? We keep a couple of bottles for emergencies. But don't tell anyone. We'd all get sacked. Some new Health and Safety bollocks.'

'No. But thanks,' whispered Emma. Then, remembering Nicole Lloyd standing there in Jason's flat, suddenly it all got too much for her and she started to cry.

'Oh flippin' 'eck!' moaned Tracey. 'I've just done your eyes!'

Saskia came running to give her a cuddle. 'Oh, you're not still crying over Jason, are you?' she cooed.

Emma looked up at the three faces crowded around her and could only sniff.

'I'll get the vodka,' said Bex.

'Morning, boys,' said Stacey as she sat down with Giles and Alex on the dining bus. 'You're not working this morning, are you?'

'No, but the fry-ups here are much better than at the hotel,' admitted Alex.

Stacey sliced her banana neatly over her muesli. 'Good day off?' she asked and, in answer to her question, both Giles and Alex lifted up their shirts.

'Have you two joined the Masons or something?' she asked, bemused.

'We've had our nipples pierced,' said Giles, and he twisted his chest around so she could get a better look.

'Oh,' said Stacey and gave Giles's small silver ring a delicate tap which made him wince with pleasure and agony. 'How sweet,' she said. 'Where did you get that done?'

'In Worthing,' said Alex.

'You went to Worthing to get your nipples pierced?'

'Yeah, at the hairdresser's on the high street.'

Stacey inspected the crusting, oozing lumps of skin and shook her head.

'What's wrong?' asked Giles. He'd expected Stacey to be impressed by his radical gesture.

'Well, it just seems a funny place to go, that's all. If you said, "We went to Brazil and got our nipples pierced", that I could understand. Or Bangkok. But not Worthing. You go to Worthing for a cream tea with your granny. You come back with a stick of rock, not pierced nipples.'

'We went with Danny,' Alex explained. 'He was getting his hair cut.'

Stacey spat out her tea. 'He was doing what?!'

'Getting his hair cut. There's no law against that, is there?'

Stacey folded up her paper and ran to the make-up bus to inspect the damage.

'I was just coming to find you,' said Saskia.

Danny was sitting in the make-up chair reading the script for his next film and Stacey could tell immediately that his hair was at least an inch shorter than it had been when they'd finished shooting on Saturday. Saskia was tugging at it to make it stand up.

'Ow,' said Danny and punched her arm.

'I'll give you Ow in a minute, Danny Parker!' Saskia snapped, hitting him back. 'What am I supposed to do with this?'

Danny turned his head from side to side admiring his profiles.

'Look, your sideburns are completely different!'

'Yeah, it looks ace, doesn't it?' said Danny.

'He'll have to wear a hat,' said Stacey.

'Leave it out, no one's going to notice,' Danny whined.

Stacey wanted to throttle him. 'Danny, on screen your head is going to be ten feet wide. Of course people are going to notice!' The problem was, she realised, that Danny's head was ten feet wide at the best of times.

'Well I could have got my hair cut in the film, couldn't I?' he insisted.

'Yes, if we started shooting on Scene 1 and finished shooting on Scene 163. But you can't get your hair cut in Scene 97, and two minutes later in Scene 98 it's grown back again. You know that. Don't you?'

Apparently he didn't.

Emma watched in silence as she sipped her vodka and orange-juice. She'd never had vodka at quarter to eight in the morning before, but Tracey was right. It really helped to calm her down.

Danny saw her looking at his hair in the mirror. 'What are you looking at, Miss Prick-tease?' he demanded.

But then again, she thought, still not quite calm enough.

*

307

'Terrific,' said Ben when Stacey told him the news. 'My leading lady's changed colour and my leading man's got new hair.'

'Could they make love with the lights out?' suggested Jamie helpfully. 'Well, me and Josephine always do,' he muttered in self-defence when Hugo glared at him.

'Can you frame him so that the top of his head's out of shot?' asked Ben.

'I'll have a go,' said Ryan, 'but he's going to be moving up and down rather a lot.' Everyone turned to watch Ryan as he made thrusting motions with his hips while pretending to hold a camera. 'Well, isn't he?'

'I don't know,' said Hugo. 'Is that how you and Josephine do it, Jamie?'

'Can't he wear a hat?' asked Ryan.

'He's in bed! He's naked!' shouted Ben in exasperation.

'Might be kind of kinky,' said Patrick.

'He'll have been wearing his motorcycle helmet in the previous scene,' Stacey pointed out.

'Maybe it's one of Emma's hats,' suggested Patrick in a faraway voice. 'He brings her home, sees the hat hanging on the wall and tries it on.' Patrick drifted off into his own private fantasy and there was silence while everyone considered this suggestion and waited for further inspiration.

The vodka had left a warm, comforting haze around Emma like a duvet. When they walked the scene through, marking out the positions where they would stand when Danny kissed her for the first time, where they would turn during the kiss, and which direction she would face as he slipped off her coat, she swayed ever so slightly as she tried to watch Will marking the different spots on the floor with coloured tape. Danny wasn't even speaking to her and seemed to be really annoyed with her about the other night for some reason. But what she hadn't expected was that Ben wasn't talking to her either. When she'd said hello to him that morning, he'd barely nodded at her and instead of coming over to talk the scene through, the way he normally did, he was sitting behind his monitor grumpily nursing a cup of coffee. It was Stacey who came over to tell her that there'd be a new line added to her script.

'Danny's going to put on your hat and you say to him, "No, don't take it off. It really turns me on." Have you got that?'

Emma repeated the line carefully and wondered why Ben seemed so stand-offish all of a sudden.

'What's the matter with Ben this morning?' she whispered to Liz when she brought her parka on set. 'He seems really quiet.'

'Oh, he's just worried about Danny's haircut,' Liz assured her. 'I'd keep well out of his way if I were you. He's very tense.' She rolled back the sleeves of Emma's coat two turns. 'Is this going to be your first screen kiss?'

Emma nodded. She hoped Liz wouldn't smell the vodka on her breath.

'Well, I'll give you a tip,' said Liz. 'Between takes, don't turn it off. Even when the camera's not rolling, keep holding Danny's hand, or stroking his neck – or whatever it is that you do. You two've got such great chemistry together.'

Emma wondered again whether to tell Liz about her rehearsal with Danny, but there were too many other people within ear-shot.

'Oh Liz, I don't know if I can,' was all she said. 'Not after Jason and everything.'

'Of course you can,' Liz whispered back. 'Put Jason right out of your head for now.'

'That's impossible.'

'Don't be silly. You're a wonderful actress. You've really got something special. You can totally do this.'

'Really?' asked Emma. She didn't feel special. She felt like a squashed bug. A squashed, slightly tipsy red bug.

'Really,' Liz promised, walking back to the monitor. Oh she knew what actors liked to hear all right. And they always believed it.

'What are you doing, Liz?' asked Jamie, who'd overheard part of this. 'You're not directing the talent, are you?'

'Talent?' said Liz innocently. 'Don't be ridiculous. I was just talking to Emma.'

When they were ready to go, Emma remembered what Liz had told her. The first shot followed Jasmine and Eddie walking into Jasmine's bedroom. The lights are off and at the same moment as Jasmine turns on the bedside light, Eddie picks up a baseball cap from her bed and puts it on. He looks at his reflection in the mirror, laughs and goes to take it off.

'No – don't take it off,' says Jasmine. Emma's voice sounded like it was coming from far away. 'It really turns me on.'

What a ridiculous thing to say, Emma thought as she gazed into Danny's eyes while trying not to look at him. It wasn't even eleven o'clock and his breath already stank of Camel cigarettes. Emma closed her eyes as Danny's tongue darted into her mouth and she tried to pretend this was Jason she was kissing, and that this was Jason's tongue that had been dumped in her mouth like a wet parcel. But that just made it worse.

Upstairs, Trisha flushed the toilet noisily in protest.

'Cut!'

'I'm sorry,' Trisha bellowed down the stairs, although she didn't sound very sorry. 'But my children do have a right to empty their bladders in their own home!'

Emma wanted to wipe her mouth but she remembered Liz's advice and forced herself to keep hold of Danny's hand.

He leaned over and whispered in her ear: 'No wonder your boyfriend dumped you. Did you give him blue balls as well?' He tickled the inside of her palm with his middle finger and Emma decided she had never disliked anyone quite so much in her entire life.

'Don't they make a lovely couple?' whispered Liz to Patrick, but loud enough for Ben to hear.

'Did I see tongues?' Patrick asked.

'That was good enough for me!' said Ben. He had no desire to watch that again. Watching Emma and Danny made him feel sick to his stomach.

'I'd like to go again,' Ryan shouted back. 'I lost them on the turn.'

'OK, we'll be going again,' called Jamie.

'We can still see Danny's new sideburns from this angle,' Stacey told Ben. 'It would help if Emma could put her hand up like she's stroking his face.'

'OK. Stroke his face!' he called out to Emma. 'Just by his ear! No, no, the other side, the camera side.'

Emma didn't know why Ben sounded so impatient with her. He must be really cross about Danny's haircut, but that was no reason to take it out on her.

They went again and this time Danny's arm was blocking Emma's face.

Ben sighed. 'Hang on,' he told Jamie and ran into the living room to give them some notes. 'Danny, could you keep your elbow a little lower next time? You're blocking Emma's face.'

'That wouldn't look natural. I'd never hold anyone like that.'

'No, it'll look fine,' said Ben. 'Trust me.'

Danny put his hand on the back of Emma's neck and let his elbow drop down in an exaggerated pose. 'It looks stupid,' he said.

'No, no. Not like that. Like this.' Ben put his arm stiffly around Emma's shoulders to demonstrate what he meant. He didn't look at her and she stared at the floor feeling like a slab of meat or a shop dummy.

'See?' said Ben and dropped his arm.

Emma's eyes felt prickly and she lowered her head to let Tracey fluff up her hair. She hated this job. She looked at Ryan behind the camera, and Billy holding the boom and Kevin who'd come in to clip a gel back in front of one of the lights. They all did things. They knew stuff. They had real jobs. She wished she could trade places with any of them right that second, but instead she had to be kissed again and again in mid-shot and close-up and extreme close-up. A whole morning of having her lips chewed and her teeth licked by Mr Camel Breath until she thought she would scream. And then she remembered that after lunch she was going to have to do it all again – only this time naked. In front of Ryan and Billy and Kevin and Hugo and everyone. She tried to remember which cupboard Tracey had hidden the vodka in.

At lunchtime, Ben found himself side by side with Danny Parker in the honey-wagon and the question was out before he even knew he was going to say it.

'Is that true about you and Emma the other night?' he asked. He hoped that Liz had somehow made a mistake.

Danny curled his lip. Had Emma told everyone that she'd walked out on him? 'Who told you?' he sneered.

'Doesn't matter,' said Ben. He didn't need to know any more. He went back to his trailer on the pretext of viewing the VHS of the previous day's rushes and found Liz already waiting for him.

'It's OK. No one saw me,' she reassured him as she locked the door behind him. 'I was fabulously discreet!' She knelt on the couch and began massaging his shoulders the way she'd seen Emma do it. 'God, you're so tense!'

'What a morning,' sighed Ben. 'I was this close, you know? I was this close to just punching him.' He couldn't get the picture of Danny and Emma out of his mind. Liz moved over and kneeled across Ben's lap, her skirt stretched taut across her thighs.

'What could Emma possibly see in him?' Ben went on. 'I thought she had better taste than that.'

'Oh come on, Ben,' said Liz, licking the soft spot on his neck the way she knew he liked it. 'She wouldn't be the first actress to fall for her leading man, would she? It happens all the time. Just not usually in a public toilet.'

And she kissed him, slowly and softly, with the sole intention of driving every last thought of Emma out of his mind.

*

As the others queued for lunch, Emma announced loudly that she'd left her sunglasses in the make-up truck. She let herself in, finding the cupboard where she'd seen Tracey hide the bottle of vodka, and filled a styrofoam cup that still had the dregs of someone else's cup of tea in it. This is what professional actors do, Tracey had said. A bit of alcohol to relax them. It made sense of course. She had a bit more. She should probably be really, really, relaxed. Maybe she'd better take the whole bottle with her – just in case.

By the time she made her way back to the dining bus, the haze between her and the rest of the world had grown to the size of a large cloud.

'Here, we saved you a place,' said Bex, patting the seat beside her. None of the boys were on set today and Danny was officially in the dog-house on account of his hair so the Daft Tarts were at a bit of a loose end, socially.

Emma made a huge effort to walk in a straight line – the aisle of the bus seemed to be banking like a jumbo jet – but she made it all the way down to the end without mishap and congratulated herself on a supreme bit of acting. But as she put down her tray, her fork slid onto the floor under the table.

'It's OK, I'll get it,' she said calmly. It was wonderful how calm she was. Nudity? It's nothing really. We've all got bodies, haven't we? They're nothing to be ashamed of. We should be proud of our bodies, she was thinking to herself as she crawled under the table to retrieve her fork. And it's not as though I've had a huge amount to drink anyway – there's still half a bottle of vodka left easily, and I wouldn't be able to get down on my hands and knees like this if I was really drunk, would I and – OWWW!'

She'd tried to stand up but had completely forgotten that the table was above her, and cracked herself hard on the top of her head.

'Emma! Are you OK?'

'Give her some space!'

There was a crowd of legs all around her. She couldn't tell

who they belonged to. Her head really hurt. Tiny little pin pricks of white light danced in front of her eyes.

I'm seeing stars, she thought. Like in a cartoon.

'What happened?' someone was saying.

'She whacked her head on the table.'

'She might have concussion,' said Tim. 'Call the nurse.'

'Can you stand up?' asked Jamie. 'Do you want the nurse?'

'Ask her if she knows what day it is,' somebody suggested and Emma knew that it was really important that she stand up and that nobody call the nurse who would realise that she'd had nearly half a bottle of vodka before lunch and then she'd be fired and so would all the Daft Tarts.

'Yeah! I'm fine!' she said as brightly as she could. 'It was nothing!' And she laughed so that everyone would know she was OK and stop looking at her. She started to eat her lunch. 'See – I'm fine!' she insisted, and waited until everybody had turned away so she could rub her head in private.

Later, she somehow found herself examining the tiny G-string that would comprise her costume. 'Is this it?' she asked Liz. It looked like flesh-coloured dental floss.

'Why? You're not shy, are you?'

It was ironic really, thought Liz that a few weeks ago she'd been worrying about Emma looking too sexy in a navy-blue shirt from Gap. Now she was encouraging her to get naked and bounce about under Ben's nose. But of course she would also be wearing the ultimate passion-killing accessory – Danny Parker. Liz was sure that the sight of Emma shagging Danny would turn Ben off her for life. Not that she need worry about that anyway, because Ben was hers now – every fabulous inch of him. This would just be the final nail in Emma's coffin.

'Do you need help putting it on?'

'No, of course not,' said Emma and giggled without knowing why. 'We've all got bodies. They're nothing to be ashamed of.' Her voice seemed to be coming from out of a deep well and she started to undress in a kind of daze, like a sleepwalker. There was a bump growing on her head and she was starting to feel very odd. More than anything she wanted to go to sleep. Perhaps she could have a little lie down on the bed between takes.

Silently, she put on the G-string and then wrapped the fluffy grey dressing gown tightly around herself before following Liz onto the minibus that would take her back to the set, pressing her pink nose up against the window.

Like a lamb to the slaughter, thought Liz. Like a lamb to the slaughter.

While Pete, Kevin and Hugo played with the lights, Danny lay sprawled out on the bed, his arms behind his head, having a kip. Emma sat in an armchair as far away from him as possible and closed her eyes. The lump on her head had grown to the size of a small egg and her hair was starting to ache. Phil was arranging the pillows around Danny's head so that his haircut would be less visible.

'Can we see you in position, Emma love?' asked Hugo.

'I don't know. What is my position?' she asked. As she leaned forward, the room tilted a little and then righted itself again.

'Right.' Ben stepped forward, but he kept his eyes fixed on the bed rather than on Emma or Danny. 'Can we have Jasmine on top of Eddie, straddling him. Are you happy with that?'

'I'm very happy with that,' said Danny, and threw open his dressing gown. Emma was relieved to see that he was also wearing a flesh-coloured jockstrap. She left her own dressing gown on and climbed unsteadily onto the bed, aware of every eye in the room watching her. Her head complained at the sudden movement but the alcohol had made her fearless.

'Bring it on!' she laughed and wondered why everyone looked at her so strangely. She climbed over Danny so that she was hovering above his stomach and readjusted her dressing gown while Hugo squinted at the shadows. Her thigh muscles started to burn.

'Come on then, girl. Slide on down there,' leered Danny. 'You know you want to.'

'That's right, Danny. Don't mind us,' encouraged Hugo, 'Just pretend we're not here.'

'Shoot the rehearsal?' suggested Jamie.

'I think that's a very good idea,' said Ben.

'All right. Final checks and then everybody out of here who doesn't absolutely have to be in here,' said Jamie. 'This is a closed set. And we're going to shoot the rehearsal.'

To Emma's alarm, Liz began untying the sash of her dressing gown. 'Wait,' she begged in a last-minute panic. 'Kevin and Hugo haven't gone yet.'

'Well they'll see it all in the rushes,' Liz reminded her. 'And so will everyone at the cinema.'

Still Emma clung to her robe.

'Come on,' said Liz impatiently. 'It's a bit late to start getting shy. Danny's seen it all before, haven't you?'

'What do you mean?' gasped Emma, guiltily. Surely Danny hadn't told Liz about the other night?

'Well, Danny's a big boy. I'm sure he's seen plenty of naked women before,' said Liz smoothly and she slid Emma's dressing gown off her shoulders and bundled it up without further argument.

Emma had had dreams where she'd be walking down the street and suddenly realise she was naked. She wondered if she closed her eyes and opened them again, would she wake up back in her own bed in Shepherd's Bush? Maybe the whole film was just a figment of her imagination. She gave it a go, but when she opened her eyes again Danny and the film crew were still there.

'The human body is a beautiful thing,' she reminded herself and felt oddly woozy – but whether from the vodka or from the bump on the head, she could no longer tell. She was aware that the house had gone very quiet as though it was holding its breath, but she could hear furtive whispering coming from around the monitor in the kitchen. She heard Ben call 'Action'. Danny's hands were on her hips but she couldn't move. She sat upright, frozen, her eyes closed as the seconds ticked past.

'And cut!'

Liz threw the dressing gown around her shoulders and Ben ran in to see what the matter was. He'd expected problems with Danny – Danny was one big fucking problem – but not from Emma.

'What's the matter? Didn't you hear me call Action?'

'I don't know what to do,' she said. 'What am I supposed to do?'

'Well, you're making love. Do whatever feels natural.'

'That's just it. Nothing feels natural. Everything's totally *un*natural.'

'Why don't you talk her through it?' suggested Patrick – a little too quickly.

'Would that help?' asked Ben. 'If I talked you through it, while we're shooting?'

'It might.'

'OK. We won't record sound and I'll talk you through it.'

The dressing gown was taken away again and Ben stood just beside the camera as a mute board for Take 2 was put on.

'OK, Emma,' Ben told her, 'Just start by kissing Danny. Danny, can you push yourself up a little bit on your elbows there and help her . . . good . . . and keep kissing . . . and Danny . . . put your right hand on her breast now . . . no, your other right hand . . . still kissing . . . and stroking her breast . . . yeah, OK then, pinch it if you like . . . and Emma, if you can drop your head back now . . . further . . . and open your mouth a little . . . you're really loving this . . . no, you look like you're in pain . . . yeah, that's better . . . and arch your back . . . oh that's great . . . keep arching . . . and keep arching . . . and tilt your head just a fraction towards us . . . that's great . . . OK and slide back down now so you're lying flat on top of him . . .'

Emma's head was begging her to just keep still but her body was responding to Ben's direction as though it was in *Showgirls* and was making her arch her back and toss her hair around like there was no tomorrow. Out of the corner of her eye, Emma could see Patrick staring at her intently while Danny grabbed hold of her hair and pressed his lips roughly against her ear.

'It's my turn now, you bitch,' he whispered. 'You're not wimping out on me this time.'

'That's great Danny,' Ben called out. 'Now grab her bottom with both hands . . . and Emma start kissing Danny's neck . . . that's it, all around his neck . . . and kissing his chest . . . that's it, bury your face in there . . . and biting his nipples now . . . go on, really hard, like you mean it . . . now get yourself into position like you're actually doing it . . . no, no, you'll need to be lower than that . . . no, lower still or we'll see your G-string . . . right on top of his . . . yeah, that's it and stay there now and pushing against him . . . and rocking together . . . make it look real . . . yeah, Danny, that's very good . . . and Emma, arch your back again . . . can you toss your hair a little . . . oh that's great . . . and keep arching . . . and toss your hair . . . now drop your head forward, then toss your head all the way back . . . fabulous . . . and keep rocking against each other . . . keep rocking . . .'

Emma didn't like the rocking. She didn't like it one little bit. Her head felt strange and her stomach felt worse and there was a curious watering sensation in her mouth and still she had to keep rocking.

'And now open your eyes, both of you . . . looking at each other like you've found the person you've been searching for your whole life . . . that's it, Danny, really staring into Emma's eyes . . . and rocking . . . and rocking . . . harder . . . and can you open your eyes now, Emma?'

Emma opened her eyes and that's when she threw up all over Danny Parker.

For a second the world froze on its axis and there was absolute silence while Emma watched, fascinated, as half a bottle of vodka and three glasses of orange juice gushed over Danny's chest, down the sides of his ribs and onto the bed. Some of it had hit him in the face – there was a little river of vodka trickling down his left ear. Danny's eyes were staring up at her in stunned fury and his mouth was opening and closing like a fish, but no sound was coming out.

In the distance she heard Jamie's voice as though he was shouting from the other end of a long tunnel: 'And cut!'

And then suddenly the earth resumed its rotation and the sound was turned back on at maximum volume as Danny leapt up from underneath her, knocking her sideways.

'You stupid cunt!'

'Fetch Danny a towel!'

'Make-up!'

'I'll fucking have you!'

'Can we have art department on set!'

'And a mop!'

'Where's the bathroom in this fucking house? I've got to take a shower!'

Emma was aware of a dressing gown being thrown around her shoulders and a sea of faces she scarcely recognised staring back at her. She did the only thing she could under the circumstances. She ran.

The laughter started the moment the front door closed behind her. The same moment as the bathroom door upstairs slammed shut behind Danny.

'Oh please, God,' Hugo was saying to Tim. 'Tell me you recorded that.'

Tim hit rewind on the video playback and the entire crew crowded around the monitor and watched as the stream of vomit leapt off Danny's chest and back into Emma's mouth.

Hugo hit play and a cheer went up as Emma threw up over Danny all over again.

'I dunno about you mate, but I'd pay good money to see that at the pictures,' said Kevin.

'I think we could still see his haircut,' said Stacey.

Hugo gave her a patronising sneer. 'Darling, if anybody's going to be looking at his hair in this scene we might as well all go home.'

'Do you suppose Emma's OK?' asked Jamie after they'd

watched the video for the sixth time. 'Maybe someone ought to go see how she is.'

'I'll go,' offered Liz quickly.

'No, you stay and calm Danny down,' said Ben. 'I'll go.'

There was no sign of Emma outside. Ben hoped she'd gone back to Unit Base, because he had neither the time nor the inclination to conduct a house-to-house search of Brighton. But, realistically, where else was she likely to go wearing a G-string, a dressing gown and no shoes?

Dominic, the second AD, was already knocking on the door of Emma's trailer when he got there. 'Emma? What's the matter?' Ben heard him asking. 'Can I get you a cup of tea?'

'It's OK, Dom. I'll sort it out,' said Ben.

'What's happened? She came tearing in here and wouldn't say what was wrong.'

'She threw up on Danny Parker.'

Dominic laughed. 'I wish. No really – what happened?' Then he realised Ben wasn't joking. 'Did we get it on tape?' he asked. He was already running towards the house to see for himself.

Ben rapped impatiently on Emma's door. 'Emma. It's Ben. Are you all right?' There was no answer. 'Emma. We need you back on set. We haven't finished the scene. Are you well enough to carry on?'

He could hear Emma get up and unlock the door. As he stepped inside, the first thing he saw was the half-empty bottle of vodka on the floor.

'Have you been drinking?'

'No,' Emma lied. She could hardly stand up straight. She couldn't remember how she'd got back here.

Ben came in and closed the door behind him. Emma was still wearing the grey dressing gown, her nose and eyes were red and her cheeks streaked with tears and mascara. He was looking at half an hour in make-up to sort this lot out. He checked his watch. It was already twenty past three. It would be at least four by the time he'd be able to turn over again. That was OK. There was still time to get this scene done.

'What the hell do you think you're playing at, getting drunk like that?' He was surprised to hear how angry he sounded. He'd meant to take the caring and sharing approach but he was still furious at Emma for shagging Danny Parker. 'It's completely irresponsible!'

Emma sat down again with a thump. 'Don't shout,' she told him. 'You're making my head hurt.'

'Oh, I'm so sorry. Do you have any idea how much this delay is costing me?'

'No. How much?'

'Is that supposed to be funny?'

'No, I'm interested. Tell me.'

'A fuck of a lot! That's how much! All because you decided to get drunk.'

'I didn't *decide* to get drunk. I thought it would relax me. I was nervous about doing the scene.'

Suddenly Ben realised that what he hated most about this was the way that Emma was turning *him* into the bad guy. Look at her, he thought, sitting there like she's so sweet and innocent, thinking I don't know what she's really like.

'Well, I don't know what you had to be nervous about,' he said cruelly. He realised he wanted to hurt her. 'I mean, it's not like you haven't fucked him before.'

Emma stood up, her eyes flashing with anger. 'What? *What* did you say?'

'Well? It's true, isn't it? You and Danny? That's what I heard.'

'Who told you that?' Emma demanded.

Ben shifted uncomfortably. 'I don't know. I can't remember. I just heard it around.'

'Was it Danny who told you?'

'Sort of,' Ben admitted.

'Oh God! And you believed him?' Emma sat down again and buried her face in her hands. 'You must think I'm complete trash!'

'You're saying it's not true?'

'No, of course it's not true! Danny said we ought to rehearse for our kissing scene. I bet I'm the first girl who's actually fallen for that line,' she said bitterly.

'So you didn't shag him, then?'

'Of course I didn't! I left him sitting on the loo with his pants around his ankles. That's why he's so pissed off with me.'

Ben thought about this for a minute. 'Actually, I don't think you need worry about that any more. I think he's got a much better reason to be pissed off with you now.'

Emma hugged the dressing gown around herself and stared at her bare feet. 'I've really messed everything up, haven't I?'

Ben sat down on the couch beside her, and realised that he had totally misjudged Emma. 'I'm sorry. I really am. I just took it for granted that you wouldn't have any problems doing this. It's my own inexperience. I've never directed a love scene before.'

'No,' sobbed Emma, 'it's my fault. I've lied to you from the very beginning. I've never done any kind of film before. All I've ever done is accident victims on TV and crappy theatre. There never was a film called *Hairdressing*. I just made that up.'

'I know,' said Ben.

'You know?' Emma stared at him in total surprise. 'How do you know?'

'I looked it up on the Internet. Asked around.' After his conversation with Flick the other day, he'd made some enquiries of his own.

'And what did you find out?'

'Nothing. Not a thing. It was like you didn't exist.'

Emma started to cry. 'Oh Ben. I'm so sorry. You've been so kind to me. I didn't mean to lie to you, but I'd been out of work for ever. I was working in a hairdresser's in Covent Garden. But I really wanted this part. I've been trying to tell you for ages.'

'That's OK. I understand.'

Emma wiped her nose on the sleeve of her dressing gown. 'I wasn't in *Titanic* either,' she sniffed.

'I know.'

For a few moments, neither of them said anything, and then Ben spoke. 'This is your last scene this week, isn't it?' he asked.

Emma nodded.

'Go home,' he said.

'What?'

'Go home. Forget about the film for a while.'

'But what about the scene? I haven't finished it.'

'That's OK. I've shot nearly three minutes and I'm only going to use about thirty seconds. I'll intercut what we've got with close-ups on Danny. He'll love that.'

Emma was certain she was being sacked. She'd lied to Ben, been drunk on set and she'd thrown up on his leading man. He must be furious with her. The word would get around that she was unstable and she'd never work again.

'Ben, please,' she begged, 'I'll come back and do it again. I feel a little better now. You were right. There are other people on this movie who are depending on me. I'll be fine, really. I can do another take.'

'No,' said Ben. 'That's not necessary. I've got enough. I think it's better if you just go.'

He wasn't about to let Danny Parker lay another finger on her.

'Where's Emma?' asked Hugo when Ben walked back on set without her. It was nearly four o'clock and Danny was showered and sitting sulkily in Ben's chair smoking. 'Is she doing a Marilyn?'

'Emma's fine.' He sidled over to Stacey. 'How long was that last take?' he whispered.

'Three minutes, nineteen,' she told him.

'Did you check the gate?' he asked Will.

'Yeah, the gate's good,' Will replied. 'We've just reloaded.'

'OK, Jamie. I want to do a close-up on Danny now.'

'Where's Emma?'

'I sent her home.'

'To the hotel?'

'London.'

'And good fucking riddance to that slag,' said Danny.

Ben ignored him. 'Danny, this is just going to be a big close-up on your face. Emma's not here, so it's all down to you.'

'Well what am I acting to?' Danny whined. 'Who am I meant to be looking at?'

'You're right,' said Ben. 'You need something to look at. Tim!'

Tim jumped. So far he'd drummed for Luke and doubled for Danny's legs but he drew the line at copping off with Danny Parker.

'Tim!' Ben shouted again. 'Run down to make-up and fetch Danny a mirror.'

twenty-seven

The rain started just as the train pulled into Victoria. Just a few drops at first that looked as though they might blow away, and then a torrent, hammering on the taxi windscreen and bouncing up off the tarmac as car tyres turned puddles into fountains and washed all of Emma's dreams away. She tried to remember what London looked like when it wasn't raining, and couldn't. Even though she'd been gone for only a few weeks it felt like a lifetime and it was still raining forty minutes later when the taxi pulled up outside her flat and she dragged her suitcase off the back seat and across the road. Donna opened the door before she could find her key.

'Aaah! You're back!' Donna shrieked. 'I heard all that bumping and wondered what it was. My God, you're soaked! Isn't this weather rubbish? So much for summer! I bet it was really sunny down in Brighton. Have you been having a great time? I'm going to put the kettle on and you've got to sit down and tell me absolutely everything. Or would you rather have a glass of wine? Have both!' Donna paused for breath as she rummaged through the kitchen drawer for the corkscrew. 'Chris has got these new herbal teabags that smell like marzipan,' she shouted over her shoulder. 'Would you like to try one of those? He's got a job in this new organic supermarket. Can you believe it? Or there's PG?' She turned around and saw Emma sitting on the sofa with her head in her hands. 'You OK? Have you got a headache? Do you want some paracetemol?'

'Oh Donna,' sighed Emma. 'Everything's a mess. I'm a

terrible actress, Jason's dumped me, I threw up on Danny Parker, I'm turning into an alcoholic and I think I've been sacked.'

Donna was at a loss to know which catastrophe to tackle first.

'Well,' she said eventually, 'you've certainly caught the sun.'

In Brighton, Ben and the band were having an eventful week. Johnny Burton, the fight arranger, orchestrated a punch-up in the kitchens of the Chinese restaurant and the following day everybody went to Lingfield to shoot the race where the Malaysian gamblers' horse, Especially Angel, wins by a nose. Hugo, who was manning the second camera for the day, shot seven races waiting for a finish that was dramatic enough for the film, and in the end Ben had to change the script so that Especially Angel wins by several lengths.

In the paddock, the band watch their horse Serenity Now finish fourth and discover that Jackson's Cantonese isn't as fluent as he thinks. They've backed number eleven instead of number nine, using ten grand stolen from Turpin's safe which they now have no way of paying back.

Danny was happy because he'd put £20 on Just Quietly to win at seven to one and the bay mare had romped home with her ears forward all the way. He wasn't so thrilled when Don't Say A Word got caught on the rails to finish fourth in the second, eating up £50 of his winnings in the process, and when Buffellina made a poor start in the third which cost him another sixty quid, he announced that betting was a mug's game and retired to the bar.

Liz was deliriously happy because, with Emma out of the picture, she had Ben all to herself. Despite Ben's efforts to keep their relationship secret, Liz was getting reckless.

She'd asked Phil Props to provide a permanent chair for her next to the monitor and when Ben was talking to Johnny and Giles about a film they'd worked on together, Liz had stood beside him and laughed at Johnny's jokes, as though they were all at a cocktail party. 'Here,' she said, 'I brought you a cappuccino', and he saw that she was wearing his lucky beige-and-red baseball cap.

'So what if people talk?' she told Ben. 'Let them.'

She wanted to hang a banner from Brighton Pier saying 'Ben loves Liz'. She felt as though the dark cloud that had been hanging over her for six years had finally lifted and she was a new person – or rather the old Liz she used to be before she'd got so screwed up. She said good morning to all the crew each day, she smiled at people for no reason, and when she almost collided with Saskia getting onto the minibus, she stepped back, and said, 'After you.' And if any further proof were needed of her new-found contentment, she received a spontaneous round of applause from the caterers when, without any prompting, she asked for chips with her lemon sole. She even considered apologising to Orlando but decided against it.

And Patrick was happy because Magda had brought him an excellent supply of soap slivers that day – two of them with tiny curls of pubic hair still clinging to their cracked surfaces.

'What for you want all this soap?' asked Magda, sitting on his bed drinking a Bloody Mary. She often visited Patrick in his room because he gave her cigarettes and it was more comfortable than standing outside by the bins which was the only place where the staff were allowed to smoke. She'd been studying accountancy in Poland and the hotel's petty rules and regulations seemed calculated to remind her that in England she was considered a third-class citizen.

'I don't think this soap is for film at all because I see it still in your bathroom,' she was saying. 'I think you are a bad man.'

Patrick's mouth was suddenly dry and his heart started to race. 'Oh yes,' he agreed. 'I'm a very bad man. I should be punished.'

'What does mean punished?'

'It means I should be smacked. Very, very hard.'

Magda laughed and Patrick grew impatient. He took a magazine out of his briefcase and showed her a photograph.

'Look,' he said. 'Like this.'

Magda's eyes widened as she examined the photograph of a naked man handcuffed to a bed on all fours as a blonde woman wearing a red bra and suspenders bent over him, brandishing a riding crop. 'You want me to do this?' she asked incredulously.

Patrick nodded. 'I've been very, very bad. I deserve to be punished.' He threw her the cord of his dressing gown. 'You can tie me up with this.'

'No,' said Magda. 'Is no good. I have something better,' and she took off her shoes and started to roll down her tights.

And Ben was happy because he'd finally figured out the ending to his movie. After a day at the races, three pints of beer, Pizza Express and shagging Liz as she leaned over the basin in the grotty hotel bathroom, he'd woken up at three in the morning as he had done so many times before and suddenly he knew what the answer was. The ending of the film had come to him in a dream – just like that. It was perfect. He switched on the bedside light and woke Liz as he slid out of bed and ran to turn on his laptop.

'What are you doing?' Liz murmured. 'It's the middle of the night.'

'Go back to sleep,' he told her and started typing in his awkward two-fingered pecking style, desperately trying to get it all down on paper before his brilliant idea evaporated.

Only Emma was still unhappy, sitting in her room, staring at the walls and missing Jason more than ever. And the more she stared at the walls, the more she realised Jason had been right about one thing at least. Her room really was depressing.

'Well, at least there's something I can do about that,' she said to herself firmly. 'If I sit here much longer doing nothing I'll go mental.'

She covered the floor in newspaper – the room was so small

it barely made a dent on the *Sunday Times* – and bought two and a half litres of yellow paint from a hardware store on Goldhawk Road – Jason liked yellow – and another, smaller, tin of white satinwood for the woodwork.

At ten o'clock on Sunday night, she was waiting for the first coat on the skirting boards to dry so she could finish the job. She was wearing her oldest pair of jeans, now covered in primrose and white paint splatters, a black T-shirt that was starting to fray around the sleeves and armpits, and a pair of woolly blue socks.

It had been one of those cold, wet August days that doesn't know it's supposed to be summer and the central heating had been on all day. Donna and Chris had escaped the painting mess by going to see a movie and Emma was watching *The West Wing* repeat on E4. She didn't understand half of it, but she was mesmerised by the way the actors could all recite huge chunks of political goobledegook really quickly whilst walking from one office to another. She was fascinated by the way nobody ever stood still on *The West Wing* but was always haring off down some corridor or another. One day, she hoped, she'd be on a show like that. Then she remembered the reason she'd left Brighton and wondered if she'd ever work again. Who would ever give her a job now? Not even the travelling children's theatre would want to touch her with a barge pole once they'd seen her bouncing up and down on top of Danny Parker.

A knock on the door brought her out of her gloom. Donna must have forgotten her key, Emma thought as she got up to answer it, because she wasn't expecting any visitors. The last person in the world she expected to see when she opened the door was Ben.

'Ben!' she gasped. 'What are you doing here?' The only possible reason Emma could think of for the director to be standing on her doorstep was that he'd come to tell her personally that she didn't have to go back to Brighton because she was sacked. He'd checked the Health and Safety regulations and she was getting the chop.

'Well it was my sister's birthday and I just happened to be passing.' He was wearing a long charcoal overcoat and looked completely different from the Ben in Brighton who wore long baggy shorts and T-shirts.

'Why? Does she live around here?'

'Er, yeah, Twickenham.'

'That's miles away. That's not even London!'

'I'm sorry, have I caught you at a bad time?' he asked.

'Oh no, I'm just watching TV.' She followed Ben's gaze and remembered that the contents of her bedroom were still piled up around the lounge like a spectacularly unsuccessful episode of *Changing Rooms*.

'I like what you've done with the place,' said Ben. He nodded towards the desk lamp standing on top of a pile of shoeboxes and CDs next to the sofa.

'I'm waiting for the paint to dry,' Emma explained, and wondered when he'd get to the point and put her out of her misery.

'I don't suppose there's any chance of a cup of tea?' he said at last.

'Sorry.' Emma tried to remember her manners. 'Do you want to come in?'

'I don't know,' he said doubtfully. 'Is it safe?' He climbed over the vacuum cleaner which was lying just inside the doorway and Emma picked it up, looked around for a more sensible place to put it down, couldn't find one, and dragged it into the kitchen with her. 'Do you like *The West Wing*, then?' he asked.

'I love it. Do you?'

'The camera work's genius, but I never know what the hell they're talking about.'

'No, me neither,' agreed Emma, and tried to keep her voice from shaking. She couldn't blame Ben for sacking her, the way she'd walked off set like that. She knew he was still working on the ending to his film and he'd probably just written her out completely. Or maybe they really would replace her with a cartoon like Hugo said. A cartoon would probably be a better actress as well, she thought gloomily. And much less trouble. 'How d'you like your tea?'

'Tiny bit of milk. No sugar.' Ben had wandered into the kitchen. 'I wasn't sure you'd be home.'

'No, I was going to go to the pictures with Donna but it was such a miserable night, I decided to give it a miss.'

'I don't blame you. It's chucking it down out there.'

'So much for summer,' said Emma, and at first she didn't realise what was happening. She was just aware of being enveloped in Ben's soft charcoal coat and his lips pressing gently against hers, and the curl of his hair falling lightly onto her cheek. And then he let her go.

'What did you do that for?' she asked, bewildered. She was still holding the spoon with the wet teabag in it.

'I've been wanting to do that for weeks.'

'You're kidding!'

Ben shook his head. 'I think I probably wanted to kiss you the first day you came in to audition.'

'Is that why you're here?'

'I guess it must be.'

'But I thought you'd come here to tell me I was fired.'

'Fired? Why on earth would you think I wanted to fire you?'

'Isn't that why you sent me home?'

'No, I sent you home because you were ill and upset and I thought it was what you wanted.'

'But you never tried to kiss me before,' protested Emma, thinking he'd obviously made some kind of mistake. Like shooting the film in the wrong order.

'Well, I didn't know if you'd want to kiss me.' He looked into her eyes and she could see him searching for the answer to his question. She thought it must be the first time she'd ever seen him properly, as though some kind of fog had been lifted. She suddenly remembered the night she'd arrived in Brighton when Ben had danced with her and how she'd noticed then – without even realising that she'd noticed – how his eyes were grey, the colour of the sea, so that in certain lights flecks of blue or green seemed to rush in and then ebb away again.

As Emma gazed into his eyes, Ben found the answer he'd been looking for and he kissed her again.

She felt herself being led out of the kitchen into the sitting room and onto the sofa and as she lay back, she felt the warmth of the desk-lamp on her cheek and remembered something else. Something Ben had told her on the first day of filming: 'When you can feel the light on your face, you know you're in the right place,' he'd told her. Was it possible that she'd been falling in love with Ben all this time and never even known it?

'I've rewritten the ending,' Ben told her. 'I think you're going to like it.'

twenty-eight

There was shepherd's pie for breakfast. It was one of those things you just got used to, Ben thought. Waking up after lunch, eating your breakfast at tea-time, having lunch at midnight and falling into bed just as the breakfast show started on Radio One. Ben had been on night shoots in winter, in the rain, in the snow, when it got so cold by 3 a.m. that he couldn't move his fingers on the focusing ring. But this was the middle of August and the days were so long and hot that his biggest problem was waiting for it to actually get dark. That and keeping what happened in London a secret from Liz.

He'd got back to Brighton just after eleven on Monday morning, lay down to close his eyes for five minutes, and woken up three hours later, just in time for the fight rehearsal with Johnny Burton who was showing Harvey and Arthur the correct way to slam Giles and Alex against a wall in the alleyway.

It was a full moon and Ben was hoping for a clear sky. He was also hoping that the Gucci body lotion he'd bought for Liz would smooth over any doubts she might have about why he'd stayed overnight in London.

His sister's birthday had been the perfect alibi. Liz had never got on with his little sister and so, when he'd asked her if she wanted to come with him to her lunch party, he wasn't surprised when she'd said she'd rather stay in Brighton. Doing his VAT return provided a suitably boring explanation for the rest of Sunday night.

'I'll make it up to you next weekend, I promise,' he'd told her when he got back.

'No, you'll make it up to me now,' she'd said and pulled him back into bed.

Ben obliged. He had to keep her sweet and if he couldn't do that now, he'd have absolutely no chance when Emma got back in town.

He'd phoned Emma every day since Sunday and just the sound of her breathy, excited voice brought a lump to his trousers. Maybe it was just a location fling, but maybe, just maybe, a little voice inside him said, it was something more. Either way, Liz would have his balls if she got wind of it.

Back in London, Emma finished painting her skirting boards and wondered how she could have spent a whole month working with Ben and been so blind to how he obviously felt about her. Or how she felt about him. Every time she remembered Sunday night, a shiver ran down her spine and the little figure skater who lived inside her stomach started doing triple toe-loops.

Kissing Ben, she'd lost all track of time. It was only when she'd heard the key in the lock and Donna and Chris coming home that she'd looked at the clock and realised it was already half past eleven.

'Hi,' she said, jumping up from the sofa. 'How was the film?'

'Excellent!' said Chris.

'Rubbish,' said Donna at the same time.

'This is Ben,' said Emma. 'The director. He just dropped in for a cup of tea.'

'Oh right,' said Donna, taking in their dishevelled hair, Ben's coat lying on the floor, and sizing up the situation in a glance. 'Nice to meet you. We're just going to bed. Come on, Chris!' and she dragged him down the corridor before he could argue.

'I should go,' said Ben. 'Because if I stay . . .'

'Yeah, you should go,' Emma agreed.

Ben stood up and put his coat on.

'You're not driving back to Brighton tonight, are you?' she asked.

'No – we're on night shoots tomorrow, so I'll go back in the morning. I'll see you on Thursday, but I'll call you before then,' he promised, stroking her face. 'Goodnight.'

'Goodnight,' said Emma, and as he bent down again to kiss her goodbye, she slipped her arms inside his coat and hugged him to her, and before they knew it, they were back on the sofa again where they'd started.

An hour later they were still there. 'It's no good. I can't say goodbye to you,' he admitted.

'I know. Neither can I.'

'But I have to go.'

'Yes. You have to go. You can't stay.'

Ben got up and put on his coat for the second time. This time they got as far as the front door where they stood kissing each other goodbye for fifteen minutes before deciding that it was much more comfortable on the sofa after all.

'I have a confession to make,' he told her as he nuzzled her cheek. 'I love kissing.'

'I know,' said Emma. 'And you're very, very good at it. You could snog for England.'

'Do you think we could qualify for the kissing World Cup?'

'I don't know. We'd have to practise and practise and practise.'

And so they did. It seemed like only a few minutes later that Ben paused long enough to ask: 'Listen, can you hear that?'

'Hear what?'

'Listen.'

Emma listened, but all she could hear was the gentle twittering of sparrows. 'I can't hear anything. Just the birds singing,' she said.

'Exactly. It's morning.'

'That means I've been kissing you all night!'

'I know. It also means I have to go.'

'Yes, you really have to go this time.'

'I'm really going this time.'

'Those other times were just practice runs. This time you're really going.'

'That's right. I'm really going.'

And an hour later, he eventually really did go and Emma had crawled alone into her own bed feeling happier than she could remember feeling in her whole life. Nobody had ever kissed her all night before – not even Jason. Nobody had ever driven all the way from Brighton to London just to kiss her. It was, she decided, the most romantic thing that had ever happened in her whole life.

On Thursday night, the crew were back in the street beside the Mongo Club, setting up for the shot where the boys climb out of the nightclub window carrying their stolen instruments. Ryan and Ben had worked out a way they could shoot Luke looking out of the window and then cut to him jumping down into shot from a carefully positioned crate – so that he wouldn't have to climb with his broken wrist.

Three teenage boys rolled up on their skateboards to see what was going on.

'What are you doing?' they asked belligerently.

'We're making a film,' said Tim, although he thought the lights, the camera and the folding green chair with the word 'Director' stencilled on the back would have made that blindingly obvious.

'Is it any good?'

'We hope so.'

'What's it called, then?'

'*Brighton Rocks*,' said Tim wearily.

'Never heard of it,' they sneered, and jumped back on their skateboards and rolled away.

'That's because we haven't made it yet!' Tim called after them, but his voice was lost on the wind.

Ben had been checking his watch all evening.

'Relax,' Jamie told him. 'We're bang on schedule for once',

and Ben just nodded and watched the minibus pull up down the road. He didn't tell Jamie the moment he'd been waiting for had just arrived. In the distance, he saw Emma get out of the minibus wearing a long-sleeved T-shirt and jeans, struggling to get her big straw bag off the back seat. He loved it when she wore her hair tied back like that. It made her look sixteen years old. He took out his mobile and dialled her number, laughing to himself as he watched her across the car park, fishing around in that giant bag of hers for her phone. He slipped around the back of the dining bus where he wouldn't be overheard.

'Hi, it's me.' He'd been planning just to say hello, but the sound of her voice was more temptation than he'd bargained for. 'Meet me in my trailer in five?'

'OK!'

'Be cool, OK?'

'Oh. I'll be very cool,' Emma giggled. 'Watch me.'

Ben hung up, walked over to his trailer and waited. He gathered up all the old call sheets and storyboards that were scattered over the couch and threw them in the bin in a perfunctory attempt to tidy up. There was a knock on the door just a few seconds later.

'That wasn't five minutes,' he laughed, when the door opened and Emma hurried in, casting a comically furtive look over her shoulder.

'I know,' she beamed. 'I couldn't wait. It's been the longest four days of my life.'

She flung her arms around his neck and covered his face in hungry kisses. As he slid his hands under her T-shirt, there was a rap on the door and the handle started to turn without waiting for an answer. Emma quickly pulled away and sat down, smoothing her hair. Ben's guilty conscience convinced him it must be Liz, but it was only Poppy with some new artwork she wanted to show him. They'd mocked up a story in the local paper with the headline: PUSH COMES TO HOVE.

'That's great,' said Ben, barely looking at it.

'D'you get it?' Poppy asked. 'It was Luke's idea, actually. I can't take all the credit.'

'Yes. It's very funny. I'm just talking Emma through the new ending of the movie.'

It wasn't quite the standing ovation Poppy had hoped for last night when she'd sat at her computer, setting out the page, long after everyone else had gone to bed. Honestly, she thought as she walked back to the set, you can slog your guts out for some people and they just don't care . . .

Ben handed Emma a sheaf of green pages clipped together. 'Here, I've got a surprise for you.'

Emma took the new script pages eagerly. Ben had been maddeningly secretive about the new ending and she couldn't wait to read it. The first page was Scene 95: 'Danny is on his scooter looking for Emma when he spots her car parked badly at the side of the road,' she read to herself. 'As he approaches the car he hears a banging coming from inside the boot.'

Emma looked up in alarm. 'But I can't be shut in the boot! It's impossible. Please don't make me, Ben. I get claustrophobic!'

Ben hadn't been expecting that reaction. Each rewrite had built up Emma's part a little more and he'd expected her to be grateful.

'You'll be fine,' he assured her. 'It's nothing. You'll only be in there for a couple of seconds, tops.'

'You don't understand, it's not something I have any control over. I feel trapped and I panic. You have no idea what it's like.'

Actually, Ben thought, he knew exactly what that was like. He'd felt like that in every relationship he'd ever been in. He put his arms around Emma and kissed her. 'I promise I won't let anything happen to you. I'll be standing right there to let you out whenever you want.'

'Do you promise?'

'I promise.'

When he kissed her again, Emma thought that if Ben was there maybe it wouldn't be so bad. Then she noticed the time.

'I haven't got time to read the rest now – I'm late for make-up.'

'You don't need make-up,' Ben told her. 'You're perfect just as you are. You're good enough to eat.' He nibbled the top of her arm to prove his point.

'Will I see you tonight? I mean, this morning, after we wrap?'

'You bet. But this should just be our secret for now, OK?'

'Why?' Emma paused with her hand on the door.

'I'm only thinking of you,' Ben explained. 'You don't want people to think you got the part just because we're seeing each other, do you?'

'Is that what we're doing?' Emma smiled. 'Seeing each other?' She hadn't been sure what to call it.

'I guess it is,' said Ben, surprising himself. He hadn't even slept with Emma yet, but he was experiencing an emotion he hadn't felt in years. He realised with a start that he actually *liked* Emma. What were the chances of that? 'But we've got to keep everything strictly business when we're in public, at least until the film has wrapped,' he explained.

'You're probably right,' Emma agreed.

'You don't mind, do you?'

'Of course not. It's only a few more days.'

But although Emma resolved not to say a word, her face threatened to give the game away.

'Well, you're looking very pleased with yourself,' said Bex when Emma dashed into the make-up bus and gave all the Daft Tarts a kiss. 'What have you been up to?'

'Nothing!' said Emma immediately, but she started to laugh. 'I'm just happy to be back, that's all.'

'Do you believe her?' Bex asked Tracey.

'Nah!' said Tracey. 'She's definitely up to something. We'll have to torture it out of her.' She picked up her straightening iron and snapped it threateningly around Emma's ears until Emma screamed in mock terror. But her lips were sealed.

That night, she had to do the scene where Jasmine and Eddie

run out of the club, chased by Turpin's goons, and she wondered if she was going to be able to act terrified and look as though she was in fear for her life, when she felt almost giddy with happiness.

How terrible to think that she might have got through the whole film without ever realising how wonderful Ben was! She'd been so wrapped up in thoughts of Jason and so overawed by the whole experience of making her first film, she'd been too busy to notice the person who was right under her nose. But it was amazing now how many little Ben moments she could remember that at the time had barely registered. Like the encouraging smile he'd given her at her first audition or the way he always leaned in and whispered when he gave her acting notes. When she closed her eyes, she could still see his mess of long dark-brown curls, smell his coconut-scented hair wax and feel the scrape of his stubble against her skin, his eyelashes dusting her cheek . . .

'Look at her, she's gone again,' said Bex and Emma jumped, wondering how long she'd been sitting in the make-up chair staring blankly into space. She remembered Ben's warning about keeping their relationship secret and realised she'd have to try extra hard not to look quite so deliriously happy.

But Orlando noticed it too. Emma had two bottles of Merlot in her straw bag for him and Liz to say thank you for looking after her during the whole Jason fiasco.

'I hope it's a good wine,' she explained. 'I asked the man in the off-licence to recommend something, because I haven't got a clue.'

'You didn't have to do that,' said Orlando.

'Oh, but I wanted to. You two have been so kind to me.'

Liz and Orlando didn't look at each other. They were still barely on speaking terms.

'Have you spoken to Jason?' asked Liz.

'No, I haven't', and Emma realised that since Sunday night she'd barely given Jason a thought. It was as though Ben had flicked a switch in her heart and Jason, who had once been the most important person in her world, suddenly didn't seem very important at all. Was it really possible to fall out of love as easily as that?

'Well you certainly look much happier,' said Orlando. 'That's the main thing.'

'Yes – I guess all I needed was a few days off.' This time Emma remembered not to smile so much – on the outside at least. If this was the rebound, she thought, she hoped she never stopped bouncing.

The Vauxhall Viva they'd found as a replacement for Patrick's shattered Saab was white and authentically shabby.

'Now this scene is a piece of cake,' Ben was saying. 'All you two have to do is run out of the club, get into the car and drive off.'

Emma nodded at him, unable to take her eyes off his lovely face. She wished that her first scene was with anyone other than Danny Parker but she was so happy to see Ben again, any other emotions didn't stand a chance. Danny was wearing sunglasses and had his Walkman earpieces jammed in his ears, listening to the music he always used to get into character for Eddie, so he was in his own little world and not speaking to anybody anyway.

'Ronald, Harvey and Arthur will run out after you, but I don't want you to look back,' Ben was saying. 'Keep looking ahead towards that street sign down the road there. OK?'

'Why's Jasmine driving? Why isn't Eddie driving?' Danny wanted to know. Apparently he could hear what was going on after all.

'Because it's Jasmine's car,' said Ben curtly.

'Yeah, but wouldn't it be better if—'

'No, Danny, it'd be better if we just did it the way that's in the script.' Ben's days of putting up with Danny's nonsense were now officially over. He held the door open to let Emma out of the car again for another run-through and she accidentally on purpose brushed her head against his arm. Ben's mouth was dry. He looked over at Liz to make sure she hadn't seen, but she was fiddling with Harvey's jacket and hadn't noticed. Nobody had noticed.

Seeing Emma and Liz together, Ben realised that Emma was the complete opposite of Liz in every way. Where Liz was cynical, Emma was trusting to a fault. Where Liz was hard and brittle, Emma was soft and yielding. Where Liz had been there, done that and customised the T-shirt, Emma needed someone – someone like Ben – to guide her through the world. Liz came ready-made, fully-formed. She'd been a woman all her life. But Emma! He imagined himself telling Emma what films she should see, what books she should read, how to wear her hair, which clothes made her look more beautiful. He could mould her. No, that wasn't the right word. It made him sound like some awful Svengali. Emma, he realised, with satisfaction, was a girl he could *direct*.

He'd really tried to give it another go with Liz and she had to give him credit for that, but it suddenly seemed obvious to him now that, however brilliant the sex was, their relationship was never going to amount to anything more than that. He hadn't loved Liz enough six years ago, and he still didn't, no matter how hard he tried. If Emma hadn't been so wrapped up in that ridiculous Jason person, he would never have let Liz back into his life at all. But he hoped they could still be friends.

He felt a little sorry for Liz, but there was no point telling her any of this just yet. If he dumped her now, before the end of the film, he knew she'd walk out and probably take Orlando with her. She might even take all the costumes. He wouldn't put it past her. No, he needed to keep his wardrobe department happy for just a few more days and then he'd tell Liz. He'd break it to her as gently as he could.

Liz was lost in thought as she slid a comb underneath the button on Harvey's jacket so she could cut through the thread without damaging the fabric. All the buttons would have to be moved almost to the edge of the material or he'd never be able to do it up. How was it possible, she wondered, that a person could put on so much weight in such a short space of time? Location catering of course – she'd seen it happen time and time again. Even now Harvey was tucking into a ham sandwich, left over from tea. If she ever let herself go to pot like that she'd kill herself.

She automatically rubbed her own stomach to check that it was still as taut as ever and for once she was disappointed to find only the familiar, reassuring peaks of her hip bones. But she reminded herself that it was far too early for anything to show. She didn't even know for a fact whether she was pregnant yet. She was just late. Eight days late, which didn't mean anything. She moved the button over and began stitching it into place, slowly and methodically, focusing all her attention on the button's smooth roundness to stop her mind from racing ahead. Oh but she knew, she just knew.

They were doing more driving shots tonight and Liz sat in the minibus with Orlando and the Daft Tarts, counting off the minutes until 5 a.m. when the sky would begin to get light and they'd have to stop shooting. The nights when you had nothing to do dragged beyond belief. She looked up in relief when she finally saw the Viva's distinctive headlights returning and Georgina started handing out the call sheets for the next day.

Both cars pulled up a little further along the road and Liz saw Ben get out and go to thank Emma and Danny. She moved over to make room for the others in the minibus and so she didn't see Ben scribble a note on the back of his call sheet and hand it to Emma. A few minutes later, he appeared at the minibus window.

'Thank you all for all your hard work tonight,' he said, and tapped his fingernails three times on the window rim which was his code to Liz to say, see you back at the hotel.

An hour later, Liz and Ben were sitting in Ben's bathtub sharing a bag of Maltesers and Emma was fast asleep in her own room, with the call sheet on the pillow beside her. 'Get some sleep,' Ben's note said. 'I'll see you at two o'clock.'

At one-thirty that afternoon when Liz woke up, Ben was already in the shower.

'Why are you up so early?' she complained. 'We don't have to be at work for hours.'

'I've got to recce the locations for the end of the movie. Do you want to come?'

'God, no. Don't you ever think of anything besides work?'

'I know, I know. But what can I do?' He turned off the shower and wrapped himself in one of the hotel's cheap white towels. 'Just a few more days and then it will all be over and we can celebrate, OK?' He leaned over and kissed her and a big drop of water fell off his hair and onto her breast.

'Shall we go on holiday when we finish this film?' she asked. It was one of her major grievances that when they'd been going out before they'd never managed to have a holiday together like a normal couple because one of them was always working. You couldn't plan anything in this business. Whenever a job came up you had to take it because you could never be entirely sure you'd ever be offered anything again. The British film industry seemed to lurch from one crisis to another and always managed to give the impression that it was liable to disappear altogether overnight.

'I'd love to, but you know I can't. I'll be up to my neck in the edit.'

'What about a weekend? We could pop over to Paris.'

Ben pulled on his T-shirt so she couldn't see his expression. 'Well, we can probably manage a weekend in Paris.' That was the way to end it, he thought. Break it to her gently, face to face – not like last time. And maybe he could buy her some French perfume or something. 'My treat,' he offered.

'OK, I'll organise everything,' said Liz, and she reached out her leg to stroke Ben's groin with her foot.

'I'll see you later,' he said, letting himself be pulled down on

344

top of her for a proper snog. The thought occurred to him that even after they broke up, it might still be possible to have sex with Liz from time to time. Just because they weren't in love was no reason to chuck out the good stuff as well, was it? Maybe he'd suggest it to her. He knew she was up for anything where sex was concerned and she might just go for the idea. You could never tell with Liz.

Reluctantly, he pulled away. 'I've really got to get going,' he told her and went to the door.

'Car keys?' Liz reminded him, and he tutted at his own absentmindedness.

'I'd forget my head if it wasn't screwed on,' he smiled.

'You work too hard,' Liz shouted after him and slumped back onto the mean hotel pillows, cross that she was being left all on her own on such a sunny afternoon, but what was one afternoon, she reminded herself, when they had the rest of their lives together? She began planning what she would wear in Paris.

Out in the corridor, Ben turned away from the lifts and walked in the opposite direction, stopping outside Room 309 and knocking hesitantly on the door.

Emma came to the door in stone-coloured shorts and a lilac singlet.

'Hello, stranger,' she sighed and pulled him inside before anyone could see.

Unlike Liz, Emma didn't complain about spending the afternoon in a stuffy hotel room. She wouldn't have had it any other way. That was another thing Ben liked about Emma. Liz was hard work, but Emma was easy. So easy, in fact, that, the first time, Ben only lasted two and a half minutes.

'Well, that wasn't bad for a rehearsal,' said Emma. 'First positions and go again?'

'You're picking up all the lingo, aren't you?' laughed Ben to hide his embarrassment. 'But you'd better give me fifteen minutes to re-light.'

'Take all the time you like. You're the boss.'

Emma's hair was fanned out on the pillow behind her and Ben stroked it thoughtfully back off her face. 'You know, you should wear your hair up all the time,' he told her. 'It really suits you.'

'OK,' smiled Emma. 'Whatever you say.'

The juggling act nearly finished him off. Each morning as the sun came up, he'd get back to his room and Liz would let herself in a few minutes later.

'Why can't I ever come to your room?' Emma wanted to know as he sneaked into her single bed each afternoon.

'Patrick,' Ben told her. 'He uses my room as his second office – I'd hate him to turn up and find you in there.' And that was more than enough reason for Emma. She only got Ben to herself for an hour every day, but he was so busy, she considered herself lucky to get that.

And Ben made sure Liz never suspected a thing. On Friday, he even went shopping with her – an activity Liz knew he rated on a par with sticking pins in his eyelids, so what better way to prove his absolute trustworthiness and devotion to her? He told Emma he was scouting for locations – a brilliant, all-purpose alibi which also scored him extra sympathy points for working so hard and would cover him should anyone happen to spot him wandering through town.

Empire magazine were still after an interview and in a flash of divine inspiration, he told them he'd do it in Worthing at the café on the cliff. While he fielded questions about Ronald Gasch's arrest: 'Ronald is a professional and he has our unquestioning support,' Danny Parker's reputation for being difficult: 'Everyone on this film has been constantly amazed by Danny's performance,' and Sophie Randall's rumoured gratuitous nude scene: 'I think when you see it you'll agree there's no such thing as gratuitous nudity,' he kept one eye on Emma, who was sipping a Coke at the table behind him, incognito in her dark glasses even though no one would have recognised her anyway.

'It's like being a spy!' she laughed an hour later as they ran down to the water. 'Did you see me looking at you?'

Ben was pleased to see she was wearing her hair up in a ponytail, just like he'd told her to, so that it bounced behind her as she ran. All through the interview, he'd been fantasising about doing it with Emma in the sea, but the water was so cold, they only made it in as far as their knees before running, shrieking, back to the shore. They lay down on the sand, eating chips, Emma resting her head on Ben's chest, safe now from the prying eyes of the rest of the crew.

'Tomato ketchup or brown sauce?' asked Emma.

'Brown sauce.'

'Me too!' exclaimed Emma. She realised there was so much about Ben she still had to find out. 'What's your favourite colour?'

'Grey. What's yours?'

'Pink. Favourite animal?'

'Dogs. Proper dogs, that is – not stupid little yappy ones. What about you?'

'I don't know – I like all of them. Except maybe cockroaches.'

'Favourite film?' asked Ben.

'*Moulin Rouge.*'

'You're kidding!'

'No – I cried all the way through. What's yours?'

Ben thought for a moment. '*Seven Samurai,*' he decided finally.

'Is that a Kung Fu movie?'

'Not exactly. It's Japanese. Ever seen it?'

'I don't think so. Is that the film that made you want to become a director?'

'No, I've wanted to make films my whole life – ever since I saw *Star Wars*. My dad took me and my brother to see it just after Christmas when I was about six and I didn't understand any of it but even then I knew it was something completely

347

amazing. I had posters all over my wall. I stole the tinfoil from the kitchen to make a lightsaber. You remember how excited everybody got when it first came out?'

Emma shook her head. 'I wasn't even born then.'

Ben stared at her. 'No,' he said, a little surprised. 'I guess you weren't.'

She was still picking bits of sand out of her hair later when he dropped her off six blocks away from the hotel.

'You don't mind walking back, do you?' he asked.

'I know you're just trying to protect my reputation.'

'And you're not worried about the scene tonight, are you?'

'Worried? What is there to be worried about?' she smiled. But as she watched Ben drive away she was already starting to feel nervous. The more she thought about it the worse it got, so she decided not to think about it at all and thought about Ben instead.

'How did the interview go?' Liz asked Ben, and he could tell by the way she didn't sound suspicious at all that she knew something was up. He'd let her sit at his table for breakfast to keep her happy.

'Not bad,' he replied.

'What did they ask you?'

'Oh, you know, the usual bollocks, favourite colour, favourite food. What's your favourite film.'

'I bet you said the *Seven Samurai*, right?'

'Yeah. Why? Do you think that sounds a little wanky?'

'Yeah. I don't know why you don't just tell the truth and admit that it's *Star Wars*. It's nothing to be ashamed of.'

That was the other big difference between Liz and Emma of course, he realised. One of them hadn't even been born when *Star Wars* came out. For the first time in his life, Ben felt old. He looked up from his baked potato to see Emma standing in front of him, holding her tray.

'Mind if I join you two?' she asked, her eyes gleaming. 'Everywhere else is full.'

'Not at all,' said Ben, and Emma slid in beside Liz, so that he was faced with the two of them. Underneath the table, he felt a foot come to rest against his own and he couldn't tell who it belonged to. Just to be on the safe side he smiled at them both.

'What did you do today, Emma?' asked Liz.

'Slept in and then went shopping.' She was really getting quite good at telling lies, she thought. She almost believed it herself.

'Best thing for a broken heart,' said Liz and Ben hoped she wouldn't notice the tiny bead of dried sand still clinging to Emma's earlobe.

It was nearly 2 a.m. when Ronald finally lifted Emma kicking and screaming into the boot of the Vauxhall Viva. As Ronald slammed the boot closed on top of her she squeezed her eyes shut and held her nose to block out the smell of oil and rubber and mildewed newspapers and tried to think happy thoughts of being on the beach with Ben. She counted to three because Ben had promised he'd always cut three seconds after the boot shut. Then Phil Props came running in with the car keys to let her out and she took a huge gulp of air and sipped the cup of tea that Tim was holding for her.

'How was that?' she asked, sitting up, glad it was all over. Really, it hadn't been so bad.

'I'd like to go again,' said Ben. 'The boot looked a bit shaky on the way down. You're not feeling claustrophobic, Emma?'

'No,' she lied. 'I'm OK.'

'What's claustrophobic?' Danny wanted to know.

'Fear of enclosed spaces,' Stacey told him.

'No kidding,' said Danny. 'I had a friend once who was scared of spiders. I used to put big plastic ones in his bed. It was ace.'

'You're a real scream, Danny.'

By Take 6, Emma's nerves were in shreds.

'You're being so brave,' Liz told her as Saskia sponged some more fake blood and bruises onto her face. 'If it was me I'd have insisted that Ben use a stunt double. Still, it's a bit late to worry about that now, isn't it?'

The idea of a stunt double had never even occurred to Emma and she wished that Ben had suggested it. To think that she'd gone through all this for nothing! And she still had to be rescued, but that wouldn't be so bad, would it?

Except, she realised now, in order to be rescued, she'd have to start off locked in the boot until Danny let her out.

'Now are you going to be OK?' Ben whispered to her. 'Because if you're not a hundred per cent happy, I'll stop this right now. You know you're more important to me than any film.'

'Really?' Phil Props had put a thick black blanket on the bottom of the boot to make it softer for her, but Ben's words were all the comfort Emma needed. 'I'll be fine,' she promised bravely and Ben was relieved. Technically, he realised, the film was more important to him than anything right at this moment and Emma came a very poor second. But it was his last night-shoot and if Emma wouldn't play ball, he was completely screwed.

'That's my girl,' he smiled and squeezed her hand quickly while pretending to arrange the hood of her parka around her.

It seemed to take ages between hearing Ben shout 'Action', and hearing Danny finding the keys in the ignition and letting her out. She was supposed to be pounding on the boot and shouting for help, but she was convinced Danny was deliberately taking his time and she started to panic, her cries for help becoming more desperate.

'What the hell took you so long?' she gasped crossly when Danny eventually opened the boot and she clambered out. It was the first time she'd spoken to Danny since she'd arrived back in Brighton and although it wasn't in the script, it was so realistic, Ben decided to keep it in.

'That was great, but we'd better do one more for luck,' he said. 'And you could maybe go a gnat's faster this time, Danny.'

Emma snuggled down onto the blanket and closed her eyes. Just a few more minutes, she told herself, and it will all be over. It was three in the morning and when this shot was finished she could go back to the hotel, make a hot chocolate and fall into bed. She felt a bit silly now for making a fuss. It wasn't really so bad in here once you got used to it.

'Hey Emma,' said Danny. 'Did you hear about this coffin they dug up a while ago? Turns out there were scratch marks all on the inside of the lid where the poor bastard was trying to get out.'

The boot slammed down on top of her and the moment she heard Ben shout 'Action' she started pounding on the boot with her hands.

'Help! Is anybody there? Let me out! Can anybody here me?' She pounded and pounded and tried not to think about being buried alive. It was impossible. She heard the key go into the lock which was her cue to pound even harder and shout, 'Let me out!' again. She waited for the boot to open, but nothing happened. She kept on pounding, and shouting, 'Help, help me!' and she heard muttering and footsteps and then Jamie yelling, 'Cut!'

'It's all right Emma,' said Ben. 'There's just a little problem with the key. Don't panic.'

The thought of panic had never occurred to her until now. 'What kind of problem?' she demanded.

'It broke off in the lock,' said Danny.

'You stupid bastard. What did you have to go and tell her that for?' said Hugo.

Emma started to scream, convinced that Danny had done this on purpose.

'Don't scream,' Danny told her. 'You'll use up all the oxygen.'

Before, Emma had only had her childish, irrational fear of the dark and enclosed spaces to worry about. Now she had the very real, absolutely normal and entirely sensible and grown-up kind of fear that comes from being locked inside the boot of a car for real. She started kicking for all she was worth.

'Emma, don't listen to Danny,' said Phil. 'You'll be all right. You've got plenty of air in there.'

But Emma was frantic. Were there any air holes in the boot? She couldn't see any.

'Just hang tight, Emma, we're going to get a crow-bar,' Phil added.

'Where are you going to get a crow-bar from at three in the morning?' she heard Jamie ask.

It was a good question, Emma thought. She was going to die in the boot of a Vauxhall Viva.

'Don't damage the car,' she heard Hugo say. 'We haven't finished shooting on it yet.'

'No, that's right,' Emma shouted back. 'Don't worry about me. Just make sure the car's all right.'

'Emma, I'm really sorry about this.' It was Ben's voice again. 'But we'll have you out of there in a jiffy.'

'Is that like a body-bag?' Danny asked.

Emma could hear herself wheezing. She was going to be overpowered by oil fumes and by the time they got her out of there it would be too late. She'd be a vegetable.

'That last take was really good by the way,' Ben added.

She kicked harder and harder at the boot, but she was so cramped she couldn't get any power into it. Her muscles were going to waste away. She'd lose the circulation in her legs. They'd have to be cut off. Amputated, like her mother's friend's husband who'd got crushed under a tractor. She screamed again. 'Get me out! Somebody, please get me out of here!'

'Are you recording this?' whispered Hugo to Billy, who was still hovering with his boom pole.

Billy nodded and made a circular motion with his finger to show that sound was still rolling.

'Emma, cover your eyes, we're going to drill the lock out.' It was Poppy's voice.

Thank God. Trust a girl to actually get the job done. Emma pulled the blanket over her head and stuck her fingers in her ears. Just a minute later – although it seemed like much, much longer – she was free.

Ben lifted the boot and helped Emma out. Her legs were shaking.

'I thought I was going to die,' she sobbed and flung her arms around Ben's shoulders.

'Hey, don't be silly,' said Ben, well aware of Liz watching him like a hawk. 'You know we wouldn't let anything happen to you. You've still got to finish the movie.' And he gave her a fatherly pat on the back.

'Come on, Emma,' said Liz, prising her away from Ben. 'Let's get you changed and I'll make you a nice cup of tea. You poor thing. You must have been terrified.'

'Are we going again?' Jamie asked Ben.

'I don't dare. I can live with the first take.'

Ronald Gasch produced a hip-flask of brandy and Emma took the tiniest sip. It tasted pretty good so she took another.

'I had no idea you had claustrophobia,' said Ronald. 'I think you were incredibly brave.'

'Brave? Didn't you hear me? I was crying and screaming like a baby.'

'Yes, but you got into the boot in the first place. People who aren't scared of anything don't have to be brave, but if something terrifies you and you do it anyway, that takes enormous courage.'

Emma had never thought of it like that before. By the time she'd changed into her own clothes, she was starting to feel a bit heroic. Her panic had woken her up and she knew she'd never get to sleep now if she went back to the hotel, so she decided to stay up and watch the last shot of the night that Ben had been so excited about.

Hugo, Damien and the boys were beside themselves playing with the crane which would swoop up and over as Eddie's scooter rode past and, with any luck, a cloud of pound notes – actually just colour photocopies – wafted up into the sky.

Sunrise was at 5:49, and they rehearsed the crane move over

and over again in the dark, waiting for the moment when the sky would change colour. In the meantime, there was soup and crusty bread rolls, coffee and muffins.

Emma sat beside Ben and Stacey at the monitor and as the first milky egg-white fingers streaked across the horizon, she felt the most unaccountable feeling of euphoria. She'd confronted her phobia and lived, she'd stayed awake all night and watched the sun rise over the sea, there were chocolate-chip muffins and, best of all, she was in love with Ben. What more could any girl want?

'Feeling better now, Emma?' asked Ben.

'Top of the world.'

twenty-nine

Emma gasped as Ben collapsed on top of her with a grunt of satisfaction. Nothing to be ashamed of there, he thought: an entire commercial break *and* almost all the first bit of *Brookside*. Those thicker condoms were a good idea. He groaned, rolled over and reached for his cigarettes, then remembered that he'd smoked the last of them a quarter of an hour ago. He hadn't meant to end up in bed with Emma – he was supposed to be going for a curry with Liz tonight. But he'd got back to the hotel and decided to just pop into Emma's room for five minutes. He'd hardly been able to see her at all this week because Liz was sticking to him like old chewing gum.

On Sunday, which was their day off, Liz had organised a picnic and demanded that he drive her to the Sussex Downs. A picnic! He really didn't know what had got into Liz these days. So he hadn't see Emma at all that day.

On Tuesday night, the moment they'd wrapped, he'd jumped in his car and driven to Worthing again where Emma was already waiting for him in a cheap Italian restaurant with candles stuck into straw-covered Chianti bottles and red plastic chilli peppers hanging from the ceiling. Ben held Emma's hand on top of the table while he ate spaghetti puttanesca and drank three quarters of a bottle of red wine and afterwards they made love on the back seat of his Golf and he drove back to Brighton at thirty miles an hour, terrified of losing his licence. He got back to the hotel at eleven and told Liz he'd been doing a boozy interview with the *Guardian*. He could feel his hangover start to kick in even before he fell asleep.

On Wednesday, four Anadin barely took the edge off, and he watched the monitor through dark glasses which made it impossible to see a thing. He refused to believe it was a hangover and worried that he might have meningitis, sending Tim to look for a glass he could roll over a spot he'd discovered on the back of his arm. They had lots of running scenes to do and during one take, as Danny ran down the pier and took cover in a karaoke bar, Stacey had had to nudge him because he'd started to snore.

By Thursday, he felt much better but he hadn't been able to shake off Liz again and today, Friday, they'd shot all of Emma's new scenes for the end of the film. He'd knocked on her door because he wanted to say hi, and good work, and one thing had just led to another.

'Have you got any cigarettes?' he asked Emma now.

'No. You know I don't smoke.'

'Don't you?' Ben was surprised. 'I thought you did.' Then he remembered that was Liz. He closed his eyes, hugged Emma to him, and waited for the craving to subside. Emma snuggled up, resting her face on Ben's chest and watching it rise and fall like the ocean after a storm.

'I've got another pack in my room,' he remembered and swung his legs out of bed. He pulled on his jeans and T-shirt and grabbed his key. 'Back in a sec,' he promised, and kissed Emma on the nose. 'Don't go away.'

'I'll order you a sandwich,' said Emma, and picked up the phone. 'Brown bread or white?' There was still so much about Ben she had to learn.

'Brown,' Ben told her as he closed the door. He padded down the corridor to his own room and put his key in the lock. He'd phone Liz while he was here and tell her he was too tired to see her tonight. He'd make some excuse. It was only one night. She'd live. And if she walked out of the film with just one day to go, then they'd manage without her somehow.

But when he opened his door, she was already sitting on his bed waiting for him.

'Where've you been?' she asked. 'I thought we said half past eight.'

'Have you been waiting long?'

'No, about five minutes. Where are your shoes?'

Ben looked down at his bare feet and realised that his shoes and socks were back in Emma's room. So were his boxer shorts, come to think of it. 'There,' he said, pointing at the grey Merrells arranged neatly by the radiator. He held his breath and hoped that Liz wouldn't remember he'd been wearing his blue Merrells today. It was exactly the sort of detail a costume designer would remember. 'I just went downstairs to send a fax,' he added, as though this explained everything.

'Well are you ready to go?' she asked.

'Five minutes for a shower?'

Liz looked at her watch. 'Oh, go on then. That Indian's never busy anyway.'

Ben locked the bathroom door and wished he'd had the presence of mind to bring his mobile phone into the bathroom. He ought to ring Emma and tell her not to wait for him, but how was he going to do that in front of Liz? He was still mulling this over when he came out of the bathroom naked, except for the towel around his waist. The clothes he'd been wearing were rolled up into a tight ball and he tossed them straight into the laundry bag in his wardrobe before Liz had a chance to see that his underwear had gone AWOL. Maybe he could get away with just not calling Emma. But then she might start calling him and that could get messy. He dressed as quickly as he could, willing the phone by his bed not to ring.

'Come on, I thought you were in a hurry,' he chivvied Liz as he pulled on his shoes.

'I am. I've been waiting for you.'

He got Liz out the door and safely down the hallway. 'Oh damn,' he said, 'I've forgotten my cigarettes.' This was his excuse to go back to his room and phone Emma but Liz said,

'That's OK, I've got a new packet.' She pushed the button for the lift.

'Great,' said Ben. He had one last chance in reception. He could phone Emma's room from the front desk.

The lift doors opened on the ground floor and Liz walked on ahead.

'I've just remembered. I need to phone Patrick,' said Ben. 'Can you give me one minute?'

'He's in the bar.'

'What?'

'Patrick's in the bar. He's right there.' Liz pointed at Patrick who, on hearing his name, got up and stuck his head around the doorway.

'Yes?' he demanded.

'Ben wants you,' Liz told him, lighting a cigarette.

'Yes? What is it?' Patrick asked.

Ben was flummoxed, his mind a complete blank. 'I am going to need Jasmine's car again tomorrow after all,' he told him.

'I know,' said Patrick. 'It's on the call sheet. We never took it off.'

'Oh. Good.'

Patrick laughed. 'Stop worrying so much. Relax.' He looked at Liz waiting impatiently by the front door and lowered his voice. 'So how's the secret affair with Liz going?'

'I don't know what you're talking about,' said Ben sharply.

'Ben, take my advice. Don't ever become a spy. You'd be completely crap at it.'

Ben tried to maintain his dignity as he walked out, but almost immediately his mobile started ringing.

'Excuse me,' he said to Liz as he answered it and slowed down to let her walk ahead. Annoyingly, Liz slowed down too.

'Ben? Where are you?' asked Emma. 'I called your room and there was no answer.'

'Right. Right. I see.' He was aware of Liz listening to his conversation and he struggled to keep a businesslike tone to his voice.

'Why do you sound so strange? Can't you talk?'

'No. That's right.'

'Are you coming back?'

'No. I'm afraid that's not going to be possible.'

'Oh.' Emma was disappointed, but a second later she'd brightened up again. 'Well, I'll see you tomorrow then, won't I?'

'Of course. I look forward to it.'

'Who was that?' asked Liz as he put the phone back in his pocket.

'The *Guardian* again,' said Ben. 'They wanted to come on set tomorrow. I told them it wasn't a very good idea.'

Ben heaved a sigh of relief and decided Patrick was right. He wasn't cut out for this double life.

When Patrick went back to his room, Magda was sitting on his bed watching *Friends*.

'You don't mind, do you, Patrick? Is my favourite programme and I don't have television in my room. I tie you up when it is finish.'

Magda had become quite enthusiastic about their games and had found a shop in Brighton that sold tasselled leather willie whips, screw-down nipple clamps and latex gimp masks. Apart from the retail therapy, Patrick was never sure exactly what she got out of it.

Tonight, after *Friends* had finished, she made him put on her white apron and her rubber gloves and crawl about on his hands and knees scrubbing the bathroom floor while she beat his bare arse with the toilet brush. She could be surprisingly inventive. Just the thought of those wet bristles gave him goose-pimples. Then she handcuffed him to the headboard, took off her knickers and shoved them in his mouth so that he couldn't speak. He whimpered a little with anticipation and breathed through his nose while she took off her lace bra and fastened it as best she could around his chest.

'You have a very small penis, Patrick. That is the right word, penis?' She tapped it with the toilet brush. 'And these, what do you call these – bollocks? These are very big. You look very funny to me.'

Patrick tensed, longing for more insults and for the moment when his punishment would begin. But instead, Magda went to her handbag and took out a small Olympus camera.

'Look what I have bought for myself with all my soap money, Patrick. Is good camera, do you think?'

Patrick struggled uselessly to free himself and shouted muffled threats through her nylon gusset while Magda snapped away.

'Don't worry, Patrick. If you are good boy and help me become actress, I will never show these photos to anyone else or send them to that magazine.'

Patrick thought she was talking about *Skin Two* but she waved a copy of *Screen International* just under his nose.

'These photos are for me only. So I can laugh at your big bollocks.' But she took the precaution of leaving Patrick tied to the bed when she took the camera back to her own room and locked it safely away. And then she returned, as she'd promised, with a rubber spatula from the kitchen, and she smacked Patrick with that for a little while until she got bored.

thirty

Luke couldn't believe that six weeks had passed so quickly or that muscles could wither away in such a short space of time. When they cut off his plaster cast, his arm looked shrivelled and white. He had the opposite of a farmer's tan – with brown shoulders and hands and a pale scrawny bit in the middle. He flexed his fingers and picked up two pairs of surgical scissors and beat out a rhythm on the instrument tray to make sure everything was in full working order. Then he grabbed the nurse – a grandmother from Barbados called Velma with a gap between her front teeth – and kissed her on the mouth.

'I love you, darlin'!' he told her and leapt out of his chair for the final day of filming.

'Is that going to be a good place to park the Viva?' asked Jamie.

'It'll do for now,' said Ben. 'Wait till we've had a look at the rehearsal.' It was only ten past eight and he'd already smoked twelve cigarettes. He had two location moves today – it was insane – and he was starting to panic. The lighting department had gone straight to the squat to light two scenes there – including one in the bathroom which was the location from hell – and then, after lunch, he was supposed to shoot two different scenes of the band busking on the seafront. They were only the most important scenes in the whole film and because of Luke's arm he'd had to wait until the very last day to shoot them. If they didn't get them done today, he was ruined because Danny Parker was on a four o'clock flight from Heathrow tomorrow to shoot his next movie in Vancouver. And now the weather report was saying 'Chance of showers in the afternoon'. Ben squinted at the clouds rolling in from the south-west and made a deal with God. 'Please God, if you don't let it rain before I finish my movie, I'll stop smoking, I'll go to church every Sunday and I'll ask Emma to marry me.'

It had just slipped out, but all at once he knew it was what he wanted. It was time for him to settle down. He was thirty-one, he was about to finish directing his very first film, and he'd found Emma. Why not get married? He looked up to the sky and prayed that God was a film fan.

In the wardrobe truck, Liz was scolding Emma with a safety-pin in her mouth.

'You've definitely lost weight,' she told her. 'You only wore this skirt a couple of weeks ago and look at it, it's swimming on you.'

'Oh well. I had two sandwiches for dinner last night, so it'll soon go back on,' she promised. 'Maybe that's what they mean by eating for two!' Emma laughed unexpectedly at her own joke and Liz froze. Did Emma know she might be pregnant? No of course she didn't. No one knew. She didn't even know herself. She was just being over-sensitive. Emma was still laughing, and Liz accidentally on purpose stabbed her in the hip with the safety pin.

'Stop wriggling about,' she told her. 'It wasn't that funny.'

'Sorry, you're right. I've no idea why I'm laughing.' Out of the window of the wardrobe truck, she could see Ben on the other side of the car park and wanted to hug her secret to herself.

'So. It's very simple,' said Ben a little later. 'The doors slide open. You come out of the store. You stop here,' he pointed to the tape marker on the floor, 'say the line and walk out camera right. That's your left. Anyway, you go off in that direction,' he explained, pointing towards a tree.

'But the car's right in front of us,' said Danny.

'It doesn't matter. We don't see the car in this shot. We don't know where it is.'

Danny muttered something under his breath.

'Sorry, Danny? I didn't catch that.'

'Nothing,' said Danny. Ben knew that he was still pissed off that he'd given his only line in this scene to Emma.

'OK, then,' said Jamie, sensing a rumble about to break out. 'Looks like we're ready to have a look at one.'

Phil ran in and sprinkled talcum powder on the trolley wheels to stop them from squeaking – everyone was running today – and Ben took his seat behind the monitor, hitting his chair with an aggrieved thump. Stacey handed him his head-phones and a cup of tea. 'Not long now,' she said comfortingly. 'Just a few more hours and we'll never have to see Danny Parker again.'

'Amen to that,' said Ben.

It was a difficult camera move for Ryan to time just right. He kept tilting up too late so that he missed the beginning of the line or he got there too soon so that the camera was hanging around and waiting for the actors to step into frame. Ben was getting impatient. He wanted to have this shot nailed by nine-thirty. 'Can you lot try to come out of the shop at the same speed each time?' he shouted. 'Is that so much to fucking ask?'

The next time, Jasmine and the boys came out of the store with their tiles and grout and they all turned at the same time as they noticed that Ollie was carrying an enormous rubber plant under his right arm.

'What's the plant for, Ollie?' Jasmine asked.

Ollie shrugged. 'I dunno. I just thought it might brighten the place up.'

They even remembered to walk off in the right direction.

'OK, moving on to Scene 74,' shouted Jamie. 'The car boot closing! Emma, we're going to need your hands for that shot in five minutes so don't go far.'

Emma had spotted the caterers laying out morning tea and

she was starving again, even though it was only a couple of hours since breakfast. The trays of sandwiches were still shrouded in cling-film and Emma delicately folded it back to sneak out two triangles of egg mayonnaise on brown. If she sealed it back up again, no one would even notice they were gone.

'Oi, you! It's not sandwich time yet,' said a voice behind her. Emma wheeled around guiltily, but it was only Orlando. He was looking particularly festive in lime-green checked trousers.

'Get us a slice of Battenburg while you're there, then,' he told her.

Emma stole two slices of pink-and-yellow cake for Orlando and a tuna sandwich for herself.

'Well, you're certainly much perkier these days,' he said.

'Am I?' asked Emma innocently, plucking a stray granary crumb from her skirt.

'What's happened with Jason? Are you two back together or something?'

'Jason? Oh no, I haven't even spoken to him.'

'Well, somebody's been floating your boat – it's written all over your face.'

'Is it?' Emma was secretly delighted. If she didn't tell somebody she was going to explode. She couldn't hold it in a second longer. She looked around to make sure there was nobody nearby to overhear them. 'Orlando, you've got to promise me you won't tell *a soul* – this is a huge secret until the film's finished.'

Orlando made a large X across his chest with his finger. 'Cross my heart,' he vowed solemnly. Even he was capable of keeping a secret for eight hours.

'OK. It's Ben,' Emma squealed, and buried her face in her hands.

'*Ben?* Our beloved leader Ben?'

'Uh huh.'

Orlando was almost as excited as Emma, but he was much better at hiding it. 'How long has this been going on?' he asked.

'Not long. Only since I went back to London. He came to see me and we spent the whole night on my sofa kissing.' She flushed at the memory. 'Oh, Orlando, it was the most romantic thing in the whole world!'

'Kissing?' Orlando was disappointed. 'Is that all you've done?'

'Weeeell,' Emma admitted. 'It's gone a little further than that.'

'How much further? Have you done the deed?'

Emma blushed but Orlando brought out her gossipy side – even when the subject of gossip was herself. 'If you must know, we did it the night I came back to Brighton. Well, the next morning, if you see what I mean. That was the first time, anyway.'

'And the last time?'

'Last night.' Emma screwed up her eyes in delight. 'God, I'm so glad I told you, I was going to burst keeping it in!'

'Well, get you!' said Orlando just as Stacey came running across the car park out of breath. She leaned over and put her hand on Emma's shoulder and whispered in her ear: 'Emma, your radio mic's still on.'

Emma's hand flew to the tiny black microphone fastened inside her jacket and Orlando turned to see who else had eavesdropped on Emma's little secret. Ben was telling Jamie to hurry up and get Jasmine's car turned around and hadn't heard a thing, but there was Tex sitting at his sound trolley with his headphones still on. As Emma's hand thumped the microphone, Tex gave a little jump.

An hour later at the squat location, Ben ran up the stairs two at a time. 'Where's the fucking band?' he screamed.

'Getting changed,' said Jamie.

'I don't care what they're fucking wearing, just get them here now!'

Emma wondered whether she should tell Ben that she'd accidentally let their secret slip, but one look at his face told her now was not the right time. Besides, what harm could it do?

In the new scene Ben had written, Alex chisels off the bathroom tiles and Danny sticks his hand into the hole in the wall to retrieve the bag of emeralds. But Ben knew that if he left it up to Danny, they'd be there all afternoon.

'Change of plan, guys,' he told them. 'Giles, can you take out the bag and say the line?' He felt bad because he'd never really got to grips with Jackson's character and Giles had the weakest part in the whole film. Perhaps Patrick had been right. Perhaps he should have made the band a three-piece.

'What about me?' asked Danny.

'Don't worry, Danny. I'm going to be on a close-up of you the whole time.'

'Oh, right. That's OK then,' said Danny and stared moodily at the tiled wall, clenching his jaw.

Ryan looked at Ben doubtfully. 'Close-up?' he mouthed at him, because he was set up for a wide shot. Ben shook his head and mimed wringing Danny Parker's neck.

After each take, Poppy ran in to stick the tiles back up as best she could. After Take 4, the wall was a mess and Ben decided he could probably live with Take 2 after all. Jamie checked his watch. They were already more than half an hour behind schedule. He'd ask everyone if they minded taking a slightly shorter lunch break in exchange for wrapping early. To hell with regulations.

The sparks started to move the lights downstairs for Emma and Ronald Gasch's last scene. Eddie comes home, having shaken off Buster and Lucky Louie, and finds Turpin waiting for him. Turpin knows that Eddie has taken the emeralds that he's stolen from the Malaysian syndicate and he's going to kill him if Eddie doesn't tell him where they're hidden. He has a gun and starts to count to three. One, two – when Jasmine, who's been lying under Eddie's duvet the whole time, sits up and smacks Turpin in the back of the head with Eddie's guitar.

Emma was wearing a pair of striped flannelette pyjamas.

'What the fuck are they supposed to be?' Ben asked Liz. He was in such a state of anxiety he forgot to be polite to her.

'Pyjamas,' said Liz. She thought it was cute when Ben got angry.

'Well they look fucking awful. Were they left over from *Terry and June*?'

'I never worked on *Terry and June*,' said Liz. She still thought Ben was teasing her.

'Well, I don't want her fucking wearing them. Get her something else. Give her one of Danny's T-shirts.'

'We haven't got any here. They'll all be packed up now.'

'Oh, for fuck's sake,' said Ben. 'I haven't got time to stand here and argue with you.' He pulled his own T-shirt off over his head and threw it at Emma. 'Here, put this on.'

'And where's Danny's hat?' asked Stacey. 'He's supposed to be wearing his hat.'

'Orlando gave it to him. He was wearing it,' said Liz, wondering why she hadn't noticed that Danny had left his hat on the wardrobe bus.

'I took it off. It was making my head itchy,' said Danny.

Jamie got on the radio. 'Can we have Danny's hat sent over? We need it five minutes ago.'

'Don't ever bring artists on set when they're not ready,' Ben told Liz under his breath.

'It was Orlando's fault,' she insisted. 'He was dressing Danny.' She'd kill him for humiliating her like this. She reached out to touch Ben's bare chest but he turned and walked away.

Emma got changed in the kitchen. Ben's T-shirt swamped her, slipping off her shoulders, hanging down the top of her thighs, and she closed her eyes as she buried her face in the soft, grey fabric, breathing in Ben's scent. When she opened her eyes he was standing in the doorway watching her with a wicked smile on his face.

'Yes, that looks much better,' he said in a loud voice and then he moved closer. 'Tonight at the wrap party, I think we should arrive separately, don't you? I'll see you in there. Let's find somewhere quiet.'

'I know,' said Emma, 'I'll meet you upstairs – in the gallery.'

'The gallery?'

'You know – the black door upstairs.'

'Ben – we're ready to have a look at a rehearsal now,' Jamie called out and Ben went back on set before he could ask Emma why she thought the upstairs corridor was called a gallery.

There were cushioned mats underneath the carpets for Ronald to land on and the art department had made a light-weight replica of Eddie's Stratocaster out of polystyrene.

'Sorry!' said Emma as she tapped Ronald lightly on the head with it.

'Honestly, my darling,' he assured her. 'I don't feel a thing. Hit me as hard as you like.'

'Yeah, really clunk him with it,' Ben encouraged her. 'Make it look really heavy.'

So on Take 4 she did – bashing Ronald on the side of the head with a double-fisted backhand. He fell to the ground looking stunned, dropping the gun, and landed face-down on the mats with a thud.

'And cut! That was great, Emma!' said Ben. 'I'll buy that one.'

But Ronald Gasch didn't move.

'Ronald?' said Emma. She crouched on the floor beside him. 'Ronald are you OK?' She tried to feel his pulse and still he didn't move. His eyes were open and glassy. 'Ronald! Ronald! Oh my God! Somebody get a doctor! I think I've killed him!' Emma looked up at Ben and Jamie who seemed to be frozen to the spot. Nobody was doing anything. 'Get Kim! Get a doctor!' Emma yelled. She was trying to undo Ronald's tie and was about to start mouth-to-mouth when Ronald Gasch sat up and hugged her, roaring with laughter.

'Oh, Emma,' he laughed. 'You are a tonic! Don't ever change.'

All the crew were laughing now as well, and clapping.

'It's all right, Emma,' said Hugo. 'We're not laughing *at* you. We're laughing towards you.'

'And if I can have your attention everybody,' said Jamie, shouting to be heard over the racket. 'That is a wrap on Emma Buckley and on Ronald Gasch, so let's give them both a big round of applause for all their excellent work over the last six weeks.'

There was a roar of clapping, cheering and whistling and Ronald kissed Emma and people were coming up to hug her.

'Nice working with you, Emma, all the best,' said Phil, picking up Ronald's gun and putting it carefully to one side.

'Emma, what can I say – you've been terrific,' said Ben shaking her hand and then, when he was quite sure Liz was looking the other way, he whispered in her ear, 'See you tonight.'

'Hey Emma,' said Danny sarcastically, 'it's been real', and then everybody seemed to drift away again, racing on to the next location leaving her standing alone in the middle of the living room. They had two more scenes left to shoot but for Emma, her film was over and suddenly she felt immeasurably sad as though a chapter of her life had ended with it.

'Oh Orlando, I'm finished. I can't believe it,' she sighed later when she got changed in the truck. Liz had gone on with the band to the final location of the day leaving Orlando to pack up.

'Just the wrap party and then we can all go home,' said Orlando. 'I can't wait to get back to civilisation. Do you have anything nice to wear tonight?'

'I was going to wear that black halter-neck top. You know, the one I wore for Saskia's birthday.'

'Oh you ought to put on a bit more of a show than that. You're practically the star of the movie, don't forget. You want to make the most of it. Come to think of it, there's a lovely dress here that might suit you.'

Orlando hopped off his stool and thumbed through the rack of polythene bags, pretending to be surprised when he found what he was looking for. 'Oh, look, here it is.' He held up a pink satin frock cut low on the back.

Emma was entranced. 'Oh, but that's so gorgeous. Do you think it would fit me?'

'There's only one way to find out.'

Emma shimmied out of her denim skirt and vest and pulled the delicate pink fabric over her head. The bust gaped open, it sagged around her waist and lay at an unflattering length on Emma's knee.

Emma screwed up her face in disappointment. 'Oh, it's too big! What a shame,' she sighed, examining her reflection. 'It's so pretty. Never mind. The black top will be fine.' She started to pull the dress off over her head.

'Hang on, missy, don't be in such a rush,' Orlando stopped her. He eased the material across her bust and started pinning along the side-seams.

'I thought this had to be returned,' said Emma.

'Oh, don't be such a fuss pot,' he said, taking a pin out of his mouth. 'Who's going to notice one tiny little dress?'

When he'd finished pinning, he stood back to admire his creation. The pink satin hugged Emma's curves, accentuating her slim hips and tiny waist.

'Wow!' said Emma. 'I've never worn anything like this in my life!'

'You shall go to the ball,' Orlando promised. 'Just call me your fairy godmother.' He'd pay for the dress himself, he decided. It would be worth £270 just to see the look on Liz's face.

Down on the seafront, Luke took his seat behind the drum-kit and scratched his arm where the pins had been taken out. Last night he'd shown Flick the script for a science fiction film he'd written and she'd agreed to produce it for him. He was going to write the music for it too, which was the bit that really excited him. Acting was all right, but he got bored with all the hanging around and this was the sixth job in a row where he'd been cast as the funny friend. He shouldn't moan – he knew he was just a fat bloke who'd got lucky, but he didn't fancy doing this much longer. He gave Ben the thumbs-up to say he was ready to rock and Ben, watching the clouds, offered up a prayer.

'Please God,' he whispered. 'Just give me two more hours. That's all I ask.'

He was going to get to shoot his busking scenes after all. They were the bookends of his movie – the first scenes he'd written before he even knew what *Brighton Rocks* would be all about. If he was completely honest with himself, sometimes he still wasn't sure what *Brighton Rocks* was really about. All that business with the Malaysian gambling syndicate didn't actually make any sense. But the busking scenes he understood. You start with nothing, you work your balls off, and you end up right back where you started. It was a metaphor for life, that's what that was.

'And action!'

The band mimed to their first track, 'Die Laughing', and then the crew moved all the gear two hundred yards down the road and set up again to shoot the second song, 'Zoomraider', in front of a dozen extras and half of Brighton and assorted paparazzi who'd turned out to see Danny Parker.

Danny leapt and leered at the crowds, Luke pounded at his drum-kit like a starving man presented with an eight-course feast, Alex looked like a choir boy on acid, Giles hit big showy power chords to cover the fact that he couldn't really play a note, and by the time the rain came at a quarter to six, *Brighton Rocks*, for better or worse, was finally in the can.

'Thank you all very much ladies and gentlemen!' shouted Jamie. 'That is a wrap!' and an enormous cheer went up. 'And to everyone who was in the sweepstake, the time now is 5:47 and eleven seconds. Thank you all for your hard work – see you all tonight at the Mongo Club.'

Another huge cheer went up – the loudest cheer of all coming from Phil Props who'd bet on them wrapping early at 5:48 and was now £39 richer.

A pensioner, taking his West Highland terrier out for a walk, had stopped to listen to 'Zoomraider' just long enough to decide it was an awful racket. Now, he put up his umbrella and came over to ask Tim what was going on.

'So what's all this in aid of, then?' he asked.

'We've been making a film,' Tim explained.

'Really? What's it called?'

'*Gladiator*,' said Tim, and the man nodded happily and went off to tell his wife.

The wire hangers rattled impatiently as Liz searched through the rails.

'Orlando, have you seen my pink dress?'

'*Your* pink dress?'

'Yeah, the one I was going to wear tonight. I left it hanging up here. Have you seen it?'

'Oh Liz, I'm *so* sorry. I didn't know that was your dress. I sent it back to Selfridges yesterday.'

'You did *what*?' Liz glared at him furiously and pushed over the ironing board. 'I told you that wasn't to go back,' she raged. 'I must have told you a hundred times.'

'Did you? I must have forgot.' Orlando refused to be ruffled.

'You complete cretin,' Liz shrieked. 'What am I supposed to wear to the wrap party tonight?'

Orlando pursed his lips. 'Something else?' he suggested helpfully.

Liz flipped. Ben had seen everything else and all the shops in this godforsaken town were closed. Tonight, of all nights, when she told Ben her news, she wanted to look like a goddess.

'That's it!' she screeched. 'This is the last straw, Orlando! I've had it with you! I am never, *ever* working with you again. Never! Do you hear me? You've had a free ride from me for too long and I'm sick of it! I'm sick of your attitude and your lack of support. Find yourself somebody else's coat-tails to hang on to because we are *through*!'

Liz stalked off, leaving the ironing board upturned with its legs in the air like a stranded beetle, unable to right itself.

'Oh dear,' murmured Orlando and giggled to himself as he wrapped the cord around his cappuccino machine and put it back in its box until the next time.

thirty-one

Tex still wasn't sure why Liz had suddenly dropped him, but one thing he did know – tonight was his last chance to find out before the crew scattered and went their separate ways.

She looked fantastic tonight, he thought, in a strapless black dress that looked very expensive. The only clothes Tex had brought with him to Brighton – the only kind of clothes Tex owned apart from the suit he wore to weddings, christenings and funerals – were jeans, T-shirts and sweatshirts. Was that the reason Liz had dumped him, because their wardrobes clashed? Would he need to start shopping in Bond Street or wherever it was you bought clothes like Liz's in order for them to be a couple? If that's what it took, he'd do it.

She was talking to Saskia, but Tex could tell she wasn't really listening to a word Saskia was saying. She was looking past Saskia, over her shoulder, looking for something – or someone – else. She reminded him of a programme he'd seen about sharks on the Discovery Channel. They had to keep moving or they'd die. He could imagine Saskia in ten years time, settled down somewhere with kids and a husband – maybe even her own husband. But it was harder to imagine Liz ever settling for one place, one job, one person. She'd always be moving, always looking over her shoulder for something – or someone. Tex knew that if he didn't go and talk to her now, he might never get another chance. He picked up his drink.

'Ladies,' he greeted them, and Saskia took that as her cue to go and mingle. He saw her heading in Danny Parker's direction but then she passed him and kept on walking over to the bar where Damien was waiting for her.

Perhaps, thought Tex, Saskia wasn't so daft after all.

'So, do you know what you're going on to after this?' he asked Liz, and she sighed. It was practically the only question she ever heard at wrap parties. Why couldn't Tex ever say anything original for once?

'Actually,' she told him. 'I'm thinking of taking a few months off.'

Tex was surprised. Liz didn't seem the type for long holidays.

'Good on you. Going anywhere nice?'

It irritated Liz the way Tex just wouldn't give up. The way he still stood so close to her when he had no right to, really got on her nerves. Didn't he get it? She wasn't interested. It was about time she shattered his little fantasy for good.

'Actually, no,' she said. 'I'm going to have a baby.'

This was the last thing Tex expected Liz to say. Perhaps he'd been wrong about her as well. Perhaps she wasn't a shark after all. 'Well, aren't you going to need a man for that?' he chuckled.

'Oh, for Heaven's sake, Tex, are you really so stupid you haven't figured it out?'

'Figured what out? I don't get it.'

Liz turned to face him so there would be no room for confusion. 'It's Ben's baby,' she said. 'I'm seeing Ben. I'm in love with Ben.'

Now Tex was really confused.

'But I thought Ben was seeing Emma,' he said.

Liz froze. 'That's ridiculous. You don't know what you're talking about,' she said icily.

'But I heard her,' Tex insisted. 'Her radio mic was on and she said that Ben had been to see her in London.'

Tex was lying. He was just saying this to hurt her – but then she remembered that Ben *had* been to London. She couldn't let Tex see how rattled she was.

'Yes, I know,' she lied. 'He told me all about it.' She'd kill Ben when she found him. Where was he anyway? She started to walk away – to get away from this conversation – but Tex grabbed her arm.

'Why can't you just mind your own business?' she demanded.

'Because I don't want to see you get hurt,' he told her and it was the truth. 'Did Ben tell you he was sleeping with her? Did he tell you he was with her last night?'

Liz felt as though she was falling down a deep well into nothingness. 'That's impossible!' and her voice came out weakly as though all the life had been wrung out of it. 'He was with me last night!'

She had to get away from Tex before he saw the effect this news had on her. She had to find Ben. And she had to find Emma. She grabbed Hugo, interrupting his anecdote about a charity football match he'd played in. 'Have you see Ben?' she demanded.

Hugo shook his head, angry at having his flow interrupted. Years of telling this story had honed his timing to shining comedy perfection. 'So anyway,' he continued, 'we thought we had Michael Owen on our team, didn't we, but it turned out to be Mark Owen from Take That . . .'

Stacey was on the dance floor with Giles, Luke and Flick dancing to Kylie. Stacey would know, Liz realised. That bitch sat there next to Ben all day with her stopwatch, not saying a word, just writing it all down in her folder. Every lens size, every aperture, every filter, every ad-libbed line, every hand position and barking dog. Nothing got past Stacey. She'd know.

Liz grabbed the sleeve of her shirt. 'Is Ben fucking Emma?' she demanded.

Stacey sighed and the mirror ball scattered sparkles of light across her face. 'I don't know, and I don't care,' she replied. She hated the tangled morass of other people's relationships and kept her own as simple as she could. She had a girlfriend called Jeni back in Brixton who looked just like her. They both stuck to what they knew. It was much easier that way.

'Where is he?' shouted Liz but Stacey just shrugged as she twirled around back to Giles.

Over at the bar, knocking back tequila slammers with Bex and Tracey, Danny and Alex knew it was their last chance to cop off.

'Which one do you want?' Danny shouted in Alex's ear. 'I've already had both of them, so I'm not fussed.'

'What are you two whispering about?' Tracey wanted to know. She was wearing an off-the-shoulder blue top decorated with specks of glitter that caught the light every time she moved, and matching pedal pushers cut low on the hips revealing the waistband of her black thong. She and Bex had spent two hours doing each other's make-up and the alcohol and the humid club gave them a sticky, sexy glow.

'We were just trying to decide who gets who,' said Danny.

'I said we should toss for it,' said Alex.

Bex and Tracey exchanged a look of horror.

'Well, that's not very fair!' said Tracey.

'Nah, we should get to pick,' said Bex. 'Who's got a coin?'

Alex dug into his pocket for a twenty pence piece.

'Right,' said Bex. 'My call.'

'Why's it your call?' demanded Tracey.

'Coz I said it first.'

'That's crap. We should toss to see who gets to call.'

'Girls! Girls!' interrupted Alex. 'I know how we settle it. Whoever can get these down first gets to call.' There were eight more tequila shots lined up on the bar.

'I ain't doing four shots,' said Tracey.

'Me neither,' agreed Bex.

'Three?' suggested Alex.

'Yeah all right,' agreed Tracey. She didn't want to look like a wimp and so Bex had to go along with it as well.

'Contestants, you will both go on my first whistle,' announced Alex, and then, because he didn't have a whistle, he shouted, 'One, two, three, go!'

Tracey and Bex were neck and neck on the first shot. Tracey looked like she was going to sneak ahead on the second, but it was Bex who slammed down the third empty glass in triumph. Alex couldn't remember girls ever fighting over him before and he wished someone was videoing it, but Bex rather spoiled the moment for him when she said, 'I pick Danny.'

Alex consoled himself with another shot of tequila and Tracey slid obligingly onto his lap. 'Looks like it's you and me, then,' she smiled, wrapping her hands around his neck.

Danny grabbed Bex's hand and she tottered after Danny in her spiky heels, her tight hobble skirt making her take tiny mincing steps.

Alex unwound Tracey's hands from around his neck and looked nervously at his watch. 'Actually,' he said. 'We better not. My wife's going to be here any minute.'

'Your *wife*?' Tracey stared at him in disbelief. 'That's so out of order.' She looked at the remaining shot of tequila on the bar and toyed with the idea of flinging it in his face. But she'd already wasted six weeks on Alex – there was no point wasting perfectly good tequila as well. She took the glass with her and hoped she wasn't too late to catch up with Giles.

As she walked to the dance floor she almost collided with Liz coming in the other direction.

'Have you seen Ben?' Liz asked her.

'Not for ages,' said Tracey. 'Last time I saw him he was going upstairs.'

Liz looked up and saw the black door upstairs – the one she'd pointed out to Emma the first week of shooting. The door that led nowhere. She knew at once that's where they'd be.

Liz ran up the stairs, dreading what she might see but not able to stop herself. She remembered how Ben liked danger and all the times the two of them used to sneak off together and feel a rush of adrenaline every time they heard a footstep or a nearby cough. She seemed to be going in slow motion, climbing and climbing, but the door wasn't getting any closer and then she was at the top and pushing it open. Ben was leaning back against the wall of the dead-end corridor, his shirt pulled out of his jeans with Emma attached to his lips.

Liz saw red, or more accurately, pink.

'That's my dress, you fucking bitch!' she screamed and flew at Emma, dragging her away from Ben by the neck. Liz's strong fingers stretched around Emma's throat and squeezed as hard as she could. She'd kill her. She'd absolutely fucking kill her. Her thumbs pressed into Emma's windpipe as she threw her against the opposite wall.

Emma gasped, more from surprise than from lack of oxygen, and her own tiny hands struggled weakly against Liz's ferocious grip. She couldn't understand why on earth Liz would be so angry about a dress.

'Liz!' Ben grabbed hold of Liz's shoulders, trying to prise her off. Emma was choking now and her eyes were terrified, but Liz wouldn't let go.

'I've waited six years for this and you're not going to ruin it for me now, you scrawny drama-school slut!'

'Let her go!' yelled Ben and Liz released one hand just long enough to fling it back and punch Ben in the ribs before resuming her strangulation.

'It's not Emma's fault!' he told her and Liz was able to see the logic in this argument because she released her grip on Emma and started laying into Ben instead. A broken mop handle was leaning against the damp brick wall and Liz grabbed it and began to beat Ben with it. He couldn't bring himself to hit her and tried to roll himself into a ball – covering his head with his arms.

'Stop it, stop it!' screamed Emma. She tried to grab the stick from Liz and was knocked backwards against the dusty red slate tiles, banging her elbow against the wall.

'You bastard! You scum!' Liz shrieked, raining down blows across Ben's back and shoulders. 'You're fucking her, aren't you? You fucked her last night right before you fucked me.'

Emma had reached out again, trying to grab the mop handle from Liz but now she froze as she realised Liz's fury had nothing whatsoever to do with a pink dress.

'Did you think you were the only one?' Liz spat at her. 'Did you think he loved you?'

Emma was speechless as Liz brought the stick down across Ben's legs.

'Liz – please – I'm sorry!' he choked and uncurled a little, pleading with her.

'I'm having your baby, you bastard,' she screamed. And there was silence.

Ben lowered his arms, staring up at her, aghast, and as their eyes met the spell was broken.

Liz looked down into the eyes of the selfish, lying, cheat cowering on the ground in front of her and knew in that instant that this man had never been her soul-mate. He was some kind of weasel in human form, a cosmic joke that had been played on her – punishment for some past-life transgression she couldn't even remember.

He was seriously bad karma.

Liz dropped her hand and shook her head slowly, surprised, as she realised that the only emotion she felt for Ben wasn't love but disgust. That for the past six years what she had been trying so hard to get back wasn't Ben at all but her own self-respect.

'Liz?' Ben stammered. 'Please?'

'You're pathetic,' she told him and slammed the handle down hard into his groin.

If Tex had not arrived when he did, sprinting up the stairs, Ben's injuries would surely have been a lot worse.

'Come on, Liz. It's all right. Leave him,' Tex told her. He grabbed the mop handle with one huge hand, tossed it aside and dragged Liz away with the other. As Tex propelled her out the door, she pulled off her sandal and as a final parting shot, she aimed it at Ben's head, the edge of the heel catching him on the eyebrow.

'You're not good enough for her,' said Tex quietly.

'Who?' gasped Ben.

'Either of them,' said Tex and went to find Liz.

It took Ben a few minutes to get his breath back. The cut above his eye was starting to bleed. When he turned to Emma, she was sitting on the cold floor with her back against the wall holding Liz's Jimmy Choo like some latter-day Cinderella. There was a grease mark on the pink dress that three attempts at dry-cleaning would never quite shift. She coughed and rubbed her neck.

'Emma, are you OK?'

Emma nodded. 'I'll live.'

'Don't listen to Liz,' Ben implored. 'She's crazy. She doesn't know what she's saying.'

'So you aren't sleeping with her?'

'No. I should have told you. Liz is an old girlfriend. But it's been over between us for years.'

'And you didn't sleep with her last night?'

'Of course not. I swear to you.' He took her hand and stroked it gently. 'On my mother's life. You've got to believe me.'

Emma looked up into Ben's dear face, that she had already grown so fond of. He smiled at her to let her know everything was going to be OK – a smile that would melt your heart – and she wanted more than anything in the world to believe him. But she couldn't.

'You must think I'm really stupid,' she said quietly. And Emma got to her feet, smoothed down her pink dress, opened the heavy wooden door and, as she walked downstairs, she knew it was the last time she would ever set eyes on Ben Lincoln.

thirty-two

Emma didn't go to the cast and crew screening that was held six months later at a preview theatre in Wardour Street. The invitation – a postcard illustrated with a still of Jasmine and Eddie on his scooter – was accompanied by a handwritten note from Ben that just read: 'Please come.' Emma put it behind the toaster. She couldn't go anyway, because Thursday was late-night closing at the salon.

'You must be mad,' Donna had said when Emma had asked for her old job back. 'If someone gave me the chance to be an actress and leave all this behind, you wouldn't see me for dust.'

'But I like it here,' said Emma. She'd missed her family at the salon and the first time she'd stepped back through the glass front door it had felt like she was coming home. If the last two months were what being an actress was all about then she didn't want to be a part of that world. She'd rather be here, doing a job she was good at, where nobody lied to her, or locked her in the boot of a car, or tried to strangle her or watched her have sex with a man she hated. It was a relief just to come to work every morning and be able to blend into the background. She didn't miss the spotlight.

'But you got to snog Danny Parker!' said Donna. 'I'd give my right arm to snog Danny Parker.'

'No you wouldn't,' said Emma. 'He's nothing special. None of them are. It's all just an act.'

'But think about the money!'

Emma did think about the money. What she'd earned on

Brighton Rocks had paid off her outstanding student loan and she was out of debt for the first time since leaving home. With the rest she bought a puppy from Battersea Dogs Home – a raggedy terrier called Scruff with a permanently optimistic expression. She felt enormously rich.

'You're wasting your talent,' Michael told her. 'It's a tragedy.' He had a spot on the Shopping Channel now and arrived at work each day on his new Harley Davidson which he thought was good for his image.

Emma just laughed. 'Actually, Michael, I'll let you into a little secret. I was never really that good.'

She was starting to get invited to audition for proper acting jobs – a small part in a TV series, a play at The Bush, a tiny part in a film – but she turned them all down. Whatever Irene said about being washed up at forty, there was plenty of time to resume her acting career. But for the next few months she just wanted to remind herself what the real world felt like.

'I don't want to pretend to be anyone else right now,' she told Irene. 'I just want to try being myself for a while.'

Ben phoned every day, leaving halting, embarrassed messages on her answering machine which she didn't return. She thought she'd been able to flick a switch in her heart and fall out of love with Jason and in love with Ben. Now she knew that wasn't possible. She couldn't have been in love with Ben because she didn't even know who he was. Everything they'd had together was based on a lie. If he'd told her the truth when she'd asked him, and admitted that he'd been sleeping with Liz the whole time, it might have been different. She would have tried to understand and forgive him. But she couldn't forgive him for lying to her face.

In March, when *Brighton Rocks* was released at the cinema, Michael, Donna and a couple of the other girls from the salon went with Emma to catch the first Friday-night show at the cinema in the Haymarket.

It was three-quarters empty – or a quarter full, depending on your point of view – and nobody queuing up for popcorn recognised Emma from the poster – in fact she scarcely recognised herself.

Emma's summer flashed before her eyes but it wasn't the way she remembered it. All of the colours seemed more vibrant and she couldn't be sure if that was because her memory had been dulled or whether it was just a trick of the light. She was dreading seeing her sex scene with Danny, but to her surprise and relief it had been cut out. All you saw was Danny kiss her, her parka falling to the floor, and then they cut to a shot of a seagull wheeling about in the sky, making a cawing noise. Donna nudged Emma in the ribs.

Apart from the music numbers which dragged on for too long – and you could definitely tell they were miming, Emma thought – the film whipped by until it reached its thrilling denouement.

'Who's that?' whispered Donna as a pair of hands, hidden by thick gardening gloves, lifted the rubber tree out of its pot, to reveal a small waterproof pouch buried in the compost.

'Shh,' Emma whispered back. 'You'll see.'

Then they're back in the bathroom of the squat where Alex is frantically hacking off the bathroom tiles. Giles sticks his hand into the hole in the wall to retrieve the bag of emeralds hidden in there.

He tips the contents out into his hand and discovers to his horror that the emeralds are gone and a handful of grey and buff beach pebbles have been left in their place.

'They're gone!' he gasps.

Cut to a close-up of a cashier's hands counting out £20 notes – maybe thirty of them, not too many to arouse suspicion – and just visible beside them is a small pile of Malaysian Ringitts. The camera pulls back to reveal that it's Jasmine being served at the Bureau de Change. She opens her handbag to put the cash inside and we can see that it's full of English and Malaysian currency. The cashier is played by Magda the Polish chambermaid looking very pleased with herself.

The camera follows Jasmine back along the street to where

her old Vauxhall Viva is parked a little distance away. As Jasmine crosses the road, she takes out a keyring, points it towards the car, and we hear an electronic beep. But instead of getting into the Vauxhall, Jasmine carries on walking and opens the door of the brand new silver Maserati Spyder parked just behind it. She gets in, puts her key in the ignition and drives off.

Emma smiled, remembering how Ronald Gasch had talked Sophie Randall into letting them hire her new car for the day. Really, he'd just wanted an excuse to drive it from London to Brighton, sitting on 110 mph down the M23 with Sophie lying across his lap on the front seat. His speeding fine, coming hard on the heels of his suspended sentence for indecent exposure had helped to hammer home his new hellraiser image. He was featured in a *Daily Mail* round-up of Sexy Over Sixties and the Bond people were already talking about him for their next villain.

Then the camera follows Jasmine as she joins the traffic in the lane signposted London A23. As her car becomes lost in the traffic, the image dissolves into a close-up of Giles's hands strumming his guitar.

The band are playing 'Die Laughing' and we hear Eddie's voiceover: 'Like I said. We were never in it for the money – it was always about the music.' After the first verse, the camera pulls back to reveal that the band are busking again on the seafront just a few yards from the spot where we saw them at the start of the film. A passerby tosses ten pence into the open guitar case. There's maybe £3 in there – all in small change.

Ollie stops drumming just long enough to tip his hat and then the screen goes black and the credits roll.

'So,' said Donna as they waited for the tube. 'Jasmine was Turpin's daughter all along.'

'Yeah. That's why she was working at the club. She'd spent years trying to find her real father, and when she finally contacted him he didn't want to know. She vowed that some-how she'd find a way to hurt him the way he'd hurt her.'

'Pretty far-fetched, if you ask me,' sniffed Donna.

'Yeah, well, it's only a film,' said Emma. 'It's not meant to be real life, is it?'

The reviews were lukewarm at best. Luke was singled out as 'wildly charismatic', the descriptions of Ben's direction ranged from 'pedestrian' through 'quirky', all the way to 'hyperactive', most of the papers used a photo of Sophie Randall even though she was only in it for ten seconds, the general consensus was that Danny was 'intense', Ronald Gasch was an old ham and whenever Emma's name was mentioned at all it was only in brackets after the name of her character, sometimes with the word 'newcomer' attached to it. A week later it was taken off at the cinema altogether and it was as though it had never happened. Perhaps its only lasting legacy was the story in a Sunday tabloid a month later in which Bex recounted her nights of passion with its star – an article which earned Danny the enduring nickname of Compact Dick.

Ben's next project, Emma found out, would be directing Luke's science fiction script. Tim the runner had told her that. He was the only person she'd stayed in touch with from the whole production and the only person who totally understood her disenchantment with the film business. The day after the wrap party he'd driven her home from Brighton and told her that when he'd checked out of the hotel that morning, he'd been presented with a room bill for £1,365.49. Apparently, Patrick had expected him to work for no money and pay for his accommodation as well. It had taken a phone-call from Tim's auntie Angela to sort it out. Patrick swore blind that it was all just a silly misunderstanding on the part of the hotel and Angela had stood over him and watched while he signed the cheque.

Now Tim was back at medical school and he'd come over to Emma's every few weeks for a free haircut and to keep her up to date with all the gossip.

A couple of months after *Brighton Rocks* was released, he

turned up with a pizza, a copy of *Withnail & I* on video, and news of Liz. He'd bumped into her in the supermarket in Wandsworth. She'd put on at least two stone and was wearing navy tracksuit bottoms and a baggy T-shirt. Tim thought she looked absolutely gorgeous. The baby was asleep in the trolley – a baby girl with brown skin, chocolate-button eyes, and glossy black hair. They'd named her Elsa after Tex's mother, Tim said.

'So it wasn't Ben's baby after all?'

'If I were a betting man,' said Tim, 'I'd have to say no. The wedding's in September.'

Emma was open mouthed. 'But does she love Tex?'

'That's not the kind of question you can really ask someone in the supermarket,' said Tim. 'But she looked really different.'

'Different how?'

Tim thought about it. 'Happy,' he decided.

'Do you think we'll be invited to the wedding?'

'Now *that* would be pushing it.'

The telephone rang just as Richard E. Grant was smearing himself in Deep Heat to try and get warm.

'I'll pause it,' said Tim, and Emma uncurled herself from the couch and went to answer the phone in the hall.

'Good, you're in,' said a voice she thought she'd never hear again. 'I'm coming over.' It was Jason. Emma was stunned. It had been what? Nearly a year since she'd seen him?

'Erm. Actually, it's not such a good time right now.'

'Why? Is there someone else there? Have you got another man there?'

Emma looked through the doorway at Tim sprawled on her sofa with his shoes kicked off and his head tipped back as he slid another slice of pizza into his mouth.

'Well, I wouldn't call him a man exactly,' said Emma. 'He's more of a boy.'

Jason made a sort of sputtering noise. 'Get rid of him,' he ordered. 'I'll be there in twenty minutes.'

Emma hung up. Her heart felt as though it was on a bungee rope.

'Who was that?' Tim asked.

'Oh nobody,' she said in a distracted voice and pressed play, hugging her feet underneath her. She wished she smoked or bit her nails. What on earth was she going to say to Jason? When the doorbell buzzed just over fifteen minutes later, she still had no idea.

'Aren't you going to get that?' Tim asked.

It buzzed again – two short angry blasts before she could get to the intercom. Emma pressed once to release the door, opened the front door of the flat, then went back to sit with Tim. She was glad he was there for moral support.

She could hear feet marching up the two flights of stairs – quickly at first, then more deliberately as he ran out of breath. Emma counted the stairs in her head. Five, six, seven, eight – then Jason pushed through the front door and was standing in her living room. His coat and hair were wet and Emma stared at him as though he was a mirage. It was only the third time he'd ever set foot in her flat.

'Oh, wotcha,' said Tim, who recognised Jason off the TV.

Jason frowned and jerked his head in the direction of the kitchen. 'I need to talk to you,' he told Emma and stomped off down the hall.

Tim looked at Emma in confusion. 'Should I go?'

'No, don't move.'

In the kitchen, Jason was wiping his black leather loafers dry with a piece of kitchen towel. 'Who's that in there?' he demanded.

'That's none of your business,' said Emma. She'd waited for this moment for months, rehearsed the scene over and over in her head, but she hadn't expected it to happen in her kitchen. None of the scripts she'd prepared would fit the bill. She'd have to improvise. 'What are you doing here?' she asked.

'Emma, I'm sorry.' He sounded humble. Contrite. 'I made a terrible mistake. I've been thinking it over and I want us to get back together.'

Emma could hardly believe that he was finally saying the words she'd wanted so desperately to hear. It was too good to be true. 'What about Nicole?' she asked.

Jason scowled. 'She's off her head. So possessive like you wouldn't believe. She's doing my head in. We're finished.'

'But aren't you two supposed to be engaged?'

Jason shook his head. 'Nah. That was all her idea. That ring she was wearing in the papers? It belonged to her grandmother. She was just winding up the photographers. She said it would be good publicity. I told you – she's a nutter.'

'Oh,' said Emma. It was exactly what she'd wanted to believe at the time. The whole engagement was just a stunt. Jason didn't love Nicole – he loved her. He still loved her. But that didn't explain why she hadn't heard a word from him in months.

'In fact,' said Jason, 'I think you and I should get married. As soon as possible.'

This was the way Emma had always known her love story with Jason was meant to turn out. She'd pictured this scene almost since the night they'd started going out, imagining how she'd accept with tears of joy pricking her eyes and a few simple, breathless words. She even knew what kind of dress she would wear, but now as she looked at Jason's wet footprints on the kitchen floor and the muddy clump of paper he'd dropped carelessly onto the counter, the only sentiment he aroused in her was irritation.

'Could you put that in the bin, please?' she told him.

'What?'

'The kitchen towel. Don't just leave it on the cupboard. Put it in the bin.'

'Don't you understand what I'm saying to you? I want us to get married.'

'Really?' said Emma. 'And how would that work exactly, Jason, when I never, ever want to see you again?'

Jason laughed. 'You're just upset. You know you don't really mean that. Get rid of that bloke in the living room and we can talk about this properly.'

'There's nothing to talk about. I have nothing to say to you.' He'd broken her heart, dumped her without a word of explanation and now he expected her to *marry* him? How had she ever thought she was in love with somebody like that?

'Emma, I'm warning you,' Jason's voice was icy cold. 'This is your last chance. If you don't tell that man to go, I'm going to walk out of this flat right now and you'll never see me again.'

'But Jason,' she said, 'you don't understand. We've rented a video.'

And with that Emma turned abruptly and walked back to the living room, leaving Jason clutching a muddy wad of tissue.

She settled back down on the sofa beside Tim, and her heart stopped lurching up and down and came to rest in its rightful position. It felt good. 'What did I miss?' she asked.

A few minutes later, she heard Jason's footsteps coming back up the corridor and the front door closing behind him. She didn't even turn her head to watch him go.

'Is everything OK?' Tim asked and squeezed her hand.

Emma smiled and turned up the volume.

'Everything's fine,' she assured him. 'I guess some people just don't know when it's over.'